The Treacle Year

Morgan Redston

ISBN-13: 978-0-9930186-0-2 pb.
ISBN-10: 0993018602 .

For Mum, with thanks for everything.

Chapter One

The lighthouse at Yaquina Head stands on rock formed by lava flows, guarding the harbour of Newport, Oregon. Very little changed for fourteen million years, until this day when the afternoon sun stroked the lazy puffins, and fifty kilometres out, fifty kilometres down the pressure increased. Silent as a gene mutates, geological time prepared to leap.

One, two, three, four, five ...

Glynn squashed the non-tartan blanket into his rucksack and gave up. Hours before, as the long twilight drifted into true darkness, and the floodlights were switched off, he climbed down to the shingle and set up camp on a rock beneath the castle. The tide turned as he waited for something beyond the long-drawn patterns of the stars, but nothing came.

Once I caught a fishalive ....

Finally, he packed up, disconcerted by two furry shadows with thick crunchy tails. He came to the top of the stone steps and could hear snatches of song,
'Six, seven eight nine ten, then I let it go again. Which finger did it bite? ...' , 'No, no, no, Liam, it's Why did you let it GO...'
Students, thought Glynn as he watched them roll by.
'Oh, yeah, ok. Six, seven eight nine ten, then I let it go again. Which fi-, No, no, no. How you doin', George Wishart?'
The singing faded and Glynn walked home past the silhouettes of ruins. He nudged the front gate quietly, jingling his keys at the lock, when a feline roar came

from behind the potted Christmas tree. 'Oh hello, Tommy,' Glynn said, and opened the door, 'Locked you out again, then? Well, you can come in, but I'm not feeding you.' The fat ginger cat lead him through the door, picked his way through the hall, and curled up on the kitchen mat, mewing like a starving kitten. 'Yes, I can see you,' Glynn grumbled. He filled a pan of water, then wrote another 'Buy Kettle' post-it note for the fridge and lit the gas. 'You cannot seriously be hungry.'

He began to unpack the rucksack, but the cat wove round his feet, miaowing, until he said, 'Oh, alright, but just this once.' He pulled a tin of cat food from the box above the fridge, and placed it in the red bowl by the back door. 'Not quite a fishalive, but this will have to do.' After a few mouthfuls, the cat walked over to the sofa and started to wash, 'Oh no, you don't!' his servant replied. 'I haven't got all night.' The cat waited, and won. 'Only outside, mind,' he said, and the cat glanced at him scornfully, as he filled the water bowl outside the back door. 'Come on, it's not cold, you daft 'appeth. There you go,' and he ushered his guest out the door. He unzipped his shoes, flopped onto the bed, and slept, safe in thick stone walls, waited out.

Only Tommy was left to look up from his bowl, feeling the first metallic tingle from the silent crashes of colour, pink, green, red, as the sky started to fall.

The next morning, making toast, Glynn banged his fist on the table as he listened to the radio. Arrived later than expected, best light showers in Fife for thirteen years; amateur photographers feel effects of Aurora-Gazing Frenzy. Determined now to have a more productive day, he left the toast and

and headed into town to buy a kettle. Two hours later he was walking along North Street, empty-handed. The sun was bright on the red mossy roof tiles, sharp against the grey stone. The kettle would be delivered on Monday, along with the waffle pan, blender and new vacuum cleaner. The sales assistant, brunette, had been most sympathetic when he'd explained how his girlfriend had moved out and stolen the kettle. Robyn, the brunette, he would later tell Rory, had quickly divined that he lacked several of the essentials for modern living. He did already own a vacuum cleaner, but the digital hygiene facilitator Robyn had shown him had been very impressive. And blue. His new life would be delivered free of charge, complete with instruction manuals, on Monday.

Planning to check the ladder at Rory's, he paused at Macintyre's Collectibles and looked at the row of quaichs in the window. They looked back at him. He wondered what a quaich was, and decided to buy one for his father's birthday. He was about to enter the shop when a man fell heavily against him before crumpling into the gutter.

Glynn looked around – a nervous group of teenagers with high beehives hurried over the zebra crossing, and a pair of golfers swerved out of sight. No sign of cameras. The man was sweating in layers of tweed, gasping, and patting a nosebleed with a white handkerchief. Glynn knelt down on the curb, and reached for his globe, 'Hang on, I'll get help,' he said. A woman's face appeared in the hologram and enquired, 'Medical, fire, constabulary?' As he formed the first syllable, the face changed to another woman, this time dressed in white. 'Self or other?' she said. 'Other!' he answered, with slight indignation.

'Please scan the patient.' Glynn ran his scanner across the old man's temple, then jumped as the image flashed 'DO NOT TOUCH VICTIM'.

And then the nurse was back. 'Dr Hughes, an ambulance has been dispatched to you. If you wouldn't mind staying with Mr. Bartlett until help arrives, that would be greatly appreciated.'
'Um, there was a message flashed up,' said Glynn.
'Och, no ignore that. Glitch in the system. Told some poor wee lad last week his toothache was an ectopic pregnancy. Mad no? Thank you, Dr. Hughes.' The image faded, leaving trees and a small, low iron gate for a horizon against the grey tarmac foreground. The old man was wracked by a coughing spasm, and spat out small fragments of phlegm. At the back of his mind Glynn noted that the loogies were the colour of serpentine; he wondered whether the man was suffering from asbestosis. His attention was wandering to the job offer he'd rejected soon after graduating – if he'd accepted, he'd now be a tanned Californian, driving a Ferrari in Humboldt County.

The old man coughed again, and Glynn refocused on the situation. By this time several passersby had stopped. A young woman with short dark hair stood in the middle of the road holding back the traffic. The easily-distracted part of Glynn's brain mulled over a joke about 'having a figure that could stop traffic', while also noting with some admiration how forcibly she directed everyone. He resolved to strike up a conversion with her, but when the ambulance arrived people drifted away, and she had strangely called over to him, 'Bye, Uncle Glynn!' before disappearing into the crowd. Glynn was pretty sure she wasn't his niece. The police pulled up

—

as the ambulance moved off, and Glynn was the only one there to give his details. Good to have witnesses, nasty fall, traffic flow problems, that sort of thing. And then they were gone, and the street was back to normal. The shopkeeper peered out keenly, scenting Glynn as a potential quaich buyer, but this was not his lucky day.

Glynn leaned back against the wall, looked at his watch, and considered his actions. He'd been heroic. He was sure the mystery girl would have said that. He'd be sure to find out who she was, in a small town like this. She seemed to know his name. Glynn considered his mental state. Discombobulated, he decided, and the traditional remedy was a good lunch. He walked back to his flat, and drove out along the coast to Crail.

As the road rose sharply up the hill out of St Andrews, the sea on his left flashed in and out of his peripheral vision. It was still the holiday season, so he had to drive around the village for a few minutes when he arrived to find a parking spot. The smell of cooking seafood rose to meet him as he reached the harbour. The girl at the hut smiled shyly, acknowledging him as a familiar face without a name, and said, 'Will you be wanting a large male crab today?'

'Spot on,' Glynn agreed, and they completed the rest of the transaction in good-humoured silence. On the way back to the car he stopped at the baker's and the greengrocer's to buy a French stick and a lemon, and placed them all on the front seat. The drive home was slowed by a convoy of caravans, but he was pulling into the car park behind the flat just as the heavy bell of the local church struck one o'clock. Plenty of time for a long, soothing lunch. He found the mayonnaise in the fridge, then unwrapped the crab and savoured the sweet, marine smell. A few barnacles were artfully arranged on one claw, breaking the smooth, glistening bands of cream, rust and black. He cracked the claws. The white meat, still slightly warm, slipped out and he bit in. 'Like making love to the sea!' was how Jera had described it when she introduced Glynn to this local delicacy. Even 'though she was gone, the experience of fresh, still-warm crab overwhelmed any lingering associations with his crazy ex-girlfriend.

Glynn wondered whether the mystery girl would be a foodie, and wondered some more about her, as he prepared his meal. The temptation was to eat as he pulled the crab apart, but the ritual was part of the pleasure. Separate the brown meat, mash with lemon juice. In another ramekin mix mayonnaise with freshly pressed garlic. Crack the legs, the claws and the body. Arrange in a semi-circle on the table, together with a basket of fresh bread, nutcrackers, a finger bowl, and the essential lobster fork for fishing out well-hidden chunks of deliciousness. And now, let us begin.

Glynn ate deliberately. It took nearly two hours by the time he had cleared everything away, hoovered and double-bagged the debris. He stretched out on the sofa, licking his fingers, and flipped through the latest news reports on the screen, ignoring the junk 3D images offering cut-price flights to Norway. He was not too surprised when one of the fjords miaowed, as Tommy walked through a tempting deal on cruises from Newcastle, blue eyes shining.

'Now how did you get in?'

The cat jumped onto his lap. 'Oi! Careful!' he yelled,

and scratched his side. 'If you had the slightest hunting reflex, you'd have realised I left you some - blue bowl in the kitchen. Go on, git!' He dozed on the second- best cushions. Tommy had lunch, then dozed on his favourite chair, and the afternoon drifted by. The sun had lost some of its edge when Glynn rolled off the sofa, repacked his rucksack and walked up the hill to Pipeland Farm. Robbie was waiting, and ran out, crying, 'Uncle Glynn, I've learnt my song!'

Before he could take off his jacket, the ten-year old began a hymn on his digital flute. When he had played the whole thing through twice, Glynn clapped loudly, 'Bravo! Bravo! Verrry impressive. Repetatio, variatio, and slight tinges of Greensleeves!' 'Do you want to hear another one?' Robbie hopped about.

'After dinner, eh? How are the bunnies?'

Robbie abandoned the recorder and sprung into the garden, 'Come and see! They're doing more to the burrow.' Becky was sat on the grass by the run, 'Uncle Glynn!' she cried, 'Look they're making their house bigger.' He sat down beside her, 'I thought they'd finished this months ago.'

'Mammy says they're getting ready for winter.'

Glynn nodded, 'Hmmn. So, how big is the burrow now, d'you think?'

Becky ran to show him, 'There's another entrance over there, but it's outside the run so Daddy put a stone over it. They might escape. And then they're digging that way I think 'cos they're bringing up the roots from the tree.'

Wow, that tunnel's long,' he jumped up, and was measuring it with strides, when Abi called, 'Can I get you a drink? We've got some fresh lemonade, lots of fizzy tooth-rotting stuff, or plenty of others, to cater for all manner of childish tastes.'

Leaving the four little ones playing, he set his rucksack down on the kitchen table, opened the clasps and said, 'Well, here it is. One super-duper, pristine rodent-repelling machine.'

'Matt said you didn't have it.'

'No, I told him I'd have to find the box, that's all. And here it is.'

Abi turned it over, 'Well, I would have preferred it. Matt's had poison down. Seems to have done the trick, but I don't like it. Much better to scare them away than kill them. Anyway, thanks for trying. Will you have a drink before dinner? We're just waiting for Matt.'

'A lager, thanks.' He sat at the table, 'Where is he then, dirty rotten stop-out?'

'Still at school.'

'Thanks. I thought they didn't go back 'til next week?'

'No, another set of meetings.'

'Ah, those mythical long holidays of school teachers of yore.'

'You're telling me! Apart from that week on Skye we've hardly seen him. Now he's got Harries working on new pilot reading schemes.'

'New initiative?' Glynn laughed, 'Demon Headmaster's become a true believer?'

Abi grimaced, as she tied her hair higher into a ponytail, salt-and-pepper grey hair now mirroring the freckles scattered all across her face. Glynn remembered when they'd first met just before Matt's wedding, dark ringlets framing her flirtatious dark eyes – she'd never been just a sister-in-law - more the slightly rebellious big sister. He liked her straight off, a little overawed, and he was sure younger brother Jamie had a terrible teenage crush on her, only soothed by her studied maternal concern for him. Now she seemed to mother them all.

'No, for once, it's not the D.H.,' she replied. 'It's Matt's idea; thinks it'll get him a headship a year or two ahead of schedule.'

'And it probably will,' Glynn muttered.

'Aye,' Abi handed him his drink. 'I know you sometimes think his life always goes to plan, but he does work hard.'

'And he has you, so there's a certain amount of good fortune involved as well.'

'Thank you kindly,' she said. 'You should see the bullshit this scheme brings with it.'

'I can tell you miss it.'

'Like a hole in the head!' She grimaced. 'Ah, here they are. About time.'

As the Land Rover drew up outside the kitchen window, cries of 'Daddy' and 'Uncle Finn' scared the rabbits back into their warren. Glynn joined them in the garden, 'Sounds like that engine's running okay now.'

'Aye, but I wouldn't like to tell you how much it cost. What can you do?' said Finn, casting an eye over the rabbits popping up in the lawn. 'Not grown much, have they?'

'They're not going to grow, Uncle Finn!' shouted Robbie, 'They're dwarfs! Dwarves! Dwarfs!'

'Well, they're not big enough yet.'

'Big enough for what?'

'Big enough to put in a pie!' Robbie laughed with him. 'Finn!' shouted Abi, 'What have I told you! Don't upset Becky. It's alright, Becky, it's just jesting, now, isn't it? Nothing to worry about, bunnies okay.

Uncle Finn's just being daft. No-one's going to hurt the bunnies. Anyway, Barbie'd bite them, wouldn't she?'

Becky stopped crying and gulped, 'Sharp wee teeth, Daddy said.' 'Absolutely,' Abi soothed her, 'now here, have some juice.' She sat Becky down at the table, then shouted out the back door, 'Oi, Mr McGregor! Come and have your tea. Enough with the pie jokes, okay?' Finn blew her a kiss, 'Okay, sis. But she'll have to get used to it sometime. Can't have rabbits up here without knowing how we treat the wild ones. Much better to shoot 'em, than have that plague of myxi.'

'Oh, come on. When was the last time you shot a rabbit, let alone had a rabbit pie?'

'I know,' Finn patted Becky's hair. 'I'm only joking, hen. Never going to be enough meat on them, now is there? That smells good. Sorry I can't stay. I've only got Malcolm helping out right now. '

'Can I come out to the farm, Uncle Finn?' Robbie gulped down his juice and was ready to go.

'Not tonight, my lad. Too much hard work to do this time of year, now your granddad's buggered off to pensioner towers.'

'Finn!' Abi threw a teatowel at him. 'Language!'

'Sorry, deluxe apartment pensioner towers.'

'Get out! Go back to your cows!'

'Alright, I'll see you next week. Bye all!'

After tea, Abi put Becky to bed and shooed Robbie into a bath with promises. He soon emerged clean and ready to seal the deal. 'Okay, time for the amazing Uncle Glynn to sing for his supper,' Abi said smiling.

'Tell me it's not more recorder practice,' Glynn groaned at her mock-innocent eyebrow. She relented,

'No, you're alright. My folks bought him another addictive game, 'Underwater Safari.' I told him you'd play.'

'Bad luck,' said Matt handing a plate to Abi. 'It seems to me, that your parents underestimate the capacity of small boys to obsess about the slightest thing. And what is it with the fish? It's not actually fishing, and why do they have these crazy personalities?'

Robbie wiped the blank wall opposite his bed, and threw a globe to Glynn, saying, 'Cool. This is ace.' A fanfare of dancing fish appeared. 'Okay,' said Robbie. 'You get a story and pick a fish. It's way cool. And you collect shells, but sometimes you get eaten. Flossie always gets eaten.'

'So, how do you pick a good fish?'

'You see their skills, but ye cannae tell what stories you'll get, so you don't always know. Agility's good, but sometimes you need to be big to scare off sharks.'

'So, it's a game of strategy?'

'Aye, but sometimes things are weird. Like there's a new shark which gets one of the best ones.'

'Ah, so you need to avoid a red herring.'

Robbie frowned, so Glynn explained, 'A red herring, something that's meant to catch you out. So it looks like a good bet, but really it's going to get eaten straight off.'

'Yeah, like when Rooster got bit by a stingray,' Robbie nodded his understanding.

'Okay, I'll take my chances. Can I be Torpedo? Fast and hides well?'

'I'll be Mercury. Agile, small enough to get through reeds.'

Glynn quickly lost to the God of Communication, as blasts of triumphal music filtered through the house. Robbie bounced on his bed, punching the air. His spirits sank just as dramatically when Matt came up and said, 'That's enough for tonight. Your mam'll be up soon so you'd better pack up.' Robbie groaned as Glynn switched off the globes, 'Never mind. Play again next week?' Glynn followed Matt down and said, 'I found the repelling machine I mentioned.'

'Oh, thanks, mate, no need now. Finn and I saw to it.'

'Poison?' Glynn wasn't sure what the family dynamic was here. Matt paused, then said *sotto voce*, 'A bit. That wasn't what solved it though. Bloody big rat. Finn and I cornered the bastard, flattened it behind the cooker. You can still smell the bleach. For god's sake don't tell Abi, 'though. She'd have a fit and want a new cooker or something. Must have been them two doors down, building their conservatory.' He laughed, 'You should have seen us kitted out, somewhere between a prop-forward and a racing driver. Gloves, the lot. Got it, 'though, that's the main thing.'

Over coffee Glynn told them about his morning's shopping. He didn't mention the ominous screen message, but Abi was still concerned. She took Glynn's temperature, and examined his eyes carefully. Matt chuckled, 'You know that's for checking dogs, right?' and reminded them of the hysteria that Spring when bird 'flu was big news. No epidemic had materialised, and he was convinced there was a government conspiracy - disinformation designed to distract from the latest sex scandal in the Department of Health. Abi humoured him, but when Glynn grabbed his rucksack from the kitchen she took a strip of pills from the dresser, and said quietly,

'Will you at least take some vitamin C, for me? Yes, I know what Matt says, but it doesn't have to be bird 'flu, or even Ebola or the coronavirus. If our antibiotics stop working, we'll be in the Dark Ages soon enough.'

'Are you worried I'll keel over and you'll have to play 'Underwater Safari' forever?' Glynn laughed. She threw the pills at him.

'Now was that *to* me, or *at* me?' he grinned.

'Away wi'ye, trouble,' she scolded, as he packed the pills in with the rodent-repeller. He chewed a pill on his way down the hill, reassured by her concern.

The next morning brought no raging fever or sudden rashes. Glynn boiled the water for tea slightly longer than needed, and chewed a few more vitamin C tablets before settling down to work on some calculations. He soon lost track of time, and only noticed his cold tea when a slight drop in light and temperature caused him to shiver. The sun was setting gently, and the sky was streaked with pink when Glynn ran down to John Burnet Hall. Rory raced down the stairs, and said, 'Felix not here?'

'No. Conference in Edinburgh.'

'Probably just as well,' Rory noted, as they set out. 'These sunsets he comes over all poetic.'

'Oh, like it doesn't make you want to get your camera?'

'Maybe, aye, but ye canna fatten the coos on't.'

'That's Gaelic for 'shut-up' is it?'

They jogged down through the West Sands car park to the beach. The sand was warm and solid and the stars twinkled through the pink as they picked up the pace. Glynn told Rory about the lovely sales assistant, without mentioning the mystery girl from the accident – Rory could trace his family back in the town to pre-Christian times, and Glynn was sure he'd know who she was and everything about her, but he wanted to enjoy the mystery for a little longer.

After a hard half-hour's run, they turned and began to jog back, when Rory said, 'Where'd she go?'

'Who?'

'The lassie in the green coat, looking out to sea. I was planning on asking if she was well.'

'Looking out to sea? Didn't see her.'

'That's cos you're struggling to keep up, wimp.'

Glynn threw the dying old man into the conversation, and was surprised when Rory paused and said, 'Cool!'

'Cool?' he jogged on the spot as Rory looked out to sea. 'That's it?'

'Well, no, but, makes you think.'

'About?'

'End of the world.'

'Right.'

'Could be like when that swan with bird 'flu turned up. Men in white plastic sealing off Cellardyke. *Chariots of Fire* meets *Twenty Eight Days Later*.'

'I don't follow.'

'Oh, no right,' said Rory, setting off again. 'Early Sci-fi night, you didn't come.'

'Too bloody right. A night of mad Lynsey trying to get her claws into me. Can't believe I missed it.'

'You're paranoid.'

'I'm not. You were there with that wand thing.'

'But she was talking literally.'

'Oh, and that's so much better. Frankly a bit of innuendo would have been fine. It was when she got out that stick with beads on, that really freaked me out.'

'Well, you could do worse,' Rory said, with a quick

sideways glance. 'She likes you, I'm sure of that, and she's no madder than Jera was...'

'Thanks, I'll pass.'

'Really, why not? Cheer you up.'

'That woman has the common sense of a whelk. Come on, you were at that graduation. Six months she spends ignoring all the signs that Brad was shagging everything that moved, and then she suddenly announces, 'He's cheating on me. I felt a tremor in the force!' Mad.'

'She was being metaphorical.'

'Bollocks. Anyway, if you're so keen on her, you take her out.'

'Well, if we're all going to die, I could do worse,' Rory sensed Glynn's reluctance, so said, 'What did Felix say?'

'He thinks Lynsey's mad too.'

'Thanks. And about the imminent viral apocalypse?'

'Oh, I dunno. I left him a message, but he's probably up to his eyes in vol-au-vents.'

When Glynn got back home, he decided that the bushes on the garden path would be a hazard for the delivery men in the morning, so he set at them with a pair of old shears which came with the flat. 'Out of the way!' he said to Tommy, who was trying to sleep, shifting slightly to keep up with the patch of fading sunlight. 'You know,' he continued to the oblivious cat, 'when I was in school a friend of mine accidentally killed a kitten, mowing the lawn. He was doing the edges with a strimmer and the kitten was fast asleep.' Tommy waited patiently for the familiar punchline. 'And you know,' I said to him, 'it's a pity you're not Catholic, Tim. You could have gone to confession : 'Forgive me father, for I have strimmed.' Whaddya think?' Tommy yawned, then rolled over to sleep again. Glynn packed up the old vacuum cleaner and drove to the recycling centre where he picked up a few copies of old yachting magazines and *National Geographic* from the top of the paper bank. He went to bed early, cursing himself for not warming up properly before the run.

Some time after midnight he drifted back into consciousness, and thought he was in his flat in Bristol. He lay in the dark, puzzled by the feeling of space. He reached for the mug of water, knocking over his alarm clock. His throat hurt, and he thought about going for painkillers, but soon fell back into bright, violent sleep. At eight he woke, groaned, sat up and immediately fell back, wrapping the blanket around him. Later he would describe it as being hit by a freeze-ray, the cold and all-over pain mangling his thoughts. Daylight grew stronger, and he moaned and moaned, and shifted under the covers until the pressure on his bladder forced him out of bed. His legs shook as he edged to the bathroom, one hand on the wall. He sat on the toilet to urinate. The bathroom cabinet had a packet of aspirins, past their sell-by date, which he threw out, the enamel of the sink slipping under his hands as he struggled to steady himself. Grabbing a toilet roll to blot his nose he staggered back to bed and rolled himself up, trying to find the warm patch he'd been lying in.

Just before midday the doorbell shocked him awake, and he staggered to the front door, gazing blurrily at the white coats through the other side of the glass.

'Late night, mate?' said the one with the clipboard, as the other wheeled the trolley up the path.

'Something like that,' Glynn grunted.

'Sign here. Physician heal thyself, eh?'

'What? Oh, yeah. Okay. Thanks,' Glynn signed and coughed. He piled up the boxes in the kitchen, whimpering to himself, before unpacking the vacuum cleaner. It was still blue, so he went back to bed.

Some hours later, when he could no longer cling to the hope of sleep, he fumbled for the 'phone, hitting the speed dial for Matt. Abi answered and shrieked, 'My god, Glynn, what's happened?'

'Can you bring me some Lempsips?' he spluttered.

'Do you think you should call a doctor?' she was clearly alarmed, 'Shall I call Felix? Oh god, do you think it's that bug?'

'He's, he's at a conference. I'm sure it's nothing, but I'm sorry, but I really feel rough.'

'Hang on,' Abi disappeared from view, and the cooker continued, 'I'll be straight there.'

Glynn rolled the 'phone away and tumbled back into the damp sheets. It seemed only minutes before Abi was there. She looked into the bedroom and caught her breath as Glynn groaned, 'Can I have a hot-water bottle? The kettle came.' She moved to his side and put her hand on his forehead, 'You're burning up. When did this take you?' She cleared a space on the windowsill, before bringing a glass of water and helping Glynn to take some painkillers and vitamin C, 'You know, this place is a germ-trap. I'm not surprised you're ill.' She filled a hot-water bottle, and closed the bedroom door. Feeling uneasy she called the surgery, and explained his symptoms. She agreed that he was in pretty good health, mid thirties, no heart problems. When she mentioned that he'd looked after an old man in the street, a few days ago, the receptionist told her crisply that that there wasn't anything any doctor could do for a simple respiratory virus, so to give him plenty of liquids and call back if he wasn't feeling better in seventy-two hours.

Abi felt silly for calling. She decided to make some soup in case Glynn felt like eating, called Emily's mum, Eilidh, to keep Becky a while longer, and arranged for Robbie to go to a friend's after Judo. By the time she took the soup in Glynn was sitting up, clutching the hot-water bottle and staring vaguely at the window. 'What if I'm the red herring?' he whimpered.

'The what?'

'It could be *his* story. I should have asked. Rory said it was strange. That Mr. Bartlett, didn't look like a golfer. You know, I used to have a schoolteacher called Bartlett. Maybe it's his story and I'm the one who dies tragically in the first act. And I've just met the woman of my dreams. She had dark hair and she called me 'Uncle Glynn', and I have to find out who she is,' he coughed, wiping his eyes.

'Oh right, well, we'll have the headstone engraved 'I said I was ill', will we?' said Abi briskly. 'That was Nia you saw at the accident, alright? So maybe she will be the woman of your dreams, but you're just a wee bit feverish. Try and go to sleep, there you go.' She switched off the light, as he mumbled, 'I'm the one who makes everyone get interested, aren't I?'

'Always,' she smiled, closing the door. The half-light framed him curled like a Henry Moore sculpture, as the sticky viruses in his blood hijacked his cells, turning his body against him. On the other side of town Nia popped a pill and drifted off to sleep.

Chapter Two

Abi saw a pair of eyes above a piece of A4 paper and stepped back from the door. She read, 'Don't Panic'. Feeling panic rising, she took a deep breath before she opened the door and realised it was Felix, wearing a gauze mask over his mouth. 'And again,' he laughed, 'Don't panic. Put the kettle on, and I'll see to the invalid.'

A few minutes later he came out of the bedroom, still wearing the mask and said, 'I could murder a cuppa, but duty calls. Now, you're not to worry, hen, but I'm taking him to the hospital. Just a precaution.' She poured the tea and said, 'He's really ill, isn't he?'

'Probably not,' he clucked, taking off the mask. 'See? Just a precaution. I think he's got 'flu, but his chest sounds bad, so I'll get him checked out – got the car outside. Now, as for you, when was the last time you saw him before today?'

'Saturday night. We all had dinner, Matt, the weans. Are we infectious?'

'Probably not, but be on the safe side, will you stay here until I know a bit more?'

Her eyes widened, and she said, 'You're putting me under quarantine?'

'Now, if I was doing that I'd be posting a watch outside the door. Look, if you've picked something up today you won't be infectious yet, but you don't want to risk spreading this.'

'You're right. Sorry. Not thinking.'

'Okay, give me a hand to get him to the car?' They threw a blanket round Glynn's shoulders and squashed his feet into slippers, before manoeuvring him out of the bedroom as he mumbled, 'I'm dying.'

When Abi closed the front door, the flat felt less solid, and she left another message for Matt, then stirred her tea distractedly before lighting up Glynn's internet connection. She was initially comforted to see no reports of strange illnesses or the much-anticipated pandemic, and relaxed slightly, skipping ahead through pages of results. Historical and literary plagues began to appear, and her chest tightened as she read accounts of sudden devastating diseases across the centuries.

They started with isolated incidents, unconnected events in well-ordered cultures, and ended with families fighting to get their relatives' corpses on to pyres. Thucydides described the plague of Athens, the confident, ambitious home of drama, democracy and medicine, turning into a wasteland where society broke down, religion and philosophy failed, and each man lived with no thought of tomorrow. Passages from Camus' fictional plague were even more disturbing, as the modern mechanics of vaccines and railroads crumbled under the threshing flail. Abi remembered something from a school trip to Amsterdam. They'd visited Anne Frank's house, and one of her friends had asked the teacher, 'Why didn't they just leave before it all happened?' Their teacher had simply said, 'Just remember, when you think you should start thinking about doing something or going somewhere, it's probably already too late.'

By this point Abi's head was spinning, with a calm, disasters-don't-happen-here, modern-medicine-is-wonderful melody playing over a darker baseline. The government advice page on planning for emergencies echoed twentieth-century advice to use kitchen tables against atomic blasts, but one detail of accounts from the Black Death rang true: The safest people were those who saw it coming, and had the money and means to sit it out, isolated, but protected.

Abi reflected on times in her childhood on the farm, minor panics over electricity cuts and the big blizzard when she was a still a toddler. The farm had lost power and they'd been trapped by drifts for days before help arrived. The animals had been fine, but preparations for the humans had been less successful. Torch batteries had soon been exhausted, and they'd lit the main room with scented candles, eating dry bread and sardines toasted on the open fire. A hole started to open at the back of Abi's mind. Matt would accuse her of paranoia, but if there was going to be an epidemic, they should expect some disruption. She decided to add some extras to the next online food delivery, but as she added candles, matches, UHT milk, bottled water, and chocolate another nasty thought occurred to her.

All the web references to recent national concerns about Bird 'Flu and possible pandemics suggested it had only been an issue of real concern eighteen months ago. She, Abi Hughes, knew that there had been a flurry of interest just that Spring, and that the news coverage had been far more alarmist than the archives indicated. Looking back at online articles the coverage seemed uniformly bland, a detail visible to any student taking Highers. After a number of scandals about corporate attempts to manipulate the internet, the party line was now that the web was too complex an entity to succumb to whitewashing, but Abi began to wonder. If a plague was coming, and information was being suppressed, civil liberties were up for grabs. Rationing, quarantine or martial law were all on the table, and if the internet had been compromised then a sudden order for firewood in the middle of August might raise a red flag.

In the space of a few minutes Abi had become convinced that something bad was happening, and that she had a brief window in which to act. She was about to call her parents to warn them, but then worried that she might worry them unnecessarily. She thought about calling Finn and Rory, but the possible 'phone calls rippled out. Who do you tell? Do you risk causing a panic for nothing, or do you risk not giving friends a chance to save themselves? Competing scenarios jostled for her attention, and she idly browsed the internet files, before a repeated motif brought her sudden clarity: Small children were found crying, clinging to the bodies of mothers who had died days before.

She left her online order on its default settings, and set up a new list for her parents, choosing the first available slot that evening. Her parents' complex had a good infra-structure, so she concentrated on getting them a modest supply of store-cupboard foods and smaller items. Then she rang Finn, and left a message telling him to get some extra food in, and sort out the livestock. She promised to call him back, and ended the message, 'Seriously, think about the blizzard.'

There was no-one at the front door, and the only eyes watching the back door belonged to a ginger cat. Feeling slightly guilty, but ninety-percent sure she wasn't putting anyone in danger, Abi locked up and drove to the main supermarket. She filled a large trolley, then paused and started putting some things back. The ordinary delivery would be along as usual tomorrow, and there was no point in stocking an emergency larder with occasional treats. She returned to the biscuit aisle, seeking out high-calorie, long-life packets. Tins of fruit, meat and fish covered the basics, then she went round again, trying to anticipate what could count as 'nearly essential', trying to plan for a few weeks of rationing, isolation or both. Fish food, toilet rolls, breadsticks, jams and batteries.

At the tills her heart sank as she heard, 'Ooh, stocking up are we?' and turned to see a girl she used to babysit. 'I was just up your way,' Maisie continued. 'We toured the new development. Lovely houses, bit small, but it's great that you can wheel a pram straight into the kitchen without touching the carpets.' Nonplussed, Abi smiled, 'I didn't realise you were expecting. Congratulations!'
'Oh, no, not yet, but doesn't do any harm to plan,' Maisie laughed and waved a very small engagement ring at Abi. 'Very exclusive. You don't want a big ring, your finger goes all clammy under the band.' Packing up the trolley, Abi was still hearing about the intricacies of gallery settings and the rarity of tanzanite. She wondered how much firewood the ring would buy in the middle of a storm. At the garage she filled two new petrol cans, then weighed down the boot with charcoal, coal and kindling, saying a silent 'Thank You' for the Scottish weather; there was nothing strange about people still wanting open fires in August.

She was about to turn off the main road when another wave of panic struck. Maybe this wasn't enough. She couldn't go back to the main store, for fear of arousing suspicion, so she drove into town and parked up near the other supermarket.

She filled a small trolley with a random collection of painkillers, plasters, tampons, tea bags, bin bags, salt and vinegar, plus two bottles of whiskey, before adding more matches and batteries, and even more bottles of water and UHT milk.

Driving back home, Abi felt as if she was on a strange version of *Desert Island Discs*. She parked outside the house and rang the home number. When Matt picked up she gave him a quick update, and was relieved to hear that Felix had just called to say Glynn was probably going to be fine. When she explained what she'd been doing, Matt laughed, but agreed she could unload and leave the goods in the garage. As she climbed back into the car Abi felt satisfied that even 'though she'd probably over-reacted, it was better safe than sorry. It was only when she turned off the ignition and Becky ran out to the car that the fear returned. She quickly rolled up the window and shouted, 'Go back inside, sweetheart, I'll see you later.'

Becky was holding up a picture for her to see, and was indignant to be locked out of the car. Abi felt the tears stinging. She wanted to reach out and stroke Becky's head, but she superimposed the memory from a few months after her daughter was born – lips turning blue, hair plastered down with sweat, clutched to her chest as Matt drove to the hospital. Becky was released after a few days with no ill-effects, but Abi was very conscious of how much equipment and medical intervention they'd needed to treat 'a nasty case of pneumonia'. Becky's lip trembled as Matt took her indoors. Abi returned to Glynn's place, resuming her self-imposed quarantine.

Three days later Glynn opened his eyes, stared at the white ceiling and mumbled, 'I'm dying.'

'Every bloody day, the same thing. No, you are not dying,' Felix replied wearily.

'It hurts.'

'That's because you have 'flu.'

'No, it really hurts. All over.'

'Aye, that's the 'flu. Good to see you're awake. That's progress.'

'Where am I?' Glynn croaked.

'Well, you're in hospital, but you're sort of here under false pretences.'

'I'm dying.'

'Have a sip of this. Look, I'll fill you in very soon. I just need to ask you a few questions.'

'Questions?' Glynn coughed weakly.

'We know you had dinner at Matt's on Saturday. What did you do on Sunday?'

'Oh, ummm, oh.'

'You went running with Rory,' Felix prompted. 'Did you see anyone else? Anyone after you got home? Monday morning, before you called Abi?'

'No.'

'Great.'

'Just the delivery men, brought the stuff.'

'All those boxes,' Felix banged his pen on the clipboard. 'Damn. Okay, everyone's okay. You rest for a while and I'll come back later on.'

Two days later the conversation continued, 'You are bloody lucky to be here, that's all I can say. You'd have been home days ago if you weren't such a good test-case.'

'Eh?' Glynn whimpered.

'You have 'flu. Simple as that. You should be at home in bed. However, you did look pretty rough, and we needed to be careful. You remember Laura, works for the World Health Organisation?' he asked,

—

'Well, once you were here, turns out we could mark you as linked to an index case – your meeting with Mr. Bartlett helps us model the spread of the virus. You are officially E2347. Matt said you wouldn't mind letting us take lots of blood to check the progress.'

'Bloody hell!' Glynn choked out, struggling to sit up. 'He's my next of kin. He'd sell me for scrap. I mean, I know I'm a donor, but I don't want them to use my eyes.'

'Right,' said Felix slowly. 'You're clear on the 'not dying' bit now 'though, aren't you? Not killer bird 'flu. We can come back to that. The main thing is, you've had lots of love and attention, and now you're on the mend we will be sending you home in a few days' time.'

'Oh god, did I infect everyone?'

'Well, you're not personally responsible, but Rory, the girls in John Burnet, one of the delivery men, possibly Abi and the kids, 'though probably not because Becky looks to have got it first.'

'Are they alright?'

'Oh aye, they'll be fine. Not well, but nothing to worry about. Matt's doing a sterling job. And she did stock up a medicine cabinet which would do a small clinic proud, so yes, they'll be fine.'

On Sunday morning the younger nurses smiled cautiously as Glynn limped out of the ward. 'You've been making them nervous,' mused Felix. 'All those ill-omened death cries.' Glynn coughed, 'I still don't feel well.' He was still groaning weakly as Felix helped him out of the car and into his flat, 'Look, your fairy sister-in-law not only did your dishes,' Felix admonished, 'but also aired that charnel house of a bedroom, and made up the bed. Food out in the fridge and someone will be round to check on you in a day or two. For now, just take it easy, don't worry. I have to dash – lots of sick people – terrible downside to this job. But you'll be fine, got it? You'll feel weak for a while, but just keep taking the tablets.'

Glynn stroked the new kettle and made himself some tea. He pulled the bed out slightly from the wall, gasping with the effort, to pick up a stray tissue and magazine, before collapsing into softer-than-hospital bedclothes. After a short nap, he got up and checked his mail. There was a circular hand-delivered from the university asking all staff to inform their line managers of their current state of health. He looked through the material he'd been working on, but his head hurt and the numbers kept moving, so he went back to bed and slept in short bursts for the next few days, waking at odd hours in light and near-darkness to eat toast and tea.

Before he called Matt he fumbled for his watch to check it was evening not morning, then checked again to see what day it was. The last time he'd tried there had been a repeated 'No service' message, so he was relieved to see the hologram light up. He jumped a little when the 'phone was answered by a tearful young woman who looked nothing like Matt. Instead it was Maisie, the radiant bride-to-be who'd accosted Abi in the supermarket. Now she looked somewhat less radiant, and probably less interested in patio doors. 'Maisie?' Glynn said warily, 'What's happened?'

She slurped back, 'It's Ron Crane, they're saying he killed himself,' her voice rose an octave, 'but he can't have, I mean his family owns half of Edinburgh and he was going to Cambridge and his mother's an MSP.'

'Oh,' Glynn stammered, 'I'm sorry, were you close?'

'His cousin went to school with my fiancé's sister. I only met him once at a party of Richie's, and now I'll never know him, will I? Why is all this happening?' Glynn wasn't sure what to say, so looked for a sensible adult, 'Yes, no, um, is Matt there, or Abi?' Maisie was pushed out of the frame and Robbie appeared saying, 'Uncle Glynn! Maisie's here to babysit,' though I've said I dinnae need a babysitter now. I'm quite well again.' Maisie came back in and said, 'Matt's at a school thing, he's running round, everyone's been sick, and Abi's still in bed and can't talk to anyone. It's alright, my wee man, I'm just a wee bit upset. Someone I know is poorly, but he'll be fine,' she grinned maniacally at Robbie before turning back to Glynn, 'I'll tell Matt you called. We're fine. You take care now.' Worn out, Glynn put down some cat food and went back to bed.

Early on Saturday morning the doorbell rang. He ignored it, then someone started tapping at his window, so he struggled to the door.

'Hi! I'm Dawn, your candy-striper.'

Glynn blinked, 'You're a stripper?'

'A candy-striper. I'm here to check you're okay, run errands?' her voice became a little uncertain.

'Oh, a home help. Thanks, but I'm fine.'

'I have to do this form to say I've checked. What's in the fridge. Temperature of the room.'

'Right. You'd better come in. No, hang on.' He leaned against the door-frame. 'Do your parents know you're doing this?'

'I'm nineteen,' she was slightly offended. 'I'm doing Art History, but they say this will count for credit.'

'Well, that's fine. Come on in.'

Clutching her clipboard, Dawn moved delicately into

the hall, and laboriously filled in a tick-sheet, while Glynn sank back into the sofa. When she appeared to have finished, and was looking round aimlessly, he said, 'Tell me what's been going on. There's not a scrap of live news on the TV. Not even on Al-Jazeera.'

'You speak Arabic?'

'No,' he smiled, 'the English version. Lots of shots of wan but happy people in hospital, and reassuring government statements.'

'Well, they've been planning for it, haven't they? So there was this announcement about 'flu and the quarantines and the rationing and all that, and people went a bit mad, buying up dinghies and stuff. But, you know, no-one's died, only the old people, and I know they say maybe the virus can mutate, but I think it's just a false alarm. But yeah, with so many people off sick, you can't get things done. They cancelled all the trains day before yesterday. People were stuck in Edinburgh, Dundee, everywhere.'

'And candy-stripers?'

'It was all set up. We're the Support Network Behind The Professionals,' she enunciated.

'What does that mean?'

'Um, well, we check things are okay, you know, that you're not dead or something.'

'So, you've been vaccinated have you?'

'Yeah, 'though they say it's not a guarantee, but what can you do? You can't just stay indoors. And those masks they're selling don't really help. I saw some ad for Chinese herbs that I might take, but I've had 'flu before, and I'm really healthy,' she reassured him. Feeling very old, Glynn said, 'I seem to recall the 1918 'flu killed lots of young people.'

'Yeah, 'Killed More Than World War One',' chanted

Dawn. 'Great pandemic. I know, I know. So they keep saying. But, well, they didn't have antibiotics and stuff then, did they? Everyone's overreacting, if you ask me. But, this is easier than the core course on sculpture, so I don't mind. I can go to the shops if you like, get some supplies?'

'What about the rationing?'

'Oh, now everyone's quieter it's fine, they still get some deliveries and you can only buy one of each of some stuff, so there are some queues, but really this week it's been much quieter. What you do want?' Glynn jotted down a short list which Dawn scanned, comparing it with a list in her envelope file. 'Right, eggs are protein, right, so yes, that's right. Oh, bread, might have to be crispbread and I'll see if there's a national newspaper, but I doubt it. Do you want an old copy if I can find one?'

'Yeah, that would be great. Is your internet connection working?'

'Comes and goes. Way not cool. I mean, I'm having to pay for telephone calls and even that old system isn't working properly. Something about not having enough people to manage the servers they say. Oh, Dr. McManus said to give you these,' and she handed over a wrapped box.

While Dawn went shopping Glynn opened the box, then called Felix and got a recorded screen with advice about staying inside and taking paracetamol with plenty of fluids. He left a message asking where the real stripper was, and why he'd sent six months' supply of anti-depressants. After hanging up, Glynn realised he should have made a joke about cutting waiting lists by making patients top themselves, but he lacked the energy to compose anything more than a feeble pun so decided to save it for another time. He took another nap, and was startled when Dawn returned with a newspaper and the wrong cat food. 'I even asked about the one you wanted,' she said, 'but the girl said people stockpiled their favourite brands as it wasn't rationed. I told you people went mad.' Glynn told her it would be fine, 'though he knew Tommy would wait all day for a free-range mouse before he'd touch that canned muck. 'Ah, you wombled a paper. Excellent!'

'Not sure it'll tell you much,' she shrugged, but Glynn was already scanning the second page, so she unpacked the food and set off on her next mission of mercy.

After Dawn left, Glynn managed to reach Matt who was being 'man who copes'. Abi was still ill in bed, and he was arranging classes for all the primary-age children in St Andrews. After the initial simplicity of closing the schools, the council wanted to utilise available resources as efficiently as possible, so any teachers who weren't sick were expected to run round looking useful. Glynn promised he'd be up to visit in a few days. It was only then that he strung together bits of the conversation with Dawn, and wondered in what sense being a candy-striper could 'count for credit' in a degree programme.

He returned to the paper, scanning the headlines. In the space of a few weeks the whole planet was suffering from 'flu or raging hypochondria. Air travel had ceased, splitting up families who had casually set off on holiday without a thought for distance. Economies were mouldering and public services struggled to cope. The editorial expressed a hope that things would soon return to normal now there were no signs of the virus being any more lethal than usual, but the long-term effects of this new pandemic could not be accurately assessed. Glynn was pissed off. He'd been stoically bearing with his illness, stoking up the blitz spirit, feeling lucky to be alive after a brush with death. Now, as this wasn't the killer bug, he was just downright annoyed about the lack of news and the general stupidity of everyone overreacting and running round like Chicken Licken. After all that, he wasn't the hero of a tragic novel, just a bit player in a short story with a boring, happy ending. He flicked through the TV channels, rejecting repeats of cop shows and enthusiastic pleas to buy craft scissors from a man called Bryn. He watched a programme about vets at an airport, before deciding to go back to bed. The cat food remained untouched in the bowl.

A few days later the paper boy arrived with the local newspaper and Glynn's mail. He had previously noted that the paper filled odd gaps in the back pages by duplicating material from the front, but never before had he read a newspaper consisting of repeats from the past six months. There was a brief, calming notice on the front and an editorial on page two encouraging everyone to get back to work, but the rest of the paper was made up of 'last year's highlights', prize-winning marrows and all. Turning to his own correspondence Glynn saw that most of the letters were final demands, so he was almost energetic with relief when he read a letter from the university offering him a full-time post for nine months, 'in light of current staffing difficulties.' He was less enthusiastic as he read the wording of 'Teaching Fellow in Sciences', and the ominous phrase 'duties and hours to be determined.' In a previous post his hourly rate had turned out to be far less than the junior cleaner's, but a job was a job. He arranged a meeting for the following day.

The next morning, feeling cheered, Glynn left the flat, and took a breath of clean bright air. A little unsteady on his feet, but mentally invigorated, he walked slowly into town, slightly spooked by the lack of traffic. As he came closer to the centre he saw that most of the shops were closed. Sounds of birds and trees seemed much louder in the central streets. A sign on the door of the Tourist Information centre gave the local hospital numbers. The cashpoint told him the machine was out of notes. Glynn saw a few others wandering aimlessly, tourists in their own town. The only sign of life was a bright tangle of ribbons half way down Market Street. He hadn't been down there for a while, since the second-hand bookshop had relocated, but he remembered there was an independent shop or two, and the prospect of people.

As he drew close he hesitated. There were rocks in the window. Not proper rocks, waiting for someone to whack them with a hammer, but shiny, teasing rocks nestling in cradles of ivy. He smelled a whiff of patchouli coming from the doorway of 'Ethereal' and almost turned back, but then he saw a girl in a yellow vest standing on steps in the window. She climbed down and when he caught sight of her dark hair he thought he recognised her. She saw him and waved, so he went in. 'Hi,' she said, folding the ladder, 'Probably can't tempt you with lucky stones?'
'How do you know that? Have we met?' he said warily.
'Actually we have, when you rescued that old man.'
'I thought I recognised you. I'm Glynn Hughes.'
'Yes, Becky's uncle,' she nodded. 'You waited outside

once when she came in with Abi, and she told me you were a geologist who said this shop was silly.'

'Ah, well, she's young. She sometimes misquotes.'

She laughed, 'Fair enough. I'm Nia. So, what can I do for you today, Glynn Hughes?'

'To be honest, I'm just relieved to see something open. I was sort of hoping there might be people here, some people. I just seem to talk to one person at a time.'

'It's a bit like that this last couple of weeks. I've only been back at work a few days myself.'

'You've been ill?'

'There's something going round, you know.'

'Really? Can't say I'd noticed,' he flirted shamelessly, spinning the card display, and stroking a bowl of gemstones on the side table.

'It's alright,' she said, 'you don't have to buy anything. Not proper geologist stuff.'

'You underestimate me, my dear,' he said and she raised her eyebrows. 'I would avoid this place, it's true, and I'm quite sure these pewter fairies are not affecting the crystalline structure of this hydrated copper silicate, but ...'

'But?' she said with a challenging glare. He picked up the large irregular blue rock, 'The real reason I wouldn't come in here is that I have a weakness for sculptural pieces such as this perfectly ordinary piece of-'

'Pretty sea-green chrysocolla,' she finished for him.

'Quite!' he continued. 'So much so, that I am willing to pay this extortionate price for these additional mystical powers which I'm quite sure it doesn't actually possess. However ...'

'You want to buy it?'

'Sorry,' he dropped the pompous voice. 'Yes, please.'

'Okay, I'm guessing you don't have this much in cash on you?' He nodded.

'Well, now the banks have stopped electronic transfers, we have to do it manually, so I'll need to write you a receipt and take your details from the card. Not that I don't trust you.'

'You know,' he said as she sorted out the paperwork, 'they used to have real cheques, actual paper ones, which you carried around with you.'

'Doesn't sound very safe.'

'And what do we have now? Electronic everything grinds to a halt when a few people get ill. You'd have thought after that debacle with Second Life someone would have listened.'

She wrapped up the rock and handed him the dockets. He placed it in his rucksack and said, 'I assume I can bring it back for a full refund if it doesn't actually turn me into a floating lotus blossom?' She smiled as the door tinkled on his way out. Standing outside Tourist Information Glynn realised he'd just spent money he didn't have on something that was extremely hard to carry. He'd planned to go and scope out the mini attic office offered in his new contract, just to get a sense of how the university was handling things, but decided not to overdo it. He walked down to the supermarket and found no signs of rioting or panic buying. Some shelves were empty and there was no bread or fruit, but the strangest thing was the lack of musak. The lighting was a little dim too, probably energy saving.

At the tills the cashier seemed subdued, but the queue was short and fast-moving. One man was wearing a mask, and others were standing awkwardly, trying to avoid too close a contact as they queued for baskets of tinned whelks and gummi bears. Glynn collected a few bits and pieces, pausing only briefly to consider whether olives in brine were still classed as fruit. As he balanced the bags he felt extremely tired, and one of his mother's phrases came to mind, 'I feel as a weak as a kitten.' He was sorry to see that Burns was still shut at he walked back and turned down Logie's Lane. He was thinking about treacle toffees when he almost tripped over a girl outside the library. She was on the ground curled up like a cat around a carrier bag. 'Are you alright?' Glynn said, kneeling beside her.

'Yes,' she said quietly.

'Can I call someone for you?' he asked gently.

'He's coming back with the car.'

'Oh, okay. You're sure I can't do anything?'

'No,' she started to cry. 'I thought I'd be alright and I was alright, and then I just started feeling so much worse, and I just can't do this any more.' She buried her head in her arms.

Glynn sat down opposite her, tired out, not knowing what to do. 'You know what I've always thought would be a good idea?' he said. 'All those online sites where people load their holiday shots and tell you what they've done. Well, I really like reading them, so I could offer my services in person – I could be an audience for people who haven't got friends, or no, not like that, but everyone gets fed up hearing what a great holiday you've had, so why not hire someone?'

The girl said nothing, and after five long minutes, a car drew up and a man came rushing over to them, shouting, 'Oi, whaddya playing at?' Glynn stood up and said, 'I was just staying to see she was alright.' The man stopped, and blew out a long breath. 'Sorry, sorry. No, of course. That's very kind, good of you. I'm sorry, I'm sorry. She's just been like this all week. We thought a bit of fresh air would help, didn't we, love? And then she got upset and couldn't get home. Should have brought the bloody car to start, but what with the rationing, crazy, isn't it? Her mam's as bad, and the lad's still hacking away. I only just got back from the rig on Sunday, would you credit it? Come on, love. Can I give you a lift?' he nodded to Glynn.

'Actually,' he replied wearily, 'that would be very kind, if you don't mind. I think I've overdone it myself.'

They drove in silence, until they were diverted to a side road by a young policeman. 'That's bad luck,' said the driver. 'Hardly anything on the road, and then to get run over – kinda funny.' Glynn said nothing, shaken by the sight of a small figure under an orange blanket, head flat on the tarmac as an ambulance drew up, siren echoing.

When he opened his front door a blast of stale smells hit him, so he let the flat air while he unpacked. He realised he'd forgotten to take his 'phone with him, and remembered what he'd heard about power-cuts and problems with services, so plugged it in to charge. He'd missed messages from Rory who looked even worse than he did, saying that he thought his doctor was trying to kill him. Glynn couldn't tell whether he was joking.

Then there was one from his colleague Eilidh, asking Glynn to ring back. He didn't think he'd ever had a personal message from her - she'd been on leave when he arrived and taught in a different area of the campus. Intrigued, he rang back straight away. 'I hear you're okay,' she said, 'You look okay. Not prying, but did you get the job offer?

When Glynn read out the salary, she said, 'You know you can ask for three times that amount?'

'No,' he sighed, 'I know the deal, scivvy for someone else's sabbatical and be grateful for the privilege.'

She looked at him intently, then said, 'But not now.'

'I don't understand.'

'Right, this line could cut out any second. You're seeing Hobden when?'

'Tomorrow morning.'

He heard a sigh as she asked, 'Can I buy you a cup of coffee first, say tennish at McGregor's?'

'I think it's shut.'

'Won't be tomorrow.'

'Okay, but what's this about?'

'You can see what's happening, can't you? And you're fine? Well, so am I, but things are going to get much worse unless I'm very much mistaken, and the likes of you and I will have a lot to do, so they'll have to pay you more. Must go, see you tomorrow,' and she was gone.

Chapter Three

The slug never had a chance. Glynn registered the physical pleasure of the squelch before any social and ethical brain cells kicked in. 'Shit!' he yelled at the ground, scraping his boot on the edge of the gate. It had rained heavily in the night and the morning air was still grey and humid. In the cartoon version of his morning, he reached the corner of Langlands Road and bubblethought, 'Wrapped Around A Lamp-post.' A red car had crashed in the night and now resembled a short, fat man embracing a tall, thin woman. The glass had been swept to the gutter, but was still scattered across the pavement. There were hardly any cars on the road.

Glynn tried to ring Rory, but the connections were down, so he'd decided to make a quick detour to John Burnet Hall before meeting Eilidh. The entrance hall was deserted; a layer of dust had formed on the reception desk. Glynn heard the sound of a shower running, but saw no-one as he walked through to Rory's room. The door opened after his first rap, and Rory said, 'Did you see a green car go by?'

'No, can't say I did. Why?'

'Come in,' said Rory rubbing his head, and he pushed a pile of papers away to free the door.

'God, mate, you look rough. Still the 'flu?'

'Didn't sleep much,' he rasped, 'Went to get some stranded Dutch lads from Dundee. Took Julie's car, and there was this crunch when I reversed.' He coughed and spluttered on, 'I had a good look, but I couldnae see anything, but then when we got back I thought, maybe, I'd scraped the other car, so I got up and went out with a torch, but I couldnae get a sense of it, so I set the alarm to get up early, have a look in daylight, and the fucking thing was gone.'

Glynn stared at him, flabberghasted, 'You had a crash?' Rory glared at him, 'I don't bloody know, that's what I'm saying, but what if I did and they haul Julie up?'

'Why?'

'It's Julie's car!'

'Hang on, who would haul her up?'

'I dunno, bloody fascist bureaucrats, and then I'd lose my job and I'm screwed.'

'Okay,' Glynn mouthed. 'Got any coffee?'

Rory slumped on the sofa, 'Dunno. Maybe.'

Glynn picked his way through the room and filled the kettle, 'Good, water, electricity, coffee. We're in business. To be honest, mate, you're not looking too bright. Still feeling rough?'

'Dunno. I was doing great, then that new lassie from the surgery gave me pills and I got worse. On edge, you know?'

'You still taking them?'

'Och no. Poisonous. Some bloody conspiracy, take over the government. We shoulda gone for independence.'

'Really?' Glynn rinsed out mugs, and glanced at the bottle of pills in the bin. 'Here, this'll do the trick. No milk, I'm guessing.'

'Ta.' Rory downed the coffee then sat upright and said, 'D'you not think something's off? I mean, it's economics. Places like Madrid, Paris, they've got diversity, they can roll with the punches, but us, whole economy's driven by the Southern City wankers – bonuses, flash cars, keeps the whole lot running. So now what? Going to hell in a handbasket or worse. Could be the best terrorist plot ever.'

Trying to divert the conversation, Glynn offered, 'I think I saw your redhead earlier, going into McGregor's'.

'It's open?'

'Just for a few hours, I'm meeting Eilidh. They've offered me a better job for a whole nine months.'

'Take it while it lasts,' Rory sighed. 'Place is falling apart.'

'Yeah, well, she thinks I can ask for more money, so that's what I'm going to do. Bound to get back to normal soon. After all, you got your people from Dundee.'

'Yeah, just what I want, trail round after bloody students complaining about the washing machines.'

Glynn finished his coffee and rinsed the mugs, saying, 'Fancy a run later?'

'Not up to it today.'

'Yeah, convalescent aren't you? Lazy bugger.'

'Fuck you.'

'Alright,' Glynn punched him, 'See you later,' and he closed the door carefully, trying not to disturb Rory any further.

The sky was clearing and Glynn felt his strength returning in the fresh, washed air. He walked up the main commercial stretch of Market Street, past closed shops still displaying banners from the Lammas Market, and met Eilidh and Emily coming the other way, blocking his view of the rest of the street. 'Hello,' he said to the child, 'That's a nice dress.' She murmured 'Thank You,' while shrinking back. 'Oh, don't be silly,' said Eilidh picking her up. 'You remember Becky's uncle Glynn?' Emily buried her head in her mother's shoulder as she continued, 'Aunty Morag's looking after you this morning, love   Let's find you a drink.

They went into McGregor's which was busy but unusually quiet. Eilidh settled Emily with crayons and paper, then brought two mugs of tea to a table at the back of the shop. 'Sorry,' she said, sitting down, 'babysitter arrived and then had to go home, she was too upset. And Bob's still hacking away.'

'Lot of it around.'

'Bright lad!' she said and sipped her tea. 'Seriously, you can see what's happening? The epidemiology? Normally you'd have things picking up by now, still get new people infected, but the first wave are back to work. Not this time. The first wave of people come back to work, and can't take it, so go off sick again.'

'What, d'you think there's something else going on?' Glynn said warily, thinking about Rory's conspiracy fears.

'Well, some people get ill and get better,' Eilidh shrugged. 'I was poorly early August, well before all the hysteria started, and I'm fine. And you're fine, no?'

'A bit tired...' he started, but she interrupted him, leaning closer, 'But not insomniac, can't concentrate, life-not-worth-living tired, no?'

'No,' he agreed.

'So, cards on the table.' She glanced round before continuing, 'I reckon this is post-viral depression, but much more than usual. I've had troubles, and I'm guessing you have too in the past.'

'Post-viral depression.'

'Aye,' she said, looking at him with maternal concern, 'Does that fit your picture?'

He paused. 'Felix sent me six months' worth of anti-depressants. And I wondered what that was about, because it's an odd thing to do, isn't it?'

'Okay,' she leaned back and stirred her tea. 'There's every chance this is going to get much worse before it gets better.'

'Why?'

'Think about it, when you were at your worst – couldn't leave the house? Leave your bed? Odd behaviour?'

Glynn frowned, then said, 'I stopped eating anything but olives.'

She nodded, 'So, take that person – would you put him in charge of a nuclear power station? Or a bus full of children? Or a car? How long until you felt better?'

'About six months.' He paused, then said quietly, 'Did Abi tell you this?'

'No. Educated guess. You got up and about quickly after the 'flu. So did I, and I've been drugged up since a nasty dose of post-natal depression. It's quite nice to realise for once I've actually made a far better recovery than most people.'

'I don't think Abi and Matt know,' Glynn said, feeling a strange mixture of relief and fear.

'Oh, I'm sure they don't. I haven't said anything. I wouldn't. Actually, you're the first person I've said anything to,' Eilidh said seriously. 'It's just with Hodders orchestrating the new Reich, he's canny, and I couldnae just let you walk in there blind.'

Glynn moved the biscuit crumbs around the plate and said, 'Eilidh, are you feeling alright?'

She took a long gulp of tea then said firmly, 'Will you listen. People are getting seriously depressed after the 'flu, and those who aren't, tend to be on anti-depressants already, no? Am I getting through to you?' Glynn considered this situation, and thought of Eilidh's position, then said, 'What about Bob?'

'He'll be fine,' Eilidh smiled. 'He has his work. To be honest, I'm more worried about Emily. She's always been sensitive, but since she got ill … well, anyway. So now, are you with me? I admit this is a peculiar conversation for us to be having, but when I heard that you were around and Hobden had his eyes on you, I had to say something. You and I may be the last line of defence.'

'Yeah, okay, I see your point. But, how come the university's been so quick off the mark?'

'Well, someone must have known this was a possibility. You know the V.C.'s got links to pharmaceuticals?'

'Oh god, don't let Rory hear you say that!'

'Well, somebody's been planning. Some of the students are around, and if they're paying their fees, something has to be done with them. You've got to be tough with Hobden. They'll have to pay you more, I'd say double wherever they start.'

'Where's everyone else?' Glynn was still cautious. He knew how complex academic politics could be, but Eilidh rolled her eyes and said, 'John and Laura are still in the States, so that two-for-one deal really worked out well. Simon's back from South Africa, but badly, and Mick's in London – may be back soon, may not.'

'Rachel?'

'Contract ended in May, back in Dublin. It's lucky, you having family here. Everyone knows it's a scandal. I'm sorry I haven't been around more,' she stirred her tea, 'but, you had an advantage. Most temporary staff have to choose – do the minimum here, try to keep life going in Birmingham, Dublin or wherever, you're never in the one place, but marking time. Or, you do what Gregor did, it was a good few years ago. Throw yourself into everything, live in the moment – I think that's better, but then it's cruel hard when your time's up and you're shut out. Anyway, you're here, and now Simon's been laid low I'm sure Hodders wants to sign you up before Aberdeen or Glasgow come calling.'

'I appreciate the heads-up. I'm not sure what I'm supposed to do.'

'I will be very interested to hear,' Eilidh laughed bleakly, 'We're supposed to start teaching next week – who and what I'm not sure.'

'Do you really think this is going to carry on? I mean, there's bound to be plans in place. Even if everyone is depressed, it's not fatal.'

'Maybe I'm paranoid, but ask for more money! And don't be fazed by the double set of eyes – he had his vision sorted years ago – the fishbowl lenses are a prop.'

'Okay, look, thanks, you might be on to something.'

'Good man!' she said, patting him on the shoulder and scooping up Emily. 'Let's be off.' Glynn followed, feeling more tired and disorientated than when he'd woken up.

As they came out into the street the sun broke through the last clouds, bright and yellow.

'Wow!' said Glynn, and Emily pulled at her mother's coat.

'What's that, sweetheart?' Eilidh said, bending down.

'Full sun,' Emily whispered more audibly.

'Yes, it is isn't it?' Eilidh replied, straightening up.

'Full sun?' Glynn said. 'You've lost me.'

'Yes, well, Daddy's been teaching you about the moon again hasn't he, hen?' The little girl nodded, looking down at pink trainers; Eilidh continued, 'To be honest, I lose interest every time he reaches those parts about gibbous phases, so I'm not surprised he's got her a bit confused. Come on, sweetheart.' They started to walk towards the sun, and saw a school friend getting out of a car. She waved, Emily looked up, and Eilidh said, 'Go on, you can go.' Emily set off, but after a few steps she tripped on a paving stone.

Glynn still wasn't used to seeing small children fall. The sight took him back to his own childhood, and he shifted nervously. Eilidh shrieked. He watched the jolt, imagined the sudden nausea as Emily's body lost contact with the rest of the world, then sensed the burning on her knees and wrists, then the pain, then the bloody smell of concrete. Emily screamed. Eilidh picked her up, patted the grazes and pulled out a piece of chocolate, which calmed them both down. They all parted, a little more restless than before they'd met.

Glynn mulled over their conversation as he walked down to the department. As he scanned the noticeboards and dilapidated door frames it seemed impossible that the great plague had come. Hobden's door was open and he caught sight of Glynn with obvious relief, 'Good news! Gonzalo's not coming back so you can have the office all to yourself. Ah, you've got the contract. Good, good.' He ushered Glynn in and closed the door.

'Why not?' Glynn asked carefully.

'Hmm?' Hobden shuffled his papers with studied nonchalance, so Glynn pressed on, looking round, 'Gonzalo?'

'Oh, trapped in Spain, wants to stay,' Hobden moaned. 'The Spanish are very big on family, you know. 'Though goodness knows how he'll finish that thesis on Kerse Loch, stuck in Madrid!'

'Hi! Who are you?' Glynn said to a young woman on the other side of the room.

'Oh, that's Maureen from HR,' Hobden nodded to her, 'here to see I don't discriminate against you for being a black Jewish lesbian.'

'Actually, Professor Hobden, that sort of remark is exactly why I'm here,' Maureen said without looking up from her notes. Hobden slapped Glynn on the back and gestured for him to sit down in a decrepit leather armchair, saying, 'Quite, quite. Admin. not happy having me here, but with Simon wallowing at home, I'm next in line. Don't be an understudy if you can't play the part, that's what I always say. Signed the contract, then?'

'No.'

'Something not clear?'

'Teaching fellow in sciences? No subject, no hours?' Glynn kept his voice low and level.

'Yes, um, things are a bit tricky at the moment,' Hobden waffled. 'V.C. very keen to start at least core courses, so we need to all pitch in. Eilidh can do the soft demographiky stuff, and then you and I can do the solid work. There's a couple of chaps back in Chemistry now, and the new girl in Physics is around, 'though looking a bit peaky, so we should be able to run a good range of courses. Might have poached a girl from up north, as well. Have to do it all manually, of course, no reliable electric or computing doodahs for all the powerpointy VLE stuff, so just start with the basics, chalk and talk. You've got a good strong voice, I seem to recall.'

Glynn sensed that his role was to nod deferentially and agree that of course he'd be a good chap. 'I see,' he said. 'I am keen to help, but not, um, not at the salary suggested,' setting the contract down on the table between them, and sitting back.

'Oh,' Hobden looked hurt. 'Fair enough, fair enough. Of course, it's a great opportunity, will look very good on your C.V., and give you good experience, some admin. work, more responsibility ...'

Before Glynn could reply, Maureen closed her notes and said, 'Not a problem, triple the salary, twelve months retroactive from start of September. Acceptable?'

'More than acceptable.'

'Good,' she stood up and pulled a new set of papers from her file. 'If you would just sign this, same contract but with the new terms and salary.'

'Gosh, you're organised!'

'We need to be. Thank you Dr. Hughes. Professor Hobden. That'll be all.'

Hobden sat down once Maureen had left, 'Good girl, Maureen, but a bit intense. So, here are Simon's teaching allocation spreadsheets. I've highlighted the things we absolutely need to cover. You're in blue. No sure what the things in purple are, can't get that off. No idea about student numbers of course, so play it by ear. Photocopier's still got some toner in it, network's down, so no email, and the 'phones aren't reliable, but we do have electricity in this building. Probably best to put up some posters, once you've decided what to do when. Maureen has a list of rooms, so just let her know, and that's about it.'

Glynn took the slim folder he offered, and sat quietly in his triangular attic office for a long time. In the middle of the afternoon, he mooched down to the vending machines which were empty apart from packets of chewing gum and brightly coloured sports drinks. Deciding to save his money he filled a beaker from a sink in a nearby lab, pondering Eilidh's words from that morning's conversation.

No-one had refilled the vending machines; not a sure harbinger of economic meltdown, but not wholly insignificant either. He started to compile a mental list of things he shouldn't take for granted. Clean water, for a start. He had only the vaguest memory of how water actually reached the tap, but he knew it was a complicated system, relying on enough people at their posts and willing to give a damn. And then, of course, there was sewerage. Glynn wondered about some sort of water collection system, perhaps a water butt for the garden. Obviously it wouldn't be a problem in Fife, but the rest of the country had been through a long dry summer. He'd driven over the Pennines in June and been startled to see the ghosts of damned communities visible in empty reservoirs. With a new-found respect for the H^2O in his beaker he returned to the office and raided Gonzalo's supply of pistachio nuts.

After a few more hours trying to define some sort of curriculum, and after he'd tried and failed yet again to contact Felix, Glynn headed home with a bag full of books and his old undergraduate notes. He saw a few groups of students wandering round the building, looking even more confused than usual for the time of year. All he could do was advise them to contact Maureen, and hope she'd managed to give herself a pay rise as well. His attention was caught by a poster of the Rector, Noel Edmonds, urging the students to work hard at the start of the new academic year. He surreptitiously pulled it down and rolled it into his pocket. Rory had a collection of the posters. He was saving them up for the day when the

Rector was revealed as a psychotic robot masquerading as an aged entertainer. He swore they'd be valuable historical documents, and had already had some promising results from a test auction on an online history site. Glynn wondered briefly about Noel's concerned grin. If not exactly causing, then was it at the least ushering in the great apocalypse of our time?

He deliberately didn't look left as he crossed Market Street, but Nia was closing up the shop, and called out when she saw him, 'How was the rock?' He sauntered tentatively down the street, and helped her carry in the stands, then turned over a few rocks on a display as she cleared the counter. 'Did you know 'flu can cause post-viral depression?' he said casually.

'Yes,' she said without looking up, 'that's the problem, isn't it?'

'Have I missed something? There wasn't anything on the news.'

'Well, no, there wouldn't be. But you can see what's happening?'

'Hmm. Someone else said that to me earlier.'

'Did she?'

'How do you know it was a 'she'?'

'Lucky guess. So what did she say?'

He walked round and twirled a stand of cards, 'Just that lots of people seem to be depressed, that's all.'

'Autumn's melancholy, isn't it? And this time of year, lots of people have problems anyway. What's the figure, one in four?'

'I never know,' Glynn said, 'whether that's one in four at any one point, which would seem pretty high, or one in four over a lifetime, which would seem a gross underestimate?'

Nia watched his profile as he puzzled over the cards, and then made herself smile and reply in a bright tone, 'Well, things are taking a while to get back to normal, but it's not as though people are throwing themselves off buildings or sticking their heads in ovens.'

'Oh, so just an increase in the general low-level misery of humanity then?' he sighed.

'You're a bundle of laughs!' she said, and he turned, shaking off his thoughts. He smiled and said, 'Sorry, just a bit discombobulated.'

'Dis what?'

'Combobulated. Mind you, I'm not sure I've ever been properly combobulated. Have you?'

'Now there's a question!' she laughed.

'Well, what about an easier one?' he said. 'Do you fancy having lunch tomorrow? I'm going to be running round the college, we could take a break?'

She paused, and said, 'Maybe. Don't take this the wrong way. Could we do it next week?'

'Sure.'

'Bit busy. We all have to pitch in. Ruth's sending these out with the candy-stripers.' She patted a small pile of boxes on the counter.

'Ruth?'

'Oh, she owns the place, and the therapy centre. I think it's a good idea, reach out to people who can't get out and about.'

'Hmmn. These what you're sending?' Glynn mused, facing the boxes, but looking at Nia's hair glowing in the evening sunlight.

'That's the plan.'

'Can I have a look?'

'Sure.'

He peered into one of the boxes and said, 'What's in

the soap? Is is some sort of herb?'

'Oh, it's a witches' stone for good health.'

He dropped it back into the box and said, 'Seriously? You're telling me that a bit of soap with a pebble in it will magically cure people?'

'Not cure them, but help them to heal.'

'Bullshit!'

'What a wonderful, rational response,' she threw back.

'Alright then, how does it work, Marie Curie? Or should I say Marie Healie?'

'You're not interested.'

'No, I am, really,' he said, trying to look cute. 'Tell me how it works.' He leaned over the counter, resting his chin on his fist.

'Okay,' she said, as she wrapped up the last boxes. 'Three things. The soap is simple, chamomile to help relaxation, but more importantly soap encourages people to wash.' Glynn raised his eyebrows, and nodded sarcastically.

'In case you hadn't noticed,' she continued, 'the first time some people realise something's wrong is when they can't be bothered to wash their hair.'

'Alright, cleanliness next to godliness.'

'Nope. But don't you feel better after a quick shower and a chance to comb your hair?' He didn't reply, so she continued, 'Well, maybe not. You're probably a man of the 'change the sheets when they get stiff approach'. But it makes a difference to some people.'

Silence. He looked up at her expectantly, so she went on, 'So, number two. The pebble. Not any old bit of rock, but a stone with a natural hole in it. Traditionally known as a witches' stone.' He gave out a stifled gurgling noise as she continued, 'not that I'm saying the stones are magic.'

'So what then?' he rose to the bait.

'How did the hole get there? Water wearing through the rock, that's how. Let me get this right, 'It's a physical manifestation of the principle that the hardest things can be broken through', even through the treacle-black cloud that's descended here. I could go on,' she carried the boxes through to the back and shouted, 'but I don't suppose you'd be too impressed if I told you how the stones vibrate with natural energy, you being a geologist and all.'

'Now I'm really confused,' Glynn said in a not-very-confused tone. 'Anyway, you said there were three things that made this work? What's the third?'

She came back in and said innocently, 'Oh, the third thing's just the magic.'

Glynn clutched his head and shrieked in a falsetto, 'I'm melting, I'm melting.'

'Cynic!' she growled.

'No,' he laughed. 'Well, yes, I suppose I am. But it's all just words.'

'You're right. How can you understand what I mean unless you've experienced it for yourself.'

'That sounds like an invitation.'

'Oh, I don't make them,' she said, 'but I can show you where they come from.' She kept her voice light, not looking directly at him, but knowing he was getting his hopes up, and he coughed before replying, 'Well, as it appears the whole town is closing its doors, and, as we may be the only people under forty left to repopulate Fife by Christmas, …
I should probably ask you your last name now, right?'

She grinned and said, 'Just call me Nia.'

'Pleased to meet you, Nia Justcallmenia,' he said, and banged his fist on the counter. 'Where do I go to get this enlightenment? Lunch some time?'

She paused. 'As I said, I'd love to, but could we make it next week? Say Friday? I've got some things to sort out.'

'Sure, no pressure. Lunch, then you can take me to the source of divine power.'

The sky was full of shreds of fading rosy pink as Glynn walked home. The prospect of twelve months on a decent salary buoyed his thoughts, despite the day's dark portents, and he decided to walk up to see the family. Things might be difficult, but he was secure in his own potential for heroism. He'd always envisaged donating part of his liver to Matt, and coping well with the universal admiration that followed. The mini-series was cut short as he turned into Largo Road and realised where all the cars were. A stationary queue for the supermarket petrol station stretched back into town. Only a few optimistic drivers had their engines running and many people were standing outside their cars or sitting on the kerb. 'Been here long?' Glynn said to one of his neighbours. 'About an hour,' came the reply. 'There's supposed to be a tanker soon, and I'm pretty much empty, so I thought I'd better give it a go. Hoping I might be able to visit my folks in Cambridge some time.' The mention of family pricked Glynn's conscience, and he pushed aside his exhaustion to walk up the hill to Matt's. He made slow progress, and stopped to catch his breath before he reached the top of the hill. Looking out towards the sea as the skies cleared and the evening light dimmed the clouds, he had a strange sensation of looking at a scene from a film.

Pushing himself to walk the last few hundred yards, he breathed a sigh of relief, then rapped on the door. No reply. He found the key from the bunch in his pocket and turned the lock. A warm, musty smell rushed into the cold air. He yelled, 'Matt! Matt!' When there was no answer he picked his way in past a jumble of toys. The house looked like a refugee camp, but a well-stocked one. He was reassured by the bottled water and stacks of firewood. The kitchen was overflowing with dirty crockery, but no-one was starving.

He walked up the stairs and met Matt coming out of the bathroom. 'Glynn!' he cried, 'Great, can you just look after things for half an hour, an hour max.? I've got to get over to see Eric.'

'Umm, okay.'

'Great. Come on then, I'll get you a lager.'

He kicked toys out of the way and headed into the kitchen, 'Seriously, help yourself, Abi got us well-stocked up, you can say that for her.'

'How is everyone?'

'Well, the kids are fine, bit restless, Robbie's watching some animal show, hard to keep them quiet now the internet's imploded. Becky's in with Abi. She's still not up to much, and to be honest I haven't got the time. It's like a bloody Greek tragedy. Every school in the area's at half staff, and we're supposed to be opening up again tomorrow – no imminent danger, all that sort of crap.'

He threw Glynn a can of lager and said, 'More in the cupboard. I won't be long. I owe you!' Then he was gone. Glynn opened the can, but felt sick and put it back in the fridge. He went upstairs slowly, and pushed open the door to the main bedroom. The room was dark, littered with clothes, and Abi was lying on one side of the bed with Becky curled up around her, covered in a large, green tartan

—

59

blanket. By the side of the bed were open books and bottles of pills.

'Abi?' he said. 'I'm just going to open the curtains a bit.' Becky sat up, then shrank back from the light and the clean air which tumbled in as Glynn opened the top window. 'Hello girls,' he contined, pulling a low chair towards the bed, 'Still got the lurgy, I see.'

'Mammy's not well,' whispered Becky. 'I'm looking after her.'

'That's very kind of you,' Glynn nodded. 'I'm here now. Shall I keep Mummy company for a while? I saw Emily earlier. She had a fall, perhaps you could go down and ask Robbie to see if the 'phones are working and check she's feeling better?'

'Is she deid?'

'No, no, ooh,' Glynn backtracked. 'Just a little fall. She grazed her knee a bit.'

'Was she covered in blood?'

'No, not really. But she still might like to hear from you?' Becky sat up, then said, 'I'm looking after Mammy. I can't be looking after everyone. I only have one pair of hands.'

She reminded Glynn of his own mother, and he adopted a suitably filial pose, 'Yes, you're doing a grand job. But I'm here now, so I can cover for you and maybe you could call Emily and check on the bunnies?' Becky was torn and repeated, 'Mammy's not well.' Abi stirred. 'You're right,' Glynn said. 'Hmmm. Mummy might feel better if she had something to eat. Do you think you could make a sandwich?'

'I know how to cut bread and spread butter. I could give the bunnies some food as well. Mammy?'

'You go on, hen,' Abi said quietly. Becky climbed off

the bed, gave Glynn a hug and went downstairs.

'Actually, a sandwich wouldn't do you any harm,' Glynn said as Abi struggled to sit up. 'Trust me, I'm a doctor!' She smiled with an effort, 'And if I was a rock, that would be useful, as Matt would say.'

'Atta girl. You alright?'

She shivered, and reached out for the glass of water. After a few sips she said, 'I'm just really tired, I don't know, I just can't read or anything.'

'It's a nasty bug,' he said.

'Everything's horrible,' she choked. 'It's everywhere, and we still haven't heard from Jamie.' Her voice fell further on every syllable, 'Matt thinks I should be over it by now, and I'm alright, I just, I just …'

'So why are you lingering in this delightful Lempsip-scented boudoir, eh?' Glynn reached out and unclasped her hands from a tissue. 'It's not just you, you know. I saw Rory today, he looks rough. No, I mean, more, more than usual. Abi, I saw Eilidh today. She thinks this 'flu bug, it's causing post-viral depression, you know, clinical depression.' Tears started forming in her eyes, 'No, it's not. Felix said that, and wanted to me to take these tablets, but Matt's right, it's just the 'flu and you don't want to go messing around with drugs.'

'And what? You're getting better are you?'

'I'm just really, really tired,' she coughed. 'If I could just get some sleep, and Becky's not right but I can't do it.' Glynn put his hand on her shoulder, 'What do I know, eh? Listen to Felix. Can I get you anything? No newspapers, but I can see if there are books.'

'No point,' she said. 'I've tried. Can't concentrate, so what's the point?' Glynn stroked her hand, exhaustion providing the only check on his rising panic as he gave her a false, calm smile.

Chapter Four

The world started to whimper. The first power-cut happened just after midnight on Monday. First the blackout, with tiny red indicator lights, which faded leaving true darkness as the burglar alarms kicked in. Glynn was still awake, trying to make sense of the first year curriculum, and quickly amused his empty flat with a cry of 'I've gone blind!' before tripping over a pile of books as he dodgemed into the kitchen.

Rummaging under the sink produced neither a torch nor candles, but there were matches by the stove. Several strikes later he found the torch and the flat swayed in shifting cylinders of light. His bookcase looked like the Manhattan skyline and Glynn wondered how his brother Jamie was coping. He'd spoken to Matt when Glynn was first ill, but all international communication was restricted. New York wasn't faring any better than anywhere else. The power came back on just before first light.

The second outage happened about the same time Wednesday morning and lasted twelve hours. Glynn had dug out an old wind-up clock, so the alarm woke him as usual, but with no electricity there was no central heating or hot water. He turned on the gas to boil some water for tea, and then realised that the freezer was leaking. Once he'd laid towels and a duvet cover across the floor he stared vacantly at the few items left in his freezer – meat could be cooked with gas, and the chips would survive until later, but the ice cream had to be eaten, for breakfast.

There was no more coffee. He was reminded of a children's book he'd read where the family had to eat odd combinations, because they'd taken all the

---

labels off their food. He wasn't sure whether that was a story of charming eccentricity or end-of-the-world desperation.

In the chaos of getting ready to teach, he hadn't thought much about his conversation with Eilidh, but what he'd told her wasn't far from the truth. His first brush with psychiatrists was linked in his memory with the taste of olives. He'd had no appetite and had decided that olives were free from pesticides. He couldn't say when it had started. Being an undergraduate in Oxford involved so many states of mind which normal people would consider peculiar. The impossible pressure to succeed academically and socially, combined with the equally impossible pressure to make it all look effortless, drove most people up some strange mental staircases. Which was more peculiar, then, staying up all night to finish an essay then going to train with the boat club, or avoiding the dinner you'd already paid for and sitting in your room eating olives? The whole town was soaked by centuries of misery. If he'd been a woman, someone might have raised the issue of anorexia earlier, but men don't have problems.

He might have stopped functioning all together if he hadn't met up with an old school friend who subjected him to some fierce mothering and took him to a doctor. Fortunately, the college had just received bad publicity over its suicide rate, so when Glynn was forced to concede that something was wrong he was allowed enough latitude to get himself back on track. That first, dark time was relatively easy to explain and he was back to normal before his final exams. The second time was more of a problem. If Eilidh was right about the new situation, he imagined anti-depressants would be in short supply, and a sudden knife of guilt skewered his ribs; he wondered whether he should hand back some of his stockpile, but the memory of the last time he spent six months in hell gave him pause. On Friday morning all thoughts of being noble were driven from his mind when a loud mioaw greeted him as he opened his front door, a little gingerly in case the world had suddenly been taken over by aliens, or possibly Norwegians, who were rumoured to be coping with the epidemic far better than the rest of the world. Tommy was back. 'Precious!' Glynn cried and scooped up the cat. He'd only seen glimpses of his neighbours who seemed to struggle out of bed solely to feed the cat, but he suspected they weren't able to provide him with much attention. As he tempted his furry friend with an assortment of defrosted goodies he realised that two years ago, when he was gripped by depression, he wouldn't have noticed how soft the cat's fur was. He wouldn't even have been pleased to see him, because nothing had mattered.

After spending two days in the sepulchral library, mugging up on his new specialities, come Friday Glynn was ready for battle. The weather was changing. In the clear early light he marched to his office, determined to have everything in order ready to teach whatever, whenever, come Monday morning. He was sure he could carry the first few lectures of each course with some basic methodology and a good measure of showmanship. With any luck, things would have settled down soon, by Week Four, perhaps, and no-one would notice how lost he felt. By the middle of the afternoon, he'd managed to produce handouts for the first day, after Eilidh had called him with a tip about a working photocopier. He was sorting them into folders when there was a knock at his door. A small, pale student unwrapped himself from several woollen layers, and blew his nose on a stringy piece of tissue. Glynn shifted his chair back slightly, and said, 'Are you alright, Floyd? Have a seat.' The young man fell into the open chair grumbling, 'Landlord's refusing to repair the window, and there's stuff dripping down the walls, and these silver things running round everywhere.'

'Silver fish?' Glynn tried to be helpful.

'Maybe. The girls are freaking out.'

'Have you spoken to the union?'

'No-one there. We're not paying rent, so one of us has to stay to make sure we're not evicted.'

'That sounds very tough.'

'Yeah.' There was a pause, until Glynn said, 'So, you wanted to see me?'

'I thought I could maybe start my dissertation, work in the library for a bit. And the sign says to see you.'

'The sign? Never mind. Dissertation sounds like a good idea. What do you have in mind?'

'Well, I really enjoyed the stuff on metamorphic rocks, so I thought maybe something on that?'

'Okay, that's a start.' Glynn took a deep breath, 'So, a dissertation needs to have something to say, a question to answer, a hypothesis, something to investigate. What do you hope to find out?'

'I thought maybe you could give me a reading list,' Floyd mumbled.

'Right. Well, were there aspects of the topic you didn't feel had been, well, satisfactorily addressed you might say, in previous studies? Is there a burning question you want to answer?'

'Not really.'

'Fine.' Glynn said heavily. 'I'll put together a short initial bibliography, so you can take a look at the most recent work, perhaps think about new angles. Even if it's a small question, you have to have something to say. You'll need to read the scholarship to make sure no-one's already done that same study, but then you need to think, 'Why should anyone read what I write?' You with me?'

'So what's *your* research about, Dr. Hughes?' Floyd tried to look interested.

'Ah, my PhD was on the stratigraphy of the Caledonian Orogeny.'

'Why should I read that?'

'Because it has a bearing on how we work with later correlations,' Glynn started before seeing Floyd's expression and changing tack, 'so, and ultimately, it affects how we structure economic exploitation of different fields. Making money from oil?'

'Oh right, sorry, I didn't mean to diss you or nothing. Oh, that wasn't meant to be a joke,' Floyd babbled.

'Don't worry, it wasn't,' Glynn threw back. 'No, no, you're quite right, can't expect you to do something I can't do myself. I'll leave a bibliography in the pigeonholes – doesn't look like email's going to be back any time soon.'

As soon as Floyd had gone Glynn dusted the bookshelf copy of his thesis. He wasn't entirely convinced of the value of his PhD, but the possible segue into the exploitation of natural resources had kept him going for four years. If academia didn't work out, he'd always be able to get a job in oil or gas, 'though he didn't fancy spending months on end living on an oil rig. He went to look for 'The Sign'. Maureen had posted a dozen hand-written notices in the central reception hall about various course units available, and there was a new notice in Hobden's writing: 'All final year students are strongly advised to write a dissertation and should contact Dr. Hughes, the dissertation convenor, as soon as possible to discuss topics.'

'Great!' Glynn thought, 'Just what I need.' He returned to his office to hunt out anything on dissertation supervision from the previous year's paperwork. When he saw Hobden and tried to have a word with him, he just said, 'Try the real attic. Lots of old dissers, just give them the same topics.'

After a fruitless hour turning up nothing but files from theology and ancient history, Glynn finally located the Geography and Geology dissertations, with an old list of topics from 2001. He decided this was sufficiently long ago to be due for recycling, and collected as many of that year's dissertations as he could find. Most topics were old chestnuts, good to review at least once a decade. After ripping out the bibliographies, he headed back to the photocopier he'd used earlier, hoping it was still working and hadn't been flashmobbed by modern linguists.

He was stopped in the quad by Eilidh's husband, Bob, who told him his intended target had run out of toner, but he was on his way to another machine Eilidh believed might be free. Glynn wasn't familiar with the admin. building believed to have the grail, so was happy to follow his lead.

'Didn't expect you'd be back so soon, Bob,' he said as they scurried along, hiding the evidence of their quest.

'I feel as weak as a kitten, but all hands on deck,' said Bob, 'and I'm hoping to do some research this evening. Always found Friday evenings a good time.'

'Hobden's pushing the finalists to do dissertations,

and they are not up to it,' Glynn moaned. 'I've just had one tell me he wants to work on 'rocks'. What do I say to that?'

'It's an epidemic,' Bob nodded. 'The last girl I saw said she wanted to work on 'perception', and when I questioned her about the precise scope, she said 'Fings wot you can see, 'n' stuff.' Am I horribly prejudiced against cockney accents, do you think?'

'No, no, not unreasonably so!' Glynn stifled a laugh, and Bob continued, 'No, I didn't think so. What I can never understand is why they do it, when you lack talent, or motivation or both. You wouldn't have met the lad who went on to be a pop star? What's he calling himself, *European Torture*? I marked his first sub-Honours papers, complete nonsense, borderline illiterate, but that wasn't his forte. Jolly good thing he quit. Now, it's not my cup of tea, but I can appreciate the musical sophistication and the instrumental dexterity.'

'On a lot at home, is it, *European Torture*?' Glynn said, raising an eyebrow.

Bob didn't notice his tone, and replied happily, 'Yes, Eilidh saw him playing at the Crown and was quite taken with the music. I imagine an early signed USB stick might be worth something one day. Aha, we're in luck,' he grinned as they reached the machine. 'Looks good to me. You go ahead, I have a batch to do.'

Glynn loaded his ripped-off pages into the machine, and Bob picked up a thin copy of the *St Andrews Chronicle* which was folded up on the windowsill. 'Still last week's, I'm afraid, but have you read the main section again? I've written to the editor. I dread to think how many of our students are close to the edge. Something like this could really tip them over. Just what we need, no?'

'Another 'pull yourself together' rant, is it? Well, I doubt many of our lot read this.'

'Normally, yes,' Bob agreed, 'but with the dearth of normal information streams, they're taking what they can, like the rest of us.'

'So Christian Marshall is abusing his position again. I've always thought there was something not right about him.'

'Such as?'

'Oh.' Glynn had forgotten that Bob was not one for generalisations. 'Well,' he burbled, 'perhaps doesn't have a social conscience, you know, beyond a political position.'

'Ah, interesting, yes,' Bob nodded. Glynn flipped through the diatribe, and agreed it wasn't helpful. He left Bob happily pottering with the photocopier, and as he walked back to his office he remembered something his ex, Jera, had once reported to him. At a faculty party, after they'd all had a lot to drink, Eilidh had apparently said that Bob wouldn't recognise his feelings if he saw them in an identity parade. Maybe that had proved an effective defence against post-viral malaise.

After a few more hours on admin., Glynn stretched uncomfortably and decided to go for a short run. He changed in his office, and jogged along the Scores. It only took ten minutes before he was feeling his chest tighten. He made his way slowly down to the West Sands, determined to do at least another twenty minutes, but gave up after ten, and started walking back. As his oxygen levels improved, he noticed that people fell into one of two categories. Either they were hunched up, walking, stopping, walking, usually in pairs, or they were running alone, and really running. Neither group was taking any notice of the watercolour sky or the gentle crash of the surf. Glynn tried to see the beauty.

The week had been taken up with teaching preparation, so he was planning to devote some time on the weekend to his own research, as well as visiting the sick and meeting Nia who had agreed to have a short lunch-break the next day. When he arrived home, he had a brief word with Felix, but the connection cut out before he could learn much. He'd said, 'Post-viral depression, right?'

'Aye.'

'Not going to tell me anything more, then?'

'What can I say? Even a mild case is debilitating.' Felix was at his desk, fiddling with Blutak, 'You know, there was a survey years ago that showed of all major illnesses, the one that had the greatest negative impact on a person's lifetime happiness was depression.' Glynn nodded as Felix continued, 'Not heart disease, arthritis, not what you'd expect. So many people struggling with low-level misery. Now, you turn up the volume, and how do you keep a society running? I'll see you on the weekend, we're meeting at the Crown to-', and then the connection cut out. Glynn wondered whether Felix was coping - he'd sounded rather distant and abstract, but that was probably down to exhaustion. 'Anyway, answers at last,' he thought as he fried the last chips and wondered how to make soup. Even 'though there was no real news, he was excited when the television moved on from its holding screen. He watched images of killer whales and US sit-coms with the awe of a child at a magic show. The previous night's offering (*Pet Rescue: Chihuahua gets stuck in a Watering Can*) had been a disappointment. He only switched

70

off when the emergency broadcast 'Nightly News' began. It had nothing new to say.

He was about to turn in when the 'phone lit up. It was only an audio connection, probably just as well, as it was Rory who started with a long moan about the unreliable 'phone services, and the impossibility of anyone doing anything without the internet. Glynn didn't have to say much as Rory continued, but eventually he said, 'You still don't sound too good.' Rory laughed bitterly, 'Everyone bloody says 'I know how you feel, you're depressed', but I'm not. I think there might be something really wrong with me. I might have a brain tumour. Seriously, I'm afeared I've got cancer, so much I can't breathe. That must mean something.'
'Do you fancy a run sometime?'
'Maybe,' Rory's voice sank lower, 'gotta go, bloody students at the door, don't want them to know I'm here,' and he cut the connection.

After a lie-in on Saturday, Glynn strolled into town. The sun was warm and bright and he was positive that everything would be back to normal very soon. Nia was handing over change to two girls, who giggled as he held the door open for them. 'Students?' he said, as she locked the till.
'Probably. Aren't they your bread and butter?'
'Yeah, I teach, but I see myself more on the research side really.'
'Oh?'
'Investigative stuff, analysing data.' Bob would have been apoplectic, he knew.
'That doesn't sound much like work to me,' she said. 'So, what do you do?' he moved quickly from defence to attack.
'Make people happy, keep the economy moving, and

I facilitate, you could say.'

'Snap. Same as I do. You think what I do's daft, so tell me what you do,' he persisted.

'I take money off people,' she said with a straight face.

'No, give me details.'

'You're crazy.'

'And so? Explain it to me. I've never been a retail bunny.' He leaned over the counter and posed on one elbow.

'Well, if I'm on my own, like today, I sort out the float, check the post, file orders, payments,' Nia told him calmly. 'If people are in, I talk to them, sometimes give advice, answer questions, take their money, wrap things up, watch for shoplifters.'

'How can you tell?'

'Groups of kids, people with large pockets, someone wearing a coat when it's mild out. 'Though Ruth's always telling me to watch for the unlikely ones, the well-dressed, middle-aged, middle-class ones who'll buy expensive jewellery then slip a little bit of quartz into their pocket.'

'Oooh, do you catch people?' Glynn asked, as she beckoned him out the door. He was intrigued by this sudden hint of criminal activity, and disappointed when Nia replied, 'No, I've only ever caught a teenager doing it for a dare, but Ruth swears she's deterred some who were on the verge. We've got this by the door which is supposed to help.' She stroked a large chunk of black tourmaline in the window, then turned the sign to 'Closed for Lunch', and locked the door from the outside, slipping the key onto a chain attached to her handbag.

'But, you're still a security guard?'

She laughed, 'And a cleaner, shelf-stacker, personal

shopper, Jack of all trades.'

'Jill of all trades? Which bits do you like?'

'All of it. Doing different things. It's good to make a big sale, but it's nice when the shop's quiet and I can get on with things. Doing the displays is fun too, but Ruth does most of that. I swear she comes down in the middle of the night sometimes to play around with things. Yes, I like doing the displays,' she nodded at the window.

'High class junk modelling then?' Glynn responded to her wistful tone and ran with it, 'I used to love junk modelling. Still find it hard to throw out egg boxes. They're good for holding rock samples, but there's always the chance I could make a spaceship out of them one day.'

She laughed again, and he said 'Lunch? I managed to get us some rather odd sandwiches from down the road, but I don't think they're serving horse meat yet…' He quickly backtracked, seeing her wide-eyed horror, 'Ooh, no, I'm joking, both vegetarian, I promise, 'though I can't be sure of the variety. And it's only crispbread.'

'Yes,' Nia said cautiously. 'Let's get some mints, while they still have some.' She cut through to South Street, and Glynn followed her like Alice. The woman at the counter did look a bit like a sheep, lost nestled among shelves of glass jars. She smiled as they entered and said, 'Usual, dear? Still got some of those! So long as you don't want chocolate gingers – all gone, they are.'

'The usual, thanks,' Nia said, as the woman reached up for a jar. 'Erica, I don't think you know Glynn. He works at The University.' She looked sideways at him as Erica took an audible breath and began, 'Eighteen years I cleaned for that lot – not a pay rise!

New contracts, new managers, more work, but not a penny more. At the top of my scale, they said. Shocking, don't you think?'

Glynn said weakly, 'And now you run a sweet shop?'

'You see,' Erica's venom subsided as she measured out the sweets, 'I got compensation after my Daniel died, hush hush stuff in the Navy he was, and I could've moved back, but I had good friends here. Hard to leave your friends. So I thought, 'What's the one thing this town needs?' and I thought, 'A good old-fashioned sweet shop.' Burns got franchised years ago. So here I am. There's your change, love. Are you a pan drops man?'

'I'm sorry?' said Glynn, as Erica handed over the bag to Nia.

'Maybe humbugs are more your thing?'

'No, I'm sorry. What are 'pan drops'?'

Nia offered him the bag, 'Try one.'

'Oh,' he said, 'mint imperials.'

'Wash your mouth out!' she cried. 'Much better than mint imperials, better taste, better texture. I can't believe you've never had them. Best mints going, and one of the greats of Scottish cuisine…'

'… along with the deep fried Mars bar, I suppose?' Glynn took a sweet from the bag Nia offered, as she said, 'These aren't so bad for you!' She turned and waved, 'Thanks, Erica. See you later!'

'Right you are, love,' Erica replied. 'He looks like a nice one, sort of a young Ewan McGregor!'

After two minutes of intense concentration, Glynn finished the first pan drop with a crunch, then queried, 'Was she flirting with me?' Nia considered this for a moment, then said, 'Erica? I don't know. Do you go for older women?'

'No. Curse of academics apparently,' Glynn sighed.

'We work with an endless stream of eighteen-year-olds, so we have trouble accepting the imperfections of maturity. What are you? Seventeen, eighteen?'

'I wish!' she said, slightly too seriously. 'So, do you have sex in your office?'

He coughed before saying lightly, 'With someone else there, you mean?'

'Uurgh!' she brightened up again.

'Well, you asked!' he shrugged. 'Actually, until last month I shared an office with an insomniac Spaniard.'

'Hmm.' She didn't look at him, although he was looking at her with some interest. 'You've never had an affair with a student?'

'Not one of mine, no,' Glynn said earnestly. 'Not ethical. You know, these aren't the sorts of questions people usually ask when I tell them what I do.'

'It's just fascinating, that's all. When you're a student, well, lecturers seem so … exotic.'

He snorted, and she continued, 'Well, not exotic, but you know, two of the girls I lived with had a bet who could bag the new History lecturer.'

'You're a History graduate?'

'Not exactly, having a bit of a break.'

'Sorry, too personal. Okay, let's go back to talking about my sex life,' he nudged her with his shoulder and grinned. She blushed and suddenly looked eighteen.

They were crossing Castle Street when Glynn yelped, 'Bloody hell!' and took a step out into the road. Nia turned to see what had ruffled him so, and saw a rubbish bin had morphed into modern art, with black bags piled around it, the contents spilling out like streams of paint. On top of the largest pile was a big rat, gnawing through a chicken bone. There was a scuffle and another rat emerged from the bag just below and stared at her expectantly.

'Fuck!' shouted Glynn. 'Let's get out of here.' He pulled her across the road, still shouting, 'God, what is the place coming to? We're going to be eaten in our beds, or die of plague!' Nia thought he was joking, but when they'd found a bench under the cathedral ruins, he settled down and said, 'I'm sorry. I just really hate rats.'

'I used to know someone who had a pet rat once, a fancy rat,' she said calmly. 'They're really clever.'

'That's the problem,' he retorted. 'I know most people think it's the tails,' and he shuddered a little at the memory of the tail curling through the chicken bone, 'but it's the eyes. I saw a documentary when I was little about rats opening doors and how they have a combined brain power which dwarfs humanity's. Gave me nightmares for weeks. And that was before I'd even read *1984.*'

'I've never read it.'

'Oh, well, there are some rats in it,' he shivered again.

'Maybe not one for the current situation, then.'

'Maybe not.' Glynn offered her a choice of sandwiches and said in a more measured voice, 'I take it you're not from these parts?'

'Manchester.'

'But not a Mancunian accent.'

'Oh, my mother would have loved that, if I'd come home calling her Muhmeh.'

'Right.'

'She hated my friend when I was little, all because her name was 'Hannuurr'. She kept trying to get me to say 'Hannaaaahr'.'

'And I bet no-one here understands a word you say either?'

'I'm picking it up.'

He left the silence for her to fill, and eventually she continued, 'Ruth says there's a sort of Gulf Stream that brings people to St Andrews.'

'Mmm,' he let her continue.

'Usual thing, came as a student, things didn't work out, Ruth gave me a job and she lets me have the other flat above the shop rent-free. She's been brilliant.'

'Sounds like. Can't say I know many alternative therapists.'

'She's great. You should meet her.'

'Is she okay? The 'flu, I mean?'

'She hasn't been down with it.'

'Lucky for her,' Glynn said with real feeling and a touch of self-pity. 'I nearly died.'

'But you're here, sitting in the sunshine enjoying a picnic,' Nia smiled, turning her face to the sun.

'You're absolutely right,' he said and stretched out to catch the last fading sunshine of the year. After they'd crunched through the sandwiches, Glynn realized his muscles had started to seize up after yesterday's run. 'Quick stroll?' he said, and they wandered round the tombstones for a while, noting the strange and ignoring the commonplace tragedies. 'After all, money may be obsolete any day now,' he said as he put in coins for both of them to climb Rule's Tower. From the top, the whole of St Andrews shone like a slide show. They tasted the hint of salt, as the wind pushed them closer together. 'My friend Rory's a sci-fi buff, do you know him?'

'Not really.'

'Well, he's always trying these alternative scenarios, you know, which is worse, seeing your town bombed and/or over-run by green lizard monsters, or having it all look good on the surface, but underneath everyone's dying or being controlled by aliens.'

'Sort of *Invasion of the Body Snatchers*?'

'Yeah,' he leaned over. 'Pretty odd, really, a town that prides itself on being full of ruins.'

He helped her down the winding stone steps, and was ready to sweep her into his arms as he guided her out, but she said, 'It's okay, I can manage,' and stepped out on her own. They walked back to the shop, on the other side of the street to avoid the rat-infested bin. 'I'm going to have my cap gun handy for those,' Glynn said, only half-joking.

As they came to the shop he said, 'This is a bit strange, isn't it? Having a charming picnic while the rest of the world's in mourning? Do you fancy going for a drive some time? I know, it's frivolous, but I'm starting to go a bit crazy stuck in town. We could even go collect some magic stones, if you like?' He was expecting her to hit him, and was a little disappointed when she said seriously, 'Actually, we could go on the bus. I'm off next Saturday.' He was puzzled, but then agreed and they arranged to meet at the bus station. When they reached the door of Ethereal he said loudly, 'Great! Next Saturday!' then awkwardly kissed her on the cheek and bounced away.

Nia let herself into the shop and jumped a little when she saw Ruth emerge from beneath a cupboard, with a screwdriver, shaking dust from her long plaited hair. 'He seems nice,' Ruth said. Nia ignored that remark, and changed direction, 'Should you really be doing that now? How did the bread go?'

'Ah,' Ruth sighed, 'so-so, not brilliant, but better than nothing, satisfies the cravings. Now, if I just had more than a scraping of butter ...'

'The farms are bound to be sorting themselves out by now. Surely can't be long.'

'He seems nice,' Ruth nudged again 'Abi likes him.'

Nia looked at her, with a slightly panicked expression, 'It's strange, with all this going on, and he's odd, I mean, I'm not sure what he's thinking.'

'Ah yes,' said Ruth, 'you need subtitles that say 'Glynn walked away thinking X or thinking Y.' Then you could relax and enjoy the romance.' Nia blushed, and said quietly, 'It's just confusing.'

Ruth put her arm round her, 'D'you know why? Well, I'll tell you. It's because men haven't a clue.' Nia laughed, as Ruth continued, 'No, seriously, you turn this into a novel and an accurate description would read 'Glynn walked away with eighteen different things going through his mind.' And I bet you half of them would be about food.'

'Thanks. I know, I should just relax.'

'No 'should' about it,' Ruth patted her on the arm. 'Rory's appointment's at three, so if I've dozed off, just send him up.'

Ruth went back upstairs and Nia dusted the next shelf of crystals. She was wrapping up some incense sticks for two more bedraggled students, and didn't notice Rory come in. He shuffled near the door, until she saw him and gestured for him to go upstairs. She was shocked at his appearance. He was clean-shaven, but his eyes were red-rimmed and he gripped the stair-rail with trembling hands. He knocked on Ruth's door and she opened it with a smile. 'Come in,' she said gently, and he slumped into a large, red leather armchair. 'Right,' he said, 'I've been getting up.'

'Great,' she said. 'Are you sleeping any better?'

'Aye, that sandalwood incense is always good stuff.'

79

He paused, then blurted out, 'Are ye sure it's not a brain tumour?'

'Sure as I can be. Have you spoken to your own GP?'

'I keep seeing this young lass at the surgery and she says there's nothing wrong, says it's anxiety and gave me a new lot of pills.'

'Persevere!' Ruth said in a soothing tone. 'Eastern and Western medicine combined can work miracles.'

'Aye, well they're saying we're all a bit wae after the 'flu, so I reckon if a few wee needles could sort out my knee, it's worth a try.' She ran through a few questions and updated his medical history in her notes, 'Just as well I never went over to online record keeping! Have you been running again?'

He shrugged and looked away.

'Well, it would do you good, if you could. If you want to move to the mat, lie on your front, we'll try to work on your Liver energies, get you back to yourself.'

Rory fell asleep just before she removed the acupuncture needles forty minutes later, and he lay there quietly for a while, his body comfortable, his mind starting to relax. He was tired, but the panic he'd been struggling to control for weeks was definitely less immediate.

'That *is* better,' he said as he paid Ruth. 'I can't thank you enough. Do you think these anti-depressants are a good idea then?'

'Yes,' she said strongly. 'Oh, there can be problems and they're not right for everyone, but you're not fit, so you should try anything that can help, do you hear me, Rory? I'm serious.'

'You sound a bit like Abi.'

'I'll take that as a compliment, seeing as how your cousin is a thoroughly sensible woman. Now, don't overdo it, you hear me?' She hugged him, and he left feeling temporarily better than before.

In the evening, Glynn walked up to Matt's and was delighted to see Abi in the kitchen making sandwiches. He gave her a hug and she looked at him sadly.

'Hey!' he said brightly. 'You're up!'

'"Better wear shune than sheets" as my grannie would've said.'

'That's the spirit. So, you're on the mend?'

'Comes and goes,' she replied quietly. 'Most of the time I'm fine, but then I start to worry about Robbie and Becky, and it just floors me. You know, I thought I was going mad.' She paused and he waited. Eventually she continued, 'Thank you for keeping in touch. You started to say something, as if you knew more than you were letting on. Really, I won't tell Matt.' Glynn checked to see they were alone, 'Nothing about all this really, just that I'm coping because I was already on anti-depressants when I got ill.'

'Oh, Glynn, are you alright? I'm sorry, I had no idea,' she hugged him.

'Yeah, I'm fine. Take the pills, restore the bio-chemical balance. I'm fine. But really, how are you? You look pretty peaky.'

She sat down and didn't meet his eye, 'I read some poetry when I was ill, only short stuff, couldn't focus, it all got fragmented, but then I read this strange piece, an introduction: 'I could stay in bed all day, working hard at staying just below consciousness, dozing in a blanket, trying not to break through the tissue paper.' It just made me cry and cry. You cry, you feel better. Not like this.' Her grip on the teatowel tightened, as she looked down at the table, 'You cry until it all dries up and then you feel the tears rising in your head, like vomit, retching out of your eyes until it's all you can taste or smell or see. Your eyes sting, you can feel the blood pumping in your eyes. And when there are no more tears, your eyes still heave, retching, empty, the nausea still in your head, no way to let it out.'

At this point, the children came back in each clutching a rabbit and Abi smiled brightly at them, 'They're alright, aren't they?'

'That's because we pay a fortune to vaccinate them against every bloody thing,' said Matt, coming in behind them. 'Ten minutes in the living room, then they go back out!' he shouted as the rabbits hurried the children in.

'It seems to me,' he announced, sitting down, 'that we need better leadership. Take the schools. Pandemonium. We clearly need to establish limits on hours and class sizes, but I can't get anyone to listen. I'll have to get promoted.'

'Things not going so well, then?' Glynn sympathised.

'Not in work, but now Abi's better we can get back to normal here.' Matt patted his wife's arm, and didn't seem to notice when she looked away.

'Did you get a note from Felix?' he said to Glynn. 'Finn and I are meeting him at the Crown in a bit. You coming?'

'Sure. Maybe he can tell us what's actually going on.'

On cue, Finn's Land Rover drew up, and he jumped out with a box. 'You see,' he cried to Abi, 'I knew all that stuff Dad said was junk would be handy one day. Cluttering up the barn, no more, coming in useful now, is it not? Five of these wind-up radios I've traded today. Want one?'

When they arrived at the Crown, there were

several groups of people at tables and a few single figures at the bar. Felix was already there, talking to Eilidh and Morag, the landlady, deciding between odd pineapple or mango. He gestured the men to a table at the back of the room where Bob was waiting, and helped to bring over a tray of drinks and peanuts.

'Thanks for this, guys, I thought you'd best know what's planned,' Felix said.

'No problem,' Morag replied. 'Eilidh'll stay and have a dram wi'ye. Sorry this is all that's left of the lager. Even the six o'clock club are having to have bottled.' She jerked her head towards a group of four men in the corner of the pub, then lowered her voice so only Felix could hear, 'To be honest, 'though, it's more like the, 'As soon as we're open' club nowadays. I doubt any one of them's going to work.' Felix gave her a small smile, as she returned to the bar. He raised a toast, 'Bannocks are better than nae breid!' then took a swig of pineapple juice and said, 'I'm giving you a heads-up, trying to keep as many people as possible calm for tomorrow. You probably know the rigmarole, but this 'flu bug, not the deadly strain we expected. What's happened instead is that the post-viral depression is far more entrenched than most people ever expected. Took most countries completely by surprise, and-'

Matt interrupted him, 'What about the 'flu? Am I going to get it? No-one's offered me the vaccination.'

'I suspect you're immune, or you'd have got it before now,' said Felix, before returning to his thread. 'What's happening is that all sorts of agencies are scrambling to catch up, but they're understaffed. The irony is, if we'd had mass fatalities, we'd have coped better than we're doing now. Plans in the pipeline for that sort of problem, just not this.'

'And now?' said Bob, keen to hear the whole story.

'There's going to be an announcement tomorrow,' Felix said. 'Most countries doing it at the same time; it'll be tomorrow lunchtime here. Making this explicit, trying to keep people calm, plus a lot of emergency plans.'

'Such as?' Finn was encouraged but wary.

'Emergency hubs for services, food, medical supplies. There'll be committees to co-ordinate things locally.'

'And the internet? International communications?' Glynn cut in. 'You said most countries are making this announcement, so not everyone's as cut off as we are.'

'Forget that,' said Finn. 'What about petrol?'

'Don't know,' Felix brushed off the interruptions, 'but long term, the UK's going for local infrastructures. Executive's bowing to London for now. Fuel supplies will prioritize emergency services. At least prices have been frozen, so we shouldn't see any blatant profiteering for a while.'

'Alright, how long can this go on for?' Matt said impatiently. 'It seems to me, most people have had the lurgy now, so you just need to get them fixed and we can get back to normal, okay? Even if they need a week or two to get the pills. Clearly people are just taking advantage of the situation, and-'

'Not that simple,' said Felix heavily, but Matt continued, 'We need to get people back in work now. They won't want to be stuck at home for long, not with only one, anodyne channel showing daytime TV anyway,' Matt sat back as if the argument was resolved, and didn't seem to be listening as Felix wearily tried to explain the range of health problems that 'depression' encompassed. He concluded by saying, 'Don't think of it as depression. Think of it as an epidemic of insomnia, grief, fear, panic attacks, agoraphobia, anxiety.'

'Anxiety!' Matt snorted. 'Clearly people need to get a grip. Look, I've seen lots of people get back to work when they had to, the undertakers for a start.'

Felix shook his head, 'You've read the latest *Chronicle* editorial, I take it. Honestly. Bloody Christian! He was one of the lucky ones. Most people take much longer to recover, and that's if it's mainly bio-chemical and hasn't triggered underlying psychological problems. So, aye, if you've got a vocation, perhaps you *do* go to work with moderate depression, but I tell you, those people are trying to drive a car with two broken wrists. You might manage it for a while, but it's torture. And mental pain is far worse.' He lowered his voice, 'Look, Matt, I know this can be hard to accept, but the figures speak for themselves. The UK suicide figures for last month jumped forty percent, most of them men.'

'What?' Glynn was shocked. 'You're joking, we'd have heard about it.'

'Would you?' Felix's eyes flashed, 'Who controls information now? I'm telling you all this now because you're all just about on your feet. Things are going to get worse before they get better.'

'Better keep that whisky back for a while then,' said Matt, 'So, this is something different? Not just all that hormonal depression stuff?' Eilidh flinched, and was about to say something, when Morag came over from the bar with more drinks, and cut in sharply, 'Who dragged you from the 1970s then?' Women get depressed, not a problem, men get depressed, national emergency? Are you really that daft?'

Matt leaned back like a peacock, 'I'm just saying, if they can get about, they need to get into work. Can't be that bad, if they're up and about.'

Morag glared and stood her ground.

'Alright, alright,' said Glynn. 'This announcement is happening tomorrow?'

'Right,' said Felix finishing his drink. 'Morag, I'm hoping you'll co-ordinate things here, you know, if people come in. Eilidh and Bob'll help.'

'Sure,' she said, and returned to the bar, throwing Matt a dark look.

As they left the pub Matt had an indulgent smile on his face, and started again, 'No offence, Eilidh, all I'm saying is people make a fuss.' Eilidh and Bob left to collect Emily without saying anything. Felix turned to Matt, paused, then said deliberately, 'What, sleeping, eating, walking, and disputing? Remember your *Faustus*, Mr. English teacher?' Matt relented and replied, 'Why this is Hell, nor am I out of it? Alright, point taken. Thanks for letting us know.' Felix got into his car, showering the street with bits of crisps as he opened the door. Finn drove back to the farm, and Matt and Glynn started walking.

'What about you, then? Dose you up in hospital did they?' said Matt.

'Yeah, Felix took care of it,' Glynn dodged the question.

'So, when d'you reckon Abi'll be able to stop taking them? I mean, she's better, but now she's drugged up she's pretty subdued.' Matt seemed more annoyed than concerned.

'They normally say about six months,' Glynn replied.

'Bloody hell, so you're ... ? Well, can't say you seem any different, so maybe she'll perk up.'

'Yeah, maybe,' Glynn nodded non-committally. They talked about the best way to conserve petrol as they walked out of town. Matt went home and had a stiff drink. Glynn went home and stroked the cat for a long time.

The announcement on Sunday was brief. The town lit up as TV and 'phone projections suddenly activated. Global pandemic was not the deadly strain everyone had feared. High incidence of post-viral depression which was unexpected and stretching medical services. Plans in place to cope with this temporary disruption to normal life. National and international government unaffected. The tone was reassuring, as the spokesman announced measures which should ensure essential services continued to run. The end of Life As We Knew It was formalised by the raft of measures, from travel restrictions to the formation of new Community Health Liaison Oversight and Evaluation Teams, but most people were too miserable to care. Bob may have been one of the only ones truly listening, as he squeaked to Eilidh, 'Six nouns? Six nouns? 'Community Health Liaison Oversight and Evaluation Team'? What next? Language is doomed.'

All Sunday St Andrews swayed with muttering and murmurs. Relief that something had been officially said was mixed with grumbles about secret committees and the distribution of resources from London. Glynn called in to his office briefly to collect some older journal articles. He was very tired, but knew that his career prospects depended on publishing. Regardless of what the universities said, they didn't actually give a damn about your teaching ability or administrative work. In the end, they didn't even care whether your research was any good. Four bland, inoffensive pieces of work, one a year, were far better than a ground-breaking argument that took years to produce. He spent the rest of the day working on calculations about the Ludlow bone bed, and was happy that he had the data prepared before he called it a day. Interpretation would have to wait until he had some clear time to think.

He rose early on Monday morning and dug out a tie. As Glynn dragged his feet to work, and braced himself for the first day's teaching, he was stunned to find a cordon around Muttoes Lane, and two young policemen struggling to control the hysteria.

Chapter Five

Death is a great equalizer, but depression creates hierarchies. Matt's failure to catch 'flu he attributed to strength of mind. Some of those already dosed up on anti-depressants felt superior, peculiarly provident. Others who had been struck with depression but responded quickly to the medication became arrogant, loudly asserting that it was down to moral fibre. Anyone can be struck by a disease, but you pull yourself together, take the pills and get back to normal. They thought themselves strong, virtuous, but they were just lucky. Before they could become a genuine threat to the fragile harmony in the town, their leader in spirit, if not in name, was murdered. One of the first influenza cases, and one of the first to recover, Christian Marshall was a man who inspired all he met to describe him with broad brushstrokes, even after he met a grisly end in Muttoes Lane on the night of the government announcement.

A textbook case, he'd grown up with adoration from any woman who happened to see his big eyes and dark curls. When he operated as an adult, some women initially mistook his flattery and studied eye contact for genuine insight and concern. People said he 'liked women', whereas really he liked women to like him. Damsels in distress he rescued, women in authority he schemed to undermine. People thought he was a lucky bastard, and some held on to this view long after he was found dead with a large hole in his chest. Inherited money had enabled him to establish businesses across Scotland, and he owned a significant stake in several local newspapers. He was a frequent contributor to letters pages, even though he had his own column in the *St Andrews Chronicle*, and gaps in the editorial staff since the summer had allowed him the opportunity to express his own feelings at greater length.

The week before he died, the *Chronicle* had given him a two-page spread entitled 'Hill walking, crosswords and depression.' He claimed that depression had become a hobby which people clung to, a topic of conversation. His final paragraph was quoted in his obituary the following week: 'They had no life before, but now their lack of animation animates them. Endless rounds of symptoms, fears and medication create a social life, a competition, a place in the world. The truth is simple: People need to pull themselves together and stop moping.'

When his body was found wrecked in the narrow alley around six on Monday morning, the news quickly spread that someone had indeed stopped moping and done something. The word-of-mouth obituaries were not kind, and often described him as 'looking like a teddy bear, but slithering like a snake.' In a brief moment of enthusiasm, Rory told Glynn later that the Leeds Armoury Museum did actually showcase a snake gun from the nineteenth century, but it was a standard shotgun that did for Christian. The culprit was unknown. Local opinion agreed that it must have been a woman he'd shafted, literally or metaphorically, coming for her revenge. There was initially some concern about depression making people violent, but the new CHLOE team issued reassurances that it was rare for patients to externalise violent feelings against others. At any rate, no-one had seen a shotgun-wielding madwoman in the area, and the precision of the shooting indicated excellent cognitive skills. Another power-cut blacked out the streetlights on that fatal night. Christian had been dead for at least six hours when he was found by a man walking his dogs, and rain had washed away any good forensic evidence. The *Chronicle* that week ran a front page spread calling on the police to draft in extra help, but conversations soon turned away. The lack of interest in a murder was surprising in a town where the main criminal activity was the theft of railway sleepers and golf clubs, but feelings against Christian had been running high, and few people attended his funeral. The space occupied by his weekly rant was quickly replaced by a new column; 'That's My Pet' was an immediate success.

The police presence in town added to the existing level of gloom, and Glynn's first lecture of the day went badly, as the students were distracted by rumours. He'd also had to start with some bad news. Without reliable electricity, there would be no powerpoint slides available after the lecture, so the students would have to take notes. He'd sighed as he saw at least half-a-dozen of his Honours students asking their neighbour for a pen. Even more faces fell as he explained the consequences of life without the internet. Journal articles would have to be read in paper copies, which would involve physically walking to the library and making notes, again with a pen and paper. The whole class finally slumped as he pointed out that without Wikipedia they would be forced to develop some old-fashioned research skills, and use a real physical encyclopaedia which couldn't be updated daily by disgruntled teenagers. To cheer them up, he reminded them of the famous incident where a Cambridge fellow had posted false information and watched how quickly it was reported as fact, not just in student essays but in national BBC reports as well. Without access to the internet, Glynn pointed out, no-one was going to be misled into thinking a new species of fossil had been discovered which proved that the Romans ate cornflakes for breakfast.

He was feeling pretty battered by the time he managed to retreat to his office, hoping to catch an hour for lunch and call in to see Nia before his afternoon classes. The morning had been spent in a pre-industrial gloom, as the electricity supply to the university wasn't high priority, and the 'phone connections were down, so it was a surprise when his globe suddenly lit up. It was a video stream, but seemed to be showing a static desert scene. A tinny, electronic voice said, 'Dr. Hughes?'

'Speaking,' he replied cautiously.

'Dr. Hughes, you have been selected as a priority customer to receive a copy of *Oil and Gas Monthly*, offering up-close access to new drill bit technology and-'

'Oh, you are bloody kidding!' Glynn cried. 'Cold calling? This is the best use of communication resources? You seriously think I'm going to buy *Oil and Gas Monthly* when...' and then he groaned, '*Oil and Gas Monthly*.' He took a deep breath, then yelled, 'JAMIE, you bastard, do you have no sense of timing?'

'Perfect timing, I'd have said,' the tinny voice continued.

'Take the bloody voice thing off, and what the hell is this I'm looking at?'

'Oh, it's the Sudan.' The voice returned to normal, as Glynn's younger brother, Jamie, appeared, giving him a mischievous grin, 'How you doing, big brother?'

'I'm fine. What about you? Matt said you were holed

up in the East Village. Stuck there, were you?'

'Pretty much. Called into the office a few days ago, we've only just got international links.'

'Are you okay?' Glynn looked intently at his brother's face, seeing only the usual enthusiasm for daily life.

'Yeah, I'm fine. It's been pretty weird round here,' Jamie nodded, 'but I managed to avoid the lurgy, stayed holed up for a while.'

'You know, Matt never got it, so you might be immune.'

'Bugger. You mean I could have been out there in the chaos?' Jamie groaned. Most people would have been joking, but Glynn knew better, 'Things been bad then?'

'New York, you know, always with the crazy. Getting some great stuff now, wanna see?' Jamie's face was replaced by a brief slide show. In the first picture a woman peered nervously out of a net-curtained window below a hand-written sign which read 'In memory of Mr. Pooky'. Jamie had blurred the shot so the only section in focus was the pastel image of the dead guinea pig. There were some black-and-white shots of people stood at braziers in Times Square, and the final full colour shots showed broken windows and looters on Madison Avenue.

Jamie's face came back, almost like another photograph, his dark eyes framed by impossibly long lashes, 'It's good to talk to you, Glynn. Is Abi alright?' he said seriously.

'She's on the mend. The kids are fine. Compared to where you are, everything's pretty subdued.'

'Gotta love the Yanks! The president's still sending out hopeful messages, but I doubt she knows what's going on. Everything's down to state level,' said Jamie. 'Look, I gotta go. I'll try and get over once the

—
93

travel situation settles down. Give my love to everyone.'

'Will do. Thanks for calling, J.'

It wasn't until the connection cut out Glynn realised he should have asked about Jamie's girlfriend, Trudie, but the call had caught him off-guard. There'd been rumours of riots in big cities around the world, and 'though he knew Jamie was frequently *sent* to trouble spots in search of a great picture, it was different if the maelstrom came to you.

While the 'phone connections were still live, he contacted Matt and Felix to tell them Jamie was alive and well, then rang Abi who guilted him into calling his father. After a long, stilted call Glynn had no time to visit Nia, so rang instead, 'You're a sight for sore eyes,' he chirped, as her face appeared on the wall. 'You okay?'

'Fine. Have you seen the notices?'

'No.'

'They're all over town. I'll probably see you at the meeting?' The connection cut out and her face faded like a photograph left in the sun.

After an afternoon delivering more bad news to groups of students, Glynn left the office and read the 'Notices' tied to street lamps. Some were handwritten and others had been produced with a rudimentary dot-printing system, but the message was the same. An announcement of a general CHLOE meeting on Thursday followed by a personal message from 'Ally, the local team leader' about the murder of Christian Marshall. Glynn chuckled at the peculiar phrasing: 'Neurotypicals are not in danger from those with depression. While this unfortunate death will be investigated, it is not part of a pattern.' Glynn wondered whether 'karma' was a pattern, as he made his way home.

The meeting was scheduled for Thursday at eight in the library, and Glynn had to rush to arrive on time. Some thirty or forty people sat quietly in small groups, mostly women with some children and a few lone men. Glynn squeezed in beside Nia, 'We still on for Saturday?' he said hopefully.

'Sure. We can get the eight o'clock bus, that one's still guaranteed.'

'Eight?' he said as neutrally as possible.

'I thought it was just students who hated early mornings.'

'Evolution, isn't it? You won't find many academics up before the sun.'

'So, you don't head out at six in the morning for a good day's geo-caching then?'

He frowned, and she continued, 'I used to go out with this guy who went geo-caching.'

He was startled, and squeaked, 'You went out with an OWKS man?'

'OWKS?'

'You know, O – w – k – s, Orienteering with Kinder Surprise.'

'That's horrible!'

'They started it. You know they call normal people 'Muggles'? Do you have any idea,' Glynn lowered his voice as people turned to stare, 'how irritating it is when you're on a field trip, you're cold, wet and hungry and some chirpy anorak goes uprooting your depth markers looking for a gonk?'

She laughed, 'A gonk?'

'Probably in an old Biscuit Tin,' he spat out the last words. 'Tell me you didn't go with him?'

'Well I quite liked the walks, but it was all the logging

and the endless tracking that got me down. That, and the fact he was a damn coward.'

'Thank god we never went for universal Wi-fi, or the whole of Scotland would be full of nerds with laptops logging their latest furry smurf discovery.'

'Not that they can do it now.'

'A real tragedy,' Glynn smirked. Nia ignored him, and gently stoked his jealousy, 'He was a nice guy. I did quite like the walking, but then we'd get back and he'd be on the net for hours crafting his narratives – the Jack Kerouac of geo-caching.'

'Wouldn't have pegged you as a Kerouac fan.'

'Different boyfriend, bit older.'

'Interesting,' he smiled and stroked his imaginary beard as he continued, 'No chance for any more Kinder surprise trails with all the GPS gone, so that's another good thing about all this.'

'Another? What was the first?'

'Meeting you,' he said slipping his hand into hers. She beamed at him. At that point the meeting was called to order, and the senior Community Health Liaison Oversight and Evaluation Team leader introduced herself as 'Ally, Senior Cho-lo–et.'

'Now that anagram is never going to catch on,' Glynn whispered, 'She's Ally Chloe.'

Ally outlined plans to conserve fuel, and encouraged everyone to use as little electricity as possible. The Memorial hospital was to be upgraded with some personnel transferred from Dundee when available, and she reminded the room that men could safely donate blood at least three times a year. The immediate plan was to assess needs, and collect resources, so she sent round a list of items required. A Central Distribution Depot was being set up at the Leisure Centre, and Ally was confident that all basic needs would be met very soon, with particular care given to the deserving poor. Glynn read the list of items, and whispered, 'Can't see anyone handing over any booze or fags.' Nia shushed him, but he carried on, 'Tinned meat, migraine tablets, yeah, okay, might have some of those, but what the hell are sanitary products?' Nia kicked his ankle and said, 'You haven't got any, don't worry. No sisters, then, I take it?'

'Two brothers,' he said. 'What?'

She whispered, 'Are you being deliberately stupid?' He looked hurt, and she mouthed, 'Tampons.'

'Really?' he said. 'They call them Sanitary Products?'

Several people were now staring at him and he was briefly silenced. The meeting covered Ally's points efficiently. In forty-five minutes she said 'Things will soon be back to normal' twelve times. As they walked back to Nia's flat Glynn told her about Jamie's report from New York, and concluded, 'I'm not sure about this 'Normal'. Things weren't looking too rosy before all this. Petrol prices, natural disasters, the race riots. Not sure what the baseline for normal is now. Mind you, my mate Rory was predicting the end of civilisation when they stopped collecting the post on Saturdays.'

When they reached Nia's flat he gave her a sombre hug and promised faithfully to be at the bus station on Saturday morning, but when the alarm went off that morning, he regretted his bravado. Glynn woke from the middle of a strange dream. He groaned, and looked around the room like Gulliver in a strange land. He struggled out of bed, still dragging Lilliputians on ropes from his head. He was barely conscious as he stumbled out his front door, and barely articulate by the time he'd reached the bus station. He hoped that some affectionate nuzzling would distract Nia from his early morning dysphasia. By the time the bus reached the village of Kingsbarns he had woken up and marvelled at the clarity of the early morning light. They walked down to the beach, passing a few dog walkers coming the other way.

'You're right,' Glynn said. 'This morning business is a good idea. Look at that, that new sky, the tide coming in. How can we be in the middle of a socio-economic disaster? Whoa, rabbits!'

The moment they came into the car park the surrounding verges hiccoughed with little white tails performing geometric tricks through the grass. 'Matt's kids have rabbits,' he tried to excuse his enthusiasm, but she just said, 'Not such a cynic after all?' They ambled along the shoreline, alternating between admiration of the wide vista and a detailed scrutiny of small piles of stones, as they argued gently about the possible healing power of rock. Once Nia had found two stones to take to Amira, she slipped her hand into Glynn's and they started to walk back in silence. The beach was deserted, and he felt her tensing up.

'It's lovely here,' she said. 'In town, I dunno, it's starting to get creepy. Everyone's so sad, I feel guilty when I feel happy, and it just goes on and on.' He tried to reassure her with the 'Things will get back to normal soon' spiel. She wasn't convinced, and said sadly, 'We should get back, it's going to rain.'

'Nah, we've got a while', he reassured her.

'What are you, half pine-cone?'

'Not at all, but the wind direction will switch before the rain hits us.'

'Seriously?' Nia was interested.

—

'Mmhmm,' he nodded, trying to sound authoritative. 'I'm serious. It actually is like nature giving you a warning, like when the sea suddenly withdraws before a tsunami hits.'

'Really, the tide turns?'

'More than that,' he said, as he reluctantly slipped his hand out of hers and concentrated to skim a stone through a lull in the waves. 'The sea can be sucked right off the shore if the trough leads. And your average person goes, 'Wow, Let's have a look!' so they're going in entirely the wrong direction when Boom, back the water comes.'

'So all the people killed by the China tsunami could have escaped?'

'Sadly, no. The draw back only gives you a brief warning, and that was such a big event there wasn't really anywhere to go. Acres underwater in minutes.'

Nia looked out to sea, 'Hard to imagine, such a big wave, how water can do so much damage.'

'It's heavy. Think how heavy a two-litre bottle of water is, then multiple that by thousands and set it in motion. Scary.'

'But we don't get tsunamis here, right?'

Glynn smiled at her apprehension, 'Not on a day-to-day basis, no!' He caught her hand and twirled her round. 'Mind you, the US eastern seaboard could be hit one day, and the south of England wouldn't be pretty. If the Cumbre Vieja smashes into the sea - it's a cliff near Spain - it could create waves bigger than the Indian Ocean ones. Then it's Bye Bye, New York, New York. Or then again, we could all be wiped out by a comet.' She put her arm around his waist and they carried on walking, 'Doesn't it worry you,' she said, 'knowing all this stuff? Seeing disaster looming at every turn? Every day could be your last?'

'Not really,' he said calmly. 'To be honest, if I was betting on an End Of The World scenario I'd have to go for the odds-on favourite, Human Beings Do Something Stupid. Or then there's the current double A-side, Epidemics with Hospital Superbug. Or there's rats. You know, if rats had conceptual thought they'd take over the planet in a trice, and then we'd be well and truly buggered. Sorry, off on rats again. No, give me a nice geological disaster any day. Much more comforting, and generally much prettier. I could see you as a disaster movie heroine.'
'Really?' she looked up at him hopefully.
'Oh yeah,' he said, placing one hand on her shoulders, and standing back with a critical stance, before he reached out and pushed her hair out of her eyes, saying with a dramatic flourish, 'Raven-haired beauty, end-of-the-world reflected in her dark eyes!' She laughed, and he pulled her towards him, saying, 'I wouldn't mind you being the last thing I ever saw.' He kissed her and the wind changed.

By the time they'd jogged back to the bus-stop they were soaked, and the downpour continued as they sheltered from the wind. 'Have to get you out of these wet clothes,' he leered as she pressed against his chest. The St Andrews bus was due shortly, so they didn't try to change sides when the Crail bus went by in the opposite direction. Glynn caught a glimpse of a man and woman both drenched, but laughing, running to catch the bus, and thought it might have been Rory's redhead, but her hair was wet so he couldn't be sure. Twenty minutes later, they were genuinely huddled together to conserve body heat. 'We should have gone into Crail on that bus, shouldn't we?' Glynn coughed. 'How reliable is this service, now?'

'I don't know,' she shivered. 'Oh, Hallelujah!'

As if by magic, a car pulled up on the other side of the road, and there was Amira leaning out the back window. 'There was a crash. The bus won't be going to St Andrews for hours. Come back with us, warm up.' They squeezed into the back of the car quickly, apologising for the sprays of water. 'This is Joe and Gracie,' she said as they set off. 'We've got a carshare system going from Crail. Last few days the buses have been a nightmare.'

'Are you the magic stone person?' said Glynn with a cocky smile. Nia jabbed him with her elbow, but Amira just smiled, 'Absolutely. And you must be the arrogant closed-minded geologist.'

'Touché. This is very good of you.'

'Nonsense,' shouted Joe. 'Do you think we'd have left you drowning, when there's room in the back for two?'

'You live in Crail, then?' Glynn said to Amira.

'On Shoregate, aye.'

'So, a proper local?'

'Not quite. My parents lived here when I was little, in 1632 ATC.'

'Not with you.'

'Marriage lintel on the big white house.'

'Marriage lintel?'

'Observation not one of your strong points, then?' said Nia, exchanging glances with Amira. As they drove along the empty roads Amira explained about the old practice of inscribing a marriage inscription when a house was built. 'It's quite romantic,' said Nia, 'they knew they'd stay married.'

'I must take a look at these sometime,' Glynn said, muzzling his sarcastic come-back. The downpour finally relented, and a small rainbow shone over the dark stone of the main square as Joe dropped them off. Nia and Amira fell into quiet conversation about people Glynn didn't know as they walked down to the cottage, but he wasn't unhappy just holding her hand. When they reached Amira's place he realised he'd walked past this row of cottages many times on his way to buy crab, and always thought they'd have great views. He wasn't disappointed by the sight of the sea, but his attention was distracted by the texture of the decoration. Every inch of the stone walls was covered with textiles, pottery and paintings, more than anyone could create in a lifetime, he thought. 'This all yours? I'm impressed,' he said when Amira went to put the kettle on, and Nia smiled as he was nice to her friend.

'Some of it,' she shouted in. 'Some was my gran's. I inherited the cottage, and the businesses.' Nia laughed and Glynn was puzzled, 'Businesses?'
'Bit of everything, really,' Amira explained. 'Gran used to turn her hand to most things, art, crafts, folk medicine, cleaning fish. You'd be amazed how much people missed what she did once she died, so I sort of took over. Not going to make me a million, but I'm happy.'
'So, you didn't have 'flu, then?'
'Oh I did, first wave, and I was really out of it, fever and everything. But the next fortnight was worse, like being lost at sea, surrounded by flotsam.' Amira waved her arms, 'But then, I was lucky. The first pills I tried helped, and I saw Ruth a few times for acupuncture, so I'm fine. Just trying to find a way to help everyone else now.'
'Ah, the soap,' Glynn nodded. 'That's why we ended up nearly getting drowned. We were looking for magic stones, you see.'

Amira ignored the whine, and continued, 'Aye, and we're trying to get things sorted in Crail, you know, car shares, visiting people on their own, making sure everyone's got stuff to eat. You'd be amazed the stuff people have in their larders.' Glynn sniffed the air, and asked hopefully, 'You still have real coffee?'

'Nearly the last, I'm afraid. Amazing how you start longing for the simple things, an orange, a piece of blue cheese.'

'Hot buttered toast,' Nia sighed wistfully, 'thick white bread, lots of butter.'

'Well, this is very welcome,' Glynn thanked Amira. 'When we're drinking Mellow Birds, that's when you know trouble's round the corner.'

It was early evening before news arrived that the bus was returning. They had to stand, and the bus groaned under the weight of a whole day's travel. When they were dropped off on South Street Nia said, 'I'd better go. Ruth might need me.'

'Okay,' he said, disappointed by her apparent resistance to his charms. 'How about dinner Wednesday?'

'Can't do Wednesday, we have a meditation group. 'Though you could come, if you like.'

'Ah. I might be a bit out of place.' He frowned. 'Saturday? D'you fancy a spot of babysitting? Robbie's birthday treat, going to some solar-powered circus in Dundee. I'm looking after the girls.'

'Girls? You counting the rabbits?'

He ignored her sarcasm, focused on his plan of seduction, 'No, Emily's staying over. Make the most of driving up there, Eilidh and Bob are going too. D'you know Eilidh?'

'Not very well.'

'Oh, you'll like her. Probably. Yeah, you will.

'It's a date. Saturday,' she agreed, blushing at his happy smile. He scribbled his address on her arm, kissed her goodnight and spent the whole week thinking about her, battling through more random lectures and scattergun tutorials as his students tried to motivate themselves in a world gone mad.

Glynn showered early on Saturday in case the electricity went out again, and used the last of his shampoo. He hoped to relax on Sunday, so tried to catch up on some reading for most of the day and was still engrossed when Nia appeared at his window, with Tommy in her arms, 'Oi!' he shouted. 'Get your own girl!' The cat stalked past him and sniffed round the kitchen as he let her in. 'Have a seat,' he showed her into the living room, while he changed his shirt.

'Nearly ready,' he called out. 'I thought we'd walk it, as it's dry. Save petrol and all that.'

'Fine,' she called back, and looked around the room. She picked up a large hardback book from the coffee table, flipped through a few pages, then closed it as Glynn came in.

'*Inorganic Chemistry: New Perspectives*?' she queried. 'How can you read this stuff?'

'I'm not a chemist,' he said, pushing it to one side. 'Some of it makes my head hurt. Some of it's nosebleed-inducing.'

'So why do it, if it's so hard? I can see why all the volcanoes and dinosaurs are interesting, but why do this?'

Glynn buttoned up his jacket and rummaged for a scarf, 'A very good question, my dear. Clearly I can't fool you with the whiz-bang, gosh, aren't earthquakes fascinating routine. Serious answer?'

'Go on. I can take it,' she crossed her arms, while he

leaned back against the door. 'Alright,' he said, 'it's deeply unfashionable, but I think these small, complicated things matter. The world *is* complicated. And on a personal level, well, the tough material is often the most fun. Intellectual satisfaction, I suppose they'd call it.' She looked attentive, so he warmed to his theme, 'Now, I don't subscribe to the 'mind is a muscle' line, but there's something about the moment when you finally see the light, solve a problem. I think it's like the sort of endorphin high you get after a long run when your muscles ache. Not that my idea of a long run is very long, of course.' He offered Nia a wool-wrapped bicep, 'Ninety-percent pure flab, as you can tell.'

She laughed, and he pressed on, 'But to return to my theme. I'm knackered after a few miles, but your Olympic athlete wouldn't be breaking sweat. They wouldn't get the high from a short run. It has to be a real test, the marathon, hundred-metre hurdles, the difficult stuff. The difficult work can be fun. I've lost you, haven't I? I think I lost the argument somewhere as well.' He grinned at her, 'Completely mad, do you think? Shall we go?'

As he locked the door behind them she squeezed his arm and said, 'I think ninety-percent's a bit unfair. Eighty-five maybe. Anyway, Einstein, your biceps weren't reading that book. I sort of see what you mean, but it does sound a bit pompous. You know, 'I'm a mental athlete who needs stimulation' and all that.'

'Oh, entirely pompous,' he agreed as they set off, 'and dangerous. A lot of people use being clever as a weapon. They're arrogant, put people down, I know that, but it's still important to acknowledge what you are. Actually, there's still a lot of discrimination the other way too. You get far more stick for being 'too clever' than for being 'too fit' or 'too fast', 'too good at tennis', tall poppies syndrome,' Glynn grabbed Nia's arm and peered at it. 'Come to think of it, this is not far off eighty-five percent either. Here am I on the defensive, as if you were the village idiot. Come on, you know what I'm on about. Inorganic Chemistry, all of it, it's just codes to learn. You could do it just as easily as I can if you put your mind to it.'

'Never in a million years', she dismissed the idea instantly.

'I'm serious, Nia. Don't do yourself down. You do a damn good job of hiding it, but I can see that mind of yours itching for a good workout.'

'Are you trying to seduce me?'

'Absolutely!' Glynn grinned maniacally at her. 'Going babysitting with a girl was half way to marriage when I was at school.'

As they walked up the lane to the house they were passed by a small car with two huge bikes attached to the back, and saw Eilidh and Emily waving. 'Isn't that Professor Urquhart?' Nia said doubtfully.

'It is. Eilidh kept her maiden name,' he replied.

Nia looked surprised, so Glynn continued, 'I suppose the students have more than enough troubling mangling the name of one Dr. Q.'

'Oh, no, not that, they just seem like an odd couple,' she said. 'I mean she seems so nice and he's a bit, well, odd. Oh, that sounds awful!'

'Well, they seem pretty happy, if you ask me. Whatever works, I suppose.'

'Yeah, I suppose,' she agreed hesitantly.

They found everyone in the kitchen, Robbie jumping about, and Becky muttering about never having such a good trip for *her* birthday. 'Where's Bob?' said Glynn, as he saw Emily was already tucking into a plate of biscuits.

'Gone to check the bikes, sorry,' Eilidh laughed. 'You know, the first time I ever met Bob he was nearly missing a train at Ely station because he was fitting an extra D-lock to his back wheel.'

'Why does that not surprise me?' said Abi, as Eilidh continued, 'Bob burst on to the train as it was pulling out, and apologised for crashing into the only free seat next to me as he was unpacking, all clips and the like.'

'Sounds very romantic,' said Abi.

'No, I was a bit put out,' Eilidh smiled at the memory, 'but then he asked me if I minded being joined with him in unholy purgatory.'

'So, he didn't have a sense of humour even then?' Matt snorted.

'Quite,' she said, 'and it went from bad to worse. Sometimes I think he carries that damned extra D-lock round as a sort of security blanket.'

'Ah,' said Glynn. 'Abi, you ever meet Uncle Fraser?' She shook her head, so he delineated his hapless uncle's character. 'He was obsessed with bikes, and with cameras. Always carrying a camera with him. He'd never really take part in family do's. He'd be circling, snapping pictures, very unsettling, but our Aunty May said it was because he was shy, gave him something to do with his hands.'

Matt sneered, 'What else was he taking pictures of, I'd like to know? Had a bad influence on our Jamie, that's for sure.'

'Also never travels without his camera,' Glynn explained, 'but you wouldn't say our Jamie was a wallflower, would you, Matt?'

'One extreme to the other,' he grumbled.

'Jamie is the Indiana Jones of photography!' Abi filled in for Nia, ignoring Matt's frown.

After they'd left, Glynn settled down to read Becky's current favourite story, a post-modern Noah's Ark. Nia stayed in the living room, but could hear the final dramatic pages as Glynn's voice rose with emotion, 'And Then...,' he said, 'Noah agreed that Lucy could bring three people with her, but one of the people she chose was ...'

'Sarah!' the little girls chorused.

'And she said she'd have to bring three people too, and one of the people she chose was...'

'Martin!' the girls joined in.

'And he said he had to bring three people too. And one of the people Martin chose was ...'

'Amy!'

'And Amy said, 'I only have two friends' but I can't leave ...'

'My old grannie!'

'So my old grannie must come too. And then Amy's grannie said, 'I can't come without ...'

The girls were tripping over the words in their excitement: 'The Kind Lady Who Does My Hair!'

'And the-lady-who-did-the-hair said she'd come, but she'd have to bring her husband and children and each of them would want to bring another three people. And then, Noah said ...'

The chorus rose to a crescendo as the girls joined in, 'Everyone has to come!'

'Exactly!' Glynn cried, 'Everyone Has To Come. Because no-one would come without their three people and eventually that would mean everyone. When he understood this Noah stopped building his boat, and decided he'd find a way to stop the melting water from the poles. And he worked so hard, and so tirelessly, that very soon he did it. And then,' the girls joined in happily, 'Everyone Could Stay Forever.'

'Quite a performance,' Nia applauded, when Glynn came back in. 'It's all in the writing,' he shrugged. 'Never too young to get them excited about environmental catastrophes. Antidote to Robbie's crazed pursuit of hapless fish – I swear he's seen *Jaws* already.'

With Emily and Becky fast asleep in the indoor camp they'd established in the dining room, Glynn rummaged through the cupboards looking for something to watch. Like most people, Matt and Abi had most of their entertainment collection online, so there were only a few old DVDs lying round. Glynn hoped they wouldn't be forced to play fish-related projection games, so was relieved to find a range of wildlife DVDs. They settled down to watch soothing scenes of daily life in the real world, as tigers roamed through forests and seals basked on warm rocks. The prairie dog wasn't quite to Glynn's taste, and Nia suddenly said, 'What you doing?'

'Umm,' he mumbled, 'I'm currently nibbling your earlobe.' He paused as he continued to do so, 'Planning my campaign South, down the neckline towards more mountainous territory.'

'What about the children?' she hissed.

'Sssshhh,' he murmured. 'Just a little recce.' She squeaked as he breathed into her ear, 'Can't be too careful in unknown terrain.'

Hours later when the car arrived home, Nia was curled up on Glynn's chest, sound asleep, but he was still wide awake, listening for any sounds from the children. As Eilidh was telling Glynn of the latest plans for exams in January, Nia yawned and said in a quiet, sleepy voice, 'Still sounds like chaos. Probably just as well I didn't go back this year. Might not fit in even more. Not that I ever did.'

She was surprised when Eilidh said wearily, 'You're too nice, not posh enough, hen. Oxbridge of the North, this is.'

'Is it?' she said, waking up more. 'My mum wanted me to try for Cambridge, but I said it was against my principles. Couldn't face the tuition fees anyway. I don't know if I regret it. I do sometimes think maybe it would have been different if I'd applied myself and gone there instead.'

'Don't torture yourself. Not all it's cracked up to be.'

'Where did you go?'

'New College, Oxford,' Eilidh said without a hint of pride. 'Sounds good, doesn't it? At least here we've got the sea to hear you crying. There, it's Hell on earth. And flat.'

'Oh come on, you don't mean that,' murmured Glynn half-heartedly.

Eilidh stretched out, then said more to Glynn than Nia, 'Every beggar watching you – go in, go out, eat, read, do your laundry. Like gipsy children hanging on you in Rome. 'Where are you off to, lassie?' 'That's a nice sweater. Have your own sheep, do you?' 'Coming in to dinner, Ay – Leee, ay-lee?' If you don't play, you're a failure,' she warmed to her theme. 'If you're not deliriously happy, you're a failure. If you object to the arcane, brutal practices, the intellectual violence, the, the, I dunno, the atmosphere of the bloody place, if you object, you're a failure. You're the one who's broken. Not good enough. So I left with my first-class degree, and never went back. Terrible how it still haunts me now, but this place can be as bad at times. It's the attitude.'

Glynn was uncomfortable, but Nia's curiosity encouraged Eilidh to continue. 'It looks so beautiful in the postcards,' she sighed, 'and I still get twinges of regret, you know? Why did I no love every minute of it? And then the old answer lurks, 'That's 'cos you're no good enough, Eilidh.' Ach, when people ask these days I generally say 'Too misty, too little sleep'. I'd never let Emily go there. She's just the sensitive type who'd work herself crazy, and break her heart.'

'Oh, well,' Glynn tried to be cheerful, 'Emily seemed quite chatty with Becky earlier, wouldn't you say, Nia?' Nia was reluctant to give parenting advice to someone she barely knew, so was relieved that Eilidh didn't seem to expect an answer, but mused to herself, 'Having the rabbits to focus on helped. She's been going on and on about having a pet. I think we're going to get a dog. Give her a bit more social contact. What d'you think?'

'I think you're a little woozy, Eilidh, and I think you'd better be off home,' said Glynn, 'before Morpheus sends out a search party.' Matt and Abi came downstairs. 'Where's Bob?' said Matt, 'Talking to the rabbits again?'

Abi leaned over to Nia and said, 'You know, the first time we showed Emily the rabbits, Bob picked Lily up and said, 'Hmm, interesting bone structure.' Well, we were in gales of laughter after that, but he didn't see why we were laughing.'

Abi hurried Robbie up to bed, and Matt slumped down on the sofa, 'Thanks for this, Glynn,' he said. 'Oh, forgot to say, Robbie got a card from the old man, post's still working down there. Abi said you rang him?'

'Right,' Glynn nodded. Matt went on, 'Bastard sent

him some cash, and a promise of more if he did well in his end-of-year exams.' Matt grimaced, and Glynn moved in a practised diversion, 'Are there even going to be exams?' Matt shrugged, and leaned back, closing his eyes. Bob pulled his car round to the front of the house. Eilidh hugged them all, then wrapped up Emily, still sleeping, in a shawl. 'I am so tired. I wish someone would wrap *me* up like this to carry me home,' she hummed, letting Nia and Glynn into the back seats before strapping Emily in. They drove home quietly.

Once everyone was gone, and Abi had finally settled Robbie to sleep, she leaned heavily on the kitchen table. 'It'll never last!' Matt snorted, opening a can of Bulgarian cider.

'You old cynic,' she said, putting the plates away. 'How can you know that?'

'Well, look at her. Gorgeous. Bright, bubbly, great to look at. Glynn'll never be able to hang on to her.'

'You managed to hang on to me!'

Matt grumbled 'Yeah,' just loud enough for Abi to hear. 'Thank you very much,' she said sharply. 'I'm going for a bath.'

There was enough hot water left to run a few inches, and she lay still, allowing her muscles to relax. Robbie had seemed to enjoy the show, but he'd kept asking questions about how the animals were treated and she hadn't been able to put his mind at ease. She consciously enjoyed the comfort of her dressing gown, as she padded quietly to the bedroom. Her heart sank as she saw the untouched bed. She walked downstairs, head aching, footsteps light so as not to wake the children. As she'd expected, Matt had fallen asleep in the lounge, two empty cans at his feet and another on the table beside him. He'd also stubbed a rancid cigar out on one of the cans, even though he was officially an ex-smoker. His 'occasional puff' was usually in the garden, maintaining the fiction that he'd given up for the sake of the children. In truth, he'd given up only briefly when each of the children was born. Now, smoked, pickled and snoring, he was not to be woken. At best he'd be intoxicated and maudlin. Abi threw the rubbish into the bin and left Matt to sleep. His shoes might mark the sofa, and his watch might leave a nasty mark where it was squashed under his thigh, but those were trivial things, not worth the risk of waking him. She went back up the stairs and stretched out diagonally across the bed, falling asleep quickly now that the fire risk had been dealt with.

Across the town, it was dark when Nia suddenly sat upright and fumbled for a light from the unfamiliar bed, only to realise the electricity was off again. 'Whatcha doing?' Glynn murmured.

'I thought I heard something.'

'S'n old house. Lots of creaks. Go back to sleep,' and he wrapped his arm around her waist. She was still tense as he opened an eye, 'Although, if you're not sleepy?' he said with a smirk and pulled her closer.

Chapter Six

St Andrews had always been a friendly town, open doors welcomed neighbours, students and tourists alike, but the waves of depression had drowned hospitality and the town closed in on itself, turning its back to the sea. The rats were indistinguishable from the rubbish they trawled. Blank, vacant faces merged with the empty shelves in dusty shops. Random cars drifted across the roundabouts. The tablets weren't helping most people, and there weren't enough people left to run daily life, let alone to give the sort of long-term support and kindness that the mentally-ill need. Although the official figures for the incapacitated were slowly going down, there was a new malaise developing, as the sole strong figure in a family found it all too much to bear, and tried to escape with good deeds, hard work or whatever intoxicant was available.

Glynn and Nia walked out from his flat in a happy bubble of their own, but the bubble burst as he saw the demonstration outside St Salvator's. These students were apparently not depressed, but possibly deranged. They were holding banners demanding more contact hours and better library resources. Glynn had often suspected that his students expected him to be on call 24/7 to answer every silly query they might have, but this seemed to be hard evidence that a certain type of student really did think the world revolved around them. The 'Say no to the BRP' messages meant nothing to him, so that was another thing to ask at the official department meeting. The lunacy continued when he arrived in his office to find a peculiar memo from Hobden, telling staff in no uncertain terms, that now

E-Learning was out of the question, they must move towards PBL or possibly EBL or CBL. Glynn had been around long enough to know that such requests might quietly disappear if you were very careful not to disturb them, so he filed the memo as if it were nitroglycerin.

The opening session was a first-year tutorial, a nerve-wracking affair at the best of times, as students struggled to adjust to the new academic styles while negotiating drinking competitions and the Fuck-a-Fresher brigade. The class was small; some local mature students, two overseas youngsters who had arrived early in the summer, plus one student who was repeating the year and was already regretting it. The seminar moved in fits and starts, and Glynn left with a pounding headache.

He gave a brief description of the session while they waited for the new geographer to arrive for the official staff meeting. When Glynn noted that at least the new Spanish student had been willing to talk, Hobden sucked in his breath. 'Ah, yes, Lopeth thomething,' he guffawed. 'Interviewed him myself. Fear he may turn out to be one of *those*.' Eilidh sighed, and Glynn said through gritted teeth, 'One of those?'

'You know the type,' Hobden waved his arm. 'Foreign students keen to show their knowledge of English by talking at great length about bugger all. Terrible. You try to give them a bit of leeway, not their native language and all that, but when you realise it's all complete drivel, damned hard to get a word in edgewise with all that funny syntax.'

'You mean they use grammatical English, rather than the textspeak most of our lot employ?' Glynn tried to broaden the focus of the rant.

'Watch out for him, that's all I'm saying. Sarcasm won't work, they don't get it. You might just have to say loudly, 'Thank you Mr DooDah. That's enough.' That generally works for me.'

Glynn nodded, somewhat bemused. He had always known Hobden was a bit odd, but his sudden rise to power seemed to have transformed him into a colonial recruiting sergeant. The new geographer arrived, clutching a pile of papers, and Hobden beckoned her in, 'Ah, yes, Tricia, come and sit down. Have you met Glynn, Eilidh?'

'Yes,' she said, sitting by Eilidh. 'I was at the meeting you called last week. And the one before that.'

'Right, right. Didn't get much done then, 'though did we?'

'So, we'd better get a move on now then, hadn't we, Malcolm?' Eilidh chided.

The meeting took nearly two hours, most of which was spent on the outdated official agenda. Glynn couldn't see how they could possibly aim to improve their admissions figures for the next five years when the whole Science Faculty was running on fumes. Nevertheless, Hobden insisted on following the agenda and writing detailed minutes longhand. The discussion of the immediate crisis had to wait until the last half hour, and there was a general feeling that they might be able to keep things going for at least another three weeks before having to reassess. By the time they reached AOB Tricia was half asleep, and Eilidh had completed forty rows of stocking stitch, so Glynn was reluctant to prolong matters, but he innocently asked, 'By the way, what's the BRP the students are protesting against?'

Eilidh put down her needles and smiled sweetly at Hobden, who patted his head with a sharp, red handkerchief. Even Tricia perked up as she scented trouble.

'Branch of the admin. system,' Hobden havered, 'temporarily, I should stress, running things rather than Senate. Can't get a quorum, you see, and these chaps are professionals.'

'So, what does it stand for?'

'Business Recovery Plan. Okay, that about wraps it up,' said Hobden rising quickly from his chair.

'Of course, what that really means,' said Eilidh, 'is that the money-making side of the university has finally revealed its second head and is trampling over any idea of educational standards in pursuit of filthy lucre.'

'This unit was in place before all this happened, then?'

'Seems so.' Eilidh was willing to prolong the meeting now there were matters of substance to discuss. 'There were rumours about this secret government for a while, but no-one expected them to take over so quickly when there was a problem. Now, there's no oversight. They do as they please.'

'And the students are protesting?' Glynn connected the dots.

'They're getting charged extra for everything, even course booklets.'

'Wow. Scary. And who's in charge?' Glynn looked over at Hobden who slumped back into his easy chair. He looked up and said, 'It's that mad woman who used to run Disability Support. You know, the one who wanted us to add extra doors at the back of lecture rooms so anxious students could have private visits from their puppies or some such nonsense.'

'Not sure there were ever puppies in the equation, Malcolm,' said Eilidh, 'but it does seem that Kath is in charge. Which cannot be good for any of us in the long run. I don't know where the students can take their complaints. I can't see good ol' Noel swooping in with his helicopter.'

'Mind you,' said Glynn, 'that *was* pretty impressive last year. I mean, until they had to give him oxygen. It was a great picture in the *Chronicle*. Surprised they're not still running it, in fact. It's the highlight of Rory's collection.'

As Hobden shooed them out, Eilidh said, 'Rory's not back to full strength yet, I see. Keeping up at John Burnet, but not able to get back in here.'

'Mmn,' Glynn nodded. 'I'll see if he fancies a run. We're going to need a tech round here soon, if only to stop those damn Chemists making acid.'

'You know the BRP's got its eye on the schools?'

'What?'

'Last governors' meeting at Greengate there was a proposal to centralise all education through the university.'

'Great, so we'll all be turned into schoolteachers by the end of the year.'

'Matt seems pretty stressed. Even Bob noticed,' she said, but Glynn was sure his brother would be coping fine.

Still mulling over the strains affecting different families, Eilidh received great thanks from several exhausted sets of parents later that afternoon when she collected a gaggle of small girls and took them up to Pipeland Farm for Becky's 'Not my birthday yet' party. The girls had the rabbits in the living room and were trying to make them join in a tea party. The rabbits were circling. Eilidh looked in, and said to Abi, 'Is your rabbit stalking my daughter?' Abi laughed, 'Yes, Barbie won't acknowledge rabbits are prey animals, not red-clawed predators. She's given the old cat a fair scratch or two. It's alright. Becky'll look after Emily. She's wise to Barbie now.'

'She's remarkably practical for her age,' Eilidh moved to help Abi in the kitchen.

'Oh, it's having an older brother, I'm sure. I can't imagine what it's like for eldest children. Or only children, come to that.'

Eilidh sighed, 'I do worry about her.'

'She's just shy,' Abi assured her. 'Life's hard for first children.'

'She was born like it, that's the thing. We barely slept for twelve months because *she* wouldn't sleep. The doctors kept telling us it was because she was bright. She needed more stimulation than we were giving her.'

'Very helpful,' Abi smiled, 'when all you wanted was a decent night's kip!'

'You're right there. Bob used to say he'd happily swap a few of her IQ points for a few hours sleep.' She paused and looked away, 'It's my fault, I know it is.' She took off her glasses and continued, 'I was in such a state, so nervous before she was born, she must have picked it up. She just shrinks from the world. So many things frighten her. I've made my own child scared and depressed, and I don't know what to do about it.'

'I think you're being a bit hard on yourself,' Abi passed her a biscuit. 'She's a wee bit timid, but she's got friends, hasn't she? And look, she's even facing up to mad rabbit Barbie, and even the vet's afraid of *her*. She's just shy, Eilidh, that's all.'

'I wish I could think that's all it was. But it's everything,' Eilidh rubbed her eyes. 'The friends, the things she likes, it's all so intense. She gets so caught, wrapped up, so invested …' Eilidh trailed off.

Abi sighed, 'If I'm honest, I don't think Becky's right after the 'flu. I probably scared her being so ill, but I cannae put my finger on it. They say that children haven't been affected by this depression, not directly, but how do you know? Matt says the ones in school are fine, well behaved, working hard, so maybe they are ok. Come on, let's go and join the furry safari. Bring your elephant gun – them rabbits can be fierce!' She gave Eilidh a quick hug, and they carried their mugs into the living room.

At the same time in town, Glynn was curious to see Nia's flat, so had arrived twenty minutes early to collect her. He had inside information that the Crown was going to be serving locally-caught fish that evening, and had urged Nia to get dressed up to go out. She was flustered, and told him to sit down while she got dressed. He pushed a pile of clothes off her sofa and said, 'Never have enough wardrobe space, you women.' She called out from the bathroom, 'Haven't got a wardrobe. Bedroom's too small. Take a look.' He got up and peered round the door, 'Oh, I admire your use of space.'

'Nicely said.'

'And a pink duvet.'

'Fuschia. Yeah, I know it doesn't go, but it's clean, and the launderette's been shut for weeks.'

Glynn was keen to explore further, but didn't want to push too far. Nia had not said much about her life, and he was hoping to glean some more information indirectly, so he went back into the living room and pulled a small children's paperback from a shelf. '*Andy Pandy Paints His House*,' Glynn read, 'don't tell me - it's a children's version, let's see, À *la recherche du temps perdu*? *The Dubliners?*'

'Oh, it's not mine,' she said, interrupting his contemplation. 'Got it from a charity shop. Look at the inscription. It's a few lines from Rilke, but look at the bit above, 'For my darling Peter. Your students are buffoons. All my love, always and whatever it takes. S., May 2000.' See?'

'So?' Glynn was confused, and distracted by the very small red dress Nia was wearing.

'Well,' she wrapped her arm around his waist conspiratorially, 'when I found this, my friend Karen and I looked up the verse on the internet, and guess what, there's a Professor Peter Elton in the Modern Languages bit, who works on German poetry.'

'Probably him then.'

'Ah, yes, but he's been married forever to a woman called Celia, works in personnel. So who is 'S'?'

'And you reckon he was having an affair?'

'And it ends badly and he gives all her gifts to Oxfam, failing to realise that there's an incriminating inscription.'

'Ooh, very Nancy Drew. Are you tailing people as well?' Glynn felt a touch of the same confusion he'd felt at their first meeting.

'No. It's just interesting,' she said, 'what gets thrown away.'

'Ah, like Bagpuss.'

Now *she* was puzzled, and he enlightened her with a theatrical flourish, 'Old children's show, girl had this shop full of random things, singing mice, and when Bagpuss went to sleep, everyone went to sleep.'

'Bit before my time, granddad!' said Nia kissing him cheekily.

'And Andy Pandy isn't?' he threw back, before she took the book from him and pushed him out the door.

There was indeed fresh fish at the Crown, together with tinned potatoes and sweet corn, a slightly odd meal but closer to normal fare than the standard rations the CHLOE team were starting to distribute. Morag, the landlady, had saved them a spot, and whispered to Glynn something about 'A nice bit of normal, nice young couple out on a date', as she showed them to their table. They could almost feel themselves in a normal situation, but for the company of hardened beer-drinkers now sipping Tia Maria cocktails with umbrellas and mermaid-shaped swizzle sticks. After a strange but relaxed evening, when they reached Glynn's flat he was annoyed to see that Tommy made straight for Nia, miaowing and weaving round her legs. 'You little traitor!' he said as he let them in, 'I'm sure you're not hungry.' He yawned widely as the cat stalked past him to inspect his flat.

'I'm shattered. Do you want to use the bathroom?' he said to Nia and put out some water for the cat. He was talking feline, and listening to the small domestic sounds of towelling and the turning on of the taps when there was a shriek, and Nia rushed out of the bathroom, wrapped in his dressing gown.

'I don't mean to be a wimp, and I'd normally do it myself, but there is a HUGE spider coming out of the airing cupboard. Do you hate them too?'

'Not as much as you do, clearly. Lay on, Macduff,' he bounced. 'I will evict the wee beastie.'

'It was coming out at the top.'

'Right, here goes.'

There was a pause, then the sound of the bathroom window opening and closing. 'All gone. Huge, but not hairy. Not too bad ...' he paused, 'Why've you put all that make-up on?' he frowned.

She gave him a hard stare, 'I haven't *put it on*. I just haven't *taken it off* yet, you fool!'

'But you weren't wearing all that earlier.'

'Oh, you innocent thing! I bloody was, and you should be grateful. Unfortunately, the evening-out face looks clownlike when I'm in my dressing gown, or no, your dressing gown. Believe me, the dressing-gown face looks a sight worse with a little red dress.'

'Not clownlike exactly. Hmmm,' Glynn moved behind the sofa, 'Amsterdam brothel owner, maybe.' She wriggled round to look at him, 'And will Sir be wanting any extras tonight?'

'He will that!' he purred as he picked her up, ignoring her squeals, and made for the bedroom.

Nia woke a few hours later in an empty bed. She was puzzled by the light from the living room and was about to get up when Glynn came back in, saying quietly, 'Sorry. Go back to sleep,' and spooned around her.

'Ooh, you're cold,' she shivered.

'I thought I told you to go back to sleep.'

'What was so important?'

'Nothing. Just something clicked; the bit I was working on today.'

'Couldn't you have done it in the morning?' Her voice drifted into incoherence.

'Nope. It would have gone,' he said, as if it was obvious.

'You're very strange.'

'Thank you. You're lovely too,' and they mumbled off to sleep together.

When she woke the next morning, Nia heard Glynn moving about in the kitchen. She stretched out, enjoying the warm luxury of the duvet. Her nose was cold. She hesitated before making a dash for the dressing gown. She was still shivering when she opened the bedroom door.

'Hello, gorgeous!' Glynn growled at her. 'You know that outfit will get me everytime. Ankle-length tartan fleece. How can a man resist! Sleep well?'

She smiled and pulled out a chair at the table.

'I can do you some porridge, only powered milk, but I do have some crusty old honey. And there's some loose tea.'

She nodded, clearing a space in front of her on the table, then focused on a notepad lying under the empty butter dish. She pulled it out and struggled to decipher half a page of scribbles and a sketchy diagram all drawn in pencil.

'Is this it?' she said. 'What you got up to do last night?'

'That's it.'

'You got up in the middle of the night, in the freezing cold, to write this? You must be mad.'

'Quite possibly,' he sat down opposite her with two mugs of black tea. 'I'm sure most people sit at their desks and write their articles properly, but mine always come in fits and starts.' She stirred the dark liquid cautiously, and stared at him.

'Seriously,' he continued, 'if I didn't get up and write it down, it would have buzzed round my head and then,' he leaned across the table, 'I'd have been tossing and turning for all the wrong reasons.'

She laughed, 'Mad as a monkey! So, what are you doing today?'

'Couple of general science lectures, an hour manning the switchboard, then I'll have another bash at this article if I have time. What about you? Anything planned, other than contributing to world peace with your general loveliness?'

'Yuk!' she brushed off his saccharine flattery. 'No. I shall be retail queen as ever. I think an ordinary day at work is quite an achievement these days. I don't know whether Ruth will be able to stay open like this much longer, 'though. Everywhere's so quiet. Maybe we'll all end up on the streets.'

'Well, I could sell my body,' Glynn patted his stomach, before leaning over the table and taking her hand, 'but I'd get much more for selling *yours*,' he said with a studied look of innocence.

'Oh', she tried to push him away, 'I'll try to take that as a compliment. Meet you for lunch?' He insisted on kissing her thoroughly before he would let her change out of the tartan dressing gown, but eventually released her to get ready for work.

As the days passed they fell into an easy routine, as the machinery of daily life creaked and juddered. When they weren't helping out with the CHLOE plans, giving blood or packing food parcels, they met for lunch comparing notes on the morning's events. Between the student contacts and Nia's connections with the smaller villages where Amira worked, they built up a reasonable sense of how different places were faring. Disturbing reports were coming from the big cities. Nia was relieved when she spoke to her parents, but worried because her mother's Legal Aid team was getting involved in challenging local CHLOE decisions. There were rumours of riots in Salford and Liverpool. Everyone was waiting, for some change, some improvement, some sign that the crisis had truly passed.

On October the fifteenth Autumn came, the temperature dropped, and almost overnight the leaves fell. Glynn volunteered for one of the clean-up weekends and enjoyed shovelling huge piles of crispy leaves. The official line was that fallen leaves would be a hazard if they blocked central drains, but the small section of the population able and willing to volunteer also agreed that it was good for morale to keep the town tidy. There had been an emergency collection of rubbish the week before, and everyone was being encouraged to reduce waste and bury anything perishable in their gardens. Glynn was due to help out again the weekend after, but it started to rain and it rained for four days, drenching the whole of the East Neuk. Crail was cut off from Kingsbarns, Anstruther was cut off from Elie.

In St Andrews the pavements slithered as earthworms gasped for air, and the gutters overflowed, flooding main roads for hours at a time. A solitary pair of council maintenance men struggled to keep on top of things, but nature prevailed. On the fourth day of rain a state of emergency was declared throughout Fife, and runners boated across town encouraging people to store rainwater and watch out for contamination. The model citizens who had tried to bury perishable rubbish in their sloping gardens, found that no good deed goes unpunished, as the failing sewerage system was choked further by resurrected scraps of food which leached out of the waterlogged soil, emerging like unseasonable rotting daffodil bulbs. There were no rainbows, except where puddles of oil leaked from abandoned cars.

As soon as the state of emergency was announced, the university was declared closed for the day and all the staff and students were volunteered to help with the town defences. Glynn tried to keep an educational focus and discuss water permeation rates with some of his students, but soon they were sorted into teams and sent to different locations. Glynn ended up at John Burnet Hall, where Rory was slowly moving sandbags around piles of weeping students. Once the immediate danger had passed, they took a break and sipped on the strange herbal tea being distributed by a junior CHLOE rep.

Perched on a sandbag, Glynn tried to make jokes about the state of affairs, but even his tongue-in-cheek praise of Kevin Costner's sterling work in *Waterworld* failed to raise more than a token smile. He cautiously enquired after Rory's health, which stirred a more emphatic reaction. 'They don't fucking work. I've been on four different things. Pink, blue, pink again. They just give me different problems, headaches, blotches, you name it. And I still feel bloody awful.'

'What are you taking now?'

'Elcazin. Ten days, dry mouth, no fucking use.'

'Elcazin. That's an old style pill. Did your doctor tell you why that one?'

'Supposed to be good. Trial and error, that's all she said.'

'That's an old style pill,' Glynn tried again. 'I don't know why you're on those. The newer ones are much better.'

Rory pressed his head hard against the wall, 'Nothing works.'

'Go back to the doctors. Seriously, mate,' Glynn had never seen his friend look so worn out and thin. 'Tell them you need a newer version. Ask them for Malthak, that's what I'm on.' Rory shrugged and slowly returned to work.

Later that day Glynn and two stout young men were sent to Queen's Gardens, where a sewerage pipe had burst and spilled black ooze into the front lawns. As he arrived, he found Tricia from Geography had been left in charge of the street, and was beginning to lose her temper as she tried in vain to get the householders to help. '*You* have a go,' she said to Glynn. 'Maybe they'll listen to a man!' He had no more success in persuading them outside, so the four of them distributed leaflets and set up Do-Not-Cross signs as the machine sucked up the worst of the mess, while the occasional white face looked out of a window. 'You know, I bet some of those houses are flooded,' she said, 'but they're just sitting there.'

'It's depression,' was all Glynn could say in response.

In several parts of the town electricity supplies had been cut by the high winds, so only some of the town received the first emergency broadcast that evening. A number of areas were believed to have had their water supply contaminated by surface water, so emergency bowsers would be distributed to key sites. Under no circumstances should anyone attempt to drink seawater. Water butts should be secured and checked daily, as rat contamination could occur.

Glynn usually enjoyed thundery weather, the shifts of atmospheric pressure distracting him from his own mental storms. On the first day of the storm he'd joked with his students about building an Ark, and regularly checked the lightning intervals to track the storm, but by day four, after he had been press-ganged into crisis management and trudged home from Queen's Gardens, he was as miserable as everyone else. He was soaked through, with no hot water, no heat, no warm food, no favourite foods, no television, and no light apart from an old battery-powered storm lantern. He brought in rainwater he'd collected outside the back door and boiled it, before dunking an old shrivelled teabag for colour as much as taste. He dried himself off with a three-week-old towel and curled up uncomfortably to sleep, thankful for the warm patch on the bed where Tommy had been sleeping all day. It was several hours before he generated enough warmth on his own to attract the cat back. He vaguely wondered, as he turned over, how he was going to cope when it turned really cold.

The next morning it was not raining, but the town was dripping and chafing. There was no sense of blitz spirit. For the first time, people began to fear the worst had not yet passed, and that that things might still be getting worse. The basic structures of civilisation were fragile. Even those hardy souls like Glynn were subdued. Under normal circumstances, they'd have said the weather was making them a bit depressed, but that common usage had fallen out of fashion. You could still be 'fed-up' or 'pissed off', but the vocabulary had shifted.

'Depression' was now reserved for the gut-wrenching pain that kept people indoors, or ran down their backs like a stalactite when they ventured out. Felix told Glynn of a report that catalogued incidents where the apparently-well had developed depression independent of the 'flu, or had simply walked out on their families. Rumours began to spread that parents were killing their children in carbon-monoxide filled cars as they couldn't cope any more, and that elderly parents were being given overdoses to end their despair. The undertakers continued to practise with dignity, but the scaremongers now started to question what would happen when the fuel at the crematorium ran out. There had been no petrol supplies for public purchase for more than a month, and getting around became more and more difficult. With unreliable communications, such that Crail for days at a time seemed like Brigadoon, notices began to appear on any flat surface in the town. 'Urgently need to contact Matty. Used to see Alison. Was a plumber then joined the army. Call Jasmine at the paper shop or Morag at the Crown.' The threads of society were gnawed away.

After weeks of avoiding the question, Glynn and Nia sat down at her kitchen table and retold the tale of how each of them had come to be on the magic pills. Nia presented her story as a classic student problem, struggling to keep up, got behind, then started panicking about going in. She told Glynn she just needed a break, but didn't say why three years had passed without returning to her studies. Glynn told her about his mother's death while he was an undergraduate, but found it harder to explain the second occurrence. He tried to explain how he'd been in his first job after finishing his PhD; what should have been the start of a great career had plunged him into a nightmare where his heart clenched every time he approached campus in his waking or dreaming hours.

'You're here for good now, 'though, aren't you?' Nia said, a little disturbed by the descriptions of his paranoia and strange eating habits.

'I wish. It's twelve months. If I can find some time to get another article out, I might get one of those magic permanent jobs that have eluded me for the last three years. I have *had* interviews,' he said almost petulantly. 'Four, in fact'

'Where?' she said, settling back in her chair and waiting for the story to unfold.

'Southampton, two years ago, that would have been a

plum job, but of course they had one of their own post-docs up for it.'

'Oh?' she raised an eyebrow, and that was all the encouragement Glynn needed.

'Gave it to Thomas Fucking Masterson, complete wanker, public school, lazy as sin, doesn't give a damn about his colleagues or his students, writes one-line feedback on essays and he gets away with it all because he has powerful friends, and he plays the game. Arrogant like you wouldn't believe. Complete wanker. Really, everyone knows.' His voice rose half an octave. 'His students hate him, except for the deranged eighteen-year-old girls who sit and simper and then write him brilliant feedback which cancels out all the bad stuff.'

'So he's due for some bad karma?' Nia tried to navigate Glynn's storms of indignation.

'You'd think. After all, he acts as though it's all a bloody meritocracy and he's just clearly the best. Doesn't realise how bloody lucky he is to have got all the jobs and research grants he had. It's just made him more arrogant, so he treats people like shit and the world keeps rewarding him.'

'But is he happy?'

'Good point,' Glynn acknowledged his audience. 'I hear he's desperate to get a job in Oxford. His wife's a harpy who wants to go back to the dreaming spires, so maybe all is not well in Masterson-ville, but it's still galling. Actually,' he said, 'I'd like you to meet her. I saw her at a wedding once when someone said something about alternative therapies for, I don't know, asthma or something. She got on her high-horse and finally said, hang on, what was it? Oh, yeah,' he rose into a falsetto, "I spent ten years of my life developing the Omega Burst 2 Yoghurts. I hold a

131

degree in chemistry from Oxford, and I am a registered nutritionist!' And then she stalked off. That was the end of that conversation. Bitch.'

Glynn was biting his nails by this point, and Nia knew she should distract him, but she wasn't ready to return to her own story, so she stoked the conversation, 'Okay, that was one job. What next?'

'London, nearly got that one,' Glynn relaxed a little. 'To be honest, that was fair. The woman who got it had just done three temporary jobs and published this amazing monograph which half the people I know don't understand.' He tensed again. 'So then there was Aberdeen, where they gave it to Postman Pat, just enough neck to attach his old school tie. Boring as hell. And finally, Bristol, where I did my PhD, where I should have been a shoe-in, but obviously not, and they gave it to some bloke from Canada who'd swanned around teaching a few hours a month, so no wonder he'd published a dozen articles. AAAAAARgh!' He kicked the wall with real feeling. 'So,' he concluded, 'altogether, it's a wonder I'm so bloody sane, with the mad family and the lousy job prospects. But things are definitely looking up for me now,' he said, kissing her and dragging her to bed. At the back of his mind he realised that he hadn't asked Nia much about her own background, but he was still hoping she'd say more in her own time, as they clung together in the dark.

And there were lots of dark places in the town that month. There were no pumpkins for Hallowe'en, and the only celebrations were reserved for the restoration of clean water supplies after the storm. A few children's parties took place behind closed doors, low key, for fear of causing offence in a world where misery was a new default setting. Some of the local churches were teetering on the edge of calling the epidemic a divine plague, and Ruth came down one morning to find graffiti on the window of Ethereal, 'Repent and turn from wickedness.' She responded by offering a ten-percent discount to all customers, and they had the busiest day for weeks, as they sold sinful geodes and evil meditation tapes as contributions to the sum of human happiness. A week later, another cause for celebration was largely drowned out. Bonfire night was usually a highlight of the social calendar, with several parties leading up to the big international firework display. This year there were no fireworks to be found, and the recent deluge had flooded all the possible wood. People were also reluctant to donate anything that could burn, as they looked ahead to a cold winter with limited supplies of fuel. Only one party took place in the grounds of Greengate School – it was intended to be a 'Community building' event sponsored by the CHLOE team. A small bonfire had been built with the dried refuse from the flood; old mattresses and warped books propped up a saggy Guy as the fire popped with heavy-duty firelighters.

Some thirty people turned up and huddled round the flames, a brief warm, bright circle in the middle of a dark, shivering town. Slowly, the party atmosphere spluttered into life, as people realised they were among friends and could enjoy themselves without being insensitive. Glynn found Becky and Robbie helping their uncle Finn to run an ancient barbecue, where he was selling charred slabs of mutton and fish kebabs. Finn's enterprises had made him an essential part of the town's non-essential life. While the CHLOE arrangements had ensured that no-one was starving, Finn was the one providing the access to old-fashioned technology, repairing items which would normally have been thrown away, and generally making himself invaluable. Glynn was about to have a good-natured go about his profiteering, but Abi caught his arm and said, 'Leave him with the bairns.' She pulled him a few feet away, and said, 'You know Malcolm, young lad helped up at the farm? He killed himself with a shotgun on the weekend. Finn found him.'

Glynn groaned, 'Oh god, he was what, seventeen was he?'

'Would have been eighteen next month. He'd been getting up to the farm seven days a week, 'though we knew he wasn't right. He left a note reminding Finn to get the pigs vaccinated next week. He won't talk about it, so I'm hoping my two can give him some comfort. Here, have some mutton.'

Glynn took the charred slice and said, 'Protein I suppose.' He looked round at the respectable townsfolk chewing slabs of meat and fish in the firelight, and saw the world returning to prehistoric times. 'How are your folks?' he asked Abi, dreading the answer, but she was calm and he saw a new determination in her face. 'They're alright,' she said. 'I got up to Dundee last week. You know they live just outwith the travel boundary, so it takes forever to get there. They're still pretty weak, but, well, it's a bit sick to say it, I think they're better for having to look after their neighbour.'

'Not well either?'

'She seemed to be on the mend, but then, it's awful,' Abi lowered her voice to avoid spreading more misery, 'their neighbour, Nance, was having regular visits, from her family, and then her daughter died of an asthma attack, inhaler'd run out, she was gasping, died right in front of her; died before an ambulance arrived. She was only thirty, and do you know, Nance got a call from the ambulance forty minutes after she'd rung to ask if she still needed it. Daughter's lying cold in the kitchen, and they're calling to ask whether she needs a doctor!'

They were both silent for a while, mulling over the unseen threats all around them, before Nia arrived and introduced Glynn to Ruth. He was being cautiously charming, when Robbie bounded up and dragged him off to help shore up one side of the fire. 'How are you feeling?' Abi asked Ruth.
Brilliant,' she replied, 'but of course I can't say that to anyone because it marks you as a freak these days, so I keep my head down and say 'middlin' like everyone else. So, is your brother-in-law treating my little Nia right?' she said, winking at Nia.
'Oh, I think so,' Abi said in a teacher's voice. 'I often think I married the wrong one. And she's very good for him.' She saw Bob carrying Emily to the food stall, and waved Eilidh over to join them.
'What was Jera like?' said Nia, cutting to the chase.
'Jera? The ex?' The three older women smiled.
'Well,' said Eilidh, 'there was this dinner party, d'you remember? And we'd invited Luce from history who'd just had a baby. So she'd been talking about how hard it was to breast-feed and said something about well, only mothers know what it's like to have little hands pawing at your chest all day long, and Jera said...' Eilidh hiccoughed, and Ruth and Abi finished the punchline for her, 'she said, 'Ah, but I do understand. You see, I have Glynn!"

Nia couldn't help but join in as the three of them laughed until the tears were running down their cheeks. Eventually, Abi choked out, 'She was a total disaster, hen. It was never going to last. You're much better for him.'

'Glad to hear it,' said Nia, and Ruth hugged her. As the laughter vanished into the darkness, Eilidh looked around and said in a more serious tone, 'Where's Matt tonight?'

Abi shrugged, 'Oh well, you know him, never goes to a social occasion unless there's booze involved, and as Finn's home brew isn't ready yet, he's still inside, writing progress reports.'

Glynn came back over with Robbie and introduced Nia to Julie, one of the postgraduate teaching assistants. Julie quickly excused herself to get back home. 'John's still not good, then?' Ruth said to Glynn, 'He's a nice lad, this is rough on him.'

'I think they're both having it hard,' Glynn didn't know much. 'Julie's family's all in Tokyo, and I don't think the communication lines are too good out there.' Huddled together against the cold and fear, they all compared their snippets of information about world events and local problems, focusing on the present, not daring to think too far ahead. As the last of the food ran out, the conversations turned once again to the meals they most missed and the best ways to combine the basic foodstuffs supplied by the authorities. As the bonfire started to die down, the party slowly unwrapped itself.

While Glynn waited for Nia to emerge from the scary small toilets, Ruth came to him directly and said quietly, 'You seem like an honest man, so I mean this kindly. She's not as tough as she looks, so be good to her.' And then she was gone, as Bob's car pulled up to give her a lift home, using his last supply of petrol. Glynn was taken aback and guilty about the stuttered reply he'd failed to give Ruth. On the walk back he tried to ask Nia more about her employer, and she told him Ruth had been a practising GP who had changed career when she inherited some money and set up shop in town. Nia wasn't be to drawn on the psychological processes that led a qualified doctor to spend more time training in acupuncture and holistic medicine, but Glynn was curious and amused himself by speculating on her motives and why she was now so secluded.

When they reached Nia's flat, Glynn was called into the shadows by a pale young man. Nia was concerned, but Glynn said, 'Just Floyd, one of my students', and promised he'd follow her up in a minute. She had just put on one light and one bar of the electric fire, when he came in grinning.

'Are you alright? What was that about?'

'Never you mind,' he said, kissing her gently on the lips, before pulling away. 'Tell you what, you have a quick shower while there's hot water and then I'll show you something.' She washed quickly before the electricity could go off again, and enjoyed the last of her shower gel. 'Hurry up!' Glynn called, and as she dried herself off and wrapped up in a dressing gown, she thought she must be hallucinating from hunger, and resolved to microwave a bowl of oxtail soup before turning in. When she opened the bathroom door, she saw that Glynn had cleared the table, lit two candles, and laid out two plates, each with two slices of buttered toast.

'Oh my god!' she said. 'Where did you get bread?'

'That was Floyd, one of my students. Lousy geologist, found his new calling as a smuggler. Should have been round earlier, but he promised he'd have it for me tonight. Tuck in.'

'Oh!' she sucked in the smell. 'I can't believe it. And real white bread.'

'Real butter too, that was easier, one of Finn's commodities. The bread I had to get by breaking into the student bartering system. And Floyd is one of the most astute dealers I've met in a while.'

She groaned appreciatively and he licked his lips, more for her than the toast, as she took her first bite, luxuriating in the crunch followed by the soft rich taste of melting butter.

'What did you have to swap?' she moaned with her mouth still full.

'I'll tell you later, just enjoy!' He bit into his first slice and they silently ate the food of the gods. Nia licked the last crumbs of the plate, and said, 'Perfect. You are brilliant.'

'I know,' he said. 'Still a bit hungry?'

'Mmmn, I was going to have some soup.'

'It's just oxtail isn't it?' Glynn grimaced. 'The great 'flu pandemic and then, even worse, The CHLOE Oxtail Soup Mountain.'

''Fraid so.'

'Ah, well, I can now be an even better boyfriend,' he said reaching under the table, 'because,' he placed the bag on the table, 'I have another four slices of bread and another pat of butter. Save them for breakfast or have them now?' She was torn for a moment, then said, 'Let's have them now. To hell with tomorrow. God, you are wonderful.' She came round the back of his chair and kissed him. 'Do you mind if I save one of mine for Ruth? It'll make her day.'

They slept well that night, and spent Sunday afternoon walking on the West Sands, wrapped up tightly against the wind. Out on the beach, watching the seagulls, it was tough to believe everything had changed so much in a few months, but come Monday morning, the quiet of the town was eerie. The day began like many others, a damp November mist hugging the buildings. A few random shops were open, and a solitary council operative trudged through the town putting up warning signs about the symptoms of Weil's disease. All across town life slowly dripped into action. Some parents struggled to find shoes, others cowered under the blankets. The older children were placed in arbitrary groups in the main school, depending on how many teachers had turned up. The younger children followed their parents to work, or just stayed curled up with them as Mummy or Daddy tried to tune in the radio. Everywhere mountains of responsibilities threatened to collapse on lone shop assistants, solicitors, farmers rattling round empty buildings. Everyone worried.

By mid morning Nia was dusting a shrinking supply of crystals and Glynn was producing copies of handouts for students on an old banda machine he'd found in the department's attic. Hobden had taken the recycling message to heart, and had produced his own version of the twentieth-century Squanderbug poster, showing Noel Edmonds with a sword fighting off the wee beastie. The students were briefly amused by this, but they needed constant reassurance that they weren't wasting their time, and that they would gain credit for work done under these peculiar circumstances. The university had collected the tuition fees from day one, but had yet to sort out all the bursaries and support funding the students had been promised. The Business Recovery Plan team was ruthless in pursuit of their objectives. Glynn tried to be upbeat, but he had to keep warding off his own anxieties and plans for his position and future prospects. Even in the middle of a global catastrophe he still worried about whether he'd have a job in twelve months' time.   Come lunchtime he was more than happy to see Nia and have a snack of rice and fish in the castle, which was suddenly open again after a three-week closure.

He would remember that lunch hour for many years, brief moments like the sudden relaxation when Nia teased him about his solemn face. More than anything he would remember standing on the ruins looking out to sea. The waves were strong and slate grey, reflecting the cloudy sky, but the sunlight kept breaking through, throwing fragments of rainbows off every splash on the sea. It was too cold to sit for long, so Glynn suggested a cup of Mellow Birds in his office. They had just come back out on to the Scores when they saw the crowd. A young man was standing on the ledge outside a third floor window, staring at the sky. The neighbouring windows would once have been garlanded with carrier bags holding cartons of milk, but now they were bare.

A siren blared out and abruptly stopped as a police car pulled up. Two officers headed towards the building. The older one moved the crowd back with a loud hailer, while the younger one went in the back door of the building. He was seen a few minutes later as a dim figure entering the room behind the silhouette on the window. The onlookers were tense and guilty, waiting, weighted down. Framed between the shutters, the glass panes reflecting the drifting cloud patterns, the man's expression was unreadable. Time passed. Then suddenly the crowd relaxed, a sigh, a laugh broke out as the figure took one single step back, and his torso turned inwards towards the policeman. The sudden blossom of hope hurt. The onlookers contracted, clutched at each other with mindless chatter. Thank God, they said.

Back to their own concerns, the figure in the window forgotten, no-one was watching, no-one saw the first move as the man in the window jumped. Everyone saw the fall as he described a perfect arc, arms gripping his chest. Brief, graceful falling, then the crash of bloody flesh.

The rest of the day for Glynn seemed to pass in silence, except for the echo of the sound of the fall. He met Nia from work and they met Felix in the Crown. Felix was restless, talkative. He bought the second round of Baileys (nothing on tap, most of the spirits gone) and started suddenly as if in mid-conversation, 'I don't suppose confidentiality matters any more. I don't know if I'm even a doctor any more. Maybe I've gone crazy, too.' Glynn and Nia could only look at him in alarm.

'Let's just say, he was, perhaps could have been my patient,' Felix said almost to himself. 'I would have written a prescription, but he didn't take them. Said he planned to pull himself through it. Saw it as some sort of test of character. A young man with gumption. I would have thought he just didn't seem the type, or maybe I'd have done something differently.'

'You mean the lad who jumped?' Nia whispered.

'There was a prescription still there on his notice-board,' Felix toyed with his drink, not meeting her eye. 'He was studying philosophy. I suppose he was used to being able to think his way out of things.'

'That is harsh, isn't it?' said Glynn. 'After all, until this all began there were loads of people who would think depression was something you should snap out of, be a man about. Moral strength, and all that.'

'Oh, I know,' Felix shut his eyes, and leaned back in his chair. 'The 'I don't deserve treatment, I should be able to get better myself' routine is part of it. I should have seen it. The trouble is, I have some sympathy. When the pills work they're great, but the principle of taking the edge off life isn't easy. You know yourself, the compromise.' He opened his eyes, but stared blankly past Glynn and Nia as he mused to himself, 'Do you take the pills to be normal, even if that means losing something of yourself? Do we really want to be blunted?'

'You musn't blame yourself,' Glynn tried to console him. 'I know you did your best.'

'Sleep, that's the key,' Felix mumbled. 'I used to think when I was a junior doctor that I'd give anything for sleep. The pain of staying awake, worse than toothache. I could snooze through the sunniest day, Royal Philharmonic playing outside my window. It was blissful, but now…,' he trailed off, 'I sleep but it doesn't do me much good.' He seemed disconnected from the conversation. Glynn might have pursued this, but he didn't know how well Nia knew Felix, so he let him be. They walked him home, made him promise to go to sleep, before going to Glynn's flat, and avoiding the subject for the rest of the evening. After they had eaten, and watched the hour of scheduled TV, they ended up gazing out the window at the empty streets. It was too early to seek forgetfulness in sleep, so they turned to the time-honoured solution. Later, warm in the post-coital darkness, Glynn whispered, 'I love you.' Nia made no response. He presumed she was asleep.

Chapter Seven

They slept late, and left the flat in a rush with no time to talk. Glynn was lost in a foggy daze as he walked to work, but was pulled back into the real world by the sight of Bob sitting in the quad. He was wearing an anorak, wrapped in a large black-and-white tartan blanket. When Glynn got closer, he saw him making notes in a school exercise book.

'Bob? Everything okay?'

'Oh yes, just doing a spot of bird-watching,' He handed Glynn a book. 'Look at this, claims to be authoritative, *Birds of Fife*, but I bet it was inaccurate when it came out. And now, with global warming, changing habitats, well it's almost useless, so I'm gathering my notes, making a few alterations. I plan to suggest a new edition to the publishers. Looks as though the internet's dead and buried, but these birds keep communicating.'

'Good idea,' Glynn paused as Bob returned to his notes, 'but you must be freezing.'

'Not really.'

He wondered whether to find Eilidh, then had a nasty thought. 'Bob, that lad who jumped yesterday, did you know him?'

'Yes,' Bob said without looking up. 'This'll be my fourth funeral in two months. Three former students, and now one of my dissertation students.'

'Four? And they all killed themselves?'

'The first two. Sensitive. Lisa was very bright, planning to come back and do a PhD after she'd had her baby. Marcus, well, nice lad, lacked direction. And Ailsa from the bank, a real fighter. Died of anaphylactic shock after one of those thought-free, CHLOE 'Helping You Through This' packages was contaminated with nuts. She had an epi-pen, but it wasn't enough. And now, a fourth.'

'I didn't realise there were so many.'

Bob put down his pen, and took off his glasses, rubbing his eyes, 'I thought this community was going to be a network for my old age, but now … Anyway, at least Rory's perking up. He looked a lot brighter yesterday. Better get back.' He shivered. Glynn didn't know what to say, but Bob continued, as if to himself, 'They said the 1918 'flu killed more than the World War, and we talk about the sacrifices in the trenches, but they weren't choosing to die. And now… no-one to fight, is there? Craig Maskell, his name was.' He didn't get up, so Glynn said he'd try to go the funeral himself and left Bob to the bird-watching.

Glynn's lectures were now exploring the areas of his knowledge marked 'Here be Dragons'. Without visual aids or complex handouts, he'd returned to basic chalk-and-talk, and was scaling back the curriculum each week. He hoped he could dress up the rambling discussions in seminars as 'Problem based learning', and hoped that the students who did turn up were getting far more individual attention than normal, which would compensate for his lack of expertise. Even on his newly increased salary, he dreaded to think how low his hourly rate of pay actually was. When he added up all the time spent on preparation, and dealing with the inevitable student chaos, his teaching week came to well over forty hours, and that was before he added in time spent on admin. and hours in the evenings and weekends trying to do some research. He suspected that he'd have crumbled under the pressure before now if it hadn't been for Nia.

After the success of the toast and butter, he'd investigated further the possibilities offered by the student exchange network, and was happy to hand over a lot of money plus a set of *Babylon 5* figurines for a dozen allegedly fresh eggs. 'How does a really big omelette sound?' he said, surprising Nia as she shut up shop that evening. 'Go on, give me the punchline,' she sighed, as she let him in.

'No, no, really,' he said and presented the box. She offered to make him a cup of herbal tea. As she drifted round the flat looking for teabags, he wondered if she was feeling well.

'You're very quiet.' He paused as he slowly realized what had changed. 'Is it about what I said last night, 'cos if it is, then it's no big deal. I'm not expecting anything. It just felt right.'

She took off her earrings and put them on the ironing board. 'No, no,' she started, 'well, maybe. What Felix said. I've heard it dozens of times, but then yesterday was so ... These pills take the edge off things, so what does that mean? Does it take the edge off everything?' She turned away from him, 'You love me, I love you, but is that love with the edge off it?'

'I'm not sure I follow.'

'Look,' she came round behind his back, and put her arms around his waist, leaning her head against the nape of his neck. 'You are a gorgeous, sexy beast. One hell of a catch, and I really, really want you, but ...' she moved awkwardly and took a deep breath before saying with a blush in her voice, 'I just never feel completely out of my mind with passion, and when I come, it's nice, but it's not exploding universe-of- stars nice. And *I'm* the problem. I just don't think *I'm* capable of feeling like that, any more.'

She desperately tried to explain, 'I mean, I've been working on my sacral chakra and everything, but it's as if the dial doesn't go high enough any more. The edge has gone. Do you see what I mean?' Any possible reply was strangled in Glynn's throat by a mixture of anger, disappointment and humiliation. She felt him tensing up and cried, 'Oh, I should have really said, 'Yes, I *do* love you too!' Sorry, I do.'

Glynn pulled her round to face him, but she couldn't meet his eyes. 'Now look,' he said, 'when I said I loved you, it wasn't a watered-down feeling, you know. Everyone knows sex changes as you get older. It can't always be explosive.'

'Glynn, how old am I? And you're hardly Methuselah! We've known each other for what, three months?' Her anger overcame her embarrassment, 'You're gorgeous, I don't scrub up too badly, and we get on like a house on fire. I know the chemistry's there, but where's the edge? What if the pills have numbed us?' He was rather disorientated, but tried to argue back, 'Would that be such a disaster? Doesn't it mean we can be sure of what we feel, not just wild passion?'

'Maybe,' she kissed him. 'I do love you. I'm just not sure that sort of love's good enough. I'm not sure I'm feeling things as I should. And if I'm not sure about myself, that makes you and me complicated.'

'A can of worms, this is, isn't it? Complicated, aren't you?' he squeezed her tight, then said, 'Would it help if I said I was joking? No. I don't love you a bit.'

'Glynn!' she pulled away.

'No, THAT's a joke. Darling, I *do* understand what you're saying, mind-altering substances, these pills, but being with you makes me very happy and that's good enough for me.' He held out his hand, and she accepted, 'You make me happy too.'

'Okay, then, back to important stuff,' he said, pulling her towards the table. 'Eggs. Scrambled? Boiled?'

While he whipped up an omelette, Nia gazed out the window. 'A good trade, then,' she reflected, 'the black market, the young bright things of The University down low with Dundee's Methadone Mothers. A victory for the middle-class, middle-aged LETS set-ups. Frankly, I don't know anyone who would even sell me a box of eggs in return for what I can offer. And obviously I don't have any of the essential skills to keep myself alive. It's nights like these I really miss the internet,' she sighed. 'You could just have a look at what the world was doing, buy a book, do some email. I'd even gotten the hang of the new auction sites after eBay collapsed.' He put down his whisk, and said, hoping a serious comment was required, 'Just like when a tree falls and all the saplings take its place.'

'Yeah,' she mumbled, but said no more. Glynn tried to stay with her train of thought as he dropped the eggs into too-hot fat and struggled to stop them sizzling over, 'I never really understood what happened with eBay. I was finishing my PhD, so I was a bit out of things, but one minute it was lovely, you could go online at 3am and decide you wanted some obscure whatjamacallit, and you could choose from half-a-dozen and get it delivered two days later. Then all of a sudden there was nothing but widgets being sold by dodgy dealers in China.'

'Capitalism, I suppose,' she said.

'How so?'

'Well, the powers-that-be wanted to screw more money from the sellers. I used to sell a few things, but it got too expensive. So, I carried on buying for a bit, but then everyone like me stopped selling and there just wasn't anything interesting to buy, so I stopped looking. Ebay pushed the sellers even more, and the whole thing ground to a halt.'

'Shame,' he said, dishing up his egg creation, 'but I suppose it was good for all the specialist sites.' They ate the half-scrambled omelette in appreciative silence, and then went out to taste the air.

The shock of witnessing Craig Maskell's death had stopped their lunchtime meetings, which they replaced with a quick stroll after Nia closed the shop, even if Glynn had to go back to the office for a few hours afterwards. On the Wednesday she was surprised to see a small group of muffled figures on the other side of the street which erupted into excited screams when they saw Glynn. When she saw a flash of red hair, Nia realised that the child waving from under three scarves was little Emily Urquhart, who talked frantically to another small woollen bundle who in turn pulled at the arm of the man shepherding the group. 'Excuse me,' he called over, 'but are you Uncle Glynn? My grand-daughter says she has something for you to see.'

'Oh lord,' Glynn chuckled. 'They're going to start thinking I'm a paedophile,' but he sauntered across the road and after a minute Nia saw him place a large orange sticker on the coat of the grand-daughter. 'What was that about?' she laughed when he sauntered back.

'I have managed to elevate Becky and Emily to celebrity status among their peers.'

'Come on. What have you done?'

'Well,' he said as the excited chattering faded away, 'Emily had a fall a while back and when I saw her next she told me to be careful because 'It was healing all by itself.' So I gave her one of these,' he pulled a small roll of orange stickers from his jacket pocket, 'and then I gave Becky one, and it sparked a craze.'

'Warning: Treat with Care,' Nia read curiously. 'Where are they from?'

'Oh, I whipped them from the Disability Support office. Crazy Kath had them made up, and they slap them on essays, which can mean everything from 'This student suffers from anxiety' (genuine case), right through to 'This student is a bit thick so please ignore all problems of spelling, punctuation and general stupidity' (not-so genuine case). I'm putting these to much better use. Becky put hers on the front of her rabbit hutch.'

'They *are* a bit scary,' Nia confessed. 'I didn't think pet rabbits were so lively.'

'Oh yeah, mind you, these two were rescue rabbits so they might be a bit nuts. They were two of Burger Bun's.'

'I'm not with you.'

'Yes you are.'

'Idiot!' she belted his arm. 'What d'you mean, two of Burger Bun's?'

'Didn't you see the *Chronicle* last year? That mad woman in Strathkinness who had a dozen rabbits and even more guinea pigs loose in her house?'

'Don't remember that.'

'Well, are you sitting comfortably, okay, standing?' Glynn began, 'Mother Bunny made her nest in an old cardboard box from the takeaway, which said 'Twelve pack of burger buns', so when the SSPCA rescued them, that was what they called her. It was a real hands-on-deck thing to find homes, and the babies were in a foster home for weeks. Pretty unsettling, so that's how you end up with a hellbeast,

149

Crazy-Biting-Baby-Bunny-Barbie, gorgeous but seriously troubled. I'm sure animals have psychological hang-ups too.'

'Oh, yeah, I'm sure they do. Don't we all?' Nia kissed him goodnight. 'I'll see you tomorrow,' and she headed back to her flat alone.

The funeral of Craig Maskell took place on a cold Friday morning. When Eilidh arrived she was holding Bob's arm, and he wasn't resisting. Glynn was surprised by the number of people there. He joined Felix near the back of the room. At the end of the service Felix said, 'Can you spare me an hour Monday morning?'

'Sure. What's up?'

'The powers-that-be think I might crack up,' he grumbled, 'so, they've given me a week off. I've got travel permission to head to Brighton.'

'Is that safe? What's happening in London?'

'I've a friend in Milton Keynes. Take the train to there, stay the night then head down in the morning.'

'Milton Keynes?'

'You know most of the government's there now, no? Centre for all sorts of disaster management plans.'

'Ah, well, living in Milton Keynes, you probably don't have high expectations of life, so maybe this hasn't hit them so hard,' Glynn quipped.

'Aye, maybe', Felix nodded. 'Too many aspirations is a recipe for disaster.' After a short service, standing quietly in the sleet they watched a small, black car pull away in place of a hearse. In the slow procession out of the church gates Glynn caught snatches of a conversation Eilidh was having with an older woman. He heard her say, 'No, he'd be no use. I know, you'd think he would, but how many philosophers do you see with wonderful lives? It's all good in theory, face up to things, think things through, but I'm not sure that really helps. If it doesn't make philosophers happier, what's the point?'

Glynn stood aside to let the family pass, and when he turned Eilidh was smiling and saying conspiratorially to her friend, 'Did you know you can get deep-vein-thrombosis from sitting in a chair working too long? It's the only way I manage to get Bob to be a human being for a while when he's into his work. Paranoid about his health, you see. Gets him every time. Mind you, he tries to get around it by doing these strange leg movements under the desk. I swear he's as fit as a yoga teacher.' The image of Bob in a leotard haunted Glynn for much of the weekend.

As he'd promised Felix, Glynn was waiting at the Crown early on Monday morning. Nia came with him for warmth, and they stamped their feet as they waited, watching warily for rats.

'So, he's off to Brighton? Seems a long way to go,' she probed.

'He has a friend there.'

'A friend?'

'That's all I know. Honestly, women.' She looked at him quizzically and he cracked, 'Alright, probably more than a friend, but you know how discreet Felix can be. So, this friend, Luke, I met him last year when he came to visit. He tried to sell me a set of orange plastic dining chairs.'

'Sounds a bit odd.'

'He calls himself a modern antiques dealer, nothing after nineteen-seventy. He's made a fortune.'

Felix pulled up in a small car; two large stickers in the windscreen read 'Doctor on Call' and 'No petrol left in vehicle overnight'. He apologized to Nia, that she couldn't come along, now even the weight of one petite attractive person burned fuel they couldn't spare. 'Thanks for this,' he said sleepily as Glynn climbed in. 'Normally you could leave your car at Leuchars with the keys in the door and no-one would rob you, but these days ... You know, we have to siphon off the petrol at night unless the car's in a secured lot? You can drop it back to the surgery.'

The roads were quiet and overgrown. Felix drove slowly. Low-lying corners still harboured patches of poisonous mud from the floods. They drove past John Burnet Hall, and when they'd cleared the checkpoint on the edge of town, Glynn said, 'I was thinking I'd go and see Rory, maybe take Tricia, the new girl, the one Hobden stole from Aberdeen? She's cute. Or there's Sarah from Physics who's covering some of the basic stuff?' Felix said nothing, allowing Glynn to ramble, 'He might want a bit of female company, but then, I know he's feeling a bit better, and they say the pills can do odd things to you, so I didn't know.'

'Okay, what's the problem?' Felix said, still keeping his eyes on the road.

'They say these anti-depressants can have a bad effect on your libido,' Glynn finally asked, 'you know, make you not yourself, so how true is that?'

'That is normally not high on most people's lists, you know,' Felix sighed. 'Many people who are depressed don't want sex. Godsend in a way, or there'd be a population explosion next summer. The pills can't take away something that isn't there. Make an appointment when I get back,'

'Nah, I'm fine,' Glynn muttered.

'Alright,' Felix said kindly. 'Purely as a hypothetical case. There can be some performance issues, in some cases with some pills, but your general love of life? Getting rid of the depression normally brings that back. And if you've been on them for quite a while, anything that's happening to you now is probably not due to the anti-depressants. Good enough?'

Glynn hummed thoughtfully. They stopped at Guardbridge to pick up two monks who were hoping for a train to Dundee, and several packages which Felix was going to deliver en route. When they pulled into the station Glynn saw two other cars unloading a similar assortment of people and objects. One of the older CHLOE reps was manning the entrance to the station, checking papers before anyone got through. Felix had been warned that the train might not actually turn up until the afternoon, so Glynn stayed until he saw the train pull in. It was one coach, already very full. Glynn didn't envy Felix his journey, but the mood on the train seemed uncannily festive.

The next CHLOE public meeting attracted the largest crowd yet and had to be rescheduled for one of the university lecture halls. Nia sat on the left-hand side of the room with Ruth and Eilidh. The first item on the agenda was the organisation of local self-help groups. Although most people agreed it was a good idea, the initial meetings had been bedevilled by arguments about eligibility for membership. Several people had objected to the presence of the more lively members, arguing that if the tablets were helping people they shouldn't be coming to the meetings. As the meetings were also used as a focal point for the distribution of extra food and supplies to those in greatest need, there was a growing problem. There was also some concern that those who were most in need of help weren't actually being enabled to go to the meetings in the first place. Ally was able to calm this discussion by announcing that a counsellor would be assigned to each of the self-help groups to set some ground rules.

The next item for discussion was a report on the medical situation. Dr. Mosely looked more miserable and exhausted than anyone in the room, even as she delivered good statistics which suggested the post-viral epidemic had already peaked some time ago, and that the numbers able to return to work were rising each week. She answered a number of questions, emphasizing wearily that there was no one-size-fits-all solution for depression. When she mentioned underlying emotional problems, there was muttering in the hall. She pressed on, talking of a 'festering layer of psychological disorders' which had been exposed by the epidemic and would need long-term attention. She warned again that if fatigue was the most prominent symptom, people should not try to self-medicate with caffeine or other stimulants.

She reminded them that fatigue was often part of the body's defense mechanism, which was another reason the anti-depressants took a while to work. Trying to remove that innate protection prematurely would press raw nerves into service long before they were ready. The audience shifted in their seats and mulled over her words.

Ally thanked her, and picked up the point about long-term management. The next item on the agenda was the provision of pay for certain services. Since so many businesses had ceased trading through lack of stock or manpower, many people had been drafted on to the CHLOE payroll to back up the patchy volunteer support. There were gasps of surprise when Ally announced that due to the central importance of the services provided by care assistants and those supporting family members, there was to be an immediate five-fold increase in the basic rate of pay, together with an allowance for those performing caring duties in their own home. Many people nodded in approval, and Eilidh said quietly, 'About time society got its priorities straight.'

Then the manager of one of the local building societies stood up, disguised in expensive jeans, and launched his manifesto for change. He argued for a new oligarchy run by the financial services, plus a system of forcing the sick to present themselves for examination, but after a few minutes Nia lost track. All she heard was a stream of, 'Clearly ... It seems to me ... This is unacceptable ... As I said to m'wife ... What I'm saying is ...' punctuating a list of unreasonable proposals dressed up as common sense. He finished in the same way, saying, 'So, we organise everyone to fill in their symptoms, get them back to work by next week, Okay?' He stayed standing, looking round for admiration.

Ally took a deep breath and started, 'We all appreciate your input, Ian, but I don't think there's a consensus to carry such drastic proposals, and while you and your brethren may feel competent to deal with such major issues, there are other things to consider such as-' At this point, Ian broke in, 'Yes, yes, but what I'm saying is, this is clearly the best way forward.' Ally tried again, 'Well, no, that isn't necessarily true, and there are people-' Once again Ian broke in, 'People without experience. I know what needs to be done, Okay? So, now we think about-', but he in turn was interrupted by Morag from the Crown, who stood at the back of the hall, and shouted, 'Shut up, you arrogant little wanker!'

Ian stopped talking, but Morag was just warming up, 'What makes you think you know better than everyone else, eh? You think you can just steamroller through what you want, and to hell with everyone else? Aye, you're clever with words, but that makes your self-will all the more heinous. You selfish, arrogant-', and she would have continued at length but was drowned out by the applause, laughter and stamping of feet throughout the hall. Nia realised this was the most animated gathering she'd seen in town in months. Ian appeared unruffled, and left the hall sneering. Eilidh leaned over and said, 'Good for Morag! High time someone objected to that self-serving tin-pot dictator. Everyone hates him. Bob thinks he's the antichrist.'

Ruth almost choked on her drink, and the whole room was laughing, high as kites. Morag recovered her breath, and waved her arms for silence. She said in a far calmer voice, 'I apologise for using such foul language,' then paused, 'But it seems to me he clearly deserved it. Okay?' Her precision mimicry had people doubled up, gasping for breath. The meeting closed on a positive note as Ally was confident there would be a major food delivery in a few days' time, and she posted a list of inspirational guest lectures planned for the next few weeks. Nia made a note to tell Glynn about the forthcoming talk on 'Rats. A misunderstood foe', but felt she'd pass over 'Coping without tampons' and 'Hunting rabbits for food'.

Glynn was propped up on cushions skimming through a pile of student essays when Nia let herself in with her new key. 'Hey, you did something to your hair!'
'Highlights,' she shrugged, 'although I wish I hadn't.'

'They're great,' he said, running his hands through her new style. 'What's wrong with them? You were excited when they opened up last week.'

'Oh nothing, just the salon was so miserable. There was this old man rambling on about god knows what. They said he calls in every day now the bookie's shut. Then this woman turned up screaming about how her *St. Tropez* tan had gone patchy.' Glynn sniggered.

'Don't laugh,' she frowned. 'It was scary. She was really mad. But the worst thing was the smoke. This Turkish burning stuff. When they started my blow-dry I had to ask them to move the ashtray 'cos it was blowing fag ash all over me. The owner said everyone's nerves are so bad she has to let them all smoke or she'd have no staff. Crazy. I had to wash my hair when I got home to get rid of the smoke. It was really acrid stuff.' Glynn murmured soothingly, 'Probably people are down to the last random packets bought in duty free and are taking whatever they can find. Why did you stick it?'

He wrapped his arms around her as she kicked off her shoes, 'Well, it sort of sweeps you along. You step through the door and they've got you. Hair in the basin, shampoo the lot.' Nia reached the real problem, and sighed, 'It's all so awful. Everywhere. That poor boy.'

'I know. I can't get it out of my head either.' Glynn hugged her tightly, 'I mean, we knew about the others, even people we knew like Malcolm, but it's not the same as actually witnessing it.'

She told him about the CHLOE meeting and he shifted guiltily when she told him about the pay issue. 'Actually, I've sort of benefited from that,' he admitted, and she looked at him, puzzled.

'Really? So I'm not the only one you've been providing personal care for then?' she teased. 'Been hanging out on Aberdeen Road offering your services, have you?'

'Hell, if I was that desperate, darling, I'd have far more luck pimping *you*! He stuck out his tongue, before the guilt returned. 'No, I've been doing some maths tutoring.'

'Oh, really evil then,' she snuggled up against him.

'You know the schools aren't really functioning?' he started, and Nia nodded as he reluctantly said, 'Well, some of the pushy parents don't want their kids to get behind.'

'Or they want them to get an advantage?'

'Yeah,' he shrugged, 'so I've been doing a few hours private tuition. I did some last year, but now the going rate's about ten times higher.'

'Wow!' she said. 'What's wrong with that?'

He shifted awkwardly and wrapped his arms more firmly around her. 'I feel a bit guilty, you know, helping the wealthy maintain their privilege and all that. It offends the Marxist in me. But then, it's only what they'd have paid their advocates or their hairdressers before this. You know, one of the houses I go to has its own swimming pool and eight bedrooms.'

She sighed, 'I think it's a good thing. Valuing education, the caring professions. Why shouldn't you get paid properly?'

'You are very wise,' he said, only half-joking, as he leant down to kiss her, 'and I do like your highlights. Right, no more guilt,' he promised. 'After all, if this keeps up all year I might be able to pay off my student loans before I'm sixty-five.' Nia continued to tell him about the meeting, covering the problems with the new self-help groups, and he pondered the possible battle lines as the anxious-depressed took on the chronically-fatigued–depressed, who all hated anyone who had the temerity to get better and resume their daily routine. Glynn was sure Rory would have had something to say about this, but their last few conversations had been stilted so he decided not to call him. After several months of enquiring after Rory's health, Rory had yet to express any interest in anything else, not even asking after Robbie and Becky. Glynn felt a bit guilty about not ringing and was left alone to battle it out after Nia went early, saying she wanted to check how Ruth was feeling. 'Never mind,' Glynn said to Tommy as he curled up on the bed. 'You still love me, don't you? You wouldn't keep bringing me dead birds if you didn't, would you?'

The next morning his 'phone was dead again, lying on his sofa like a battered ping-pong ball, so he went to find one of the guaranteed 'phone connections which had been installed around the town in solid red boxes. He called Rory on the main line at John Burnet Hall, and was relieved to see he was more alert, almost wide-eyed, and willing to talk. 'Aye, I saw Dr. Mosely. Told her what you said.'

'Ah, so you got the Malthak,' Glynn noted with some satisfaction.

'That was the plan, but that posh Ally lass said 'Oh no, he needs the best, needs to get better straight away. Give him Halvass,' so I got the best stuff going.'

'Ally? You mean the CHLOE liaison woman? What the hell was she doing there?' Glynn was confused, but Rory seemed keen to give him good news, 'Dunno, but she got me top stuff, so I said, 'That'll do for me.' That Dr. Mosely wasnae keen. Said they were new, but I said, 'That sounds good to me,' and I got 'em. You know, I might even fancy going for a run in a day or two.'

Glynn was encouraged, but cut the call short because of the queue of people sighing loudly outside the box. He steeled himself for the next departmental meeting, where they were joined by Sarah, the hostage from Physics. Hobden was still in charge, and began in a presidential tone, 'Welcome, welcome. As you know, we are supposed to be scrutinising the exam papers for semester one. Also, to welcome back Simon, who's going to take a back seat for a while, settle back in before he takes over my job,' he nodded to Simon who was nursing a mug of something hot in the corner. 'But,' Hobden announced, 'before we do this, we have the problem of Special Circumstances. For the new girls,' Eilidh glared at him, and he coughed, 'oh, sorry ladies, the new women, let me say that normally we have a Special Circumstances meeting at the end of term to consider pleas for mercy, late essays, needing extra time in exams, the usual stuff, dyslexia, broken legs and so on. Unfortunately, this year eighty-nine percent of our students have submitted special circumstances forms, so we have a bit of a problem.' 'Well, that's it then,' said Eilidh solemnly. 'Genuine cases or no, the Lunatics have taken over the asylum,' and she started to laugh so hard that even Hobden had to join in. Eventually Glynn said, 'Do they have reasons?'

Hobden was deadly serious again, 'Maureen has categorised them A-J. About a third are in these first categories A-D, illness affecting a piece of work, dyslexia needing extra time in the exams. We have to grant all those, 'though to be honest I'm not sure how much good an extra twenty minutes in an exam can do you if you're just stupid or lazy.' Eilidh frowned at him, and Hobden coughed then continued, 'Alrighty, then there are categories E and F where the student claims the current pandemic has exacerbated some other problem.'

'Such as?' Glynn was confused.

'Take your pick,' Hobden read down a list. 'Irritable Bowel Syndrome, Eczema, Backache, Insomnia, Fatigue, Headaches and something called PCOS, not sure what that is.'

'So, pretty much like the rest of us? What sort of special considerations are they asking for?' Glynn was still puzzled.

'Oh, you name it. Everything from 'Excuse my late essay', to 'I find exams too stressful, can I just write another essay?' There's one here somewhere where she wants to take the exam in a hotel room with a jacuzzi or something.'

'Really?' Eilidh murmured a warning.

'Here it is: Must have extra time allowed and be seated in a quiet, relaxing atmosphere with access to fresh running water.'

'Why?' Tricia and Sarah said together.

'Anxiety. She finds exams stressful.'

'Do we have to allow these as well?' Glynn was not happy.

'I'm very reluctant myself,' Hobden agreed, 'but Maureen says the students will appeal and then we'll have the Disability mafia on to us. Kath, you know.' He looked at Glynn pathetically, and Glynn relented, saying darkly, 'So, what about the rest?'

'Ah, now this gets more complicated,' Hobden said apologetically. 'About two-thirds of the requests fall into categories G, H, I and J. Start with G is 'affected by illness of a family member', then H is 'affected by illness of a friend'. Again, requests for extensions, mitigation of poor performance and so on.'

'So, again that could apply to everybody. What about the others?' Glynn was picking up the tune.

'Category I is 'am on medication but still not feeling quite right', mainly Honours students who think their grades this year will be lower, so want extra marks.'

'And how can we tell?' Eilidh sighed. 'Many students do better in Sub-Honours, because then the work gets harder.'

'Yes, so what do we take as a baseline?' Hobden was on a roll. 'And then there's category J, 'am suffering from depression, but do not want to take medication or have counselling.'

Eyebrows were raised.

'Lots of sick notes from overworked practice nurses saying 'X appeared to have one or more symptoms of mild depression when I saw him or her on this date.' Maureen chased them up, saying we'd need more medical evidence about their diagnosis and treatment, and in every case they said something like 'I don't like doctors', or 'I don't want to take mind-altering pills.' So, something of a conundrum, no?'

Eyebrows were raised even further.

'So, they're ill, but they're fit enough to come to university, and then they submit forms for special treatment, but they won't take treatment. So, how do they know which treatment they need?' Glynn was disorientated.

'Frankly, I think they're swinging the lead,' Hobden agreed, 'but we have to respond. We have your husband to thank for that, I think, Eilidh. Isn't it Bob's work on free-will behind this policy somehow?

She shrugged her shoulders, 'You can't force people to accept help, and when it involves taking drugs which can have nasty side effects, what can you do?' Tricia tried to make sense of this, 'So, we have to take their word for it that their performance has suffered because they're ill, even though they won't get help?'

'Well, that's the question,' Hobden had nothing to offer. They were all silent for a few moments, then Sarah suggested, 'If they were, say, diabetic and refused to take insulin, would we give them special dispensation if they kept asking for it?' Simon suddenly joined in and said, 'Thank You! A voice of sanity from Physics. It comes down to personal responsibility. If they're well enough to come to university, and not ill enough to get help, then they can't expect special favours. Yes, we need to show compassion, and as many of us now know to our cost, depression is particularly insidious, but at some point you have to say 'Either you're here, or you're not.' And if you're not well enough to cope and you won't take help, then you need to leave.'

Eilidh nodded her agreement, as Simon continued grousing, 'I've always fancied going in for the London Marathon, but I don't have an ideal physique.' Tricia and Sarah exchanged glances, as Simon stretched his legs out, saying, 'Oh, I could probably do it, if I put myself through a punishing schedule, but I wouldn't expect to say to someone, 'I find it too painful to train, so could I just run a couple of miles and we could say I've done the marathon?' I imagine Bob would say the analogy is misleading, but in the end, what about being realistic? As for the 'I have a family member or friend who's ill', that's life, no? I'm not sure we're doing students any favours by accepting all these excuses. We're infantilising them. Even if we reject the last categories and gear up for a lengthy appeals process, we've still got half the buggers getting special treatment, and I bet you the rest will claim retrospectively, so I can't honestly see how there is any hope of maintaining academic standards. These exams are meaningless. What is the point of a university education any more?'

'Yes, well,' said Hobden, 'that's the next point. The Business Recovery Plan team has some very interesting ideas about how the university could take point in co-ordinating all levels of education in the town, consolidate our forces so to speak.'

'I am not going to be a fucking school teacher!' Simon snapped.

'Oh, I don't think it will come to that,' said Hobden, looking hurt, 'no, it's more about using our resources as best we can, offering people what they want.'

'So, no more expecting the kids to think for themselves. We just give them Noddy lectures and spoon-feed them interesting facts about Dinosaurs.' Simon drained his mug of tea.

'It could be a chance to develop more individualised research-led teaching,' said Hobden hopefully, as Simon walked out.

Glynn nodded through the next tutorials; if someone wanted to talk, he let them. If there was silence, he started talking almost to himself. His lecture handouts were becoming simpler, and he'd started teaching mainly from the core textbook. He had heard from Tricia that Hobden was simply sitting in lecture halls, reading out chapters from his forthcoming book, so he didn't feel any need to exert himself too much in a world gone mad. Occasionally he'd be startled by a conversation with an enthusiastic student who turned up to discuss a dissertation or an essay topic The rest of the day would then be spent in a grey fog of pointless paperwork and half-hearted marking, with an occasional well-paid lesson in the evening with a student sighing to keep his or her parents happy.

Throughout the UK there were reports of social disarray and outbursts of violence as people's frustration leaked out. A skeletal infrastructure was still operating, but the cold snap was a problem. News from overseas was far less reliable, but there were stories of whole communities confined to mental hospitals in Germany, and huge pilgrimages from all of Italy to Vatican City. The Norwegians and New Zealanders were hailed as mythical figures, who were allegedly immune to the plague, and had been holding global communications together, but no-one in St Andrews had seen or even spoken to such a being. For most people, life shrank to the basic principles of survival. Only when they were fed and watered could people begin to contemplate the lives of their small communities, let alone the global forces which controlled them. For those still in the grip of depression, trying to think about anything was like trying to walk in treacle. Those who were gradually recovering still found themselves caught off-guard by sticky, trailing misery.

Celebration and overt joy were frowned upon, so Glynn was thrilled to offer Nia a chance to tag along to Cambo Sands one Saturday when Finn was taking the family to fly kites. As a birthday treat for Becky, Finn had arranged a minibus to Kingsbarns when the weather was expected to be perfect. He was officially dropping off three people who had been discharged from the Memorial Hospital, but as he'd done so much behind-the-scenes community work the CHLOE team had allowed him to keep the bus for a few hours and to take a full load of passengers.

When the bus pulled up outside Glynn's flat late Saturday morning, three wan ex-patients sat in the front seats. Abi, Matt and Eilidh waved, and Nia was shocked to see Bob in the middle of a sea of excited children, having ribbons tied in his hair. 'He's like catnip for children,' Glynn whispered. 'They think that bemused expression's something out of *Harry Potter*.' As they climbed in, they saw that Bob already had been painted with a lion face, and Eilidh said nonchalantly, 'You know, I have just the thing to finish this off!' She pulled a large sheepskin scarf from her bag, and Emily cried, 'A mane! A mane! Thank you, mammie!'

'Now, you have to keep it on until we get there, mind,' Eilidh warned her husband. 'Cannae waste such a work of art, can we girls?' As Nia settled down she saw Bob mouth to Eilidh, 'I'll get you for this,' but his eyes were twinkling, and he adjusted his mane with studied vanity.

Becky's friends squeaked a great deal during the drive, and Nia was glad to escape for a quick walk with Glynn while the others set up camp. Clouds were dragged across the sky at great speed by gusts of wind which whipped up the surf as the tide came in. Nia waved when she saw Amira coming the other way from Crail, and they compared notes on the local situation. Amira was part of the coastal support team, and had walked from Crail ensuring a minimum safe path stayed open to the public. 'That's a long walk,' said Glynn. 'D'you want Finn to give you a lift home? I'm sure he won't mind.'

'No, I'm fine,' she said. 'It's a nice walk back. Anyway, don't want to disturb you two love-birds. Oh, aye,' she said as Glynn raised an eyebrow. 'I know all about the last time you came here.'

'Ah, the rain,' he said.

'Something like that,' she smiled. 'Keep your eyes open for me. Have a good day.'

She set off back to Crail at a brisk pace while Nia and Glynn turned to head back to the family. Nia was scanning the ground from time to time, looking for witches' stones, when Glynn said 'Aha!' and stooped to pick something up.

'Did you find something for Amira?'

'No, for you,' he said, and brandished a large limpet shell with the top missing. 'I reckon this will fit,' he said, taking her hand and slipping it over her middle finger. 'Perfect!'

'You know, I could do serious damage with this, like a knuckle duster.' She raised her hand in mock aggression.

'I'd be better be good then, hadn't I?' Glynn teased, as he wrapped his arm around her waist and they meandered back towards the picnic site.

'I still think it's odd, him and Eilidh,' said Nia as she watched Bob patiently trying to teach Becky and her friends to build elaborate sand castles.

'They do seem pretty happy,' Glynn replied.

'Oh, I'm sure, but I'd have sort of expected they'd adopt or something'

'Eh?'

'Well, I can't imagine Bob fathering a child.'

Glynn grimaced, 'Can't say I'd thought about it.'

'But come on, yes, I'm sure they have this great emotional bond, but I mean, look at him, not exactly the touchy feely type is he?' she said, so he replied, 'D'you think like the literary chap who freaked out on his wedding night when he discovered women weren't quite as smooth as marble? Ruskin? Milton? Abi would know.'

Nia ignored the footnote, 'Yeah, I mean, I can see them getting married for companionship and stuff, but not the other.'

'Well, I can't say I really consider my colleagues' sex lives too often,' Glynn began tactfully, 'but I don't see Eilidh as the type to get married just for the sake of it. And they do have Emily, after all.'

'Yeah, that's why it's so weird.'

'I dunno, maybe he's just uncomfortable with public displays of affection.'

'I think it's more than that,' she persisted, lowering her voice as they came closer, 'he just looks really uncomfortable with any sort of physical contact.'

'This is fascinating you, isn't it?'

'Yes. He's just so ... intellectual. Maybe she seduced his mind and his body came along for the ride.'

'They do say still waters run deep. Maybe, and this is a very disturbing thought, but maybe he's an animal in bed. He's probably very meticulous and conscientious, after all.'

She giggled into his shoulder, 'We're being horrible, aren't we. People are probably saying horrible things about us, too.'

'Oh, I don't know,' he said lazily. 'I'm sure no-one could doubt what a firecracker you are! I'm a very lucky man.'

'Too right!' she poked him. 'Anyway, I think it's our turn to battle those kites!'

Finn had unpacked three large red and blue competition-style kites, and half-a-dozen small, agile ones which he was now helping Robbie to set up. Glynn joined them, taking off his coat and rolling up his sleeves. Nia appreciated the view, and unconsciously licked her lips, before she exchanged a brief amused glance with Abi - he didn't realise the effect his gesture had. As the wind rose, Abi took on one of the adult kites and soon had the girls clapping and jumping around in admiration as she controlled the pressures, making the kite circle like a bird of prey. Robbie had soon mastered the small kite and was running along the shore. He whooped and yelled happily as he was almost lifted off his feet. 'Take over!' Abi shouted to Eilidh, 'My arms are breaking!' The women swiftly changed places, and Emily jumped around shouting, 'Mammie, Mammie!' Bob helped her to take a photograph, saying, 'Look at her go!'

Glynn and Nia managed to get one of the other kites airborne, and rocked wildly as they used their combined weight to stabilise the swooping forces. The kites flew freely, as the clouds parted in the cold, blue sky.

When the adults brought the kites down exhausted, Robbie was still running up and down the beach, now chased by Becky and her friends, determined to disturb his concentration. 'You know,' said Glynn he surveyed the sandcastles, 'that large one looks a lot like a Ya dan.'

'A what?' Nia looked at him, waiting for a punchline.

'No seriously, a Ya dan, Chinese sand dunes get whipped into odd sculptures. I went to a lecture on them once. They have these massive sand-dunes, five hundred metres high. Need a camel to get up them. Quite a sight.'

'Don't let Becky hear you saying that!' Matt laughed,

'or she'll be wanting a camel herself.' He'd set out a few plates, and was offering round bottles of Finn's home brew.

'Bit early, for me, thanks,' said Glynn sitting down. 'Maybe later, but I'm not sure I trust that gut rot.'

'It's got a kick to it, alright,' said Matt. 'Nia?' he offered her a bottle.

'No thanks,' she said.

'Oh come on!' He gave her a little shove.

'Thanks, but no, I don't really drink.'

'Really?' he said. 'Only time I've known women to swear off is when they're pregnant.'

She ignored his comment and focused on the food instead. Abi had managed to create a fairy-themed cake with lots of silver balls. 'No butter-cream,' she said sadly, 'but plenty of E-numbers.' It was too windy for candles, but when the children came back, they sang 'Happy Birthday' and toasted Becky while she happily her presents. After they'd eaten, the wind dropped a little and the adults spread out to teach the girls to fly the smaller kites. By the end of the afternoon even little Emily had managed to control one for a few minutes, and the children were exhausted and half-asleep as the light started to fade. 'Time to head back,' said Finn, and started to pack up. Matt helped him, taking the last bottle from the coolbag. 'Shame to waste it,' he said, twisting the top. 'You've done us proud here, mate.'

As she packed up the children's kites, Nia said to Glynn, 'Is he alright?' nodding towards Matt, 'He's had a lot to drink.'

'He's pretty stressed, that's all.'

'Hmm,' she said. 'That's not really going to help though, is it? God knows how strong that stuff is, and he's had at least five this afternoon.'

'Are you checking up on him?' said Glynn puzzled, 'or me?'

'No,' she said, 'but you had one earlier on, and Finn did and Bob and Eildh, but there were ten bottles in there when we arrived.'

'Iron constitution, that one,' Glynn shrugged. 'Not like he's knocking back the scotch now, is it?' Nia let it drop, but watched with some concern as Abi tried to take things out of Matt's hands and pack them away. As they prepared to leave, the mackerel sky suddenly lit up with the last rays of the sun and everything was bathed in a deep raspberry-pink light. 'Cool!' said Nia, and Abi and Eilidh woke the sleeping girls to let them watch. They all stood at the side of the minibus and watched as every face, stone and wave was shifted into another colour spectrum.

When they got back to St Andrews, Glynn and Nia were dropped off at her flat, and she offered him first go in the shower. When he came out, she said, 'Where's home for you, these days?' He shrugged, 'Home is somewhere I leave my stuff. Since Mum died I haven't really been back to Brecon much. I suppose Bristol was home for a while, but I always knew I'd have to move on, and since then, well, wherever I lay my hat. I really should sort things out. I know there are boxes of my things all over the country, but it's one hell of an effort to get it all to the far side of Fife. And who knows where I'd have to shift it to next. I should have bought shares in Pickfords. What about you?'

'Don't know,' she said sadly. 'I don't think my mother's ever felt Manchester was her home, so it's a problem. I suppose my family home *is* home, but I sort of think there must be a place for *me* somewhere. Maybe I'll just stay up here, try to put down roots, give myself somewhere to dig down.'

'What a horrible image! I can just see you, sprouting like a potato.'

She laughed, 'I was thinking more like asparagus, but maybe you're right. Potatoes settle down good and proper.'

'Until they're dug up and eaten.'

'Well, yes, there is that. Mancunian exile found eaten in Fife. Front page of the *Chronicle* for sure.' She hesitated, then said in a rush, 'Matt drinks too much. Is your father an alcoholic?' Glynn jumped, and shouted without thinking, 'No he bloody isn't! And Matt isn't either!' He took a deep breath, 'Sorry, sorry. Seriously, you're a kind, good person to worry, but Matt's fine. Really he is. You worry too much. Tell you what, have a shower and I'll see what I can rustle up. Gives you an appetite, all that sea air.' She kissed his nose and let the subject drop.

Life continued to splutter along, and December arrived with no Christmas cards in the shops. During a very slow tutorial in which three of his students had mispronounced 'iridium', Glynn was barely feigning interest while he idly watched Tricia outside the window. She was talking patiently to two female students, each wearing a full dark burqa, but Glynn noticed they were also wearing heavy mascara, which seemed to defeat the object of the exercise. He was saved from this thought-crime by a knock at the door and a tall curvaceous young woman panted, 'Dr. Hughes! You have to come quickly!' He recognised her as one of Nia's frequent customers, so was not unduly alarmed by her state of distraction. 'What's the matter?' he said, 'Are you alright?' 'Dr. McDonald ... She says ... you must come ... right ... right away... lecture room B3.'

'Is she alright?'

'She said to come straight away … It's Mr. Dunbar
…. he's having some sort of fit, or something,' she
gasped. 'You really have to go!'

Glynn directed the group to consider the
next set of data, and left one of the mature students
in charge of the discussion. He left the messenger to
catch her breath and raced over to the lecture room,
where he was met by a small group of crying
students who told him Eilidh had sent them to call
an ambulance. He heard muted chatter and scared
whimpers from inside the room, and slowly pushed
open the door. The remaining students were frozen
in their seats. Eilidh was pressed flat against the
blackboard, and Rory was prowling round the front
of the room with a large hammer. His shirt was
drenched in sweat. He was red in the face and
muttering rapidly as he peered along the rows.
'Thank God!' he cried when he saw Glynn. 'I was
looking for you.'

Glynn took a deep breath, then ran down the
stairs and grabbed Rory by the shoulders, 'Okay, I'm
here now. Throw this lot out and we can get
everything sorted.'

'Oh no, I cannae do that,' Rory pulled away. 'Some
of them are here. *Her* probably.' He jerked his head
towards Eilidh, then lowered his voice, 'I've been up
all night but I've finally figured it out. How come
there are all these women running things now? Will
you listen? I'll tell you why, they were taken poorly
like normal people, but then they got better. This is a
conspiracy.'

'Um, I see,' said Glynn. 'Right. We might as well
throw out the men, hadn't we?'

'Collaborators,' hissed Rory. 'I've seen them. I've bin

haaavin, bin haavin visions. Some of them are here.'

'Will you at least sit down?' Eilidh said, before Rory turned to glare at her, but she continued, 'You don't look well.'

'I said, Shut Up, Bitch!' he yelled, then staggered slightly and groaned. His face went from red to white in an instant, and he collapsed. Eilidh rushed over, as Glynn kicked the hammer to one side. 'Stopped breathing. No pulse!' she cried. 'Where the hell's the ambulance?' One of the students from the group outside came in and shouted, 'They said they'd try to come, but couldn't promise it!'

'Right!' Eilidh shouted up to them, 'Jessica, Damian, run to the surgery, tell them his heart's stopped and he's no breathing. He'll need a defibrillator. The rest of you, any of you who can do CPR, get down here. The rest of you, skeddadle.' She knelt down and moved Rory into position. 'You do compressions?' Glynn nodded, and they started the hopeless attempt to revive him. Most of the students fled but five lingered, two stepping forward quickly to take over from Eilidh and Glynn. He rubbed his wrists as Eilidh recovered her breath. She waved the other students over, but they held back and one girl said, 'I only did a short course in Guides. I don't know if I can do it.' The lad next to her said, 'What if I do it wrong?'

Glynn screamed 'You selfish fuck!', but Eilidh put her arm around him and said quietly to the students, 'He's already deid unless we try. We have to hope help will come. Two breaths, thirty fast compressions. Tomas, you should have greater upper-body strength, will you take over the compressions?' The two speakers took over, before they were relieved by Glynn and Eilidh.

'How long?' Glynn gasped. 'It's not working.' Eilidh handed over to one of the students, and murmured, 'We cannae restart his heart, remember? We're just keeping the circulation moving. Now, Roisin,' she said calmly to the remaining student huddled in the front row, 'go out into the quad, find anyone who can do CPR.' Like a startled rabbit, the girl raced away, returning in sixty seconds with three men in suits. Eilidh's heart sank when she saw them, but they rolled up their sleeves and took over. When it was Glynn's turn again he was almost as white as Rory, but he muttered over and over, 'Come on, you bastard.' As his strength failed, he gave a final effort and cracked one of Rory's ribs. The students gasped, but Eilidh glared at them and said, 'Aye, that's the pressure you need.' The group was fracturing when two elderly women sprinted in with a defibrillator. 'Stand back!' the older woman ordered, as her colleague wired Rory up. After two rounds, Rory took a sharp breath and moaned. 'Good,' said the younger of the pair, as she injected him again in the thigh. 'Have to get him up, car's outside, we'll have him to Ninewells.'

The three men in suits carried Rory out and disappeared as the car sped away. Eilidh hugged the students who had helped, and joked that it would look good on their C.V., before she sat down heavily. Glynn sagged against a wall, digging his fingernails into ancient mortar. Eventually he said, 'Are you hurt, Eilidh? Who were they?'

'Wee bit shaky. I know he wouldn't have hurt me, no violent bone in his body, but, well, I was scared,' she said, before shaking her head to clear her thoughts. 'The older one's Dr. Petch, she was my doctor when I was a wee lass. It's an ill time now if they're putting grannies to work. Come on, hero,' she said, getting up. 'We need a strong pot of tea. I've an inkling Bob has some, and some milk. Contraband, I know, but he'd be no good without his tea. Come on,' she took his arm and led him to Philosophy. 'We've done all we can. We just have to pray.'

Chapter Eight

'I am so cold,' she shivered as Glynn gallantly gave her his scarf. 'Would it kill him to put that fire on?'

'I think he's cold blooded,' whispered Eilidh who was already wrapped up against a blizzard, 'related to lizards.' Tricia laughed, pulling Glynn's scarf tight, and then stifled it into a cough as Hobden scurried back in followed by Maureen. She was carrying a thermometer, which she placed on the desk before handing out three handwritten copies of notes. 'Sorry,' she said, 'no toner to be had for anything this week.' She picked up the thermometer and said, 'Professor Hobden, your zeal for energy conservation is admirable, but you are now breaching Health and Safety regulations, so if you don't put that fire on I will declare this room unsafe until the ambient temperature in the building rises.'

'Oh,' he looked hurt, 'a chap does his bit, and then it's held against him.'

'He should be so lucky,' Tricia whispered to Glynn, as Hobden reluctantly switched on his halogen heater. They all hoped that the meeting would be as short as possible, but the contents of Maureen's memo put paid to that. It was a summary of drastic changes to the education system in St Andrews, bringing all children over the age of seven under the control of the BRP team, with resources and teaching spaces all centralised into the main university buildings in town and on the North Haigh. Statistics indicated that current schooling arrangements were on the point of collapse, with unreliable staffing levels and inability to heat the buildings. The final paragraph was bleak, and disburbing: 'Learning Outcomes are not being met.'

Eilidh slammed the paper down on the table, 'I knew it. I knew when they cancelled the last governors' meeting. No consultation, no nothing. That bloody CHLOE team. What does this mean for us?' Maureen looked at Hobden threateningly, and he stayed silent. 'Cards on the table,' she said. 'Official university policy is that undergraduate teaching continues as normal, but I think you've seen how it's going. Unofficially, this change will guarantee an income stream via the BRP, so they don't care what you do.'

There was a stunned silence.

'You mean we could just get on with our research?' said Eilidh.

'Or just swan around?' said Glynn.

'I suspect you'll need to be seen doing something with the undergraduates,' Maureen shuffled her papers sadly, 'but beyond that, it's up to you how much you can salvage. You've actually got some good students in your lot. Not like those feckless modern linguists. Some of them might want to stick it out, get through this year somehow. I don't know. All I know is that for now, the BRP won't bother you.'

'But will it come back to bite us on the bum later on?' Tricia said, thinking of the long-term prospects for her and Glynn.

'Most things do,' Eilidh got up to leave. 'I suggest we carry on as we are until the end of term, then re-assess. Okay with you, Malcolm?'

'Very wise, Eilidh.' He nodded, looking very tired. 'We can only hope Simon will be back by then. He's off with food poisoning again, you know?'

The force of inertia kept the university machine running over the next week, as the BRP got started, moving people and furniture in preparation for the new world order. The mood in town brightened considerably when sacks of mail were finally delivered. Glynn came home one evening to find a black bin-bag of post outside his door, and spent a happy hour sorting out the gems from the junkmail. There was a postcard from Jamie, sent in the summer from Capetown, and several magazines which he devoured like a starving, literate lion. The next day he was given the task of sorting through the latest delivery to the Geography and Geology departments. This was less entertaining, but there was a certain satisfaction in throwing out all the requests for statistics and daft queries which had been sent before the world ended.

Six days after Rory was rushed to Ninewells Hospital, Nia surprised Glynn by turning up at his office mid-morning. 'I've got good news!' she said, 'Rory's better! They're transferring him to the support unit at the Memorial.' She looked at Tricia who had been sitting on the desk and now closed her file with a smile. 'Bloody hell,' said Glynn sitting heavily on his desk. 'That is the best news I've had in months!' He took a long breath, 'Oh, Tricia, Nia, Nia, Tricia.'

'Hi!' said Tricia. 'I'd better be off. That's great news about your friend. Nice to meet you,' she smiled at Nia and squeezed past her out the door.

'Finn dropped off Dr. Petch at Ruth's,' Nia explained. 'Did you know she stayed up at Ninewells all week to make sure they took care of him? She's been amazing.'

'Thank god for that. I know Abi's been taking in food, but they're pretty short staffed. Have you seen this? Latest edition.'

He tossed her a thin, well-worn copy of the *Scotsman* dated 'November 21st – 28th'. The headline read 'Government stands firm on pipeline negotiations.' Nia flipped through to the central page, ignoring the political and financial crisis which threatened to cut off petrol supplies across Europe. She looked through the local city reports and then said, 'Damn! I knew my father was hiding something.' Glynn looked at the report of a fire in Manchester.

'That's where my Mum's friend, Laura, lives.' Nia banged her fist on his desk. 'When I got through last week Dad said she was visiting people at the hospital. That was it.' Glynn looked at the full report: Electrical fire in a warehouse fanned by high winds. Spread to residential areas of Withingon. Limited response from understaffed fire service. Water supply failed. Eight streets gutted. Sixteen dead. Forty-eight injured.

'Like a bloody third world country. Anyway,' Nia said standing in front of him with her hands on her hips, 'I have even more good news.'

'Really?'

'Well,' she began, waiting for his full attention, 'you know we've all been on starvation rations for a while? Not that it seems to have done Tricia any good.'

'Eh?'

'Well, she must be a size eighteen. She got a secret supply of sugar or something? Anyway, I was doing some washing for Erica this morning- '

'Why?' Glynn wasn't quite sure what he was asking.

'Oh, her hands are getting more arthritic. So, I was there when she got this massive delivery, stuff she'd ordered from the States for Hallowe'en.'

'Are you telling me there are sweets in town?'

'Oh yeah, baby!' Nia kissed him quickly. 'A CHLOE team looked, but weren't interested, 'cos they said it wasn't food!'

'I'd have thought bubblegum eyeballs were full of goodness,' he deadpanned.

'So,' she took a step back and smiled, 'I'm going back this evening to help her sort things into little bags before she can sell them, sort of rationing, one bag per person I think, but because I've been helping out, she gave me all this!' She reached into her pockets and threw handfuls of sweets into the air.

'Oh, wow!' Glynn jumped up. 'Darling, you always make my mouth water, but this is too much.'

'What do you fancy? Gummy pumpkins? Vampire teeth?'

'Are you sure you want to share?'

'Of course. Anyway, we can join the queue tomorrow to get some more. This is a freebie.'

She popped a bloodshot candy face into his mouth and he groaned softly, 'Oh, the sugar rush. You are amazing, Ni!' She smiled, and he took her hand, 'No, really you are amazing. Have you been getting your carer's allowance for helping Erica?'

'God, no,' she said. 'No need. I just pop round now and then. She wouldn't want all that official fuss.'

'Well, this is pretty good payment, I'd have said. You know, this is almost as good as the news about Rory.'

'Here,' she said, putting half the sweets on to his desk, 'you have these. I've got to get back, Ruth's covering for me. 'Phones aren't working again.'

'Tell me about it. There's only two fixed lines for the whole university and a few in the Halls.' He sighed. 'Thanks for all this. You're a star!'

'Any time,' she gave him a juicy, sugar-filled kiss. 'I'll see you tomorrow? I'll be helping at Erica's tonight.'

He managed to save most of the sweets until the end of the day, and walked past the shop on the way home. There was the sad little notice which had been up for the past months: 'All I have left are mint toffees and root-beer balls. Open Saturdays 12-2pm only.' Above it was now a large sign which Glynn recognised as Nia's elegant handwriting: 'New Hallowe'en stock. Open from 1pm Friday, one bag per person limit. 400 bags only.' He walked up to Matt's before he went home. Matt was still at work, so he told Abi about the delivery and was pleased by hysterical screams from Becky and Robbie as he handed over an assortment of vile green sweets with the promise of more tomorrow. After he'd played a long, complicated board game involving fish, and lost badly due to his failure to recognise a shark before it ate him, he strode home, feeling that life was getting better.

The next morning, he made it to the office while it was still dark, a little creeped out by the extra layers of silence that had fallen in the night, thankful for the clockwork lantern Finn had sold him. He was rewarded by a Technicolor display as the sun came up, waves of colour gently lapping at his window, and the world seemed a better place again. He left for an early lunch and wasn't surprised to find a long queue already outside Erica's at midday. Whole families had turned up, and there was heated debate about whether babes-in-arms would qualify for their own ration. He saw Abi with the children near the front of the queue and waved conspiratorially. Nia came out to count the queue, and hugged him, saying, 'Thought you'd be back. Did you give them all to the kids?'

'Not all of them, but I'm here for them today. Spill it.

What's the inside story? Are they all mixed bags, or are there any specials I should know about?' Nia answered him quietly as those next in line listened in, 'About half the bags are mixed sweets, and then there are six individual types of bags, some toffees, some mints, some gummy teeth, that sort of thing. We were up 'til all hours to get them labelled. D'you know, two families turned up at midnight to start queuing. We were just finishing up, and Erica took pity on them and gave them a couple of bags. If people are that desperate for a bit of sugar …'

'Yeah,' he said, 'she's making lots of people happy today.' By the time the shop opened, Glynn reckoned there were at least two hundred people in the queue, with more turning up in droves as the word got round. He felt that a mixed bag would probably be the best investment, but changed his mind when he saw the last bag of 'Congealed blood treacle toffees'. When he came out, Abi was waiting with the children who had spread their bags of sweets out on their laps. He was happy to agree to look after them, as Abi wanted to run a quick errand.

All along the street were the sounds of frantic bartering and once Glynn had conferred with the children about their strategy, they set out to forage. An hour later, they had made some good deals and were satisfied with their haul. The sweets were now changing hands for money, and Glynn held tightly on to Becky's hand, as disappointed parents turned up late, and had to explain to the children there was nothing left. As they started to walk back to Glynn's office, he saw Bob sitting with a group of unhappy children. Emily was cuddled up to him, sucking her thumb and two of her friends were sobbing. 'Disaster!' Bob groaned, 'They found out. I promised I'd take them, but the car ran out of petrol. I feel awful, getting their hopes up. Disaster.'

Robbie and Becky shifted nervously, their previous exhilaration, turning to defensive, guilty anxiety as they clutched their bags in their pockets. Glynn paused, and said, 'I only have treacle toffees … but I have an idea. You two, stay with Professor Urquhart. I'll just be a bit.' After ten minutes' frantic bargaining, Glynn had spent his last week's earnings from tuition in exchange for seven half-bags of sweets, and returned in triumph to the small group. He sorted the sweets and gave them to the children, with one bag for Bob, saying quietly, 'Need to keep your blood sugar up!' The children screamed with delight, and Becky and Robbie relaxed. 'How much do I owe you?' said Bob, *sotto voce*. 'Nothing,' said Glynn. 'Seriously, these are the most expensive sweets you'll ever eat, but worth every penny.'

He took Becky and Robbie back to the university to escape the escalating chaos, as Bob walked the little ones home. They met Abi coming out of the main quad, and she was looking far brighter than he'd seen her for a while.

'I've got a job!' she cried.

'Wow, that was fast. What you do?'

'You'll never guess,' she said joyfully. 'Matt told me they were looking for English teachers; he said my skills were too out-of-date, but I went to see the organiser and she said I'd be perfect. I'm going to do two afternoons a week teaching for Highers from next week, and they'll take Becky in the under-sevens crèche for free after Christmas!'

'Under-sevens crèche?'

'Over-elevens are starting here next week, then after Christmas, the Seven-to-elevens will have their basic classes. They've given up on early years altogether.'

'That's great news,' Glynn hugged his sister-in-law warmly. 'Thanks,' she smiled broadly, 'I know I'll feel much better once I'm doing something productive.' She set off for home with the children, and Glynn felt she was finally on the road to recovery.

The town was cheered by the sudden jolt of sugar, and when a second delivery of mail arrived Finn collected boxes of items he'd been promised and set up a small stall near the Westgate, selling everything from tins of pretzels to magazines with advice on how to choose the right bikini. Glynn went through the motions of revision classes, 'though the students were distracted by the constant moving of furniture. He'd been worried that the influx of school children would turn the quad into a noisy playground, but the classes were surprisingly well behaved. After a particularly pointless day teaching, he was planning to do something useful, and was on his way to see Rory when he ran into Abi who had just finished her first week of teaching.

'Hey, how's it going?'

'Brilliant!' she laughed. 'I'd never thought I'd have missed it so much, but you know, I did. Oh, it's going to be a struggle and all, but I really think I might get them through.' He hugged her, 'That's great. I'm really pleased. I'm just off to see Rory.'

'Don't expect much. He's shattered, slept most of the time I was there yesterday, but I'm sure he'll be glad to see you.'

As Abi had warned, Rory was asleep when Glynn arrived, and still asleep an hour later when he left. He was cheered to see the range of home-made cards, and messages of support from all the students at John Burnet Hall. On the way out, Glynn caught sight of Felix, and managed to catch him before he was dragged off by the hospital administrator. 'Just a minute,' he said, 'I won't keep him long.' The administrator narrowed her eyes and said, 'You have two minutes. We need him in this next meeting.'

'What's going on?' Glynn pushed Felix, as the administrator left the building.

'Cannae say yet. Rory's on the mend, 'though.'

'Yeah. What happened?'

'Ah, that's sort of what the meeting's about. He's not the only case.'

'So is this something else going on?'

'Nothing to worry about. Look, I'll tell you as soon as I know anything, but he's in no danger. I've seen to that. Will you trust me?'

Glynn was both reassured and concerned by Felix's cryptic clues, and went round to Nia's to see if she knew anything more. 'Not really,' she said as he took off his coat, 'but there are rumours about one of the new anti-depressants, serious side effects. Might be that Felix meant.'

'How do you know this?' he said coming round to nuzzle her neck. 'Oh Shit!' he shrieked. 'What the fuck is that?'

'Glynn!' she hissed. 'You'll frighten him. There, there, poppet, it's all right,' and she carefully unwrapped a Russian hamster from her scarf. 'I'm looking after him for a friend. She's gone to Edinburgh, in a bit of a state. I was cleaning out his cage, and Jenna said he liked being snuggled up, so I've kept him in my scarf. Don't be such a baby!' She put the hamster back in its cage and gave Glynn a hard stare. 'You're not seriously scared of hamsters?'

'There's something unnatural about a, a furry ball like that,' he said darkly, 'You know, they fall off things?

186

I've seen them before, toddling along and then, Whump, off they fall.'

'Okay,' she laughed, 'I'll make sure he's in his cage when you come round, deal?'

'Thanks,' he said, sitting down awkwardly. 'Is your friend coping?'

'Not really. But she's concerned about her hamster, so that's a good sign,'

'Hmm,' Glynn nodded. 'Even drug addicts still take care of their animals. I used to help at a shelter in Bristol. I've seen people spend their last penny on dog food, or take in a stray moggie and care for it like a show cat, when they themselves look like the wild man of the woods.' She nodded and he came back to his earlier enquiry, 'So, where's this rumour come from, about the anti-depressants? How did you find out, when I don't know anything?'

'Oh, I don't know. I just talk to people.'

'You have a gift, Ni.' She blushed, and he looked at her with a serious face, saying, 'Really. You could do anything you want to, you know? Have you thought about doing a psychology degree?'

'Who knows where we'll all be by this time next year,' she said and cuddled up beside him.

'This wouldn't be so bad,' he stroked her hair warily, still on the look-out for hamsters. 'Anyway, Erica's supply of Christmas sweets might turn up by April, and that should keep us all going for a year or two.' He glanced at the book by the side of the sofa, 'Whatcha reading?'

'It's a sort of romance-come-psychological thriller. Got it from the library, now it's open again. It's a bit flowery, but it's got some serious stuff in it. Most of the characters are really believable, I mean, I'm worried about them.'

'Hmm.' He flipped past her bookmark, 'If I read any more than a few pages, I'd find the word 'perforce', wouldn't I?'

'Maybe. Go on, you can laugh. Idiot!' she poked his nose. 'Maybe it's not brilliantly written, but it's a good story. The narrator, this middle-aged man has terrible things happen to him, and he's trying to explain it all to this woman, Margaret, who's going through the same stuff, but he can't promise her it'll be alright, because his life is still awful.'

'Oh, great. Who wrote this? Louise Fauver,' he flipped to the back cover, 'Mother of three, lives in Devon. So she's really going to be convincing, writing as a mad, middle-aged man.'

'Cynic. Scientist.' She jabbed his chest. 'What about George Eliot?'

'Yeah. Right.'

'So what, a woman can't imagine what it's like to be a man? Or vice versa? And men are so much more complicated to write, yeah?'

'Oh, alright, I'll back down. Can't argue with feminist logic.'

'Actually, I went to lectures in theory. They suggested that men and women can't inhabit the other gender's world, but I don't agree. Surely, it's more complicated than that.'

'Write an essay on it, by any chance did you?' Glynn teased. 'Come on, I can spot an opening paragraph at fifty paces!' She glowered, and he laughed, 'I give in. But don't let this depress you, you hear me? I think we all need comedy in these dark times.'

Temperatures stayed below freezing during the day, and one night fell to twelve below. Elecricity and gas supplies were unreliable, and people unblocked fireplaces all over town. Glynn's landlord came down from the upstairs flat, and took out the living-room radiator, to open up the fireplace. After they'd managed to check the chimney wasn't blocked, Glynn was glad he'd bought a new vacuum cleaner at the end of the Summer, as his flat was coated with soot. But it was worth it. Finn had a coal bunker at the farm and brought round a sack of wood, so Glynn was able to get a real fire going. When three people died from hypothermia in town on a single night, the CHLOE team changed tack, setting up warm safe houses and shelters for the night. They also started to distribute fur coats, which had been stockpiled over many years by the charity shops. They'd previously distributed them to homeless shelters, but had been unable or unwilling to sell them because no-one wanted to wear animal fur on point of principle. Now that people realised there was a chance the cold could kill them, the choice of wearing fur for practical, rather than fashion, reasons seemed easy.

'Wow!' Glynn cried, when Nia opened the door to him one evening, wearing a dark mink coat with a smear of red paint down the side. 'This makes me a bad person, doesn't it?' he said, staring at her with darkening eyes. 'I have to admit I'm imagining you with nothing on underneath it.'

'Now that would rather defeat the object of the exercise, wouldn't it?' she sparkled. 'But they are incredibly warm. I went to get one for Ruth, and they insisted I should take one too. I can't believe I'm doing this. I never thought I'd ever wear a fur coat, and do you know, it's rather nice. It's so warm and I feel all film-starry. It's really nice. Am I a bad person?' Glynn didn't think so, and said, 'Shall we promenade?' He took her arm, and they giggled as they hurried through the dark streets. Suddenly Nia shrank back, 'Oh! Oh no, she spotted us!' A couple waved from the other side of the street and started to pick their way towards them across the patches of black ice. Nia smiled a frosty smile at them, and said quickly through gritted teeth, 'Shared a flat with her when I first arrived. She put up all these hearts with motivational sayings. Already engaged to loverboy there. Said she'd had a vision of their future children, back seat of the BMW, a girl with blonde hair and dark eyes and a boy with dark hair and blue eyes. She used to take a taxi to lectures.'

'Ah, got you, say no more,' Glynn smiled as the couple approached.

'Nia, darling!' the woman emoted. 'You remember Torrin?'

'Of course,' Nia nodded. 'Anna, this is Glynn.'

'Pleased to meet you. I'm so glad you got someone.'

'Glynn's a lecturer in Geology.'

'Oh, Torrin's been thinking about an academic career after his MA. We're in Edinburgh now, thought we'd come back see how things are.' Anna pulled in her stomach, as Torrin said to Glynn, 'How are property prices doing?' Glynn psyched himself up to psych Torrin out, 'Few places sold last autumn, not much movement recently. Hard to judge, probably going back to using the Register of Sasines after a while.'

'Ah. Oh.' Torrin paused in a brief moment of confusion, before asking, 'We thought we might find a good deal, what with all this hoohah. What do you reckon, Glynn?

'Not my area of expertise,' Glynn said with deliberate indifference. 'All rather small scale. I could put you in touch with my broker, if you're looking for something in a long-term investment portfolio.'

'You're thinking of moving back?' Nia stayed calm.

'No,' Torrin continued, 'but it could be a good investment, and we have a sentimental association with the place.'

Anna fluttered her eyelashes at Glynn, 'We were married at the Royal and Ancient. Such a great honour, a wonderful place.'

'Ah,' said Glynn. 'That's the thing about being academic staff - you have access to some of the most unusual, and intimate parts of the university for a wedding. I've always thought I'd go back to get married in Merton Chapel, old boy and all that.'

'Gosh!' Anna simpered and tossed her hair, 'Well, you want to hang on to him then, Nia!'

'Good to meet you,' said Glynn, 'but we have places to be.'

'Oh, oh, well, yes it was good to see you, Nia, and lovely to meet you, Glynn.'

Glynn hurried Nia away, and said, 'Was that alright? Too alpha-male? Sorry if I overreacted.' She stopped, pulled down his scarf and planted a kiss on his forehead, 'You were bloody brilliant! I've never seen her wrong-footed like that. She always looked down on me like some sort of lower life form, and you played her at her own game.'

'Glad to oblige,' he said, pulling her hood back up. 'The one good thing to come out of my time at Oxford - I can ponce with the best of them. So, were you at the wedding? Did you see this global event?'

'Lord no, I'm just this pitiful drop-out. They had this marquee, and apparently they showed a constant powerpoint loop with pictures from their latest Caribbean holiday.'

'Ooh, tacky!'

'I know! But she's always so self-assured, infuriating!'

'Tell you what,' he said as they reached her flat, 'let's make little voodoo dolls of them, and we could get the hamster to savage them. Would that help?'

'You are very strange,' she smiled, 'but I do like you.'

The cold persisted, so Nia stuck with the fur coat when she called round to Glynn's before the Christmas party. 'Was that you I heard singing?' she said, when he opened the door.

'Damn,' he said, 'caught out being callously festive. I imagine a few rounds of *Good King Wenceslas* could get you lynched these days'

'Was that what you were singing?'

'Um, no. *I Wish It Could Be Christmas Every Day*. It's like a compulsion, and this year I can't even blame in on musak in the shops. I just start singing.'

'Yeah, not very Christmassy around, is it? No lights, no decorations.'

'No advance displays of Easter Eggs in the shops,' Glynn did up his coat, then paused before opening the door. 'Look, I'd better tell you,' he said quietly, 'but keep it to yourself. Matt's been suspended.'

'What happened?'

'There was this end-of-term party, a sort of 'Thank You' for the teachers who've kept things going. So it went on until quite late, there was a lot of moonshine, and something happened. I'm sure it was all innocent, but a window got broken, and then this woman made a complaint against Matt. The BRP team suspended him until it can be sorted out.'

'That's awful. What did he do?' Nia was startled.

'Nothing. He's denying anything happened. He says this woman's a bit of a trouble-maker, not a sense of humour, and she's been gunning for him for a while. Anyway, don't say anything. I just thought I should tell you, in case it came up. Abi's pretty upset.'

192

'And they're still going ahead with the party?'

'Well, it's for the kids, and I think Matt's wanting to keep things quiet. It'll all blow over, I'm sure, and then he'll be back at school in the New Year. No need to give the gossips any more to talk about.'

'Yeah, I suppose,' Nia was not convinced. 'He does like his drink, your brother. Not giving him scotch for Christmas are you?'

'No. As you can see from the cunningly wrapped present, this is clearly a DVD, but what of, there's the poser.'

'101 favourite breweries?'

'Now who's the cynic? Go on, guess.'

'Oh alright. I guess it's a football video.'

'Ohhhh!' he wailed, slapping his hand to his head. 'So close, but just glanced off the crossbar. It is, in fact, a compilation of the best bits from last year's Irish Rules Football season.'

'Never heard of it,' Nia rocked to stay warm.

'It could just as well be called Irish No-Rules Football, because they seem to do whatever they like. It makes for a spectacular game, but it's hard to follow the scoring. I know.   You're impressed,' Glynn waggled his eyebrows before putting on his hat, 'and you're thinking, 'Oh, I hope there's one of those in my stocking tomorrow morning.' No?' She threw a glove at him, 'I do hope not. I'd hate to break up with you on Christmas Day.' She kissed him and wrapped her scarf around his neck. 'I'm not sure pink is your colour, but you'd better wrap up. It's freezing out there.'

As they set off, a bag of presents on each arm, everyone they saw in the shadowy streets seemed to be going in the same direction, voices low, clutching presents and small children. Not that there were many people about. They arrived in a convoy, and struggled to reach the kitchen, through the carnival of balloons, hair ribbons and small plastic ponies. 'Hallelujah!' Abi cried as they came in. 'Unencumbered adults! Our child-to-adult ratio was reaching critical. Without Finn we're short of stories, and the quiet ones are running out of corners to hide. We'd normally have Bob and Eilidh as well. Take your coats off, get a drink, then get out there!'

The company was good, and people were happy not to feel guilty about being cheerful. Abi was running the circus, enjoying the distraction. 'Nia!', she called, 'can you give me a hand with these?' She passed over three plates, and collected another four. As they moved towards the kitchen, Matt shouted from the other side of the room, 'Never run with cacti!' Glynn replied, 'Delicate plants…' then they both chuckled.

'Cacti?' said Nia, rinsing the plates under the tap.

'Och, pay no notice to them,' Abi brushed it off. 'It's just some mad Welsh family thing. Their mother loved her houseplants, or something.'

'But what does it mean?'

'No idea, but they seem to think it's conversation, so it's best to leave them to it.'

Felix arrived looking brighter than Glynn had seen him for a while, and quickly entranced all of the children with a series of grotesque plastic finger puppets. Abi finally shooed the children upstairs, settling the younger ones to sleep and leaving the older ones practising their 'What do you call a man with a shovel on his head?' routines. When she came back down, Abi saw that the adults had adopted the puppets. 'And I suppose these have a medical purpose, do they, my lad?' she said wryly.

'Abi! Take a look,' Felix threw one over.

'What are they?'

'Viruses.'

Glynn wrenched off his finger puppet in disgust, and threw it at Nia, 'Ych a fi! You didn't tell us that!'

'No, well, they were made up by a pharmaceutical firm, promoting an anti-flu drug that missed the boat. I've got a whole box. And …' Felix pulled out another plastic bag from his briefcase, 'now that the bairns are out of harm's way, do you want some inspirational notepaper?' He passed round pink and blue notepads. Abi deciphered the ornate calligraphy, 'Be confident. Live Free.'

Everyone paused, then Felix said, 'Look closely at the logo at the bottom.'

Everyone started turning round the pads, until Glynn choked, 'Oh lovely - inspirational condoms!'

Everyone was left nervously clutching their notepads as Abi said to Felix, 'You're a bad influence, you know!'

'I know, but good for a laugh, no? We just have to get through Christmas and New Year, and everything will be okay. Always the biggest suicide flash point. You know they're closing off most bridges this week? We're on the way up, hen. Not to worry.'

By ten o'clock the party was buzzing with blitz spirit. Recurring conversation noted how strange it was to be normal, to be having a Christmas party while the town was sunk in mourning. An oasis of light in a desert of darkness, even a mirage of an oasis was welcome. Glynn was relieved to see Jon and Julie arriving as part of a crowd of younger people. He'd heard that Jon was still in a bad way and that Julie hadn't been out much, not wanting to leave him in the house alone. Glynn made a point of greeting them, and asked how they were. 'Oh, much better,' Jon said strongly. 'Had things bad for a while. Whole world gone mad, sort of thing, but I'm feeling fine now. Full of the Yuletide spirit. Can I get you a drink?'

'No, I'm good for the moment,' Glynn smiled as Jon headed for the drinks table, then he lowered his voice and softly asked, 'And how are you Julie? Are things really better?' She looked sad, but said confidently, 'I'm tired, but yeah, things are looking up. These last few days he's been a lot brighter. It was his idea to come tonight, 'though that may have been just to escape from his mother. So, point me to the mince pies, professor. I am in the mood to party.'

Now there were fireworks, and after several people had disgraced themselves with tuneless renditions of favourite carols sung along to old CDs, there was a move to venture outside and set the sky alight. Glynn was gingerly opening another of Finn's home-brew potions, and Nia was helping Abi slide tiny mince pies into the oven, as Matt and three of the younger men carried a large box into the garden. 'Matt!' Abi shrieked. 'What about the rabbits?'

'Oh, they'll be fine,' he shouted back. 'Do 'em good anyway, wake up the dozy little bastards. We should have got our money back, should have signs on 'Require batteries and personal vet,' or something.' Abi rushed out after them, shouting, 'Maisie, give me a hand!' They came back a few moments later, each clutching a soft, wide-eyed rabbit. 'We're going to put them in the guest room for now,' Abi said to Nia. 'Can you keep an eye on things for a minute?'

'Of course,' Nia closed the oven door warily, then stood near the open back door, and watched several large rockets emerging from the box.

'This should be fun,' said Glynn.

'This could be dangerous,' she replied. 'Don't you think you should get your brother away from there? He's had far too much to drink.'

'Drunk in charge of a firework, do you think?'

'I'm serious, Glynn. He shouldn't be doing it.' He took another swig from his glass, so she stormed into the garden shouting, 'Matt, Matt. Let them do it, alright? Come back in, it's freezing.' The night was clear, but the moon was only a crescent, so Glynn could barely see dark outlines of the figures each sending out a cloud of breath, as the conversation heated up. 'Nia, lovely Nia, stand back, this is men's work,' Matt cried.

'Fine, but you're not the man to do it. It's not safe!'

'Safe, safe? I've blown up rockets ten times the size of these. S'no problem,' Matt slurred.

'You're drunk. It's not safe. You're not safe,' Nia turned to his companions. 'What about the rest of you? Can't you see he's half-cut? He shouldn't be playing with these things.'

The other men muttered, then one of them said, 'Okay, Matt, you've set them up, I'll light them?'

'You're not going to listen to her? You saying I'm drunk, that I can't hold my grog?'

'Matt, please,' Nia said. 'You've had too much this evening, it's dangerous.'

'Oh, so you're checking up on me, are you? What are you, my mother?' Matt snarled.

'I just think it's not a good idea for you to light these fireworks in your condition.

'Oooh!' he sneered. 'In my condition. I'm not bloody pregnant.'

'Come on in? I want to help you. You could maybe take some milk thistle to help your liver.'

'Milk thistle? Ha! Look, love, you're the one needing help, obviously. Not me. Now fuck off.' Nia stepped back, 'Fine. Blow yourself up. See if I care!' She ran back into the kitchen, ignoring Glynn and pushing through the crowd of people who'd assembled to watch the fireworks.

The rockets went with a bang, followed by cascades of pink and green showers glowing in the stars. Distress flares all round. Glynn left the crowd and poured some more dried mango slices into dishes in the living room. He looked up as Felix came in, but said nothing. After a few minutes Felix began cautiously, 'You know I like Nia. She's great. It's just that not everyone will share her enthusiasm about things, particularly this New Age stuff.'

'Yeah, I know. But she's so sorted for her age, I start thinking there must be something in it.'

'Glynn Hughes, druid? Really?' Felix picked at a piece of mango, 'I'm sure there is something in it, but it's not for everyone. And if I'm honest, I'd say they're right to be sceptical of a twenty-something-year-old with all the answers.'

'What are you saying, Felix?' Glynn glared at him woozily. 'First off you like her, now you're suspicious.'

'That's not what I meant. Don't get all drunk and disorderly on me. I *do* like her. But she needs to pick her battles. Don't see your brother as a likely convert any time soon, do you? Not an easy sell, at the best of times.'

'No. Sorry. You're right. I will collect my pesky child bride and remove her from harm's way.'

'Good idea. Give her my love.'

'Will do. Enjoy! Don't eat all the strange snacks!'

Glynn found Nia in the hallway, simmering

with righteous indignation. He heard Julie trying to cheer her up, and caught the end of the conversation: 'So, we were at this graduation party, sitting round in the blazing sun with just these decorative balloons for cover, and Jera screamed, 'What's the matter with you, Glynn? You're sweating more than when we have sex!'

He took a deep breath before coming round the corner. Julie was both relieved and embarrassed to see him. He collected their coats and scooted Nia out the door, waving discreetly to Abi who was sat half-way up the stairs. After a silent drive home, they were just inside the flat when Nia said, 'I'm sorry things turned out like that.' He switched on the light and took her fur coat, 'It wasn't your fault. Matt gets these moods. The suspension's really got to him. You just picked a bad time to join the temperance movement.' Nia stretched out on the sofa and said, 'He's an alcoholic, in denial. He needs help.'

'Don't you think that's a bit over dramatic?' said Glynn sitting at her feet.

'Were your parents alcoholics?' she said, watching for a trigger.

'No they bloody weren't!' he snapped back, 'and neither's Matt. It's not a problem, Nia. I know you want to help, but he's fine. I'm sorry he had a go like that, at you this evening. I should have said something, but it's usually best to just leave him be. Maybe he has been drinking a bit too much lately, but who hasn't with all this going on?'

'Whatever,' she closed her eyes. 'I'm sorry it turned out like that.'

'Forget it. Let's go to bed.'

Twenty minutes later Glynn was lying on his back, Nia on her side, both awake but not talking as the street lights went out again. The town sank as the darkness signalled the end of the Christmas party. After a few half-hearted attempts to start a sing-song, the guests filed out, Abi locked up and Matt passed out in the kitchen, dreaming of fireworks and cacti.

Days ticked by, and the New Year came unnoticed. Glynn and Nia accepted an invitation to Pipeland Farm on the evening of the third to play Edinburgh Monopoly. A set of board game conventions was established, and the evening proceeded carefully. Glynn was winning when he landed on Robbie's hotel and the child punched the air loudly, disturbing the table. Silence swooped as the bottles rocked and fell.

'Is your arm connected to your brain?' Matt wiped a froth of scorn from the corner of his mouth, 'Stupid boy!' Nia set the bottles straight and said sharply, 'It *was* a mistake. I really don't think you should be so horrible to him.' Matt shifted his focus, gearing up as he turned towards her, 'Bloody hell! I was joking, alright? You can take a joke, can't you son? You people have no bloody sense of humour, that's your problem.' Nia looked at Abi and Glynn, but they avoided her eye as Matt switched back into conversational mode, 'Fetch us another bottle, son. Mind the butterfingers! Okay, where were we? Abi, love, your go, I think.' Nia watched from the table as Robbie angrily took another bottle of home-brew from the fridge.

Matt won. The girls began to clear away. Nia started to scrape the plates into the compost bin. Abi crossed Matt's path, as she came to collect dishes and glasses, and he went into the kitchen. It happened in seconds. A sudden pressure, an aircraft firing its engines at the edge of a runway. The burst of air as the arm swung, the explosion of sound, glass and blood, and then Nia shattered on the ground, the bottle splintered around her. Looking back, as he gave a statement to the police, Glynn reshaped it into a slow-motion film. The bottle in flight, the brief flash of horror before impact, then freeze-frame, a halo of green glass, and a slow drip off-screen.

Chapter Nine

Glynn sat with her in the ambulance and wandered dazed into the waiting area while they rushed her into an operating room. He couldn't get his bearings, and stared dumbly at Julie who was already there crying when he arrived.

'It's Jon,' she said blankly. 'He tried to kill himself.'

'Oh Julie!' shouted the woman next to her, 'I won't have you saying things like that.'

Julie turned on her, 'What should I be saying, Marsha? He cut his wrists in the bath, he left a note, Dear J., I can't go through this again. I love you, Jonathan. What is this, then? Accidental death?'

'He's dead?' Glynn gulped, as the older woman stood up with a cry and walked off.

'No. They don't know,' Julie sobbed. 'He's lost a lot of blood. He's in there now.'

'My god,' he said, sitting beside her. 'I'm so sorry. I thought he was getting better.'

'Oh, he was.'

'Did something happen?'

'No, he was just getting better again, thinking more clearly.'

'No-one tries to kill themselves if they're really thinking clearly.'

'You don't believe that.'

Glynn looked at her and said, 'Talk to me.'

Julie pulled her hair back behind her ears and looked away, talking to an unseen distance, 'You know, he'd been through it before, and he really tried. Really tried, not just the self-help positive-thinking crap. He'd been through counselling, spiritual stuff, turned himself inside out, 'cos it was supposed to help. All the, Don't Rely On Medication crap, being strong, he kept going. He was in hell, Glynn.' She turned to face him. 'Yes, he was getting better, but it's not all 'How wonderful, I can see the sun again'. He was on borrowed time. It comes back, over and over, and he thought I didn't understand, but I do. I do. And he was strong, so many times he was in pain, you'd put an animal to sleep, but he kept going. But when he started to feel better, calmer ... well, who would wait around for it to come back? Because nothing stopped it, and he worked so hard, but nothing worked, and who the hell would tell him he had to put up with it? What gives Marsha and all these fucking do-gooders the right to tell him he has to suffer eternal pain, and be glad of the cool days while he waits? Why the hell would you wait? Why not decide enough is enough? There's no point. You'd put an animal down.' Her knuckles were white as she clung on to the chair.

Glynn offered her a hankie, 'It's not very clean,' he apologised, as she twisted it in her hand. 'I'm so sorry', he said, 'I don't know what to say.'
'Oh, it's alright,' she said. 'It's alright. Really, I'm alright. It's just Marsha is so determined and so collected and she doesn't understand. She's so bloody arrogant and I'm so angry I could kill him,' and she started laughing, choking on her words. 'You know, people laugh at funerals. I never believed it.' She handed back the hankie, saying angrily, 'You know what I think, unless you've really been at the edge, you've really thought about it, not just as a possibility, but pulling at you like the tide, I don't think anyone has the right to judge. No-one knows what that pain, that life is like. He thought I couldn't see it, but I could, I could. How dare people say he 'should' and 'ought' and 'better'? How can they judge

him?' she gulped, 'How can they judge him? How could he leave me?' She cried silently for a few minutes, her head in her hands, then sat up and said, 'Oh! God, Glynn, what are you doing here? What's happened?'

'It's alright. It's Nia. She's hurt, but she's not in danger, I think. Look, is there anyone I can call?'

'No. That was his mother. She's already assembling the clan, telling them all about this dreadful accident,' She laughed bleakly at Glynn's puzzled look. 'She wouldn't accept he was depressed, so how could he commit suicide, no?' He patted her on the arm, as she said, 'We were going to travel, d'y'know? Backpacking this summer, Asia, be hippies and the like. He always wanted to travel. And then he couldn't leave the house. Dundee might have been the other side of the world.'

'As it is for many locals.'

'Aye. You're right,' her smile collapsed back into tears, 'I just, I just don't know what I'm going to do without him.'

They sat together for a while, and Marsha came back quietly with three cups of coffee. She placed them on the chair next to her, and watched them grow cold as they waited for news. Two hours later Julie smiled for Glynn when the doctors came to tell him Nia would recover. She'd lost a lot of blood, but they'd repaired the damage and were hopeful she'd regain the sight in both eyes. 'Give her my love,' Julie said quietly as he went in to see her.

The waiting room and everything else vanished for Glynn when he saw Nia's bruised and bandaged face. He sat beside her stroking her hair, thanking all the gods for the miracle. By the time Abi and Ruth arrived to shoo him out to get some sleep, the waiting room was empty. It was only days later he found out Jon died that night.

Nia lay quietly in the dark, listening to metal instruments in plastic trays. She tried to take her mind off the itching pain under the eye patches, and focused on the pleasure of clean, soft sheets. She didn't know how many days it was before she caught a hint of her mother's perfume and heard her stifle a gasp before greeting her cheerfully. She let her mother hold her hand when they took the bandages off, and once her vision cleared she saw realised how serious her injuries had been, as her mother was bracing herself to cope with Nia's blindness.

'It's alright, mum,' she said. 'I can see. I'm fine.'

Her mother hugged her, 'I do wish you'd come home, Nia. Your father's worried sick.'

'Maybe,' she said. 'Maybe.'

Once it was clear that Nia's sight had returned and the doctors began to talk about discharging her at the end of the week, her mother reluctantly went home. Ruth came in to tell Nia she had seen her off on to the train without incident, though she had urged Ruth again to try to make Nia go back to Manchester. As Ruth was walking back through the hospital grounds she saw Glynn clutching a nervous bunch of flowers. 'I hear she's properly awake,' he said. 'She was still pretty drugged last time, so ...' Ruth nodded and went to walk on, but then paused and said, 'You may not be the person she wants to see right now. She hasn't said she blames you, but some people do.' Swept up by a storm of guilt, Glynn lashed out in words, 'To be honest, Ruth, this is none of your damn business. You're supposedly helping us to be more holistic, helping people, 'n'all, but you've kept one low profile these last few months, haven't you? I mean, maybe crystal healing's good for some people, but Matt's been out there on the front line. I haven't seen you pumping out drains or looking after the sick and injured.'

She said nothing and walked away, leaving him twisting the flower stems tightly between his hands. He gathered his composure before approaching the ward, and was slightly nonplussed when the smell of disinfectant receded as he came over to Nia's cubicle. Before she could say anything, Glynn took a deep breath and smiled, 'Ananya,' he lilted, 'by The Body Shop.'

'Yes, I know it's corny,' she said. 'My mum bought me a bottle and squirted me. But how do you know this?'

'Ah, when I was doing my A-Levels it was the height of sophistication, the retro thing. I bought a bottle for this girl once. I kept it in my rucksack and I'd sniff it and think of her. Soppy, eh?'

'So did she like it?'

'Oh, I chickened out. Kept it until I went to uni, then chucked it. Just another tragic tale of unrequited love and cheap perfume.'

'So, I'm taking you back to your tragically well-spent youth?'

'Sort of. Um, I brought you some flowers,' he said, cutting the banter dead. 'I don't know what to say, but I'm so sorry.'

'It wasn't your fault,' she said quietly. 'They'd better go in some water.'

'How are you feeling?'

'Not so bad. My mum told me I looked like a boxer, which cheered me up.'

'Nice of her to come, 'though?'

'Yeah, maybe …'

'Do I sense a 'but'?'

'It's hard to talk to her. I'm a disappointment. I'm glad Ruth's been here.'

Glynn expressed his disapproval that Ruth hadn't been more visible over the last few months, and was taken aback by Nia's reaction, 'Do you really think she should've been doing more in her condition?'

'What? What, is she ill?'

'Are you bloody stupid?' she said weakly. 'She's five-months pregnant. She's been doing all she can, but you can't really expect her to be shovelling leaves, for god's sake.'

'Oh,' Glynn stumbled. 'Isn't she a bit old? I just thought, you know, um. Ah, well, that explains a lot. Sorry.' Nia shut her eyes, 'I'm tired. It's good to see you, Glynn. Maybe tomorrow …'

He left her to rest, then sat outside the hospital feeling a complete fool. He'd never thought Matt was capable of violence. He hadn't realised Ruth was pregnant, hadn't really considered her at all, 'though he knew how important she was to Nia. He'd let Rory get into such a state he'd nearly died, and all the time he'd been focused on his own little world, thinking he was coping well despite the external circumstances. Now he didn't know where to go next. He decided to try to start with his immediate *faux pas*, and walked round to Ethereal where he found Ruth and Nia's temporary replacement just opening up after lunch. Before Glynn could say anything Ruth smiled and said, 'Will you come up for a moment? Jenny'll look after things here.' As he followed her up the stairs, Glynn heard a voice in his head say defensively, 'Well, better not to realise, than to ask a fat woman if she's pregnant.' Ruth settled down, and invited him to take a seat. He took a deep breath, 'I was unforgivably rude, and I apologise. The truth is, I need your help.' Glynn leaned back against the door, and Ruth said, 'The past is the past. Have a seat. What seems to be the problem?'

He sat down. 'I'm trying to be there for Nia, but I have these headaches. Not quite bad enough for painkillers, I've only got a few left, but I wake up with them every day. Now I may be the cynical child of science, but I do know a bit about depression. I know depressives dream more than normal and I've been having pretty strong dreams.'

'So you think the dreams are, what? Causing the headaches, connected to them?' Ruth was interested but clearly not alarmed, so Glynn continued, 'I don't know. I called my old shrink and told him about the dreams I could remember. He said they were too fragmented to be of much use and that maybe I should take a muscle relaxant.'

'Well, yes, if you're tense you could be grinding your teeth in your sleep. That could be causing the headaches,'

Glynn looked sceptical, so Ruth went on, 'but you still think the dreams are the root cause rather than a side effect?'

'Well, basically, yes. There's this one where I'm walking along a row of houses-'

'Let me stop you there,' Ruth smiled at him kindly, 'Your dreams are *your* dreams. How can I untangle them if you can't?'

'Symbols. Jungian archetypes?' he said hopefully. 'There's so much I don't remember, but the feeling.'

'Bingo!' said Ruth. 'Let me tell you a story?' She gave

Glynn a pan drop. 'Let's say you go to a big city, first visit, maybe. - Follow my finger. - Paris, Amsterdam, sun shining, money in your pocket. You go for a wander, and you come across a side street, you have a lovely meal, listen to a brilliant busker, browse in a little artist's shop. You're relaxed, happy, at the end of the day you ramble along, find yourself back in the centre or near your hotel. - Stand up and shut your eyes. Hold out your arms. Hold it there. - Now, weeks later you're back home, could you tell me exactly where that little street was? Probably not. - Okay, put your arms down. - Now, next time you're in that city maybe you could find it, navigate by signs you didn't know you'd remember, street corners, shops. Say you found it again, I bet it wouldn't feel the same, even if nothing had changed. - Sit down, open your eyes. - You might find the same street, but it won't feel the same, even if nothing physical has changed. Same with dreams. Once you're asleep or under hypnosis all you can retrace is the feeling. And your dreams feel like the source of your headaches.'

She paused, with her hand hovering over Glynn's head. 'End of story?' he looked up at her hand with suspicion. After a few seconds she moved away and said, 'End of story. Professional advice, something is troubling you, and it's affecting your sleep.'

'So you'd agree with my shrink? Take a muscle relaxant?'

'Not entirely. You need to relax your mind and your body together. I can give you something to help, and then you need to take a good look at those feelings you're waking up with. Don't force yourself, but look at them. These dreams, these headaches are coming from you, so you're the only one who can solve it.'

'I feel as though I've just opened a fortune cookie,' Glynn said, but his sarcasm was overlaid with real sadness.

'No simple prescription, I'm afraid. Wait here a minute.' Ruth spent a few minutes at a desk on the other side of the room, then came back over with a small paper bag. 'I'd suggest you start simple: Camomile tea. Drink before you go to bed. Lavender oil, few drops in the bath or a footbath. And finally, if you haven't got one at home already, go buy a piece of quartz downstairs. Keep it in sunlight in the day and hold it in your hand for thirty minutes before you go to sleep. Encourages alpha waves – fast food meditation, so to speak. But, of course, don't put it on your computer's hard drive.'

He raised an eyebrow.

'You'd be surprised how many people are caught out by their cynicism,' she continued. 'They say they believe crystals can work, and thank you what a lovely piece of quartz, but they're still surprised when they put one on their computer and it buggers up the connections.'

'People do that?'

'Oh, aye We forget how powerful bits of quartz, silicon, diamond can be. It's not all symbolism. Well, you being a geologist should know that. What's magnetism if not magic?'

'I will take your word for it, oh wise one. Oh, no, seriously, thank you, I'm sorry, I'm just really off,' he mumbled.

'Try these out, simple things first. If the headaches don't pass there are other approaches. Don't overdo the painkillers. They'll just mask the source of the pain. Here endeth today's lecture.'

'Thank you. I'll think about it. But you don't think

210

I've got a brain tumour? To be honest, you're sort of my second, no, third opinion. Felix said I had rampant hypochondria.'

'And there's nothing worse than a hypochondriac with a headache,' she teased, before saying with calm authority, 'I don't think it's a brain tumour, but there's something wrong, clearly, and you need to track it down.'

As he left he said awkwardly, 'I wouldn't have been so judgemental, um, Nia only told me today that you're expecting, and in my defence you look great so I just didn't realise, but I'm sorry I was so rude. Congratulations!'

'Forget it,' she said 'You have a lot on your plate.'

'Thanks, how much do I owe you?'

'Whatever you think,' she smiled. 'People just pay what they can.'

He left a generous amount of fraying notes on the side table, and bought an extra piece of quartz on his way out. He was nearly home when his 'phone lit up, and he saw Abi's exhausted face appear. 'Are you at home?' she said, peering at the background.

'Nearly. What's up?'

'Well, I was hoping you could do me a huge favour …'

'Anything. What's up?'

'Finn has the rabbits in the minibus, and the hutch and the run, and I was hoping, well really Becky was hoping, you could have them in your garden for a while.'

'Um, sure, I suppose. What's going on?'

'I'll tell you when I see you. We're coming now.'

He saw the minibus draw up a few minutes after he arrived home, and Abi and Finn both jumped quickly out, and started to unload. They'd set everything up in Glynn's back garden and brought the rabbits in from their baskets before saying anything. Finn went back to the bus saying, 'Don't be long, hen. We've still got a way to go.'

'Abi?' said Glynn, watching Tommy peering at the rabbits who stared threateningly back at him. 'Want to tell me what's going on? D'you want a cup of tea? I have milk.'

'Thank you,' she wrapped her coat closer round her, 'I can't stop. Glynn, I'm leaving. I'm packing up, taking the children to Dundee with me. They're at Eilidh's right now. Finn's taking us in the minibus once I've packed things up.'

'Oh, umm,' he stuttered.

'It's complicated, I'm sorry to bring you into this, but Becky freaked out when she thought Finn was having the rabbits - one too many jokes about rabbit pie - and I don't feel right leaving them with Matt, the way he is now.'

'What's he said?'

'He doesn't know I'm going. He's been out of it, drinking a lot. After what happened with Nia I just couldn't stay, but I think he'll react badly and I want the children away from it. He's in Edinburgh, had to go for his disciplinary hearing. We're moving all we can now, and I'm going to leave a note. Don't look at me like that. You saw what he did. I can't risk a confrontation.'

'He'd never hurt you or the kids!' Glynn was rather shaken by the strength of her resolve, as she said, 'I'm not so sure. Finn's not sure either. He had some pretty heated words with him, after Nia, and they're not really talking. I've told the children Matt's not well, so he needs lots of peace and quiet, for a while. I'm doing this for them as well as me,' she sighed.

212

'How long d'you think you'll be gone?'

She put her hand on his shoulder, 'Glynn, I'm leaving him. He nearly killed your girlfriend. My son knows his father smashed a bottle over a woman's head. I'm not coming back. I'm sorry.'

'No, no,' he hugged her, 'I'm sorry, I'm just such a mess. Of course I don't blame you. You have to do what's right for you. Will you be alright?'

'I will. Finn's going to take me back to pack some suitcases, then take us up to Dundee. I'm sorry I haven't time to bring the bairns round. Finn hoped to get the minibus sooner today, and then we had trouble getting fuel, and now we really need to be gone before Matt comes back.'

'I understand. What will the hearing decide, d'you think?'

'No idea. There's something else to it, something Matt wouldn't tell me, so I cannae tell. Maybe ...' she trailed off. 'Anyway, look after yourself, Glynn. We'll be around. I'm not planning to cut the children off from their friends.'

'Now, look after yourself too?' He hugged her more tightly, then waved sadly as she and Finn drove off.

When Glynn called Matt later that evening he was surprised at how calmly his brother was taking things. 'She'll be back,' he said, 'Just needs to let off steam. She knows how sorry I am, you know, alright? I was really ill that night, and she kept pushing. Accidents happen. She's alright now, isn't she?' Glynn said nothing, and Matt continued, 'Women, eh? Can't live with 'em, bloody true, not so sure about, Can't live without 'em, 'though. Know what I mean?' Glynn ignored the question, and said, 'What did the hearing say? When will you know?'

'Well, the chairman seemed a decent sort, so I'm not

too worried, but I think they're going to give me a slap on the wrist just to keep the PC brigade happy. But …, ' he said waving a glass cheerily, 'I did get some proper scotch while I was down there, so come round and we can put the world to rights.'

'Okay,' Glynn nodded. 'I'll join you later. I've got some stuff to sort first, but I'll be along. Don't start without me. Don't want to have to go back to the home-brew, oh, bye!' he said, realizing his mistake.

The brothers spent an odd evening together, as Glynn tried to water down the scotch. He left Matt apparently in a happy mood, telling him everything would be fine, and thanking Glynn profusely for his fraternal support. The bottle was empty by the end of the night and Glynn slept for most of the following day, only getting up when the sun was setting.

His head was hurting again, and he tried to focus. He pulled on his thickest sweater and a pair of gloves. He enticed the rabbits out of their hutch and put them in the run. The early moonlight and the dew brought them out in frantic dashes and aerial acrobatics. He laid out a rug next to the run and stretched out on his stomach. 'If it was only twenty degrees warmer,' he thought, 'this would be paradise.' He mentally traced the constellations starting to appear above him, and took deep lungfuls of the clear air. As he was about to go inside, he realised he was being hunted. A barely visible, thick black leg stretched out from the hedge, followed by glaring eyes. A strange cat slowly formed in the darkness, inspecting the spectator. Turning to lie flat on his back, Glynn felt a twinge of the fear which shapes the lives of prey – low to the ground, sharply watching for any movement, oppressed by silent, elegant aggression. If he'd had longer ears he'd have poised them, just as the rabbits were doing. The shadow started to slide towards the run, and as he turned his head slightly Glynn saw the familiar dance begin. Lily retreated to a safe distance, while Barbie advanced, stretching out her body, stalking the predator. Glynn didn't know whether this particular cat had yet learned of the danger posed by fluffy bunnies with less-than-fluffy claws, so he decided to forestall trouble. Cats with scratched noses make a lot of noise. He sat up and shooed the cat, who sneered at him, then dematerialised. Tommy had already chosen to ignore the rabbits and curl up in the kitchen. Glynn rolled up the rug, and went indoors to make a cup of tea. The single bulb in the kitchen lit up the run in the garden, so he stood at the sink drinking his tea, watching the rabbits for a while. Then he scooted them into the basket and put them back into the hutch. They were rearranging the new hay and fighting over pieces of the long grass stalks as Glynn pulled down the insulating blankets and tucked them in for the night.

After a visit from the ophthalmic specialist who was covering the whole of North East Scotland, Nia was allowed home under Ruth's supervision. She concentrated on simple actions, appreciating each degree of improved movement, when she could turn a tap on fully, when she could tie shoelaces. She could feel the skin around her eyes starting to smooth out as her peripheral vision returned to normal, and it became more of an effort to avoid glimpses of herself in mirrors. The whole population was finally benefiting from better food supplies as distribution networks were slowly re-established, and as a medical priority, Nia received better food parcels than most, which gave her some small comfort. For a few minutes as she luxuriated in the taste of Brie on crackers, she forgot what had happened, and forgot to worry about what would happen now. She was scared when Glynn arrived at her door, even though she'd almost begged him to come over. He had another bunch of flowers, and this time she was thinking clearly enough to question their source. 'Greenhouses in Dundee,' he explained, 'some of them survived the winter, and these are from the weeds. Romantic, eh?'

She made him some tea, 'Nice to have regular milk again,' he nodded. They sat on the sofa, and discussed the recent slow improvements to local services, and the caution optimism of the CHLOE team that life would be back to normal before the summer. Even though Glynn was the most obviously perturbed, it was Nia who pulled off the plaster, saying, 'Ruth tells me Abi's gone to Dundee.'

'Yes,' he said cautiously. 'Don't know for how long. May be for good.'

'You'll miss her.'

'Well, she'll be around. She's doing some teaching here, after all. So,' he burbled, 'it seems the kids don't get off school that easily. Maybe things are getting back to normal. They even had some local brew on tap when I had a drink at the Crown yesterday. Morag saved some special, and Matt was over the moon.'

'You're still seeing him!' Nia stood up and walked to the window.

'He's my brother,' Glynn coughed. 'What can I, what do you expect me to do?' He stood up but stayed by the sofa.

'After what he did to me?' she gasped.

'I know, I know, but he's confused, he's upset. He's family, Ni. I can't just wipe out thirty years.'

'And what about the last thirty days? Can you forget about them?' She stared out the window.

'Baby,' he circled, 'what happened to you was awful, and I've told him that, but I can't cut him off. Abi's left him. He's in a bad way. He needs me.'

'And what about *me*?' She turned round, eyes flashing. 'Don't *I* matter? Look at what he did to *me*!'

'Of course you matter. I love you. You matter to me more than anything,' he said wearily.

'Then I don't want you to see him again,' she spat.

Glynn wouldn't meet her eye, and shifted his weight awkwardly from one leg to the other. Finally he said, 'I can't do that. You must see, he's family.'

'It's him or me,' she shouted, 'Your choice!'

'No! That's crazy! You're making it sound like I'm seeing another woman or something.'

'It's the same thing, isn't it? Loyalty? Trust? You can't play both sides. Not after what he's done to me.'

Glynn slumped on the edge of the arm chair and gazed at his hands, 'I'm supposed to choose between the woman I love, and my own brother?' He looked up at her bruised face, 'How can I make a choice like that?''

'Maybe this isn't about you!' she screamed. 'Maybe this isn't your bloody story! I'm the one who's just had her face smashed in! What about me? Will you promise not to see him again?'

'Nia,' he said heavily, 'I can't promise you that. He's my brother.'

She cried, 'Then you've made your choice!' before running into the bathroom, locking the door behind her. He hammered on the door as she wept.

'Nia! This is crazy! Open the door. We have to talk about this.'

'What is there to say?' she screamed back. 'You don't care about me. You just care about your wonderful brother. Your wonderful, alcoholic brother, who tried to kill me. You said you loved me. Go away, just go away and leave me alone.'

He leaned his head against the door, lost for words. Eventually he heard her sobs subside and he said quietly, 'I'm going to go now. I think we've said enough. But I mean what I say. I love you, Ni. I don't want things to be like this. Nia? Alright. I'm going.' There was no reply, so he collected his things and left.

When Ruth came round to see her that evening, Nia was calm and shivering. She told Ruth briefly what had happened and Ruth tried to reassure her that it would work out, that Glynn was just in shock and that he needed time to think. Nia insisted that it was black and white and that she couldn't see him again if he continued to talk to his brother, but Ruth stroked her hand and said, 'We'll see, we'll see. After all, what can be possibly talk to his brother about? How are you, Matt? Hit anyone else lately?' Nia sobbed into her shoulder, 'No, it's over. He had to choose and he didn't choose me, so he's dumped me. What more is there to say?' Ruth stayed with her until she fell asleep.

Glynn tried to focus on his work while the chaos twisted in his head. On Friday afternoon he was taking another slim pile of exam scripts down to Maureen, when he saw Tricia sat on the floor of the main foyer. He moved to her side, 'Hey Tricia, what's wrong?'

'Have you seen the bloody questionnaire digests , the

ones from last semester? I've just got mine back.'

'Did we do questionnaires?'

'Hobden sent out these batches to the students individually.'

'And thus invited only the moaners to return them.' He sat down beside her.

'D'you think?'

'Oh yeah. Longest questionnaire response I ever had was basically a three-page call for my resignation. What did they say?'

'I haven't seen them, but Hobden just called me in to see the digest. Lots of whinging about how the essay titles were too hard, and how I put pressure on people to contribute in tutorials. Some of them even said I wasn't approachable.'

'Oh, so not the ninety-percent of your students who are regularly camped outside your door to talk for hours on end then?' Glynn tried to be supportive, and Tricia opened up a little more, 'The real pain is half of them had come to me to complain about Hodders, but I did the professional thing, tried to make them see their expectations were unreasonable and so on. And now, he just goes and stabs me in the back.'

'Were they all bad?'

'No. In fact my biggest course had lots of good things, that made me feel I'd really achieved something, but that won't be what the university sees, and if there's a permanent job comes up here, it'll be this negative stuff they see.'

'Have you talked to Eilidh?'

'Yeah. She said I can't win.'

'That's a bit negative.'

'She said, first off, the questionnaire's all leading questions, so statistically, it's useless for qualitative analysis, then secondly she said women always get lower scores than men.'

'Really?' Glynn was intrigued.

'Lots of factors, apparently. More women than men fill in the questionnaires, and they tend to be biased towards the men they fancy.'

'Ah, that's why I always do so badly then,' Glynn moaned, and she smiled weakly before explaining further, 'Also, female lecturers are supposed to be endlessly nurturing and supportive, so any time you give a student a stern warning, or you're not being grateful for the privilege of teaching them, they think you're a bad lecturer. Whereas men are expected to be bastards, so any sign of humanity is taken as an indication of sainthood.'

'And of course, questionnaires are useless because true education only shows its value later in life,' he agreed.

'Oh I know, and I could just laugh it off, but when you've got someone who's using this stuff to get at you, it's hard not to take it personally. I need Hodders to write me a reference after this.' She looked up at him, wide-eyed, wiping away her smeared mascara.

'Come on,' he said, 'Let me you take you for a coffee. I hear there might even be cakes in Taylor's.' She shrugged and looked away. 'Oh, come on,' he said, 'to be honest, I'm having a really crap time lately. My girlfriend's freaking out and I don't blame her, but I don't know what to do. You're a woman, come on, be supportive and help me out.' She finally agreed, and he poured his heart out over a weak cup of coffee. She patted his arm comfortingly.

Nia was relieved to have survived her first morning at work. She spent hours in front of mirrors with her make-up, trying to hide the scars Matt and Glynn had caused. None of the customers had seemed to notice anything, so when Ruth had suggested she pop out to hunt for some change she'd agreed, and was feeling pleased to be coping so well as she headed back to Ethereal. Glynn's absence was still thudding in her head, but she had let Ruth assure her that Glynn would be feeling just as bad and that they'd work things out. As she passed Taylor's she saw Glynn sat in the window, smiling with a woman's hand on his arm. She felt the glass cutting her skin again, and all the bones in her hands and wrists fused together as she watched him until she was blinded by tears and ran back towards Ethereal. She felt sick and slumped against the side wall. She wanted to scream like a baby, hysterical when its mother dies, and it screams and screams but mother never comes back.

Chapter Ten

'How could you? How could you, you bastard?' Nia bawled at the image flickering above the globe. 'I saw you today with that slut. You go straight out and screw the nearest woman you can?'

'What?' Glynn spluttered. 'You threw *me* out, remember?'

'You fucking bastard!' She smashed the off-button, and he sat by the now-silent globe, shell-shocked. He remembered what Tricia had said over coffee, 'You're being an idiot, Glynn. Go round and apologise.' He'd shrugged, thinking maybe he'd go tomorrow, but after that 'phone call he wasn't sure. His pride reared up and he felt hurt by how little she trusted him.

Amira came round to see Nia and witnessed her waves of rage and despair with a quiet compassion. 'I'm sure there's nothing going on, Ni,' she said, 'I'm sure of it.'

'But he said he loved me,' she choked through her tears. 'It was just yesterday. And now … How. Could. He. Do. This?' Amira could only put her arm around her and try to tell her it would all be ok, but she shook with the force of Nia's misery. As she walked away to wait for the bus back to Crail, Amira kept hearing a line from a reading at the the small Christmas concert, 'I should be glad of another death.'

Glynn determined to get on with practical tasks, and was relieved his car was still functioning after its long hibernation when he bundled up the rabbits to visit the vet. There was a massive square marquee in the car park and the whole area looked like a show ground. He slowly manoeuvred through the crowd to the reception desk. 'Hello, Glynn!' he was greeted cheerfully. 'Didn't know you had pets.'

'Mary! What are you doing here?' He put the carriers on the makeshift desk.

'Doing my bit, you know? Don't worry, I don't actually treat the animals.'

'I should hope not, after that business at the aquarium,' he said knowingly, but she didn't rise to the bait, so he changed tack. 'May I present Lily and Barbie Hughes, here for their combined vaccination. We do have an appointment, but would you say we were in for a wait?'

'Ah, here you are,' Mary found the entry in the well-thumbed appointment book. 'Well, we're trying to see pre-booked clients quickly, but it's busy today. It might be a while. Don't stray too far. I'll give you a shout when Peter's free.'

Glynn looked around for a spot without too many dogs, and settled down against one of the marquee flaps, just within eyeshot of the desk. He looked into the carriers, 'Well, bunnies, I hope you appreciate the effort I'm putting in.' A small voice came from one side, 'Are they bunnies? We've got a bunny, but we've bringed our Harriet today. She's my guinea pig. She's feeling badly.' Glynn looked round and saw a small girl with red shoes looking at him fixedly. 'Are you with your mummy?' he said. She dashed off, 'Mammy, mammy, come and see the bunnies!' Moments later she re-appeared, stepping more gingerly around the cat basket. She was followed by a tall, tired woman carrying a cardboard box and a tiny baby. 'Mammy! Bunnies! Wee bunnies!'

'Hold your horses!' The woman slowly put down the box, sitting next to Glynn, 'You don't mind, do you?'

She's mad about them. I can't keep hold of the reins with these two, so we tend to go where she leads.'

Glynn smiled, 'What's wrong with Harriet?'

'She has a lump. Growing. I do feel daft struggling through all this for a guinea pig, but Moira worries. Best to get the vet to check her out, no?

'What are their names?' asked little Moira, who seemed less focused on her sick pet and more distracted by the novelty bunnies.

'Lily and Barbie.'

'Barbie,' she giggled, crinkling her nose. 'That a doll's name,' and she started rolling around, singing, 'I'm a Barbie girl, in a Barbie worororld.'

'Wow,' said Glynn. 'I haven't heard that one in years.'

'Lucky you,' replied her mother. 'You've picked up all sorts from your Auntie Kay, haven't you, Moira? She's still got a working CD player and loads of old discs.' She raised her eyebrows at Glynn, 'Anyway, why are you here?'

'Looking after them for my brother's kids. They're due vaccinations.'

'Good idea. It's high risk for myxi up here. Were you here a couple of years back when they had the big outbreak? Nasty. Are all of these animals ill?' she looked around. 'I can't believe it's so crowded. Are some of the vets off sick, d'you think?'

'I suppose so. Queues everywhere these days.'

'Tell me about it! We spent three hours yesterday queuing for petrol when they had a delivery. My husband's had to go to his mother's, major hypochondriac, and I have to take these two everywhere. Did you know the school's only taking them from seven? I thought Moira'd have been settled in school, well before this babbie came along.

Now, well, now I've got both of them all day long.'

'And now a sick guinea pig,' Glynn commiserated. She raised her eyebrows in reply, 'Och, I know lots of people are worse off than us,' she said, 'but it just seems to drag on. It's crazy. The councillors should be doing more about it, and our so-called government. Handing things over to London sounded all good and proper, but nothing seems to get far north of Leeds these days.'

Glynn nodded, and the conversation was drowned by an outbreak of barking from the other side of the car park. Little Moira remained gazing into the carriers until Glynn heard Mary calling his name. He looked up and saw her beckon him over. 'Well, I hope Harriet gets better soon,' he smiled, then picked up the carriers and made his way to the main door.

Inside the building the foyer was unnervingly quiet. A man in a green tabard came out and said, 'Lovely Lily and Biting Barbie, back again I see. And you're…?'

'Glynn, the uncle.'

'Ah, Felix's friend. I'm Pete Barnett. Pleased to meet you. Just come through, pop them up on the table. Great. Any less biting going on?'

'Not that you'd notice.'

'I told them to get them spayed, but I gather the father objects?'

'My brother. I could see that he might.'

'Never mind. Okay, let's do Lily first. Is this her?' he opened the carrier door, glanced across at the other carrier and said, 'Yes, I think it is. A more good-natured expression. Come on, sweetheart. What a lovely rabbit!' and he lifted Lily on to the table. 'Right, let's top you up!' After a quick injection, Pete

225

settled her back back in the cage, then said, 'I think I'll need you to help with Barbie, if you're up for it. Normally I have a nurse to help, but we're doing what we can.' As he opened the second cage there was a loud growl, followed by furious scrabbling. 'Well, this won't be dignified!' said Pete, as he firmly clamped his hand over Barbie's head and slowly inched her out. The minute he shifted his grip she twisted her head and tried to bite him. 'Whoah!' he said. 'Give us a hand!' When Glynn had Barbie firmly pinned with both hands, Pete drew up another syringe. 'Need to keep her still. Need to be precise. Have to get some in the skin, as well as the main injection.' He was swift and determined, and Glynn was relieved to get Barbie back in her carrier as quickly as he could. 'Thanks,' he said. 'My niece and nephew will be pleased.'

'Any time! Join me and Felix for a drink tonight, if you like. He's got some grand new plan to save the planet. More the merrier.'

'Yeah, if I can,' said Glynn. 'Shall I let your next patient in?'

'Ah, the endless stream of the suffering. And their pets. Just see Mary on the way out. See you tonight, maybe.'

The university exams were strange that year. Often there were more invigilators stationed at the desks than there were candidates. When Glynn went to collect one batch of scripts from the exam hall, he noted one student sitting on a beanbag, another with two friends sitting next to her, and a third who'd been placed at a desk at the very back of the hall so he could get up and pace around, occasionally returning to his desk to scribble a few sentences. The last few minutes of the exam ticked by, and let Glynn reflect cynically that at least the exam marking wouldn't be difficult. After another emergency meeting it had been decided that everyone should contribute one lecture and one seminar per week on a core subject for the next few months, and then it was up to individuals whether they offered anything else, at undergraduate level or just to the general public, depending on demand. Hobden was hopeful that at least some of the dissertation students would complete enough work to graduate in the summer. After the meeting Eilidh caught Glynn and Tricia in a corridor and said, 'You need to get your heads down and get on with your research. Do the teaching you have to, and if you think it'll help your C.V. do some other lectures, but don't kill yourself. You'll no get any thanks for it.'

'What about you?' Tricia was concerned.

'Ah, well, I'm going to give all my favourite lectures. Bob's doing the same. He's going to do 'Epistemology with Puppets' once a month. You're welcome to drop in.'

That evening in the Crown Glynn told Felix how the university was becoming more like a self-service cafeteria each week. He told him about the trip to the vets, before saying none too casually, 'So, how did you two meet?'

'My brother was at uni with his. Oh, it's not like that. More's the pity. His girlfriend left him a few months ago - she was a social worker up in Dundee, saw some really awful stuff, fell apart and poor Peter couldn't cope. So, I'm putting him up for a while.'

Pete arrived, his hands raw from disinfectant. He smiled wanly at Morag as she passed over a clandestine packet of pork scratchings, before he joined them at the table. 'Drich,' he said, staring into the foam on the top of his glass.

'Aye,' Felix replied.

'Not just the weather, mind you. This whole situation is so damn boring. Waterlogged. Like you just want to walk out and start again.' He started to stir the foam with his index finger.

'I've only ever walked out of a film before the end once,' Felix mused, 'but it was in Winnipeg and there was really nothing else to do at all, so walking out was quite an event.'

'What was the film?' Glynn enquired with brotherly solidarity.

'*The Terminal.* No, really. That appalling picture with Tom Hanks and Catherine Zeta Jones. God, it was worse than *Zorro*.' They paused as the magnitude of Felix's statement sunk in.

'So, plan to save the world, eh?' said Pete, without any real enthusiasm. 'How is the world, anyway?'

'Now the military's back in action, the heavy work's improving. No major epidemics, and the forced evacuation of town centres down south seems to have worked,' Felix stated flatly.

'And why was that again?' Glynn had been following the news, but wasn't sure about the bigger picture.

'Ah, well, as all the Southern isolationists in their swanky penthouses got stuck when the power cut out and the lifts didn't work,' Felix began to brighten up, 'you had miles of shops selling digital toast racks and chi-chi baby carts, but nowhere to buy a loaf of bread. They might have starved, been eaten by wild animals. Seriously, it got bad from what I've heard. Mind you, we've had it easy. They've cholera in Spain and Portugal.'

'So all those expats didn't make such a good move after all. Well, that's something,' Glynn grimaced.

'Medically, we seem to be over the immediate crisis. Suicide figures jumped at Christmas, as expected, but not dramatically, and once we get past Valentine's Day, we should be good.'

'Valentine's Day,' Glynn said heavily. 'Joy to the world.'

'Yeah, one more reason to kill yourself,' Pete sighed. 'A few years ago we had a cat left on our surgery door on Valentines's day. One of our patients, so we called the owner, and it turns out she'd topped herself, but had wanted the cat to be safe. She'd even left his favourite toy and instructions about what he liked to eat. Tragic.'

Glynn was horrified, and said in a higher pitched voice than he'd have liked, 'So, Felix, Pete tells me you have a plan to save the world?'

'Plan To Save The World. I just keep hearing, 'Oh aye, much better, doctor. I just don't feel quite meself, wee bit peelie-wallie, if you take my meaning.' People aren't throwing themselves out of windows so much. It's more they're settling into a low-level depression, functioning, but not quite right. I suspect the drugs have done all they can, but then … what's left?'

'Existential angst, you think?' Glynn tried to sound interested.

'Well, that wasn't the phrase on the tip of my tongue, but maybe. So much gets buried, and depression brings it all out to be aired.'

'And now it's oxygenated, it's hard to bury again, if I'm following the metaphor?'

Felix nodded listlessly, 'Yeah, I'm sure there's something poetic there about bellows on a coal fire, but I think I'm losing the thread. And the will to live. You're not a damn poet.'

'So what can be done?' Glynn asked the ether.

'I'm not sure there is anything. Did you see those old stamps they re-issued a few years ago? Cartoons, with a man in a doctor's, saying, 'Do you have anything for the human condition?' Counselling would help a lot of people, but overstretched is not the word. No-one's going to prioritise counselling for people who seem to be doing well on the drugs, back at work but a wee bit out of sorts. Okay,' Felix roused himself, and carried on in a more forceful tone. 'you know Laura, my friend at the WHO?'

'Ah, the angel who got me hospitalised?'

'That's the one. There's this new WHO survey, looking at people who are actually well, seeing what helps on a day-to-day basis in local communities. Turns out St Andrews isn't doing too badly at all, so they're coming here, survey, psychiatrists the lot. You both might get invited for an interview.'

'Not much good, that would be. I feel pretty shit right now,' Glynn grumbled.

'But miserable's not the same as depressed. So, the plan is to find out what really works and how we can pass on this useful information.' He took a swig from his glass. Glynn looked at his watch, then said, 'Hasn't that all been done? I mean surveys that show that forty minutes' exercise a day helps depression, that sort of thing?'

Pete grunted, 'Nazi fascist gym bunnies!' and Felix slumped further into his chair.

'Too theoretical, that's the point,' he said, 'not useful. Take exercise. Absolutely right, if you can take regular exercise it helps. Trouble is, it's a Catch-22. Some people can barely take a shower, let alone get down the gym for forty minutes a day. And some people who do it, actually feel worse because they get so stressed out by the whole business.'

'Too fucking right,' said Pete. 'Nazi gym bunnies.'

'So,' Felix continued, giving him a concerned glance, 'what we need are more specific ideas. Let's stay with the exercise thing; if forty minutes a day seems like a marathon, wouldn't it be more helpful if someone could say to you, 'What helps me is to decide I'll walk for a block, and if I feel ill I'll come home. Some days that's exactly what I do, and I only walk for about three minutes, but sometimes I feel better, and I do another block or twenty, and when I get back then I do feel a lot better.' Or maybe it helps to go on your exercise bike with a favourite film in the background.'

'So making suggestions, not being so prescriptive, you mean?' Glynn leaned in.

'Aye, and making it clear that these are not 'You should do this, you bad weak people', but other people trying to be kind and offer you something to help because they've been through it themselves.'

Pete and Glynn both pulled themselves together. 'That actually sounds like a good idea,' Glynn nodded.

'Agreed,' said Pete. 'Having a pet is damn good for you. I'd like to see that written in black-and-white somewhere. Count me in.'

'Me too. I'll get my students rallied, those that are still around, that is. So, now are you going to tell me about Rory.'

Felix glanced round to see they weren't overheard, 'It'll be in the papers soon enough, I imagine. You know there are a number of practices, but we've tended to centralise since the outbreak. There've been memos about treatment protocols, the schemes trying to get people well as quickly as they're able, and as cheaply as possible. Lots of them, especially from the CHLOE people. Mostly what you'd expect, form-filling, priority-setting. Anyway, when you told me about Rory I noticed something odd. The party line has been to use older anti-depressants first. Longer research history, better understood, that sort of thing. And generally cheaper. So that's how people like Rory got fobbed off on things that clearly weren't working. It's true that it can take weeks to see a difference, but basically we weren't encouraged to pick the most appropriate drug for the patient. Then it gets more complicated.'

He glanced around again before saying in a low voice, 'The memos about preferred treatments started advising that we prescribe one of the newest drugs on the market, Halvass. Being as it's new, it's odd to see it so readily endorsed. And when I looked into it further, turns out it costs nearly three times as much as the next on the recommended list, and before this happened it was only licensed for some very specific conditions, mainly some bipolar disorders. Someone is pushing this drug, and Halvass just happens to be made by Hal-Merchant.'

'WHAT?' Glynn shrieked, putting down his Babycham with a jolt. 'What? Are you telling me a pharmaceutical company engineered this 'flu bug so they could market a cure?'

'Not so fast, Sherlock,' Felix laughed bleakly. 'The truth, I fear, is less global conspiracy and more low-level greed and corruption. Final piece of the puzzle. Not all areas, even in Scotland, are recommending Halvass. The ones that are, they have one thing in common. Their CHLOE overlords, yes, you know it already, the overlords, like our very own Sir Leo and

Ally, are all shareholders in Hal-Merchant.'

'The drug's dangerous?' Glynn's hysteria calmed slightly.

'When not properly prescribed, absolutely. Anything that alters brain chemistry can be dangerous. Developing anti-depressants is a nightmare. You know depression often comes with exhaustion?' Felix paused as Glynn and Pete nodded, then continued, 'We think it's a sort of basic defence mechanism, to stop the body going ballistic as the mind struggles. In Rory's case, it caused tachycardia and mania, leading to a full-blown cardiac arrest. There've been at least eight other cases locally linked to the drug in the last couple of months. Basically, our senior CHLOE enforcer, who has no medical training, was looking to line her pockets. She was leaning on a harassed, overworked junior G.P. and helped her to prescribe a very expensive drug when it wasn't indicated. The good news is it's out in the open, and the Executive's planning an inquiry.'

'So Rory was right about a conspiracy,' Glynn let out a short whistle, then explained to Pete, 'He was sure something was going on. Mind you, he thought we were being taken over by oestrogen. What?' he said catching Felix looking away. 'What? You're going to tell us we *are* all being neutered?'

Felix grinned at the alarm on Glynn and Pete's faces, 'Not at all,' he said, 'just that Rory's right about one thing, there *are* more women in power now than there were before, but that's mostly because they've gritted their teeth and got on with it. We may be seeing a new world order growing, a new standard of what counts as physical strength. Anyway, I'd better get back. Spread the word about the survey, if there's a way you can. I think it's worth a shot. And it means we get some professional support round here for a week or two.' As Glynn moved to leave, Felix said, 'You and Nia had a fight?' 'I don't want to talk about it.'

'She's a good lass, she doesn't deserve your shit,' he said. 'Think about it.' Glynn promised to add it to his list.

After several months living in Scotland, Glynn had learned to think of Monet with more respect than he usually accorded the posters draped across student rooms. He could see first-hand how the changing light made you paint the same scene over and over. Every evening now he went for a walk on his own. As the dark rose around him, the snow stopped falling, and lay in blankets of light, charcoal pink along the Lade Braes. A new landscape of snow papered over the cracks. He saw a well-muffled couple on the path ahead of him, and heard a woman's voice say, 'Look! There's one! You could almost miss it, couldn't you? D'you remember last year? How you took those pictures, Harry? Look, just there.' As Glynn drew closer he could see that the man was frowning, looking into the distance towards the children's swings. Seeing Glynn approach, the woman took her companion's arm and turned to walk on. The snowdrop burst from the ice, stood firm, framed by brambles. The petals glared blue between green knives. As they passed, the woman gave Glynn a well-practised half-smile, but said nothing. He watched families sledding on Martyrs' Monument, and didn't know what to do.

She'd given him an ultimatum and now was blaming him for not choosing, and then he'd tried to get some advice from Tricia, and that apparently only made it worse. And now everyone was telling him he should apologise, but he didn't know what for. 'Alright,' he thought, 'let's think about this rationally. Who knows what's going on? Well, probably Ruth, but she'd probably castrate me. Abi, maybe, but this is all too damn close. Erica, and how do I start that conversation?' After mulling this over for several days he decided the least painful option would be to talk to Amira, so he threw caution to the wind and drove to Crail.

The snow had been cleared along the main roads, but was still knee-deep as he struggled down from the car park. He took a deep breath before knocking, and adopted what he hoped was a serious, genuine face. He heard laughter as the door opened. Amira was barefoot, wearing a white cotton dressing gown. 'Am I interrupting?' he said, taking a step backwards.

'No, no,' she said, opening the door wider, 'we're just finishing.'

'Oh, I *am* interrupting!' He took a further step back.

'No, no,' she laughed. 'Come on in. Really, I'm having my portrait done.'

'Oh. Great,' he rocked back and for, then followed her inside.

In the shadowed half of the room he saw a picture-perfect pose, a woman with dark curls leaning back on a stool and contemplating a canvas by the window. She looked over at him and smiled.

'Glynn,' Amira welcomed him, 'meet Marcie. A rising star from Canada who has taken on the ridiculously small commission of painting me. A great act of kindness.'

'No, Mira, it's your kindness to me,' said Marcie. 'It's such a beautiful place to work. Hi!' she greeted him warmly, 'You're Nia's friend, am I right? Pleasure to meet you. I wondered if we'd meet, while I was here.'

'Good to meet you too, Marcie.' They shook hands, and he said, 'Is that the picture?'

'It sure is. Not quite finished, but if Mira don't mind, you can take a peek. I always welcome an objective view.'

'Go ahead,' said Amira. 'It'll be up on a wall soon enough. Go on! You can laugh at my vanity, but when I get to sixty I want to look back on a wrinkle-free version.'

'I'm no art critic …' Glynn said as Marcie turned the easel round to face him. 'Wow! That's amazing!' He looked more closely, then stepped back, 'It reminds me of something. Should it?'

'It has many creative influences,' said Marcie, 'but probably what you can see, being British, is the echo of a the Hepworth sculptural style, combined with a little European twist.'

'Yeah, I don't know how to describe it.' Had he been forced to articulate it, being a verbal person Glynn would probably have struggled to explain in the canonical thousand words. He might have noted indications of a classical nude, fragments in perfect alignment, Amira lying on her couch, the curve of an arm, the Venus rings highlighted around the neck, the flexing ankle, her smile. The rest of the form was hidden by a barely defined shimmer, a pale translucent blue and green, dragonfly wings. All the soft shapes were enclosed in a tilted, three-dimensional egg, angled to reveal the copper green gold running inside the grey stone outer edge, a metallic injection to a pebble. The picture appeared to be made of multiple textures: cold granite, warm metals, flesh, water, yet sharing the same movement, suspended for one instant on the canvas. If he came to write down his impressions, Glynn would probably have wanted to use an old fountain pen, but standing there before the picture, his response was one of still, wordless admiration. His greatest praise was the desire to look, which was only slowly overtaken by embarrassment. 'It's lovely,' he said, and he turned away, moving the conversation to less physical subjects. Marcie went to make coffee, and Amira gestured for him to pull a chair towards the fire. As he stared into the sparks flying from odd bits of timber and sea coal, Amira said, 'So, you'll be wanting to ask me what to do?'

'Pathetic, eh? I swear to you there's nothing going on with Tricia. I just want things back the way they were.'

'Glynn,' she said slowly, 'she was violently attacked. That sort of trauma lasts. Quite apart from the fact it was your own brother who did it.'

'So what can I do? She wants me to cut him dead, but he's family!'

'And he's a violent man who caused her serious harm. I know she's not thinking straight, but you have to accept this might not work out. She has to be able to trust you.'

'I'd never hurt her!'

'You just *have* hurt her! I know you didn't mean to, but it's of no consequence. She needs someone who can put their own needs aside for a while and look after her. If you can't do that, then you need to give her space, or you'll just end up hurting her more.'

'My head hurts,' he moaned. 'This is such a mess.'

Marcie came back in with coffee and maple syrup, 'Duty Free shops still had the weirdest items for sale, business is strange,' she shrugged. 'Glad I could get here. My boyfriend got stranded here, but he liked it, so I bartered my way onto a flight.' Glynn gratefully accepted the coffee and asked about the situation in Canada. After a few minutes, he drained his cup and said, 'I've taken up too much of your time. Thanks. I'll think about what you said.'

'Good,' said Amira coming to the door, 'but don't go sitting in café windows with attractive single women any more. Seriously, Glynn, you'd be surprised how little effort it takes to be kind, thoughtful and caring – that's all she needs.' He drove home, muttering, 'It wasn't as though I was locked in a juicy snog with her, or anything.' He was a little encouraged by the conversation, but a new layer of guilt was forming over his heart. Marcie finished the portrait, and she and Amira talked into the night about failures of communication.

Then the team of psychiatrists arrived, and Glynn encouraged his students to fill in the questionnaire during his first lecture of the week. It was a long form, with different sections to complete, depending on your current state of health. He studied his form over coffee with Tricia in her office, and was pleased to see there was at least space for comments, unlike the university tickbox versions. 'Mind you, I'd like to have seen it,' Tricia laughed. 'My state of mental health is a: Excellent, b: Not Excellent, c: Don't know. I try to kill myself, a: Always, b: Sometimes, c: Never.'

'I've been invited for an interview,' he said, without meeting her eye.

'Well, you should go. Just make sure you don't get hauled in to give blood again. You didn't look so hot last time, remember? No-one could forget that.'

'Ooh, don't remind me,' he moaned, hand on head. 'Which is worse, do you think? Seeing a psychiatrist or a phlebotomist?'

Tricia looked up and said sweetly, 'Don't suppose it matters if you're feeling bloody awful.'

'Terrible!' he groaned. 'No more puns, or the biscuit supply dries up!' He left a few on her desk on the way out.

The town was buzzing with the arrival of the WHO survey team. Nia heard about it from her regular customers who continued to visit even though stock was running low. When Amira came round for lunch she jauntily made her promise not to mention the survey - anything for a new topic of conversation. Amira perched on the edge of the sofa. 'So,' she said, 'stupid question, but how are you feeling?' Nia's mask slipped and she started to cry again, feeling force of the throw, the blow, the insult of rejection. Most of us take each punishment, each judgement and walk away, but the sentence is only suspended. Sometimes there comes a final rejection, a final judgement which rolls all the previous convictions into one. Nia saw her lifetime imprisonment behind and ahead of her – every slight, every mistake she'd made, or suffered, projected from the past into the future. Glynn hadn't rejected her, she was a reject. The relationship hadn't failed, she was a failure. Not loved, so unloveable. While Amira looked on helplessly, she sobbed, 'I just can't bear this. I had this one chance to put my life right and I blew it, I wasn't good enough. I wish I could rip my self up, start again. I'm no use to anyone.'

Amira tried to reason with her. She argued that the view of one man was not a good basis for a choice of sandwich, let alone a sensible foundation to base your whole self-image upon, particularly when that man sang Elton John songs in the shower, alone.

Glynn wasn't Mr. Perfect, it wasn't her fault, but soon Amira realised that Glynn wasn't really the problem. Recent events had triggered off a whole set of memories, rising like a hydra. When Nia seemed calmer, she said to her gently, 'Glynn came to see me, typical bloke really, looking for help to understand the mysteries of the female psyche.'

'What did you tell him?'

'Nothing much. Told him he was an idiot, and that I thought that brother of his was a menace.'

'What did he say?'

'Asked me what he should do.'

'And?'

'I told him you needed time. I hope that was the right thing to say, non-committal. I told him I'd tell you he'd called by.'

'Thanks,' Nia got up and watered the plants on her windowsill. Amira waited for a few moments, then said, 'I do think he cares about you.'

'Not as much as he cares about his brother. Oh, I don't know. It's such a mess,' Nia sat back down heavily on the sofa. 'I mean, I'm trying to stay calm, I'm taking herbs, I'm trying to meditate, but it's too much. They're such bastards.'

'Hey, come on,' Amira comforted her. 'You've had a terrible time. You're bound to be upset.'

'It's not just Glynn, it's all of it. It all feels so chaotic, but maybe there's a pattern.'

'Boy meets Girl. Boy acts like idiot?'

'No, fate or something. Maybe I'm just not seeing it.'

'That sounds dangerously theoretical to me. Maybe you should take philosophy? When you get back to college?' Amira gently tried to add a note of optimism to the conversation, but Nia was stuck in her distress, and replied, 'And end up like Bob, mad

Bob, the great philosopher, Dr. Q? No way! I may not even go back. Why do you think I'm going back?'

'No reason. I just think you will. Anyway, Bob may be peculiar, but he's still going strong. Wife and child, a job he loves. There are worse ways to be.'

'Does Dr. Q know the meaning of life, I wonder?' Nia smiled, 'but I doubt it's the philosophy. The other tutors all seem to be perpetually miserable and multiple divorcees to boot.'

'Oh well, maybe not philosophy. Or maybe not university. You do have all these options, Nia. I know it doesn't feel like it, and this business with Glynn is horrible, but you might look back one day and see it as just a blip in your long, successful life.'

'When I'm accepting my Pulitzer Prize, you mean?

'Who knows? Who knows?' Amira said, relieved that Nia could at least contemplate a brighter future.

'Okay, give her time, give her time,' Glynn said to himself several times an hour, as he stopped himself from 'phoning Nia or calling by the shop. Determined to be of some use to someone he went to visit Rory, who was due to be released in a few days' time. He found him looking alert and more talkative than before. 'Hey, you just missed Bob!' Rory greeted him cheerfully.

'Really? What did you talk about?'

'The pandemic. You know he's researching bird migration? Turns out there's this theory that the virus came from space.'

'Bob told you this? Real 'It Fell From the Sky' stuff?'

'Aye. Seems the Himalayas are the first place the atmosphere picks it up, and then you get birds carrying it, which is why most epidemics start in Asia. Cool, no?'

'I suppose.'

'That's why,' Rory continued, 'or so they say, the 1918 epidemic started simultaneously in lots of different places. It actually fell in lots of places. Mind you, this time we brought it on ourselves with all the air travel, like.'

Glynn pulled up a chair and was about to offer Rory some contraband fruit pastilles, when his attention was distracted by the projected images on the wall.

'You've got an internet connection! How d'you get that?'

'Hospital perks. They asked me what I wanted to do, and I told them I wanted to write.'

'So, pen, paper?'

'Nah, this is online fan fiction. Who d'you think got the super servers back up? The fan communities, that's who.'

Glynn leaned over and peered at the screen:

His fingers took the place of his lips, and he kissed his way back up her still-quivering body.

'Quite a hors d'oeuvre. And interesting background music.'

He reached her neck and pressed her harder against the door. As he felt her temperature shoot up and her breathing grow shallow again he pulled back, 'Oh, don't stop!' she cried. 'Oh, I don't intend to,' he smiled smugly. He pushed her back again and thrust into her, pulling her up on tiptoes, 'I ... don't... intend to stop. I ... don't ... intend to stop until you're screaming again.' She dug her fingers into his shoulders, as he licked her neck and continued, 'And I might not stop even then.' As she shuddered and whimpered against him, he had to drop the mask, and as he looked into her fluttering eyes he said breathlessly, 'I can't ever stop now. I fact, I don't think I could stop this now even if a fleet of Goa'uld mother ships was bearing down and this was the end of the world.'

'Oh my god,' Glynn cackled. 'You're writing *Stargate* porn!'

'No,' Rory said mildly. 'I'm just adding some pictures, favour for a friend in South Africa. Their image hosting's not too hot yet.'

'And have you actually met him, this friend?'

'Her.'

'HER?'

'All the best hard core stuff's done by women.' He looked a little puzzled, but nowhere near as puzzled as Glynn whose lower jaw was hanging open. Rory looked back at the screen, 'Some of it's because the women want more background, context, romance, that sort of stuff, but you get through fifteen pages of narrative and then it's …, well …, creative? Dynamite, really.'

Rory was lost in his own thoughts and peered at the screen, 'Some of it's rubbish, as you'd expect, but this is J.T.'s stuff and I asked her, 'If you can write like this, why not just cut to the chase, and not write all the chitchat?' and she said, 'If you want the paint finish to be right, you have to spend most of your time on preparation.' She's an amazing woman.'

'Amazing, as in nymphomaniac?'

'No, no. J.T.'s got three bairns. Her author profile has a recipe for muffins. Look,' He scrolled through the last five-thousands words of the story, 'These are just ordinary women.' Glynn didn't like the sound of that. Rory said, 'I'll make us a brew', and left the author bio on the screen. Glynn sat down gingerly, and couldn't resist the last paragraph of the story above the author info:

'She waited until he was on his last gulp of water then said casually, 'I never expected you'd be so talkative.'

He choked as she'd intended, and spluttered, 'ME? ME?

And what about all the X-rated stuff coming out of that delicious little mouth?'

She looked at him with an amused, feigned ignorance.

'Oh, gone coy now, have we? Well,' he settled his head on to her chest and traced circles on her hips, 'maybe I'm not the only one whose memory's failing, because I distinctly remember someone saying 'Touch me until I'm screaming.'

Then there was a recipe for blueberry muffins and an invitation to email the author with suggestions for keeping small boys occupied on rainy afternoons.

Rory brought over a mug and said with a rueful smile, shaking his head at the screen, 'Preparation apparently. I'd happily do *thirty* pages of narrative to get that sort of result, I can tell you, but I'm more into the action stuff. *51 Traitors.*' He clicked on a link. 'Transfer the jump point to St Andrews, write the story, then I can work in all the local shots.'

'Hey, that's good,' said Glynn, still a little dazed, as a stylised image of three alien guards lurking outside St. Salvator's appeared on the screen.

'I'll print this one out for you,' Rory said, 'I've had some good reviews.' The printer whirred.

'Wow, like the old days, being able to print off the internet,' Glynn was impressed. 'Won't be long 'til we're getting our car and tax bills by email again.'

'Doubt it,' said Rory. 'Entertainment, socialising's one thing, but finance, government, I doubt it. So much was lost for good when the system crashed, I doubt there'll be much confidence. Even these connections are patchy.'

After a cup of tea Glynn rolled up the printed pages and left Rory to his illustration. He didn't tell Rory that he was combining visits, going to to the newly-established, Norwegian / New Zealand mental health outpost. The psychiatrist he saw was friendly but distant, and Glynn was disorientated. Sometimes the questions demanded a simple 'Either/Or' answer, (Do you feel better after eating? Is the image clearer on the red or the green?), but sometimes the answer provoked a longer discussion, as when he was asked whether he generally felt more positive when he woke up or as the day wore on. As this was a simple one to answer (I often wake up feeling crap, but tend to feel better once I get going), Glynn was surprised it merited further exploration. By the time that question finished he'd discussed his sensitivity to light and the best form of alarm clock. He'd agreed to the proposition that he would work more effectively if his day could start at lunchtime, but didn't see much chance of any career offering him that option, although the next generation might get it. As students, they were managing to control what they did or didn't do with a simple note from a doctor saying, 'X has problems', so maybe they'd receive the same treatment when they came to paid employment. Somehow Glynn doubted it, and it gave him some satisfaction to think of his laziest students getting fired from jobs for turning up without their presentation because their hamster had died.

The unit was arranged so individuals arrived through one door and left through another, so it was a matter of chance that Glynn saw Eilidh and Emily walking into the grounds. 'Tricia said you'd been summoned. How was it?' she asked, uncomfortably. 'You know, lots of ink blots. They let me go, that's the main thing.'

'I, oh, ' Eilidh paused. 'Could you not tell Bob you've seen us? I haven't told him, yet. They're only seeing seven-year-olds up, but Felix got a slot for Emily, my piece of mind, to tell the truth. I'll tell Bob once we get back, but I'd appreciate it, if you didn't mention anything for now.'

'Of course. Is everything alright?'

'I think so. But I'll feel better, you know?'

'Sure. You could call in to see Rory. He's on good form. Oh, but make sure he switches off the computer before Emily has a look.' He smiled at her puzzled look and went back to work.

A few days later, Glynn 'phoned the main line in John Burnet Hall, and saw Rory's cheery grin appear.

'So, you're back home?'

'Yeah, chucked me out now they've had their fun. Terrible timing, you know Valentine's Day. Half of them swooning over bunches of flowers, and the other half contemplating suicide because they've no sweetheart.'

'I sent her a card.'

'Which one?' Rory said, genuinely confused.

'Which one? Whatcha mean, which one?' Glynn cried. 'Nia!'

'And?'

'She didn't send me one.'

'And you're surprised?'

'Perhaps I should have sent chocolates as well.'

'Hmm.'

Glynn waved the printout at him, 'Anyway. This is good. Why don't you write a real novel?'

'Too much pressure,' Rory waved it away. 'This way you've got the characters, speech patterns, models to work with. You can just relax and have fun. And you don't get people speculating about which bits are the real you, you know? Mind you, people get a bit antsy if you make their favourite figures do things they're not expecting, or don't like.'

'That alien prison guard who had his eye out, was that based on Hodders?'

'Too obvious?'

Glynn laughed, 'Not really, it was just something about the way he turned his head in surprise that gave it away. Anyway, I'm sure lots of writers use their work to put the world to right. And you obviously can't go round taking advantage of your subordinates when you're stranded in space.'

'That's it. I never go for anyone gratuitously. Just putting right a few wrongs, the pea-splittin' injustices that make life such a struggle. And I did just kill him off painlessly. It's out of respect, really. Now wait 'til you see what I've got planned for good ol' Noel.'

'God, mate, you're sounding more like a writer by the minute.'

'Thanks. Some people have published with proper ISBNs, but who knows in this new world order. Have you seen the *Chronicle* headline?' Glynn shook his head and his eyes widened as Rory held up the front page to the 'phone: Psychiatrist Says: Our Children are Crazy.

Chapter Eleven

Nia looked at the handmade card on her mantelpiece, trying to re-interpret the phrase, 'Lots of love, Glynn.' Stumped, she looked at the front page of the *Chronicle*: 'Psychiatrists Say: Our Children are Crazy.' Within days of the first round of interviews, there had been so-called 'leaks', and it seemed the child psychologist had expressed concerns about the mental health of *all* the children she'd interviewed. They'd all been very polite and working hard at school, but when pressed they tended to exhibit deep-seated fears about household objects, and obsessions with sharks and similar livestock. An emergency CHLOE meeting was called and the new liaison supremo tried to calm everyone's nerves. Most of the parents wanted to know what they could do to help their children, but a few disputed the results of the survey, claiming they were seeing problems where none existed.

The child psychologist spoke in elegant English, confused at people's reactions. She explained that depression often manifests differently in children, and that as they have very few options in life, they often apply themselves to their academic work, the one area where they can exert some control. She continued to explain that many of the children were showing signs of repressed anxiety, manifesting in sudden outbursts, night terrors or physical symptoms such as asthma or bed-wetting. Although some cases could be linked to existing family traumas, in most cases there was no apparent trigger and the change in behaviour had been subtle, after an episode of 'flu. She reported global concerns that an entire generation might grow up to be highly successful academically but suffering from serious emotional problems. The town had just begun to hope that the world was righting itself, and now there was a vision of a future where all the adults were dysfunctional, damaged, unable to maintain a stable society, scarred by a childhood illness no less debilitating than the physical problems an earlier generation carried after polio. Combined with new warnings about antibiotic resistance, the long-term future began to look very dark.

The psychologist promised that the problem would be addressed, and spoke of an action pack, which would be distributed to schools. In the meantime, she advised parents to stick to a routine as far as possible, but to encourage their children to discuss any difficult issues that had arisen, such as the death of a family member. She said that medication would not normally be appropriate for children, but that fresh air and healthy exercise could do wonders. Most parents left the room feeling encouraged, if a little guilty.

The classrooms in the university were re-organised again, as the CHLOE team established counselling centres for all age groups. The decision to ignore the under-sevens was revised, and it was decided that two days a week there would be classes for four-to-seven year olds, with one day for nursery age children. The rate of pay for teachers was quietly raised again, as the BRP struggled to find enough qualified people to cope. As public transport became more reliable, Abi agreed to take on more hours, bringing the children with her from Dundee three days a week, until they could sort out accommodation in town. As the bus stopped to collect people from Leuchars, Abi wondered whether she should have brought the children with her. They were sitting quietly in the seat in front of her, playing cards. She'd promised they'd see Matt today, if he was well enough, but wasn't looking forward to the encounter.

She shrank towards the window as an older woman settled herself into the seat beside her. She unbuttoned her tweed jacket, and put her small black hat on top of one of her bags. Then she pulled out two small, pink, satin ballet shoes and placed them on her hat as she continued to rummage in the bag. She swapped the shoes for a Dickensian notebook, and unclipped the pen from the front cover. Out of the corner of her eye Abi watched the woman carefully write something at the bottom of a page filled with numbers. The woman started as if she were an old friend, 'I'm not sure what to believe, but it doesn't seem to be getting better.' Abi murmured her general assent. 'Have you heard the latest?' the woman continued, shutting the notebook and re-attaching the pen. 'They say the infrastructure's getting back to normal, but I don't see much sign of it here. Can I get an examiner to come from Edinburgh? No, I cannot.'

'An examiner?' Abi played along.

'Daarnce,' said the woman. 'I've kept the classes going for the girls – their parents thought the stability was good for them, so things have been jogging along. But now, we've had one delay after the other. I can't get an examiner for the girls to take their exams, and the parents feel it's no use continuing. As if exams were the only thing that counted.'

'That must be very difficult for you.'

'My dear, you can't imagine. It's not well-paid work

at the best of times, but there is a certain, well, creative satisfaction,' the woman briefly smiled, before her frustration returned. 'Now I'm reduced to seeing the whole business in economic terms, and it's not a pleasant position. I'm having to supplement my income with work from the CHLOE team, although I hear most of them are in disgrace.'

It seemed to be Abi's day for unwanted chance encounters. After a long, irritating bus journey, and a soggy walk through town, she was trapped with nowhere to go as she saw unwelcome neighbours, Gary and Denise Rogers, strolling towards her, wearing matching cream fisherman's sweaters. 'So good to see you out and about!' said Denise, air-kissing her, 'So brave!' Abi nodded and tried to move past, but Denise stopped her, looking at the children. 'How is Robbie now? This can't be easy for him, after failing that reading test last summer.'

'Actually, Denise, you can't fail a reading test at that age.'

'Yes, yes,' she soothed.'That's what we say to Gavin. He's always saying 'Did Keira score as high as this when she was my age?' and I tell him not to think of it like that, but it's natural for boys, isn't it?'

Her patience fraying, Abi said, 'And how have you two been helping out with all the relief efforts? Haven't seen you around much?'

'We've been putting the children first,' said Gary sombrely. 'They're very forward, not at all disturbed by all this business.'

'Must be harder when your children were already falling behind,' Denise simpered sympathetically.

'Must go. I have a class to take.'

'Oh, they're letting you teach?' said Denise.

'Aye, that's because I'm a teacher,' Abi snapped back. 'I've been an Assistant Teacher myself,' Denise said, and Abi finally cracked, saying quite brusquely, 'No, actually, I think you were a teacher's assistant. I have a PGCE and a Scottish conversion qualification. Now if you don't mind, I have to get to work.'

She could hear them adjusting their self-satisfied sweaters as she stormed into the main quad, and was working up quite a head of steam by the time she'd settled Becky in the playroom and seen Robbie into his first class. Trying to collect her thoughts for her own day, she was taken aback to see Glynn as she walked into the makeshift staff room. 'You're white,' she said coming over and looking at him carefully. 'What's happened?'

'Got roped in,' Glynn said, clearly relieved to see her. 'Said they'd only be a few minutes and could I look after the class? I sat them down to read a story, there were only ten of them, and I said to the one in the front, 'That's a nice bag, is it Peter Rabbit?' Then one of the other ones piped up 'Robbie Hughes has a rabbit!' and it was like an avalanche. They all wanted to tell me things about rabbits, and when one of them said, 'We had rabbit pie last night,' half of them started crying and then they started hitting each other.' He laid his hand dramatically on his forehead.

'What did you do?' she smiled.

'Mrs Pertwie came back. She shouted 'Sit down at once!' and they did, but I did too. Then she snapped, 'Not you, you fool!' Turns out she wasn't talking to me. Lost all my authority there.' Abi tried not to laugh, as Glynn continued, 'Oh, she got over it, she was very nice in the end, said she hadn't seen me, she thought the kids were all alone, or she wouldn't have come in like that. That was really embarrassing.'

'Maybe you'd better stick to the big ones,' Abi grinned. 'Hard work, the wee beasties.'

'Hell, I'd need danger money to go back in with those eight-year-olds again. Perhaps I'd be better off with the little 'uns doing, 'Wheels on the Bus',' Glynn moaned.

'No,' she cautioned. 'Don't be fooled. The smaller they are, the worse they are.'

'Oh, like hamsters.'

'Maybe,' Abi was a little thrown by the comparison, so returned to the topic at hand. 'I'll see you tonight. Off to do *Romeo and Juliet* with a bunch of fourteen-year-olds who think it's all fanciful to do mad things for love. And they don't understand the 'Modern English translation' anymore than the Shakespearean text. We need it in Scots.'

'Ah, and Juliet cries 'Keep away fae they windys, Romeo', would she?'

Abi cringed, saying 'That's meant to be Scottish?'

'Oh, I'm hurt,' he pouted.

'I know, you've had a bad day, now run along, ma wee man!'

The teaching gave Abi a chance to focus her mind, and after several challenging sessions she stepped back out into the salt-tinged air and breathed deeply, ready to listen to her own children's narratives as they walked over for their meeting with Matt. 'Oh heaven', she sighed, seeing Matt's glassy stare as she approached McGregor's. She had asked Finn to join them, and she saw his Land Rover parked at a safe distance. She beckoned him over, and Matt caught sight of them. Matt threw his arms wide open, 'Hey, superstars!' he shouted, as Robbie and Becky ran to him. Finn and Abi took a table on the other side of the room, where they could keep an eye out for trouble, but Matt ignored them and seemed set on amusing the children with gifts. The hour passed without incident, and Abi was just about to breathe a sigh of relief when Robbie said at the door, 'Daddie's all well now, so we'll be going home.'

'Not tonight, hen,' she said trying to move them on.

'Oh, come on, love,' said Matt. 'For the children's sake. I know I need to apologise. I've been ill.'

'We are not talking about this here.'

'Then they're coming home with me, and you can high-tail it back to Dundee.'

'No. They're staying with me.'

'I don't think so,' Matt picked Becky up, not noticing her quivering lip, and took Robbie's hand. 'We'll be alright, won't we son?'

'Aye,' the boy said nervously.

Abi clenched her fist at her side, 'You're in no fit state to look after them. You said yourself, you're ill.'

'I said I've *been* ill. I'm fine now. I'm going to take care of my children.'

Becky started to cry and as he approached from the other side of the square, Glynn saw Matt reluctantly hand her over to Abi as he came up behind the group. He heard Finn say, 'Let's leave this for now, Matt. Come on, Robbie lad.' Robbie stayed by his father's side. 'Come on,' Finn said again. 'You can sit in the front seat. Don't want to leave Becky all on her own, d'you?' With a furtive spurt, Robbie pulled his hand out of Matt's, and ran to Abi's side. 'You bastard!' Matt yelled and took a swing at Finn. With the advantage of sobriety, he neatly dodged the blow and pinned Matt against the wall. 'In the car!' he shouted to Abi, who hurried the crying children away. Glynn wasn't close enough to hear what Finn said before releasing him, but half the town heard the rage of insults Matt threw after him, 'You bastard! What are you, some kind of idiot? Can't see she's playing you? She's losing her mind, going nuts, making stuff up about me.' As the Land Rover pulled away he screamed, 'I'll get you, you bitch! Nobody takes my kids from me. I'll make you wish you'd never been born!'

Glynn pressed himself into a stone wall, out of sight, and stayed there for a long time, ignoring the stares from passers-by, until the blocks were cutting into his shoulder blades and he was sure Matt would have gone.

He was calmer by the time he got home. The stars were bright and he steadied himself by tracing the constellations. 'Okay,' he said to himself as he lit a fire, 'you screwed up your relationship because of your fraternal loyalty, so why aren't you being more fraternally loyal?' He'd taken Matt out for a drink shortly after Abi'd left, and had called when he could, but he wasn't sure they were really communicating. Matt kept insisting everything would be alright, and that Abi would be back. Taking a deep breath he rang Matt who was now several sheets to the wind and greeted Glynn's face with cheerful confusion. 'Not just a brother,' he rambled, 'A friend. And friends are good. Friends are happy. Are you happy? You've always been there for me, mate and I appreciate it. Good, happy people.' He swayed back and for, and Glynn wondered what exactly he'd been drinking. Making what little sense he could of Matt's conversation, he promised he'd ask Abi to bring the children back, but was still shaking slightly when he cut the connection. He threw some old water-damaged books on to the fire, and sat enjoying the blaze by in the makeshift fireplace, enjoying the heat and the light, as he let the rabbits in and watched them stretch out their back legs on the hearth rug, toasting their soft, white bellies in the shifting firelight.

While Matt was plunging into a hell of his own making, the town was starting to make progress. With reliable electricity and 'phone connections, normal routines were being established and the pace of change seemed more predictable. There had been few suicides reported since the New Year, and even those who were still walking round in shock, like Julie after Jon's funeral, were still functioning in some limited capacity. Glynn only realised that the ambient state of emergency has lessened when he saw it roar back into life a few days later. He'd been happy with his last lecture, which had been attended by a good range of town-and-gown enthusiasts, and he was enjoying a brief, controlled, adrenalin high when he found a group of anxious students camped outside his office door and down the stairs. He'd caught odd phrases all morning about some disaster in the US, but had put it down to the usual, unreliable rumour mill. The truth began to drown him when the first student to see him cried out, 'Dr. Hughes! You're a geologist. They're saying there's been a huge earthquake and tidal wave in America, the Pacific North West.' The students waited for his reply. 'The Cascadia Subduction Zone?' he said cautiously, and the group started moaning.

'So it's true?' one of the girls screamed. 'My sister's in Los Angeles. How bad will it be? They're saying it's worse than China.'
'Look, I don't know anything,' Glynn stammered, 'I'm just saying there's a big fault line off the West Coast which has been on everyone's watch list. Sorry,

I have no idea whether anything's happened. It might all be a false alarm. Look, come down to the common room, I'll try to find out what's happening.'

He found Tricia and asked her to stay with the students while he investigated. He 'phoned the Memorial Hospital, but they wouldn't let him talk to anyone, so he called Rory who went round in person to find an internet connection. When he came back to Glynn's office an hour later his face was drawn.

'So, it's true then?'

'Seems like,' Rory said, rubbing his bloodshot eyes, traces of tears still on his cheeks. 'Can't contact anyone on the edge of the West Coast. Best I can make out, there was a huge shift in the Cascadia fault and then the tsunamis hit. I've spoken to Meryl, she's inland, North East of Vancouver, and she's only had bits of information, but Seattle and Vancouver are still standing.'

'They're on inland waterways,' Glynn said slowly, 'Everywhere else, depends on the locality and magnitude, but could be casualties into the hundreds of thousands, millions maybe, not much help coming.'

'Looks like it,' Rory murmured.

'That's it, then,' Glynn said. 'I'll tell the students.'

Suddenly Glynn and Hobden were in a glare of publicity. After the Met. Office was overwhelmed with requests for information about earthquakes, the government in London issued a general call to the CHLOE teams to improve the state of the nation's scientific understanding, specifically to explain that 'Weather' wasn't the same as 'Geology'.

The local team had suggested the university should provide public talks on the disaster, with such information as they could gather, and the talks were so popular they had to be given each day for a week. Glynn suspected some people were coming for the novelty, as they might go to see a science fiction film, but he was touched by the amount of compassion still to be found in a town struggling with its own demons. Although a few strident voices from one of the churches tried to present this natural disaster as a punishment for loose-living hippies on the West Coast, most people donated money to charity, and took time to care for those who now had missing relatives. The inconveniences of food rations and local government procedures seemed insignificant as people contemplated the pictures which started to make it into the *Scotsman*. Whole towns smashed to pieces, families trying to pick food out of stinking dustbins, cities in ruins.

At the start of the third lecture Glynn saw Nia in the back of the hall and had to wrench back his concentration when it was time to take over from Hobden. The first half of the lecture was a mechanical survey of the geological situation, the general explanation of the Cascadia subduction zone and its place in geological timelines. Glynn's section was a reconstruction of what they thought had happened, with limited information from the monitoring sites, as an 8.5 mag. earthquake caused shock waves over thousands of miles, triggering waves which rose to over seventy feet high. From the scattered information coming through it seemed that the waves had reached up to four miles in land, overwhelming cities from Vancouver to south of Los Angeles, as waves spread out to hit Hawaii and Japan. Questions always started with the dry, illogical outrage about how this could have possibly happened, before the personal consequences came to the fore. Glynn found himself being asked disturbing questions about what people would have experienced when the waves came, did it hurt, and what would happen next.

He struggled to answer the simple, 'What were anyone's chances of survival?' He told people that there was a good chance in some areas, and that he had heard directly from survivors in Vancouver, but he didn't know whether he was causing more pain by holding out false hope. In the morning when he ran along the West Sands Glynn noticed a sharp drop in the numbers on the beach, as if a superstitious fear of the water was keeping people away. He'd explained in his lecture that the aftershocks from Cascadia had largely died down, and that Fife was not in any danger from this catastrophe, nor likely to be hit by anything similar, but the debris scattered by the spring storms floated menacingly on the waves, a reminder of how fragile human existence could be.

The new-found celebrity brought more students back into the Geography and Geology departments, and Hobden started talking about a field trip or two. Unfortunately, most of the students found their interest waning when they realised there was lots of chemistry involved, and the answer to the question, 'How do you stop a volcano from erupting?' was 'You Don't.' After long days of impossible questions, Glynn was exhausted. One morning he'd given in to the need for comfort and called Nia, but she'd only reluctantly spoken to him. He'd managed to say something callous which made her cry, and she'd hung up on him. He called Matt that evening, and in his weakened state he'd ignored Matt's grunted lack of concern, grousing about how upset Nia was and how he didn't know what to do. He knew there was a note of reproach in his voice, and that Matt's drunken brain was unlikely to say anything kind in response, but he was too tired to keep up the pretence.

Matt's voice changed. It overtook Glynn like an eclipse. The light drains away, the temperature drops and silence rises up from the earth. He could hear Matt's voice contorting as he sneered, 'You don't know what you're talking about. *I* am the one who's suffering here. You're just like the rest of them. A spineless, whining cunt. You should have killed yourself when you wanted to. Done us all a big favour. You won't win. I'm in control, and I say grubbing little fuckers like you don't win.'

Glynn struggled to draw breath, his chest constricted from the blow. The menace in Matt's words hovered around him, until he found his voice, still shaking with fear and anger, 'You are a fucking bastard. D'you know that? Well, I've had it with you. You're on your own, brother.' He jabbed the off-button, but continued shouting at the little globe, fists clenched, tears steaming from his eyes. After a few minutes he sat down on the floor, back against the wall. It was like trying to watch twenty different television channels at the same time. Anger and indignation fought for his attention with the fear and distress caused by Matt's voice, the feelings of inadequacy caused by his insults. On the margins were guilt that he had provoked this outburst, and guilt that he had let Nia down. But beneath it all was the emetic horror, the realisation that Matt, his own brother, the man he'd defended, made excuses for, Matt was actually the monster. The violence, the hatred, the contempt, was all for real. He'd passed it off before, put it down to the drink talking, but now, in the spotlight, he felt it all. The force of the words, the choice of sentiments, they all came from Matt, not something he'd drunk. The venom was personal and heartfelt. Suddenly there were more shadows in Glynn's world.

For the next few days the television screens around Glynn flickered on and off. Anger gave him energy to teach, to clean the rabbit hutch, to run miles every evening, but he slept badly with dark lullabies. Lack of sleep made him vulnerable. Gradually, anxiety took over, and anxiety had guilt round for supper. Maybe he *had* provoked Matt. He began to think that Matt hadn't meant what he said, began to worry he was in a bad way, all alone, deserted. After four days he reluctantly dialled Matt's number. There was no reply. Nor was there a reply that evening or the next morning. Glynn queued for bread on his way to work, stiffened by a cold dribble of fear down his back. He struggled to smile when Becky brought him a paper daffodil for St. David's Day, and played with it, twisting it aimlessly all day as he taught. He almost gave the daffodil to Tricia when he met her walking out into the dusk.

'Fancy a drink?' she said. 'I hear they've got quite a lot in at the Crown this week.' He almost said yes to her, but went home and called Nia to apologise instead. They had a slightly awkward conversation, sharing information about the practicalities of life without saying anything. Glynn switched off his 'phone, a little happier. Nia was confused and rang Amira, 'I don't know what to say to him. I just want to tell him everything that's going on, but then I think, no it's not like that now, so I just tell him bland stuff, and I think I'm going crazy.

He left a paper daffodil on my doorstep.'

'That's quite sweet. Do you want to get back together?'

'I don't know. I don't see how we can, if he's still sticking up for his brother.' Amira agreed that it was tricky, but encouraged her to keep talking.

Cheered by his good gesture, Glynn gave thanks for cheese and bread, made a cheese sandwich and ate half of it, but then his resolve finally crumbled and he decided to walk up to Pipeland Farm, worried that something might really be wrong with Matt. The scenarios played out before him as he trudged up the lane. Matt dead in a corner. Matt fine and raging. Matt fine and apologetic. Glynn imagined his own responses. He rang the bell, rapped on the door. No reply. He found the key on the bunch in his pocket and turned the lock. A rotting stench rushed into the cold air. He fell back gagging, then pulled his sleeve over his nose and yelled, 'Matt! Matt!' When there was no answer, he picked his way in. Downstairs was the now-familiar tangle of old clothes, congealed food and empty cans. No corpse.

He walked up the stairs, struggling to breathe as the smell increased. The source was obvious as he reached the landing. A trail led to the bathroom which had witnessed an explosion of bloody vomit and liquid excrement. Glynn stepped between the patches, and pushed open the door to the main bedroom. It was untouched, probably just as Abi had left it. Glynn opened the door to the guest room and found Matt. He was lying half-on and half-off the bed, his trousers soaked with black diarrhoea. His face had a yellow tinge and his mouth was caked with brown liquid. He lay like a vision of death, surrounded by old, empty, green bottles.

Glynn's first thought was that he must be dead. But when he called 'Matt' once more, the carcass stirred, then struggled to focus, then to move. Glynn pushed him on to the bed then stepped back. Matt moaned and rocked his head. Glynn backed out of the room, muttering, 'It's alright. I'll call an ambulance, Okay?' He ran down the stairs and out of the house, gasping for air. After a moment he pressed the emergency button. He realised he wasn't making much sense to the operator who was looking at him suspiciously. He tried to explain why he couldn't transmit Matt's chipped data, how he had a drinking problem, but finally he just repeated the address and said that Matt needed help. He didn't know whether anyone would come.

Basic instincts provoked small, deliberate actions. He stepped back into the house, poured a glass of water and took it upstairs, reeling again from the smell. Matt rolled himself into a sitting position and reached out his hand, spilling the water as his muscles whimpered into life. He sipped it, taking barely enough to free his voice. 'My house,' he said indistinctly. 'Give me back my key. Give it to Mum.' He sank back and the glass smashed on the floor. 'I'm a sick man,' he moaned. 'This is my house, my house.' His eyes closed, and he shrank into the bed, shivering. Glynn stood at the bedroom door, his teeth gritted. His 'phone rang and he went downstairs to answer it. The face told him there was no ambulance coming. Shortages of staff, self-inflicted alcoholism was a low priority, call the family doctor, arrange an appointment. Glynn descended further into shock, murmuring, 'But what about me? He's dying. I don't know what to do.' The calm face repeated the instructions then vanished. Glynn stared at the overcast sky, then went into the kitchen and filled another glass of water. He sat by the sink, watching the tap drip. As he sat in freeze-frame, time passed around him.

He was dragged back into the present by a crash, and he marched back up the stairs. He saw Matt kneeling on the floor outside the bedroom, unsteady as baby's first outing. Glynn tried to help him stand, but even holding on to the doorframe his legs gave way. He was sweating and shaking. Silently Glynn dragged his brother back to the bed and propped him against a clean patch. He wasn't sure whether Matt was still conscious, until the deadweight opened its eyes. He was seemed to be lucid, his eyes focused on Glynn and he said, 'I'm a sick man, and you're to blame.' Glynn pulled away and left him.

As he walked down the lane, away from the house, he called the surgery, told them that his brother was dying and that the ambulance service refused to come. He gave them the address, and went home. When Felix called round that evening he had to let himself into Glynn's flat with the key hidden under the cat's new water bowl. He picked his way around a broken mirror, and found Glynn curled up in a chair, shivering. He gave him some sleeping pills, told him Matt was in Ninewells Hospital; he'd spoken to the neighbours and called an industrial cleaning firm. Order was imposed on the external chaos. Glynn slept blindly, cocooned by the drugs. He took two days off work, and arrived back to find another huge pile of old mail had been delivered. He threw it all out without opening it. The fallout from the Cascadia quake was felt globally, and even the *Chronicle* contemplated the economic impact and speculated on the likely fate of the refugees. International agencies struggled to cope with the scale of the disaster. People had begun to think the worst was over. Now they wondered whether this was the eye of the storm. Rumours circulated that there was a worse 'flu pandemic lurking, that antibiotics were failing. Once again, people wore tight, white masks on the street.

Desperate for a reason to smile, Glynn felt all the muscles in his face finally start to soften when he opened an envelope marked 'Top Secret.' There was no note, and he couldn't tell from the handwriting, but he took a chance and called Tricia.

'Where did you get it?'

'Turns out Bob's been collecting them all year and thought we could do with a laugh, but it's all hush hush because the Business Recovery Plan team wouldn't approve. Which were your favourites?'

'Well I quite liked the one from Anthropology.'

'Ah yes, 'they became aquatinted with the local moles', instead of 'acquainted with the local mores'', she read from her own copy of the Top Secret 'Quotes from student exams.'

'I'm surprised any of our lot were aware of 'mores' as a word. I really liked the Restoration comedy one about 'guests being buried under a collapsing canapé', complete with accent. Or 'Mr. Knightly had a worm comforting manner' – do worms normally need comforting? Or 'Antigone displays baldness and carriage' – what on earth does that mean?'

'Ah, got that one, it's 'boldness and courage,' Mind you, our great scientific minds aren't that hot,' Tricia sighed, reading out, "The first mineral deposit was caused by the second'. 'Geological calculations do not always correlate with the aspidistrical."

'Is that actually about plants, do you think?' Glynn was beginning to choke on his laughter, and said, 'Hard to tell, I suppose, but how on earth did Bob get 'Socrates was born in Preston'? I mean, how can you account for that? Thanks, really, I needed something to cheer me up.'

'Well, I might be able to go one better,' she ducked out of view for a moment, then reappeared in the image waving a feather boa. 'Fancy coming to my birthday party on Friday? Nothing fancy, few friends, few drinks. I'd love it if you could come.'

'That's very kind of you. Yeah, I'll try to make it. What time?'

'Seven, eight, whatever suits you.'

'Great, I'll see you there.'

And so, on Friday night Glynn made his way through a maze of new-build flats until he found the door hung with pink tissue ammonites.

'Cool,' he said to himself, ringing the bell, then 'Wow!' as Tricia opened the door. He couldn't work out why she looked different, apart from the tight jeans and the black velvet corset. He thrust his present forward, and she warmly invited him in.

'Wow!' he said again, looking round. 'This place looks really lived-in.'

'Is that a polite word for 'cluttered'?' she said, as she poured him a Turkish cider.

'No, no, I meant, it's individual. You have pictures on the wall.'

'Yeah, complicated procedure involving a hammer, a ruler, and nails. Come on, I think you know most people.'

Glynn was surprised to find he didn't, and realised Tricia had been making friends very easily since her arrival. Sarah was still introducing him to a bunch of modern linguists when he saw Tricia open her present and gasp slightly, holding it up to the light. 'Wow!' she mouthed to him. 'Thank You! I love it!'

'You're welcome!' he mouthed back.

After the final guests had arrived, Tricia insisted they all sing along to the 'Best of Eurovision DVD' she'd received. Glynn embarrassed himself early on with a too-enthusiastic impression of a Belgian cowherd, and had been sitting back enjoying the cabaret.

'Okay. Now for some real music,' said Sarah from Physics, struggling to cope with the primitive technology of an old CD player. Glynn helped her, and was strangely moved to hear the first strains of her twentieth century pop classics mix.

'Dance?' said Trica from behind his shoulder as the first notes of Abba's *Mamma Mia* began.

'Very badly,' he grimaced.

'Ah, but it's my birthday,' she pouted, one can of cider too far gone to care.

He surrendered and gamely spun her round, banging into the other uncoordinated couples twirling round the CD player. As the song drew to a close, she said, 'I'm sorry about your brother. Look, if you want to talk, I can get rid of this lot.'

'Oh god, no, it's your birthday.'

'Well, you could help me celebrate it at the same time?' She was happy, relaxed in his arms, and Glynn pulled her closer, breathing in the hint of perfume, just before gathering himself, and stepping back, 'I'd behave badly, and you don't deserve that. I've screwed up enough people's lives already.' Before Tricia could protest, he kissed her on the cheek, said 'Happy Birthday', and left without his coat.

'Good Decision. Right Decision,' he mumbled on to himself as he walked quickly down towards the harbour. He sat down heavily on a bench, pausing to read the plaque, 'For Mum, who loved this place.'

'Happy families, eh?' he thought as he started to shiver. 'Accidents waiting to happen, more like.' He thought about the brief moment of blissful oblivion he'd felt as he danced with Tricia, and was tempted to go back to the party and try to forge ahead, regardless, but then an image of Nia, fragile and bruised in hospital, came to his mind; how she'd allowed him to talk about 'the accident' instead of calling the police; how she'd brought him strange Hallowe'en sweets to brighten up his day. 'So,' he thought as he stamped his feet to keep warm, 'How would Nia react if I went out with Tricia? Would she, [a] Be happy for me? [b] Not care? [c] Cut my balls off? Umm, probably [c], but is that because she still cares about me and wants to get back together, or is it because she hates my guts and doesn't want me to be happy? Ow,' he thought as he contemplated the last possibility. 'I'd be pretty cut up if she didn't care about me, even if Tricia does. Okay, need to get this sorted out. If she tells me to fuck off, still time to go back to the party.'

With the syllogism barely holding him together, he 'phoned Nia and groveled, telling her he owed her a huge apology. 'I know it's late,' he said, 'and I'm not expecting anything from you, so how about we meet on neutral ground and I can try to explain?' He was encouraged to see her smile, despite herself, before she agreed to meet him outside the department in half an hour's time. As he waited, the fog thickened, and he worried that he'd been a little insensitive to suggest she walk on her own at night, but he hadn't wanted to turn up at her door and impose, and the street lights were on again. He noticed she was wearing her fur coat, and wondered whether Abi had brought it back that night.

'Is this alright, being here?' she said, as he turned the three locks.

'Yeah, sure. All the electronic surveillance stuff's been turned off, and anyway, they sort of expect us dedicated professionals to be here night and day. The students seem to think we live here. Umm. Common room, probably best. I might even be able to offer you some coffee.'

'Where's your coat?' she said, as he turned on the lights. 'Oh, um , left it at Rory's, having a party, had to get some air, went for a run. There we are, black coffee okay?'

'None of that Mellow Birds muck, then? '

'Thankfully not.'

She brushed crumbs off a decomposing sofa and sat down to survey the devastation. 'Bit of a mess I'm afraid,' he rambled. 'We've had loads more people in here since the Cascadia business. Oh,' he paused, still with his back to her, 'I didn't ask, I mean, did you know anyone there?'

'No,' she said, 'but Amira's friend Marcie, her parents retired to Santa Monica. No news.'

He brought over two mugs of coffee and they sat in silence for a few minutes. She waited for him to begin. 'I'm not good with words,' he sighed, 'I just wanted to apologise, and I understand if you never want to see me again, but I wanted to apologise, so I, no, so *we* can both move on. I treated you very badly. And you were right about Matt.'

'What have the doctors said?'

'He's quiet, for now, but long term … Apparently 'Alcoholism Is A Disease', they keep telling me, but maybe he's just had a breakdown and this'll snap him out of it. He'll have been sober while he's in there. I suppose he'll have had withdrawals, and be over the addiction by the time they kick him out.'

'Maybe,' she said. 'It can be complicated.' She paused. 'My father drinks. He's what they call a 'functioning' alcoholic. Holds down a good job, pillar of the community. Just can't cope without a drink and gets out of his head every now and again, then goes promising the world to everyone around him.'

Treading carefully Glynn said, 'Is that why you've had such a hard time? Ruth told me there was more to your being here than just not getting on with your course.'

'Maybe. Counsellor said I had deep-seated trust issues from growing up with an unpredictable parent, but then, who has perfect parents?'

'Right,' he nodded. 'I don't suppose I really got over my mum's death that well. They said it could be a bio-chemical imbalance, but my shrink kept wanting me to talk about my family. All a bit cracked, aren't we? How's Ruth getting on? When's she due?'

'Early May. Not long now.'

'She'll be glad to have you around.'

'I hope so.'

They drank their coffee, then Glynn said, 'I don't want to keep you. I just had to let you know how sorry I am for how things worked out. I'll understand if you don't want to see me again.'

She started to cry, and he gulped, holding back from touching her. 'I don't know,' she whispered. 'I don't know how I feel. I was so angry and then when I saw you with her …'

'There was nothing going on. I'm sorry I hurt you again. I don't want to pressure you. I do love you, Ni, but I understand if you don't want to see me again.' She started crying even harder, tears bouncing off her dark fur, 'No, no!' she sobbed. 'You don't understand, I don't 'not want to see you again', but I just don't know what to say or do, and I don't want to feel like this.'

He cautiously pressed his hand over hers and let her gather her breath. 'It's late,' he said quietly, 'I shouldn't have asked you to come out like this. I really didn't mean to upset you or put pressure on you, I just had to apologise. Come on, I'll walk you home.' He closed up as she wiped her eyes, and he told her all about the Cascadia fault on the way back to her flat, before kissing her on the cheek and bidding her a goodnight.

When Nia told her about the night's events, Amira was wary, but conscious of the sparks of hope lighting up her young friend's face, she simply said, 'That's great. Just, next time you talk, make sure he tells you what he wants and make sure he tells you exactly what he's apologising for.' Glynn's mental canoe had barely righted itself when two days later he was drowning again, catching sight of Nia coming out of Taylor's with Tricia. Nia was smiling as she walked back to Ethereal and Glynn debated which one to talk to first. As Tricia was walking directly towards him, the decision was made for him.
'Maybe this is none of my business,' he shifted nervously, 'but can I ask what you were doing talking to Nia?' She smiled at him brightly and they started to walk back to the department. 'She asked me for coffee to apologise for being so suspicious. She's a very nice young woman,' Tricia said calmly.

'Ah, yes,' he murmured. Trica waited until they were out of earshot of passers-by, and then said in a matter-of-fact tone, 'I like you. We've had some fun together. I thought there was a possibility of us having a deeper connection, but you obviously still have feelings for her, as she does for you, so I'm not getting involved.'

'Well,' he stuttered, 'I don't think it's quite like that.'

'And there's your problem,' she half-shouted. 'You don't know what's going on, and you're content to leave it in this ill-defined state, no matter who it hurts. What d'you think, this is somehow noble, all this tragic suffering and misunderstandings? Grow up, Glynn. She's only young, but you're old enough to know better. Either patch things up or tell her it's over. She deserves that.'

Glynn studied the notice-board in the foyer as Tricia went upstairs. He was puzzled. He'd always seen her as a junior colleague, because she was a couple of years younger than him, but now she'd made him feel like an gauche teenager being told off by a kindly teacher. He didn't like the feeling. For the rest of the day he was sharp with his students, distracted when he tried to write up his research. He 'phoned Abi and talked to Becky about the rabbits. He 'phoned to check on Matt and was told he was comfortable. He wanted to call Nia but he wasn't sure how to patch things up or tell her it was over. Lost in another pointless weekend, he walked for hours out to Crail and back, before ending up exhausted at John Burnet Hall. He staggered into Rory's room, and Rory told him to relax on the beanbag.

'Bob told me about Matt,' he handed Glynn a cup of tea. 'Bad luck.'

'Yeah, he's in a secure unit in Ninewells, probably for another week or so.'

'God awful place.'

'Really?'

'Oh aye, I was there for a few days before they realised I wasn't a loony and transferred me back to the Memorial.' He tore off a piece of sellotape with his teeth and sealed up another large cardboard box.

'Are you moving? I don't blame you.' Rory shook his hands in the air and shouted, 'New York, baby! Jamie got me a job.'

'My Jamie?'

'Mmhm.'

'Bloody hell. Really? You know he's coming over in a couple of weeks?'

'Yeah, I was hoping he'll keep Abi's mind off things. I think she might be upset I'm leaving.'

'What sort of job?' Glynn was shocked by his friend's news, and the apparent involvement of his absent, younger brother.

'Creative editor for a fanzine. Wanna see the prototype?' Before Glynn could answer, Rory removed a magazine from a solid plastic wrapper, 'I'm on page three. Yeah, don't even think about jesting.' Glynn flipped through the pages and instantly recognised Rory's photography, although he wasn't sure how true-to-life the pictures were - they showed silver-suited space rangers prowling the lanes of the East Neuk.

'They want me to transfer it all to New York, and oversee all the fiction stuff. Cool, no?'

'Not more porn?' Glynn punched him manfully.

'Scout's honour. No PWP.'

'PWP? What? Porn ... without a plot?'

'PWP – Plot, what plot? Normally porn, but are you

kidding? Even Bob knew that one!'

'Bob?' Glynn shrieked. 'Bob, who thought *Sex and the City* was an ESRC funded research project?'

Rory shrugged as Glynn shook with laughter, 'Bob, who thought Ann Summers sold medical supplies!'

'Well, they do have nurses' uniforms in their window. Anyway, this isn't that. Take a look.'

Glynn returned to the cover and read *Alternative Realities: Philosophy, Fantasy and Science Fiction. Issue Zero: A new Firefly story, Godzilla in Chicago, Aristotle on the Good Life and Daily lessons from a galactic fighter pilot.* He put it down and said, 'I think I'm having a stroke.'

'Bastard!' Rory grinned, and punched him back happily. 'They said my stories showed 'Great philosophical sensibilities', no less.'

'So, this magazine is a mixture of sci-fi and what, philosophy-lite? Is it going to sell?'

'Doesn't matter, that's the beauty of it. The US government's bankrolling it for a year. Free distribution, at least in the North East.'

'Run that by me again.'

'Okay,' Rory sat down. 'You know the WHO survey? Well, the American ones turned up all sorts of things, and apparently somebody made a connection between sci-fi fans and some complementary therapies that involve contemplating alternative realities. God, that was a mouthful.'

'So,' Glynn said slowly, 'this is meant to help people get through their depression?'

'You got it! Seems there was going to be one in L.A. too, but after Cascadia, not happening…'

'Yeah. Well, J.'s always said it's a mad place. Are you really going?'

'Too bloody right. Chance of a lifetime.'

'You know you can't drive in their cities. What was it Bill Bryson said, 'mobile hysteria?'

'I think that was just Boston Seriously, 'though, I've always wanted to travel. I've really made a mess of things here, anyways.' Rory suddenly became more subdued.

'People know you weren't yourself.'

'But some of it was me, y'know? And I don't want to be that person.' He put down the sellotape and sat looking out the window. 'You know, I finally ran into that gorgeous woman with the red hair, she had the saddest dark eyes, and was just nursing a coffee in McGregor's. And I couldnae even go up to her and say 'Hi', because she might know what a jerk I am. So I walked out, and then after five minutes I thought 'To hell wi'this, she looked really miserable, I should have at least said 'You okay'?' So I turned round and when I got back she was gone.'

'Not meant to be, then.'

'Aye,' he sighed.

'Well, J's always said the yanks let you start a whole new life. I'm really chuffed for you, mate. How's Abi gonna take it, 'though?'

'She'll no understand. Her whole life's here, she likes having it all the same. I want to walk out of an apartment and down a street where I don't know anyone. I think I'll take better pictures.'

'You haven't told her, then?' Glynn knew she'd be upset, and wasn't surprised when Rory asked, 'I thought maybe you could break it to her?'

At the end of the week Glynn waved Rory goodbye, but Abi was too upset to join him. He rang Tricia by way of an apology, telling her to bring some boxes to have first pick of the leftovers. Rory had left most of his possessions behind, too much to take on the boat, and he'd told Glynn to distribute what he could. Without the internet, Freecycling had been replaced with a more *ad hoc* system, just leaving any useful items in a particular section of the town dump. There was no sense in being too noble, so Glynn took all the odd bits of food and had a good rummage with Tricia, before pinning up a 'Take what you like' sign on Rory's door. He was met within minutes by an overjoyed Australian student who told him of a native tradition, Kerbside Collection, where everyone in a town left out stuff to recycle on a particular day. By the end of the afternoon the room was empty and Glynn handed over the keys to the incoming warden.

After a weekend of admin., and a tiresome Monday's teaching, Glynn decided that the bunnies were having things way too easy, so he gave Tommy pride of place on the hearthrug. He was trying to take stock as he poked the fire, stiffening after a long run, thinking what to say to Nia, envying Rory his good fortune, contemplating his own career and wondering whether he could suggest adopting Tommy, when the 'phone lit up, and Matt's face appeared, haggard, with large bags under his eyes.

'Out of hospital, then?' Glynn said.

'Yeah, fighting fit. You saved my life, little brother.'

'Yes. I probably did.'

'I'm really sorry you had to see me like that, mate.'

'You could have died, Matt.'

'Yeah, I know. They told me. Liver disease. Nasty.'

Glynn took a deep, dark breath and said, 'No. It wasn't a liver disease. You're doing this to yourself. For some god-unknown reason, you're Hell-bent on on drinking yourself to death, and unless you wake up and see what you're doing, you'll end up like-'

Matt cut him off. 'Bullshit! I had a bloody awful illness. I deserve some fucking sympathy, and all I get is people droning on about 'Being An Alcoholic.' Don't you start on, as well. I thought you'd be on my side.'

'Matt, if you don't stop drinking it'll kill you. You need help. I hate to say it, but you're well on the way to being an alcoholic.'

He saw Matt squint and adopt the 'How to explain the obvious to someone very stupid' tone of voice, 'Now look, Glynn. I was in a hospital with some very sick people. I nearly died. They have all the specialists there who deal with those alki types, and they never said a word to me about it. Alright? I'm not the one with the problem here. Maybe you should get some help, little brother. You've needed it in the past.'

Finally a large metal grill fell down across Glynn's train of thought and he said, 'And you are a fucking alcoholic, you fucking arsehole. You are in denial, Matty boy. Get some help.' He bounced the 'phone against the nearest wall, and went to make a cup of tea.

Chapter Twelve

'Why does an earthquake in America mean people need to give blood here?' Robbie squirmed. 'If they've all drowned, how can they need blood? Don't they need air?' Abi wasn't sure whether he was being deliberately provocative or was seriously troubled. 'Mini-series for the child psychologist, this one,' she thought darkly. She'd reluctantly allowed Matt to see the children at a mutual friend's house, with her own father there to watch them. She wasn't keen on leaving them so long, but had promised to go to Ruth's baby-shower, once she finished teaching. The day passed slowly.

At lunchtime, Glynn turned up at Ethereal, slightly puzzled by the banners. 'Do you fancy a quick lunch break?' he said to Nia before he lost his nerve. They walked to the harbour and found an empty bench. 'I love it here,' was his opening gambit. 'So, you went and talked to Amira,' she said neutrally. 'Uh-huh.'

'She's been a great support. Not just to me. How they'd have managed without her in Crail even before this, I don't know.'

'Yeah, well I'd be more altruistic if I'd inherited a free house and a sinecure,' Glynn moaned. 'Not so easy if you have to work for a living.' He bit into a pollock niçoise sandwich.

'She doesn't have an easy life, you know.'

'What, making soap, gardening? Hard life.'

'So, if you inherited a cottage, you'd do what Amira's done? Go back to Brecon?'

'God, no. Live in your hometown in a different house? No way. Rent it out, make my life a little bit easier.'

'So, you wouldn't change your life?'

'And become a hippy? Nice dream, but not terribly secure, is it? Anyway, I've been working too hard for too many years to give up on this now.' Glynn realised this conversation wasn't taking the path he'd plotted, and he asked after Ruth's health. Unfortunately, Nia took that as a sign to return to the shop to prepare for the baby-shower. They parted awkwardly, both a little puzzled about what this lunchtime meeting meant.

Tired from her teaching, Abi felt her spirits sag when she saw Denise Rogers, sans fisherman's sweater, making her way to Ruth's party, carrying an ostentatiously ribboned basket. She feared the worst, as she heard the pitying A-sharp, C-sharp lilt of 'Aaa biii'. The only mercy was that Denise was alone. 'Oh, I'm glad I'm not late,' she sighed. 'I never received my invitation, but it must be a drop-in thing. Rather unwise, having this so early, but I understand Ruth's cousin Hannah is visiting, so I suppose she wanted to be the one to hold this quaint event.' Abi was relieved to talk about the matter in hand, as they debated the spread of this American custom and agreed that it was probably no bad thing.

Denise showed her the paraphernalia, noting the need for practical things, 'As the father's not in the picture'. Knowing what was coming, Abi feigned ignorance, partly to stay off her own situation. 'Oh well, it's common knowledge, I'm afraid,' Denise displayed gleeful concern. 'There was this architect, nice chap. Met him at the church barbeque, you would never have guessed. Married. Had a wife in Edinburgh, and poor old Ruth never knew a thing. So, when she found out, she sent him packing.   And, well, you couldn't make it up, poor Ruth, I mean, oh, so, a fortnight later, she finds out she's pregnant. She seems happy about it now, 'though to be honest I don't think being a single parent will be pleasant. Children need both parents. Oh … I didn't mean that. Of course I wasn't meaning you, it's just …'

'Yes, I know exactly what you meant!' Abi said briskly, and was glad to escape to the kitchen when Denise settled down to receive congratulations on her gift.

Nia was dishing up another set of mini-Christmas puddings. 'So I wasn't seeing things', said Abi as she poured out some sherry glasses of fruit juice. 'There really were Rudolph pictures in amongst the baby banners outside.'

'Celebration's a celebration, that's what Hannah said. And I am actually starting to get excited. She brought all this Christmas stuff up with her.'

'You okay?'

'Yeah. You?'

'Aye. Not doing too badly, you know?'

'I hear Rory left. That must be hard, family and all,' Nia wanted to express her support without mentioning all the complicated history.

'Keeping busy,' Abi played the game. 'Lots of teaching, and we've got our Jamie coming over next week, so that will be interesting.'

'So, is this true, he's this famous photographer or something?'

'Something. Do you really want to hear about another of my twisted in-laws?'

'Oh go on,' Nia said. 'Might give me some insight.' They took a seat in the living room and Nia called Ruth and Hannah over from Denise's huddle, 'Abi's going to tell us about her jet-setting brother-in-law.'

'Ooh, this should be good!' Hannah hadn't heard any

good gossip for some time, and enjoyed the company.

'Where to start?' Abi began. 'So, he was about thirteen when I first met him, typical teenager, scatterbrained, wee bit gawky, blushed every time a woman looked his way. After Lou, his mother, died he went really quiet, stayed in his room, so we all assumed he was just doing what teenage boys do. Matt and I were back in Brecon quite a lot then, never heard a hint of a girlfriend. Odd really, 'cos he was a nice-looking lad, even then. So, their old man was pretty out of it for a while, but he sobered up about a month before GCSEs started, and promised Jamie something for everything he passed, not sure how much, hundred quid or something, and double that if he got an A, thinking he'd maybe pass a few if he was lucky.'

'And?'

'And ...,' Abi shook her head, remembering, 'you should have seen the old man's face when Jamie handed over his result slip, cool as a cucumber. Thirteen A-stars and one boring old A.'

'Wow. That's good going,' Hannah commented.

'Aye,' Abi smiled, 'he'd been working himself into the ground, locked in his room. Brilliant he is, and then instead of going on to A-Levels he banked the money and took off round India. Never went home again. Met some grizzled old journalist and went round as his apprentice. He got this great job in New York a few years ago, and he's made quite a name for himself.'

'That's quite a story,' Nia was impressed.

'Hope springs eternal, eh? I just hope things work out so well for Rory. He should have just about arrived by now.' Abi stayed lost in better memories, while the conversation moved on, swirling around her, with balloons and tinsel.

Towards the end of the evening, Ruth's cousin Hannah stood up, chinking her sherry glass, and thanked everyone for coming, 'We haven't had much to celebrate, any of us, lately, so preparing for a new life is an important moment. I'm glad I could be here.'

'I'll be celebrating when I sleep on my front again,' Ruth said, *sotto voce* to Abi.

'Oh no, you'll not be expecting any sleep for a while!' she chuckled back.

'Then how about, I'll be celebrating when Denise goes home tonight.'

'You won't be the only one,' Abi shared her grumble. 'I'm sorry I have to leave early. My dad said things have been quiet with Matt, but Robbie's a bit unpredictable these days.'

'I really appreciate you coming. See you at Eilidh's?'

'Aye.' They hugged at the top of Ruth's stairs and Abi smiled at the snowflakes and pumpkin balloons hanging down the hall.

And then nothing happened for a while. No new disasters. No change. No new hope. Once she'd heard that Rory had arrived safely in New York, Abi relaxed a little and began to look forward to Jamie's visit. 'There he is!' shouted Robbie, as they drew up at the station, 'Pull in there, IN THERE!' He leaned out the window and shouted, 'Uncle Jamie! Over here. Let me out, let me out here!' and he kicked the car seats in frustration as Abi drove on to the car park. As soon as the car stopped, Robbie jumped out, ran over to Jamie, and threw his arms around him before he could even take off his rucksack.

'How you doing, butt?' Jamie greeted him joyfully.

'Let me look at you! Grown up, haven't you? Almost as big as this!' he said, pulling off his rucksack. 'Abi!' he beamed, as she came over with Becky. 'How are my beautiful girls?'

'We're doing fine. Good to see you! The car's over here. Glynn's just finishing his teaching.'

'You alright?'

'Yeah, we're fine,' said Abi. 'Throw your things in the back. Robbie! Do your seat belt up. Glynn promised he'd have some food in. You must be starving. I warn you 'though, you'll have to wait until the rabbits are fed. He's more obsessed than these two.'

'You haven't met the rabbits, have you, Uncle Jamie?' Robbie shouted.

'They're called Lily and Barbie,' said Becky.

'Daft girlie names,' Robbie bounced on the seat. 'They need proper names, like Fang or Bruiser.'

'I look forward to meeting these remarkable creatures,' Jamie winked at Abi as she turned on the radio. While Becky started to sing along, she said to Jamie quietly, 'Glynn suggested I should drop you off so you can see Matt in daylight. I'll just take you to the end of the track if you don't mind a walk – give me a ring when you're done and I'll pick you up.'

'Sure,' he said. 'Don't expect I'll be long.' Abi nodded and didn't say anything more until she dropped him on the main road.

Glynn was waiting when she pulled up at his flat. His apron read, 'For best results, add wine.'

'Excellent! Here you are!' he said. 'Well, I've been pushing the boundaries of my culinary expertise, so you're in for a treat in honour of the prodigal's return. But first, nephew, niece, we have pressing business to attend to!'

'Feed the bunnies!' shouted Becky.

'Absolutely,' he replied picking her up. 'Robbie, care to pull a carrot?' Robbie harvested two tiny carrots as Glynn opened the back door.

They were still watching the rabbits fighting over the baby carrots Glynn had lovingly grown next to the fireplace when there was a ring at the door and Felix arrived. 'I invited him along,' Glynn said, as Felix gave Abi a hug. 'Not often I get to cook at the best of times, now is it?' He was making tea when the door rang again. Glynn frowned, 'Now I'm sure I didn't say this was an open house.' He smiled broadly as he opened the door, 'Mate! Good to see you!'

Abi frowned and said to Jamie, 'You must have come straight back. Wasn't he in?'

'Oh, yeah, he was in, alright. Done my duty.' Jamie didn't meet her eye, but turned to the children, 'Now then, where are these rabbits?'

Jamie was introduced to Lily, Barbie and Felix in turn and expressed a suitable degree of interest in fur and claws before coming in for tea.

'So,' said Glynn, 'what brings you back to these shores?'

'This and that. Get the lie of the land.'

'And Trudie?'

'Ah, well, we broke up,' Jamie said with a sigh.

'Oh, I'm sorry,' said Abi. 'What happened?'

'Well, she wasn't too happy that I didn't visit her when she got 'flu. But I mean, I'd gone to such trouble to stay out of its way, I wasn't going to get deliberately exposed. I've seen some of these bugs all over the world, they get nasty.'

'So, what,' said Glynn, 'you just kept yourself in isolation?'

'Pretty much.'

'And you do this every time there's some bug going

round, do you?' Abi looked at him curiously.

'No,' he said slowly, 'but I've kept an eye on these things. I saw some pretty nasty stuff in Hong Kong that year, and when Jo in my local juice bar told me he'd had a run on echinacea blasters, I knew this was the real thing.'

'Jo In Your Local Juice Bar? You are SO New York!' Glynn scoffed, but Jamie was unruffled, 'I keep my ear to the ground. So, I've always thought that when you start thinking 'should I do something?' it's already time to act, so I stocked up and sealed myself in. This flat's brilliant, one of the new T340 systems, radiation-proof, own water system, generators, air filters, the works. So I waited, and when half the East Village went down with 'flu that weekend, I was damn glad I did.'

Glynn started to say, 'Ooh, a T340, does it-' when Abi interrupted, 'And Tru?' She wasn't going to let him get distracted in technical details, and Jamie looked at her, slightly shamefaced. 'Yeah, well, she thought I was overreacting. Called me a 'paranoid doomsday merchant', I think were her words. And when she came down with 'flu, it was early days, we didn't know how it was going to pan out. For all I knew it was going to be the big lethal bug that wiped out half of humanity, so I'd have been pretty stupid to risk that just so I could take her flowers, wouldn't I?'

'Hmm', said Abi. 'Fair enough', said Glynn. Felix drank his tea.

'So, is this true?' said Jamie, holding up a copy of the *Daily Telegraph*.

'Nice find!' Glynn congratulated him. 'A real English newspaper? Where'd you get it? Is it recent?'

'Got it at the airport. Is this right?' Jamie prodded the

headline, 'Hard Work is good for you.'

'Again, leaks from the WHO survey. Half-truths and statistics,' Felix shook his head.

'So, hard work is bad for you?'

'You were never going to take the risk, were you, Jamie, old son?' Glynn twitted him.

'I'll have you know this shutter finger is one of the most hard working in the business,' Jamie wiggled his finger at Abi, who batted it away with a smile.

'Got it insured, have you?' Glynn bit back.

'Boys, boys,' Abi scolded. 'Felix was going to tell us something.'

'Thank you, Abi,' Felix continued. 'Yes, well, a superficial reading of the first stats might suggest that some people reckon work keeps them sane, and as the powers-that-be are most concerned with getting people back behind the wheel, they'd like to think it's a causal link.'

'But?' Glynn prompted.

'Well, lots of these workaholics actually are still exhibiting symptoms of low-level depression.'

'I knew it!' Glynn thumped the table. 'Look at Bob,' he said to Abi, 'works like a demon, but tense, tense. I bet he'd say work was good for you.'

'Yes, well, the WHO survey is not just meant to get people's bodies up and about.' Felix sighed. 'We have a real opportunity to improve mental health across the board, Gross National Happiness and all that. It's frustrating, these leaks simplifying everything.'

'Anything useful turned up?' Glynn said without any great enthusiasm.

'Maybe. I know some countries have come up with some novel ideas.'

'Like Rory's wild goose chase to New York,' Abi frowned.

'I'm hurt,' Jamie moaned. 'I thought you'd be pleased for him.'

'Oh, I am, but I miss him.'

'Sorry,' he put his hand on her wrist. 'I didn't think.'

'Och, you're alright,' she said, patting his hand. 'So, what *is* the good news, Felix?'

'Well, it seems that contact with nature helps.'

'That's it?'

'And then it's down to context.'

'Such as?'

'Right,' Felix began, 'let's take one of the big ones. Prayer, meditation, contemplation, all shown in this survey, as in many others, to help people recover from depression.'

'But?' Glynn waited for the next line.

'But, it can be taken to extremes, or abused. People can end up thinking something bad's going to happen if they don't meditate for a certain length of time, or if they miss a set of prayers, it can just feed into paranoia. Or then there's all the simple escapism, watching old Bond movies, reading detective novels, all well and good, can give people a break, let them catch their breath before facing up to reality again.'

'But?' Glynn asked again.

'Some people go too far,' Felix warmed to his topic. 'The world of their fictional detective starts becoming more real than their own life. They start neglecting their own lives, thinking the characters are real. Even before this I've seen some fragile patients go completely off the rails when their favourite soap character dies. They really feel it like a death in the family. So, we can't just say to people, 'Read some of these good novels' because it might backfire. That's why the WHO survey is supposed to be different,

287

contextualised, but that makes it much harder to analyse, and it doesn't quite fit the instant packet soup answer so many people are after.'

'Is it all a waste of time, then?' Glynn was hoping for something more.

'I'm an optimist. I even think we may survive the end of antibiotics, when it comes. For this, if it ultimately introduces one person to something that can help them, then it's not a failure, but it could be so much more, there could be so much more help. Treating mental illness in this country is like the torture of Sisyphus.'

'You been talking to Rose in the library?' Glynn was surprised by the sudden mythological reference.

'Yeah, that's one of her metaphors for this.'

'What's her solution?'

'She meditates and knits.'

They paused to contemplate this combination treatment, before Glynn dished up the casserole. Felix enjoyed being part of his adopted family, and relaxed properly for the first time in months, feeling greatly cheered when he left with Glynn to take Robbie to football. Jamie had gone to lie down after taking a few bites of his meal. Becky was playing with the rabbits in the garden, and Abi was enjoying a few minutes' peace, when Jamie came back out of the bedroom, yawning.

'I thought you'd crashed out,' she said.

'Jet Lag. Lie down for ten minutes, then, POP, up again. I'm gonna take some melatonin. It's the only thing that works. Where's everyone?'

'Glynn's taken Robbie to football, Becky's going crazy with too much bunny excitement.'

'It's sweet she's so concerned,' he rubbed his eyes in unconscious imitation of the furry creatures. 'Did you know Glynn had a pet woodlouse when he was little?'

'A woodlouse?'

'He was desperate for a pet, but the old man wouldn't hear of it, so he kept this in a matchbox for a week or so.'

'Until it died?'

'Hmm, yes. Not such a good story, that one. Sorry,' he said, looking to see if he'd upset her, but she just asked him directly, 'Are you sure you're alright?'

'Oh, yeah,' he reassured her. 'I'm normally fine until I've been awake for about twenty-six hours, that's when I start getting sweaty and achy and seeing things out of the corner of my eye, and not sure whether I've dreamt people or done them. Anyway,' he reached into his rucksack, 'Present!' He offered her a small box.

'Oh, but you've already given us all these things,' Abi smiled. 'You'd shouldn't have.'

He shrugged, 'This one's just for you.'

She opened the box and gasped, 'Wow! Chocolate Brazils! I love these! Where did you get them?'

'Had to wrestle a grizzly bear,' he said deadpan, before breaking into a wide smile. 'Amazing what you can get in New York, even now. I remembered we'd had them that Christmas after mam died.'

'Thank you! I don't know what to say,' Abi felt tears starting to well up, as he said seriously, 'Promise me you'll have some yourself, not just share them all out. I know what you're like.'

'Alright, I promise,' she said. 'D'you want one?'

'Thought you'd never ask,' he said, jumping on to the sofa beside her.

'Should your teeth be that white?' she said, opening

289

the box and inhaling the rich chocolate smell.

'Teeth can never be too white,' he said calmly, 'and never run with cacti.'

When Glynn came home with Robbie, trying to knock some of the mud out of his hair before letting the boy see his mother, he was taken aback to find Jamie in the middle of an anecdote about a hooker with leather trousers, 'And it looked like the cut outs were designed to show every type of cellulite you could imagine,' he heard, as they came into the living room. 'I'd never even understood what cellulite was before then, and this was like a horror movie. Glynn, mate!' He put on a serious face, 'Just telling Abi how I nearly got lynched taking some street-life shots last month.' His façade cracked and he fell back laughing again, 'And then she said, 'It'll costya if ya wanna see more!'' Abi had tears rolling down her face, and was laughing too hard to talk. 'What have you two been drinking?' Glynn snapped. 'Chocolate Brazils!' Jamie hiccoughed. 'Not a drop, seriously. I don't. Sorry, jet-lagged, glad to be home. Look, I'm gonna crash out again. Robbie, tomorrow, butt, okay? Abi, a delight as always. See you tomorrow.'

The next morning Jamie was still fast asleep when Glynn crept in to collect some clothes. He left an egg and a little milk in the fridge, then set off for a day of meetings with his dissertation students. After a good eighteen hours sleep, Jamie rose refreshed and was briefly contrite when he met Abi and the children off the bus from Dundee. His presence heightened Abi's awareness of the changes in town. About a third of the shops were permanently closed, their aluminium shutters pasted with announcements from the CHLOE team. Feral cats hunted through abandoned cars and hanging baskets were overgrown with straggly brown slugs. They passed a few people who looked sideways at Abi and her new man.

'Wanna give'em a show? We could pretend you've hired a gigolo,' Jamie whispered. 'I could just slip my arm round your waist and shout, 'Darling, zis eez lovely, but you have only paid for four more hours'?' His mock-Spanish accent made her smile despite herself, but she hissed back, 'Don't you bloody dare, Jamie. This isn't Times Square, remember?'

'You know, I thought something didn't look right. I was thinking maybe it was the colour of the taxis …'

She hit him gently with her teaching folder, 'You be good, today. We're the centre of too much clatter, as it is.'

'Okay, hang on a sec,' he said, as they passed Market Street. 'I'll just be a minute.'

'Jamie!' Abi shouted, exasperated, but he just winked and sprinted down the road. 'Oh no you don't!' she said to Robbie, who had started to follow, noting with some satisfaction that he immediately came to a dead stop. 'Pity the schoolteacher's voice doesn't work on adults,' she thought wryly.

Jamie took a deep breath, then calmly pushed open the door to Ethereal. A few minutes later he was back, and swept the children off before Abi could question him. She was trying to catch him alone for a moment when she collected the children that evening, but Glynn's flat was small, and they could easily be overheard. Her frustration caught her out, when he re-appeared from Glynn's bedroom, saying, 'Love you and leave you all, see you tomorrow, ankle biters. Won't be late.'

'You have a *date?*' she hissed, her voice a little too shrill for her liking.

'Jealous?' he raised an eyebrow at her.

Glynn grinned at him, 'Well, don't do anything I wouldn't do.'

Abi groaned, and shouted at Jamie's back, 'I will bloody kill you if you do anything stupid! D'you hear me, Jamie?' She would have been even more worried if she had seen him swipe a handful of flowers from a garden on his way to pick up Nia. He was charming and polite until they were settled in the Doll's House, and Jamie had beamed at the slim, sixteen-year-old waitress.

'Your type?' Nia said, with an edge to her voice.

'My gran would have said, 'Bag of spuds tied up ugly,' he said lightly. 'Pretty, slim, but white cheesecloth shirt is never a good idea, slightly see-through, slightly too tight, and she has buttocks like puppies fighting in a sack.' Nia was taken aback, but gamely tried to play it cool, 'That's your view as a hot-shot photo journalist, is it?'

'Damn. Rumbled. When did you work who I was?'

'Minute you came through the door at lunchtime.'

'And there I thought I was being mysterious,' Jamie sighed.

'Ah, but everyone's been talking about you for weeks. Becky thinks you're a great astronaut or some sort of superhero. And you do have a pretty strong accent.'

'I know,' he moaned, puzzled. 'Can't shake it. I'll stick with the water,' he said to the waitress and then to Nia, 'would you like some wine?'

'No thanks. You not having any?'

'No, I don't drink. Not good for focus. I need to keep a clear head in my job, catch people unawares, get the real picture.'

'So, you're taking advantage of people?' she said.

'I see what you're thinking,' he agreed. 'So, I snap the

award-winning pictures of a starving child, then rush back to my air-conditioned limo? Hand on heart, I don't. I spend time in these places. I have permission whenever I can, and I can live with the times when I can't. But I know what you mean, it can be intrusive.'

'Are you working now?'

'Do you see a camera now?'

'No. You're very well-behaved.'

'House trained.'

Nia choked on her drink, and dropped her guard a little as Jamie leaned back in his chair. 'So, my dear,' he continued, 'you have nothing to worry about.'

'What's with the 'my dear?' she said when she recovered her breath.

'Distancing technique. Proves I'm not trying to seduce you. Not that you're not lovely, 'cos you are, but blood's thicker than water.'

'And you've got a girlfriend in New York.'

'Alas, no, the lovely Tru wisely decided I'd done one stupid thing too many and refused to take me back.'

'So is dating in New York as mad as it pretends to be?'

'Wouldn't know. Seriously, it seems a weird mixture of fantasy and gut-wrenching honesty.'

She looked at him curiously, as he continued, 'You go from 'Handsome, romantic thirties male seeks princess to sweep off her feet' right through to 'Bald solvent thirties male seeks very attractive size zero blonde (Nordic preferred).'

'And the women?'

'Tend to the brutally honest.'

'Such as?'

'Oh you know the thing, lonely early-forties female, given up on romance, seeking solvent male for stable relationship. Single fathers, alcoholics and pets welcome, but please, no smokers.'

'Pets welcome?'

'Big thing in the States. First thing Tru asked me, when I first met her, was what my favourite breed of dog would be.'

'It all sounds pretty bleak.'

'Yeah,' he swirled his water carefully, appreciating the tiny sliver of lemon. 'You know, before all this broke out, I'd just been on a whistle-stop tour of Africa, looking at communities where a whole generation of men had been wiped out by civil war. And after a few days I was pretty happy with my shots. They struck the right heroic note, or so I thought, you know, strong women battling on, rebuilding, not just coping but actually making things better. So I sat down to compare notes with Sophie, the real journo, she was a Fulbright scholar, and she said, 'These are pretty. Where are the real pictures?' Turns out I'd been doing Mother Courage, and she'd been talking to the women and getting a completely different story. It was about about how the older women who *did* have husbands were shunning the younger ones because they thought they'd steal their men with witchcraft, and how these whole families of sisters, in their teens, some of them, were working themselves into the ground to send the youngest one away to college so she might find a husband. It was too late for the others.'

'Yikes,' said Nia. 'No feminist revolution, then?'

'Not a bit,' Jamie said sadly. 'The really awful thing was the research Sophie'd done that showed it was just the same in this country after the First World War. A whole generation of men killed, and the women left stranded, 'cos they'd grown up believing marriage was their destiny.'

'I remember this from History,' Nia said. 'These women all took up arms and changed society for the better.'

'But at what personal cost?' Jamie was genuinely troubled. 'The tabloids of the day referred to them as the Surplus Women. The lonely hearts were full of 'Attractive girl, mid-twenties, seeks marriage with injured veteran in return for nursing duties.' What a bargain!'

'That's horrible. Did they have no self-respect?'

'That's the thing. It wasn't just what they felt about being single, it was the fact that society saw them as somehow tainted. So any form of marriage, even to an incontinent geriatric with only half a leg, was better than being a spinster. And the men were willing to put up with all sorts of stuff too, just to have a live-in nurse. Misery all round.'

'Thank heaven things have moved on,' Nia wasn't sure where this conversation was going; it seemed that rambling was in the Hughes family.

'It's an interesting piece, if you'd like to see it,' Jamie continued. 'The paper was looking to publish it, but decided in the current climate they'd better stick to a story of plucky heroines and communities all pulling together. Which is sort of where St Andrews comes in. They might send me over here for a while. No riots, lower than average mortality rates. Can't just be the devotion lavished on pets, whatever that survey says, or New York would've been a model community. D'you know, my neighbour has a cat which she keeps in her apartment, and she takes it for walks on a lead. Abi nearly burst a blood vessel laughing when I told her that.'

Nia enjoyed the evening. She didn't quite know what to make of Jamie, not least when he asked the chef for a vegetarian option, which wasn't on the menu. Nia had the fish, relying on the proximity of the sea. At the end of the evening Jamie walked her home and said, 'I've had a great evening. Thank you, but the real reason I wanted to buy you dinner was to apologise on behalf of the whole family. Matt is an idiot. Glynn, also an idiot, but I think he cares about you. I think he'd like another chance.'

'It's complicated.'

'Yeah, I heard.'

'He says Matt might be getting some therapy.'

'Think we can introduce him to his inner child, and he'll be a new person?' There was an edge to Jamie's voice she hadn't heard before, but then he smiled again and said, 'You may be right, therapy or something, but I don't know. Maybe it's different here, but in the States, there's not enough to go round, and frankly I think the people he's hurt deserve help more than he does, don't you?'

Jamie walked back to Glynn's and spent the rest of the evening discussing global economic forces. Nia put the flowers in water and washed her hair. She invited Amira round for a chat the next day, slightly discombobulated by the week's events.

'I met Glynn's brother, Jamie.'

Amira raised her eyebrows.

'He seems, I dunno, different, more sensitive,' Nia went on. 'He told me that after the First World War all the women who couldn't find husbands were called the Surplus Women.'

'Ouch!' Amira wrapped her arms round her body.

'Yeah,' said Nia, 'It wasn't just how they all suffered because they wanted love, and babies, and the whole family thing. It was society turning on them, treating them like outcasts. They would marry anyone, just to be married. It's terrifying. Tragic, really.'

'Well, it's still happening.'

'But why? I mean, financially it makes no sense now, so what's the point?'

'Status, jealously guarded by those inside the circle,' Amira said with a sigh. 'Oh come on, you must've seen it, early-forties single women, probably had a great passion in the past, get hitched to some halfway-presentable bloke and suddenly turn into a North Oxford wife, talking about how hard it is to get 'OUR children into good schools', or how they can't possibly work late because hubby's picking them up.'

Nia laughed, 'Or those mad women who start having strong opinions about teething toys!"

'Oh, you were there for that one?'

'How could I forget? She told me at the end of the evening that I should make the most of my youth, and then went 'Tick Tock!'

'That Denise is not a nice person. I'm only safe because she thinks I'm a witch. Or a lesbian. Or probably those are one and the same thing to her.'

'Yeah, I'm glad she didn't stick around.'

'I don't think Ruth would've coped much longer. I mean, I know she's really good about saying meditation's for everyone, and we don't have religious prejudices, but when she stood up and said 'Tonight let us send the light to Venezuala', I could see Ruth was trying not to laugh.'

'You know she started her own meditation group? They have a quick five minutes of breathing, then they start chanting for what they want.'

'So not just ecumenical, but basically mad?'

'Yeah, I'm not sure what sort of religion she thinks it is,' Nia was genuinely puzzled.

'I see that's one of the things that comes out in the WHO survey. Along with pets and exam marking wasn't it?'

'Yeah, I didn't really understand that. There's supposed to be another meeting.' Amira was still worried when Nia said goodbye, but hoped Ruth's presence would be a calming influence on her.

There was a welcome improvement in the weather on the day of the next CHLOE town meeting, and Nia saw her first solar-powered car of the year driving slowly past the Cathedral. She debated whether to go to the meeting, but didn't want to run into Glynn until she'd had more time to think. Ruth promised to fill her in on anything she missed, so she stayed home and settled down with an old novel. 'Can I join you?' Ruth said quietly, sitting down beside Eilidh, and looking at the tufts of red hair sticking out from the bundle curled up on the seat beside her.

'Oh, speak up,' said Eilidh. 'Dead to the world, she is now.'

'Babysitter ill again?'

'No. Change of plans. We went to see the psychologist again. I've been getting more and more worried.'

'And?'

'Well, she said she's not depressed, just very sensitive. And alright, I've heard this before, but when I asked what I could do about it she said, 'Sensitivity is not a character disorder', and lectured me about how society *needs* people to be sensitive and thoughtful.'

'Can't argue with that.'

'So, she suggested we forget about sending her to any school for a year or so, and forget about trying to make her more sociable. She said if Emily wants to stay with me, just let her.'

'Good for her,' Ruth said earnestly.

'You know, she was right. I feel better, Emily's sleeping better. Bob was worried for a while. I think he was pretty isolated as a lad, doesn't want her to be the same, but he's coming round.'

'That sounds like a very good outcome. No idea what sort of a parent I'm going to be,' Ruth rubbed her bump a little, feeling a gentle kick. Eilidh patted her arm as the newest CHLOE team leader called the meeting to order. There were strange mutterings as the new CHLOE commander introduced himself. A few people wondered out loud whether a man was really up to dealing with such complex issues, but he made a strong start and won most people over by the end of the meeting. He passed round a briefing paper from the Executive addressing longer-term planning into the next Autumn and Winter. A new building programme was envisaged to create extra storage and distribution facilities, and farmers were encouraged to use their land creatively, to reduce food miles. He was asked who was going to be running all this, and he coughed before replying, 'Ahm, we're redeploying lots of civil servants.' There was a quiet period of surprise, so he pressed on, 'As you know, local government has become rather a blunt instrument, rather haphazard, and the Executive decided that rather than keep employing all these people who would just try to make everything complicated again, they'd actually put them to some good use. I mean, would you prefer two strong lads unloading food deliveries or measuring the size of road signs? Some

299

patent officers, or someone to collect the rubbish? Someone to monitor water quality in rivers, or someone to make sure there's clean water in the taps? It's all about priorities. Of course, these people will be allowed to return to their normal duties once the situation stabilises, but it could be a while before that happens. We need to focus on important skills.'

'You know,' Eilidh whispered to Ruth, 'it's like the old joke, how many Oxford dons does it take to change a lightbulb?'

Ruth looked expectantly, as Eilidh said lightly, 'Change? Change? Whaddya mean, Change?'

'We're not exactly high priority, 'though, are we?'

'You're a healer. That's an A-plus in my book,' Eilidh wasn't ruffled, 'and actually this whole Cascadia thing has really brought what we do into focus. Not just the practical sciences either. Bob's had far more interest in his courses on charity, and I know History and Classics have had lots of people wanting to know about previous quakes. The internet made knowledge cheap, but now it seems like scholarship might be proving useful after all.'

On the way out Ruth said gently, 'Can I ask how it's going? Everything okay? If you don't want to talk, that's fine.'

'Aye,' said Eilidh, waiting until they were somewhere quieter, 'I'm sorry I was in such a state before. They did a biopsy. Said it's a duct, just as you said.'

'Glad to hear it,' Ruth wasn't surprised, but was still relieved for her friend.

'I feel a bit daft, going on like that,' Eilidh apologised. 'I mean, it's not as if I'd never thought about it. But with things the way they are … You hear all the stories about how the oncology wards went into melt-down, and you think, this is about the worst time possible to get a diagnosis like that.'

'Sobering, aye,' Ruth nodded. 'All these layers of life, what to eat, how to get clean clothes, how to educate the young, and then boom, you get cancer, or your family gets wiped out by an earthquake. One foot in front of the other. Not that I can see my feet any more, mind you.'

'How's Nia?' Eilidh asked. 'Glynn seems to be running about fifteen miles a day lately, from what I can tell. Not a happy bunny.'

'She's bearing up. Amira's been a great help.'

'It's true what they say, no use having money or beauty at times like this. What you need are good friends. Who knows what's coming next.' She patted Ruth goodbye, then gathered up her sleepy child more securely into her arms.

Chapter Thirteen

Jamie's parting words to Glynn were cryptic. He'd hugged the children and Abi tightly, promising to be back soon, then said, 'Nice little shop, that Ethereal. Might call in there next time I'm here.' Then the train arrived, and he was gone.

'What's he done now?' Glynn moaned to Abi, as he drove her and the children back into town.

'I don't know. Have you seen Nia lately?'

'I like Nia. She said the bunnies were cute,' Becky joined in.

'Yeah, but she dumped you, right?' said Robbie.

'Robbie! That's rude!' Abi turned round and scolded him.

'Sorry,' he mumbled.

'Nah, you're alright,' Glynn said casually. 'She did dump me, but all is not lost. I'll keep you posted. You can be my wing man, young Robert.'

'Cool!' he relaxed and started pulling at Becky's hair. Chastened to be caught out by his nephew, Glynn decided to be a man and went round to Nia's after work. The shop was shut, but she was willing to let him in.

She made him a drink and they discussed the latest CHLOE directives. He was debating whether to mention Jamie and ask whether she'd met him, when she suddenly said, 'Shit! Sorry!'

'What?' he said, confused and a little scared.

'Look at this!' she waved her fingers at him. 'Chipped already. Two hours I spent doing these yesterday and now, look!'

He looked, and said cautiously, 'Life is hell without a decent manicurist in town?'

'I'm serious. Every damn thing is out of control now.

I can't get a grip on any of it. Any of it.' She banged her mug down on the table. Glynn observed her warily, 'Hey, come on,' he said, 'lots of people your age haven't got life plans set in stone. You've got plenty of time to work out what you want to do.'

'That is not the point. Every bloody thing is out of control.' She stood up and walked over to look out of the window, 'I can't keep my flat tidy. I can't stick to a diet. I plan to take more exercise but I never keep it up. I plan to read more books, but I don't. I want to learn French, but I don't. My ironing basket is always overflowing, and the recycling bin. I plan to get up early, but I'm always running late. I can't even keep my nails tidy, so what hope have I got of ever sorting out the big stuff?'

Glynn reacted decisively, 'Why are you on a diet? You're gorgeous!' She remained staring out the window, back to him, 'Frankly, I've put on a stone in the last year. I feel fat and horrible. So I decide to be good, and I am for a few days, but then I get this overwhelming urge for something I shouldn't have, and I give in. It used to be chocolate, but there's not much around, anything will do. Then I eat too much again and feel sick, and I feel pathetic 'cos I can't even stick to a diet. Okay?' She turned and glared at him. He jumped up and hugged her, 'What's this about, eh? What's the matter? You're not telling me you're all worked up about some stupid diet? And you shouldn't be dieting anyway. You're beautiful.' She pulled away, 'But it's all of it. I can't get to grips with any of it. I don't know how it all went wrong. I was so organised at school, and when I first came here. I keep thinking if I could just get one thing sorted out, even clear the ironing, it would all sort of fall into place again, give me a good base. I could be disciplined, keep on top of it. All this clutter, it's bad for the chi. But I can't do it. I'm just warding off one disaster after another. I never seem to get anything sorted out completely.'

She slumped on the sofa, and Glynn sat down slowly beside her. He waited for a few moments, then said, 'I suspect sorting out your ironing wouldn't help. I don't do any ironing at all, and it hasn't held me back. But then again, what do I know? Early thirties, no fixed job, no home, and then you came along and I messed that up too.' She turned her body away from him. He pulled her gently back to face him and continued, 'You are the best thing that ever happened to me, and I nearly got you killed. All for a brother who always tried to shit on me, metaphorically, and is now doing so literally as well. I am so, so, sorry, Ni. Forgive me. That's why I'm here. I've been trying to tell you for weeks. I know I've been mind-bogglingly stupid. I've hurt you, 'though I never meant to. You have every right to hate me. You were right all along, and I cannot tell you how sorry I am, but if we take things slowly, I'd really like to try again.'

The words crocheted in the air between them. She looked at him, then looked away and said, 'We can't just pretend nothing's happened.'
'No, no, of course not. I wouldn't expect that. I just can't bear for you to hate me.' Without making eye contact, she leaned her head on his shoulder, 'I have missed you, Glynn. But I'm scared.' He stroked her hair. She said nothing, but the silence was warm, and when Glynn spoke again it was in a lighter tone, 'If I could make a little suggestion? I could to help to tackle the chaos a little.' She sat up, 'You iron?'
'Oh no. What you need is to get to the root of these

problems, focus on what's important first.' He jumped up and went into the bathroom, emerging with a roll of cotton wool, and said, 'Chipped nail varnish is never attractive on a woman.' She laughed and accepted the gift. By the time he left they'd arranged to meet for lunch later in the week, and Nia had half-accepted an invitation to join a trip to Edinburgh later in the month, depending on how well Ruth was doing.

'What did you say to her?' Glynn asked Jamie over the 'phone that evening. 'Who? Me?' Jamie feigned surprise. 'Oh alright, I just told her you were an idiot.'

'Ah, well the honest approach seems to have worked. I owe you one.'

'Don't think anything of it, mate. She's lovely. Too young for my taste, of course, but you could do much worse.'

'Thank you for the advice, oh guru. Gonna tell me what really happened with Tru?'

'Pretty much what I told you. I was an idiot, took my eye off the ball, took her for granted, all that stuff. So I got what I deserved. Anyway, I'm stuck on this wretched tug for the next week, so let me know how you get on.'

'Not gonna happen.'

'Glad to hear it. Give my love to Abi.'

After the excitement of Jamie's visit had died down, Becky and Robbie were grumpy and distracted. Abi was glad to leave them with her parents, playing a calming game of cards when she left for her second social engagement of the year. Bob opened the door, 'Abi! Great! Come in. Eilidh's putting Emily to bed. Food won't be long. Here, let me have your coat.' He led her into the living-room, and said, 'Can I fix you a drink?' We're down to the Madeira now, if you fancy some?'

'No thanks,' she said, settling into the sofa. 'A cup of tea would be great.'

'No problem,' said Bob, 'that's just what I was going to have myself.' He poured the tea, added some powdered milk, then set them on the coffee table before sitting opposite her. 'There we go,' he said. 'Now, how are you doing? Eilidh told me what's been happening. Are you alright?'

Abi reached for her tea, and swirled it with a spoon to help the milk dissolve, 'Actually Bob, no, I'm not alright. This is a bloody nightmare. I don't know whether I'm coming or going. But really, I appreciate you asking. I do. You've no idea how people are about this. I get everyone asking about Matt's health, all with some veiled, or sometimes not so veiled, accusation, that I'm to blame. Nobody thinks what things are like for me. D'you know, mad old Miss Butler came up to me in the street last week and told me I should go back to him because he's a sick man and he's given me two lovely children. That's what she said.'

'Oh, but she *is* mad,' said Bob soundly. The doorbell rang, and they heard Eilidh running down the stairs, whispering loudly, 'I'll go.' Abi sipped her tea, 'I know, but everyone's thinking it. I'm sure they are.'

'It must be very frustrating,' Bob nodded. 'I think you're coping remarkably well. Have you thought any more about the practicalities?'

'Well, as soon as there's some sort of order restored I'll file for divorce, force him to sell the house. But I can't do anything for now. I spoke to someone at the council and the best he could offer me was a place in a women's refuge. And here's Matt sitting in a four-bedroom house which my parents helped us buy. It makes my blood boil.'

'Surely there are some procedural steps you could take? Wouldn't he leave if you asked him? Or is that a naïve question?'

'No, it's not. I know there are women who throw the husband out, or ask him to leave and he goes. Finn told Matt that the kids needed their home and suggested he move out. It wasn't pretty. A mixture of 'They can wander the streets barefoot, for all I care', and 'She can come back to live here any time', but of course, only if I go back to him and pretend nothing's happened. And I'm the one in the wrong, according to all the local gossips. Poor sick husband, deserted by his wife, no wonder he needs a drink. Hi, Ruth, don't mind me. I'm just sounding off. I don't know. I get so angry, but I should have left him years ago, so I know it's my fault.'

'Oh yes,' said Ruth, lowering herself into the armchair, 'all your fault. After all, you're the one who's been knocking back the White Lightning, hitting people with bottles and generally being a grade A bastard. Must be your fault.' Abi smiled and her eyes flashed for a moment, 'I will try to remember that. How are you?'

'Fat and sleepy,' Ruth groused.

Bob was agitated, trying to find more cushions to make Ruth comfortable, but she shooed him away and said, 'So, Bob, what's this I hear about you trying to stick electrodes into Emily?'

'Oh, oh,' said Bob, clutching a cushion to his chest. 'What did Eilidh say?'

'Something about you experimenting with babies and kittens. And killing all baby boys under two. Oh no, that was Herod,' Ruth winked at Abi as they watched

Bob's response. 'Oh well, yes,' he started, pacing around the room, 'it's fascinating. They've done experiments with kittens which prove that visual perception does vary among individuals, and can be artificially manipulated. Of course, kitten experiments are notoriously unreliable. In boys they've shown that different chemical make-ups mean that some men do see colour spectrums differently. It's fascinating for how we understand reality via perceptual content. Not that I'm an experimental man myself. It's the implications that interest me. But,' he continued seriously, 'I never suggested putting electrodes on Emily, or any other child. I was merely pointing out that boy babies gave more useful data to interpret. Fewer variables, and so on. D'you know, in boys you can actually pin down colour perceptions. Depending on whether a child has A or B in their genetic make-up, they'll perceive the shift from red to orange at one point or another on the spectrum. And colour blindness is another one – more common in boys because it's on the X chromosome, so girls need two mutations for it to show up. Did you know there are some valleys near Glasgow where nearly twenty percent of the men are colour blind? Astonishing!' He was almost as astonished as his audience members.

'And this isn't to do with the amount Glaswegians drink, I suppose?' Abi hinted. 'No, no,' Bob rolled on, 'No, it may be an evolutionary trait which helps to see in twilight. Incidence of colour blindness falls sharply the closer you get to the equator.'

'Well, that's fascinating Bob,' said Ruth. 'Pity I'm having a girl, really.'

'That's exactly what I said about Emily! Ah, yes,' he

paused. 'I may have been misquoted. Do not fear, Ruth, I have no Dr. Frankenstein interest in your unborn child.' They laughed, and Abi relaxed as the conversation circled round safe, familiar topics. Only once over dinner when the topic came up did she remark on how people were treating her in town.

Eilidh was strong in her defence, accusing her critics of reading too many Aga Sagas, 'You know how it is. They think the crisis was months ago, so you must be nearly at the final chapter by now. Everything neatly tied up, apart from the odd fly in the ointment for realism's sake. Except it's not like that. You'd have thought by now more people would have grasped that. This whole year, the 'flu, the depression, it's not a mini-series. Things drag on. Hell, it gets boring. It's not dramatic with some well-crafted plot line. Our lives won't be neatly tied up in fifty pages' time. I am truly sorry I haven't been more support. I just had no idea how bad things were.'

Bob started to wash up, and Ruth broke the brief moment of awkwardness as they moved to the living room, by saying, 'I was in the shower thinking, what colour shall I paint my toenails when I can see them again. I am so longing for a bath, it's driving me dotty. Even if we had reliable hot water, I couldn't fit in the tub. I never knew I liked baths so much!'

'Ah, long baths,' Eilidh sighed. 'I can't relax any more. I end up looking at all the bottles of bubble bath Bob's bought me over the years, and I realise I'm thinking 'Cube, cylinder, blue, yellow, white, one, two, three', even when Emily's not even in the house. Tragic, no?'

'Are you feeling well, in general?' said Abi, as Ruth squirmed in slow motion, trying to get comfortable in her chair. 'Oh, I'm lucky, it's only now I feel I can't move around much,' said Ruth. 'I'd look pretty strange on a bike right now.'

'I was really ill with Emily,' said Eilidh, 'but probably just as well.'

'How so?'

Eilidh lowered her voice, 'Bob was like a mother hen – delighted to wrap me in cotton wool and run around while I was swooning. I swear his blood pressure shot up every time I went upstairs. He'd probably have had a heart attack if I'd wanted to carry on as normal.'

'Well, you're both lucky,' said Abi. 'When I was carrying Robbie I was supposed to rest up for a few weeks after a scare. I'd had a miscarriage the year before, so I took time off work, and at the end of the first week Matt came home, saw me on the sofa watching television. You'll never guess what he said.'

'Why are you lazing around?' Eilidh guessed.

'Almost,' Abi sighed, 'he said 'Why haven't you vacuumed?' Really.'

'What did you say?' Ruth gulped in astonishment.

'I cried a lot, then rang my mother, and she came round and had a stiff word with him. He was fine after that. You know, you look back, and think, bugger me, what was I thinking, letting him carry on?'

'Well, maybe it's a blessing in disguise that I'm doing this on my own,' Ruth said with a frown.

Once the washing up was finished, they took their time to enjoy the first chocolate éclairs of the year. Abi felt safer for a while, more determined that she would move back into town and reclaim her community. She'd offered Ruth a lift home, but she preferred to walk, so Bob gallantly insisted he would accompany her. They were at the door, saying their goodbyes, when Eilidh said, 'Oh hang on, I've got some sweeties for the bairns in the kitchen. You head off, Bob, no point keeping Ruth out in the cold.'

'Okay. I'll be back in about thirty minutes, dear,' he said, escorting Ruth down the path.

Abi moved to do up her coat, but Eilidh came back with the dish and said, 'Hang on a minute. I mean, would you mind? I'd really like it if you could stay a bit longer.'

'Sure. What's up?'

'Can we sit down for a moment? Let me take your coat.'

'I'll have another éclair, if you don't mind,' said Abi, settling into the chair.

'Oh, of course, of course,' Eilidh leaned against the wall opposite her. She took a deep breath and said, 'I want to apologise. I haven't offered you as much support as I should have through all this.'

'It's fine.'

'No. I want to explain,' She looked at Abi who nodded. 'You see, I left Bob a few years ago. You've been so brave with it all, and I wasn't.' She rocked slightly, and Abi paused mid-éclair, 'I had no idea.'

'Well, no-one knew. I was only gone a few days. Rang Bob from my mother's to say I was leaving him, and then three days later I came home, and that was that.'

'He must have been persuasive.'

'Actually, he didn't say anything. Not a word. And I still came back.'

'I'm not with you.'

'Do you mind me telling you this? It's probably the last thing you need right now.'

311

'No, it's fine. Really, I'm happy to listen. I don't understand. What happened? Why did you leave?' Abi finished the éclair, and Eilidh took a swig of Madeira. 'Emily was two – lots of tantrums, usual stuff. I felt I was going mad, and Bob just didn't see it. He was calm, and he was rational and he was beautifully detached from it. It was so cold, I just left.'

'And he didn't say anything?' Abi queried.

'When I rang him to say I was leaving he said, 'Thank you for telling me.' When I got home, he just said over dinner one night, 'Marriage is difficult.' And that was that. I tried telling him, but he couldn't see that there was a problem. I might as well have been speaking in Latin for all the sense he thought I was making.'

'Yikes. But if you were so cut off, why did you come back?'

'Stupidity?' Eilidh laughed briefly. 'Part of me said it was for Emily, stable family and all that. He's not a bad father. But I suppose the main reason was that I just couldn't tell anyone. What could I say? My husband deals calmly with our crying child, doesn't lose his temper and brings me flowers once in a while. He's not a bad husband. And frankly, I'd spent so much time convincing my friends he wasn't a cold fish, I think I was too proud to admit I was wrong. It just all comes up again when someone is brave enough to leave, I just can't deal with it, that's all.'

'Is he really that bad? Any time I see him he seems to be laughing,' Abi tried to offer some consolation for a problem she didn't quite understand.

'It's empty, Abi,' Eilidh forced out. 'He relies on clever bits of information and lines from the old *Fast Show* scripts. When I married him, I thought he had hidden depths. There's a line in Yeats about the 'pilgrim soul', and I thought I'd seen it in him. Then I found out he's not an iceberg after all, just an ice floe. Terrible mistake for a geographer to make.' She was smiling, but said sadly, 'He just doesn't communicate.'

'I'm sorry, that sounds really rough.' Abi didn't know what to say.

'So, I came back and decided to make the best of it for Emily's sake, but now I'm not so sure it is what's best for her,' Eilidh continued. 'He cares about her, but she's so tense. I know I get too caught up in her fears and worries, but I don't think it touches him at all. And how is that going to take her as she grows up? Looks fine on the surface, but actually her father's an emotional cripple.'

'That bad?' Abi winced slightly.

'Sounds awful, I know. Alright, women are much better with emotions, but more and more I think Bob is simply acting it out.' Eilidh glanced at the Madeira, then took a gulp of cold tea, and sighed, 'When we got together, I was having problems. He said the right things, listened, made thoughtful gestures, but I don't think he was really engaged. He's learned how to have some social graces, but it's not enough.'

'I'm so sorry. It sounds awful.'

'Oh, it's alright,' Eilidh took a deep breath, 'I just felt I hadn't been honest with you. I just wanted to explain why I've been a bit off. You've been so brave and stuck to your guns. Here I am supposedly with this perfect life, and I'm pretty pathetic, stuck, feet of clay. It all looks so good on paper, but underneath, well, …'

'Are of thinking of leaving again?'

'No. No, I don't think so. There's the disruption for Emily, and in a strange way I do love him. He does try – he will let me be affectionate ...'

'Oh, that's an awful thing to say! You can't live like that!'

'I do love some things about him. The only thing that truly worries me is what might happen if I met someone else, someone who might, I don't know, truly connect, you know?' Abi nodded, and Eilidh went on, 'but then, how likely is that, eh?'

'I'm not the one to ask. Not sure I know anyone who's been lucky in love. I think hard work does it for some, but as for the magic, well, call me cynical, but maybe it doesn't exist'

'Aye, that's where I've got to as well!'

Abi gave her a hug and said, 'I feel bad I didn't realize. Things always seemed so good between you, like proper grown-ups. The romantic ideal, meeting on a train and all that. Or isn't that the whole story?'

Eilidh sat down and fiddled with the baby monitor, 'Not really. We did have that odd meeting on the train, and he was good company for an afternoon. Then a few weeks later there was this awful Staff Development course with role-playing. Half-way through Bob stood up and declared the whole thing a parody of education and led a walkout to the pub, which obviously endeared him to me. And then, well, I kept seeing him a lot, not obviously sitting beside me in meetings or anything, but sitting opposite me, little conversations. And this went on for months and months, and I wondered about it, but only a wee bit. He's a very private person. You don't really speculate about someone like that. At least, I didn't, before.'

'So, what happened? Did he just jump you?'

'Oh lordy,' Eilidh laughed, 'could you imagine it? That would be a sight! Well, I was pissed off one evening, everyone I knew was out and I just thought to hell with it, so I rang him at home and asked if he wanted to go for a drink.'

'Ah, you jumped him.'

'No, because he said 'Thank you for asking, but I've just put a lasagne in the oven.' No, honestly, he did!'

The two women laughed until they cried. Finally Eilidh said, 'So, I thought, that's that then, but two days later he sent me a gift-wrapped copy of his latest book.'

'Oh, now that's romantic. What does he write on? Ethics, isn't it?'

Eilidh nodded, 'It was called 'The Ethics of Intervention', snappy title, I know, but I opened it and saw that he'd dedicated it, as part of the printed acknowledgements, mind, 'To Eilidh', and he'd written by hand underneath, 'No, I don't know any other Eilidhs'.'

'Wow, that is pretty dramatic. Hardback copy, was it?'

'I know! Apparently his publisher begged him to reconsider, but he wouldn't. I was a bit confused, sent an email saying 'Thanks'. So, then he sent me *another* copy, two days later, and under the inscription he'd scribbled, 'Marry me?' Just like that.'

'Bloody hell. So what did you do?'

'I know. So I went to see him, and did the, 'What the hell are you playing at?' line, but he was so obviously tortured, inarticulate actually, that I took pity on him and suggested we have dinner, and we sort of went from there. So, this went on for a couple of months, and I was staying at his place a few nights a week, and he went away for a month, Princeton, and then, well, he called me all the time and left me these adorable little emails.' She looked sadly at her feet, 'and I thought I could be in love with him. It's my fault. I'd lost the love of my life when I was in college, leukaemia, and I wasn't looking to replace him, but I suppose the nice, casual relationship wasn't enough. I wanted to have the whole package again, so I convinced myself it was the real thing, that we were soulmates. Maybe if we'd taken longer over things, it would have worked better, but I didn't want to go through all that 'getting to know you stuff'. I wanted to be living happily ever after, and then he came back and he proposed again, with a ring, hidden inside a book. And I went to buy a wedding dress.'

'That *is* very romantic,' Abi said. 'With me and Matt it was more like, shall we get hitched then, but we already had Alexis on the way by then.'

'Alexis would be the child you miscarried?'

'Aye, five months along. But we were talking about you. So, go on!'

'Alright,' Eilidh told her the rest, 'so, yes, all the warning signs were there, but I convinced myself it would be okay, I was thirty-five, and he's a good man. In fact, sometimes I think he's the most moral, honourable person I've ever met, because he wants to be kind but doesn't have instincts. He doesn't understand what people need, so he tries to rationalise it,' she trailed off, 'and he grieves it …'

'And now? said Abi quietly.

'I don't know,' she mumbled. 'Saw a counsellor once who told me I smile when I talk about him.'

'Actually, you do,' said Abi, 'that's true. Whereas Matt's name makes my face contort into a gargoyle.'

Eilidh smiled sympathetically before saying, 'She got

me to write him a letter spelling out all my frustrations, not to give to him, but as a way to vent it all, really have a go, but when I read it back, I realised I'd just written him a love letter, so I think I'm stuck with it. Thank you.'

'What on earth for?'

'It's a relief to tell someone. I'm sorry to add to your troubles.'

'Not at all. I'm very glad you told me. I think you're very brave,' Abi told her sincerely.

'I don't think I am,' Eilidh sighed, 'but it's good of you to say so.' Abi left for the night, sad for her friend's life as well as her own. When Bob came home, Eilidh kissed him and they checked that Emily was sleeping soundly before Bob settled into his study to catch up on a few hours' work. Eilidh had a long bath before turning in.

Nia was nervous but excited on the morning of the trip. She hadn't been further than Dundee since the previous summer, and a trip to Edinburgh had been a big deal even before then. She'd found an old cotton shirt, and felt slightly odd out of her usual winter gear. She pulled the sleeves of the cardigan down to cover her wrists as she walked down to the meeting point. The trip had attracted a full house, in addition to the official reps who were gathering to discuss the admissions crisis for the coming September. While the universities were trying to carry on, setting exams and marking dissertations, the exam boards for A-levels and Highers had arranged for *ad hoc* granting of qualifications, based on reports of coursework and teachers' recommendations. The universities were struggling to make offers, and the science faculties were particularly worried. The medical schools had refused to take any new students without a serious review, and most university administrators were pressurising the other departments to compensate by taking more students, regardless of qualifications. This, Glynn had explained to Nia, could be a problem.

She knew most of the people on the bus, and Glynn introduced her to Rose from the library, and Nick from Biology, 'He's the one I told you about - tried to superglue his sunglasses and got his eye almost fused by the fumes.' Nick was wearing a short-sleeved check shirt, but most of the men had simply rolled up their normal shirt sleeves. Funny how much of a difference that made.

The roads were quiet, but the journey was slow. A universal fifty-mile-an-hour limit had been imposed to encourage fuel conservation, and the roads before they reached the motorway were in a poor state of repair. Twice they had to turn round and backtrack several miles because the minibus couldn't make it down the main road. This circuitous route allowed them to see how other places were faring. Some of the smaller villages were abandoned, as services had been centralised in larger communities, linked to the outlying regions by a single daily bus service.

Nia and Glynn sat in the back seat, cuddled up in silence, watching the new landscape unfold. The motorway had more of a *Mad Max* feel to it, with traffic down to one lane in places where accidents had simply been moved to the side. Everyone was driving cautiously. As they drew near the Forth Road Bridge, traffic ground to a halt. Tuning in the radio, Nick found a local station which told them the tailback was particularly bad today. Only one lane was open, due to repair works.

'I was thinking,' Glynn said, stroking Nia's hair, 'I'll see you for lunch, but I'm going to be pretty busy all day. When we get back, why don't you come back to my place? I'll make us something to eat.'

'Not your famous casserole?'

'Something much better.'

'You're on,' she said, matching the twinkle in his eye.

The minibus slowly made its way towards the bridge, dovetailing into the main queue behind a red van advertising a touring performance of *Ariadne auf Naxos*. Nick shouted from the front, 'Hey, Rose, was Ariadne the one who got eaten by a sea monster, or the spider woman?'

'Moron,' Rose shouted back. 'Ariadne was the classic helper maiden, helped Theseus get out of the maze once he'd killed the Minotaur. So he took her away with him, promised to marry her, and ended up dumping her on Naxos before they made it home.'

'Cheerful!'

'Yeah well,' Rose continued, 'some versions of the story go on to say Ariadne gets rescued by the god Dionysus and lives happily ever after. Theseus, however, the great hero, doesn't exactly have an easy life. He's sailing back from Naxos, maybe dumped her deliberately, maybe forgot about her. Actually, he's terribly forgetful. Forgets to change his sails to show he's killed the Minotaur and so his father thinks he's failed and tops himself, so good old Theseus. Should have had a sign on his head saying, 'Ooh sorry, didn't mean to do that.''

'Cool!' Nick agreed.

'Sorry,' said Rose, turning round to Nia with an apologetic grin. 'I used to be a lecturer. Old habits die hard.'

'Used to be?'

'Long story.'

'We could be here for a while,' invited Nia, nodding to the stationary queue.

'Okay, short version,' Rose began, 'I came up here for a two-year job. Half-way through, my mum comes to stay, she'd split up from my loony stepfather and he was being, let's say, very difficult. Cancelled her credit cards, that sort of thing. So, start of my second year they have a permanent job come up, my field, everyone says, 'Oh yes, you must apply, you're doing such a good job.' So I apply, thinking this could work out well, and then they don't even shortlist me. They didn't even have the decency to tell me. I just got the round-robin email saying, 'Please attend the interview presentations next Friday. Candidates are presenting in the following order.' And I wasn't on the list.'

'Ouch.'

'Yeah. They gave it to some girl from Cambridge who was married to a bloke in the English department. You know, she even had spelling mistakes on her presentation handout. And, you know, jobs are jobs, but it was the way they handled it that really got to me.'

'So you quit?' Nia was surprised, given how dedicated Glynn seemed to be in pursuing his goal of a permanent job.

'Not quite,' Rose replied. 'I got talking to Howard, senior librarian, he offered me a job for when my contract finished. I could have applied for more temporary teaching jobs, nothing else permanent that year, maybe got one, but then I'd have dragged my poor mum all over the country with me. She likes it here. I'd have felt rubbish about making her share a poky little studio in the back end of Birmingham, or

Lampeter. And anyway, that horrible business with the job here left a nasty taste in my mouth. I thought, 'Do I really want to spend my life working with academics who behave like this? Oh, individually some of them are great. It's a cultural problem, I suppose. So, I took the library job and I'm taking some courses. In a year or so I'll be a fully qualified librarian, and then I can go wherever I please.'

'Footloose and fancy free.'

'Libraries everywhere,' Rose agreed. 'I could actually choose where to live, not get thrown around at random, ending up in one of the few places that have Classics departments. Not many of them are in places I'd care to live, so this is going to work out far better. And d'you know, I do miss the teaching sometimes, but I'm still working with books, and you don't have to take the work home with you.'

It took nearly two hours to cross the bridge and approach the city centre. Everyone fell quiet as they drove along Princes Street, contemplating the change in the city. Rose had already been dropped off to meet a friend at one of the out-of-town DIY stores, which had been turned into a giant car boot sale. Nick had been due to get out with Nia at the Scot Memorial, but had yelped and demanded the bus be stopped some two miles, earlier when he'd caught sight of an open branch of Dungeons Workshop. 'He paints little model men, and then acts out the Hundred Years war,' Glynn had told Nia with a straight face. 'Don't imagine he's had any new men for a while. We need to check he doesn't have a stroke if they've got new stocks!'

Nia stood beside the Scot Monument, slightly disorientated by the crowds of people. She felt jostled, and shrank back against a wall, trying to get

321

her bearings. Apart from a thicker than usual layer of moss, the structures of the architecture were unchanged, and would probably look much the same for a hundred years even if humanity disappeared overnight. Street level was a different matter, as a new organic layer of commerce had spread out over the old. Many of the larger stores were still trading, but the window displays were ragged and fading, and most business seemed to be taking place in the first ten feet around the main doors. In some of the doorways the main shop floor could be seen in a dim haze, problems with power supplies, flooding and general neglect had shrunk the shop floor areas to those easily illuminated by daylight. It was more like shopping in a large market than a major commercial centre. Her meeting with her friend Jenna was short and awkward. Nia had reassured her that the hamster was well, but clearly Jenna wasn't. After sharing a shallow cup of tea, looking out towards the castle, Jenna had sat there without talking until she shrugged listlessly when Nia suggested shopping, and simply went home.

Although she felt guilty about her relief when her friend left, Nia was soon distracted by the prospect of some retail therapy. She hadn't had much opportunity to spend any money in months, and Ruth had somehow managed to keep paying her as normal, unlike many people who'd been fobbed off with promisary notes and ended up in hock to the CHLOE administrators, just to keep eating. Nia wandered along, overwhelmed by the sudden choices confronting her, until her attention was caught by a small stall tucked into an alcove. She turned over a few coloured blocks of soap, while looking surreptitiously at the range of pills on sale with labels promising to ward off 'flu, cure depression and help with weight loss. 'None of that herbal nonsense here, love,' said the man behind the table. 'Real pharmaceuticals, straight from Europe. Now,' he looked at her closely, 'not that you need it, mind, but this has been a hard year for us all. Wanna get back into those skinny jeans? I'll do you a two-for-one deal on weight loss pills. Lovely girl like you shouldn't be on her own.'

Nia looked at the price list and wavered, thinking about the evening ahead. Before she could answer, a woman in a red uniform tapped her on the shoulder and said, 'Could I have a word?' The stall-holder rolled his eyes and settled back to read his newspaper as Nia stepped away.

'Hi!' said the woman. 'You're not local, right?'

'No,' said Nia cautiously, looking around, but no-one was paying them any attention.

'Good. I'm a street warden. Nothing to worry about. He's not peddling heroin, 'though he is technically breaking a number of laws. Now, the Executive's not going to do anything, so we have this volunteer force trying to give people advice about all sorts of things. Basically, he's selling vitamins, but there have been cases of some real medical pills getting into the system, and that can be nasty. And we still have the antibiotic resistance to worry about.'

'Oh,' said Nia, feeling very uncomfortable.

'No problem, for now,' said the woman, 'not to worry. Not everything's gone to pot. I imagine you're looking to perk yourself up a bit, no? Well, I can tell you if you take the money you might have given to that shark, go and ask for Rachel in Jenners, she'll make you look a million dollars in a couple of hours, chemical-free, guaranteed.'

Nia paused under the faded grandeur of the Jenners façade, and walked into the main foyer, illuminated with large glowing candles. As she ran her hand over the smooth, curved banisters, she couldn't quite work out why it felt so strange. Certainly there were very few people around, and a few rails of clothes for men and women spread through the halls. She saw two teenage girls, adjusting their outfits in front of two large mirrors and admired their style, but she couldn't see any similar clothes out on display. She pulled a short, flowery dress off the rail, noting that the warden had been right – even with price fluctuations, the dress would set her back about the same as the pills she'd been offered.

She held it up in front of the mirror, trying to imagine her shape under the jeans and baggy shirt, but the colour wasn't quite her, and the shape wasn't quite right. She sighed, feeling very bedraggled.

'Hi, can I help?' a voice said from behind her, and she turned to see a very young man wearing a tie. 'We're accepting all forms of credit including LETS,' he said.

'Oh, that's okay, I have money.'

'Ah, that's why you came in the main door,' he gave her a wide smile. 'Not many people do nowadays, but we like to keep the show. Nicholas Gray, how can I help?'

'Ummn, I saw someone who told me to ask for Rachel.'

'Ah, yes, looking for something customised.'

'Oh, no, I really haven't got that much money,' she backtracked.

'Nonsense,' he said steering her towards the back of the store, 'Rachel will set you up for half what you'd need for that cardboard-cut-out dress. Come along.' Nia was surprised, as he led her towards the back of the store, and she smelled rich cooking flavours rising up. 'Cholent,' he said, 'isn't it wonderful? It's been like a mecca for Jews round here. We've been so lucky.'

Nia realised why most people were coming in the back of the store. In one section was a large café with about forty people all tucking into bowls of stew. She saw an advertising poster on the far wall: 'Fed up with CHLOE parcels? Try CHOLEnt at Jenners.' Nicholas led her past the smells, saying, 'Make do and mend, you see. Rachel's been doing this all her life, and her mother before her, so it was a godsend having her here.' They paused outside a bright red door, where a tall woman with long silver hair was sitting on a chaise longue, sipping from a mug.

'Ah, Rachel, a young lady in need of our services,' Nicholas introduced her. 'Tell her about your mother's dress.'

'Oh, I don't mean to disturb you,' Nia backed away.

'You're not!' Rachel nodded for her to sit down. 'I'm merely having a break. I never mind telling the family story. Well into my anecdotage, if you get my meaning.'

Nia sat down, and Nicholas sat at her feet, looking up at Rachel expectantly. 'Well?' he said, 'And make sure you start at the beginning.'

'My mother was eighteen in nineteen-forty-five,' the old woman began, 'living in Levenshulme in Manchester. There was a dance planned for the town hall, but my mother and her sister had used up all their coupons. There was an article in the paper that the council was selling some old parachutes, so mum and Sylvie queued up for two days outside the Council offices. So, there were about thirty people by the time the office opened, and everyone said my mum was mad, they'd never get the parachutes, but they did, these big tattered sheets of silk. So, they got out their sewing machine and made two gorgeous dresses, and at the dance my mother met my father. Fairytale ending. And after that my mum set up a tailoring business, and we've been going ever since. Looked like we might retire for a while, when the disposable fashion was in, but this last year, business has been brisk.'

'Tell her about your mother's cousin,' Nicholas encouraged, enchanted.

'Oh yes, so same dance. My mother's cousin who'd been pretty scornful of the parachute queue, ended up queuing herself to get some cotton sheet they were selling from the undertakers.'

'Ewh!' said Nia.

'No, no, you haven't heard the best bit yet!' Nicholas chuckled.

'So, she made her dress, carefully using the best bits, but the lights at the dance were so bright it showed up places where the fabric had been embossed, even though it was on the underskirt. She turned up with 'R.I.P.' on her backside!'

Nia joined in their giggles and Rachel said, 'Come on, let's get you sorted out. Lovely girl like you shouldn't be hiding in those clothes.' She opened the red door, and Nia gasped, looking into a magical cavern where rails of clothes were lined up against stacks and bolts of fabric. On one side of the room were a dozen sewing machines, some operated by teenagers. 'Amazing the number of hand machines still around,' said Rachel. 'Of course, lots of them are tiny, which is why we've got the youngsters in. Nicholas here has some potential, as does Martin over there, but really, we need the girls for the detail, they've got a much better eye.' Nia looked enviously at a bank of tables with boxes of buttons, ribbons and trims where a dozen or so women were trying on different outfits.

'You just wait, dear Rachel! Mrs. Donnelly's suit is looking *so* hot already!' said Nicholas, before turning to Nia. 'Over there we have second-hand clothes, some very nice items, mostly dropped off on a LETS basis, but as you have actual money, you can go to town!'

'What do you mean?' Nia was confused.

'Nicholas, thank you. Now, off you go,' Rachel shooed him out, before turning back to Nia. 'Lovely lad, very keen, but sometimes comes on a wee bit too strong. Now then, dear, what can we do for you?'

'Umm, I've sort of got a date tonight, my boyfriend, it's complicated, and I don't have anything to wear, I mean, I've put on a lot of weight, and I thought maybe I should buy something. Someone on the street sent me here.'

'Excellent,' Rachel rubbed her hands together. 'Let's get started. I think we might have something out the back we could work with. But first, we need to sort out the foundations. Not exactly working your assets, my dear girl. We can do something about that.'

'Really?'

'Oh yes, full service. We can even get shoes done with a few days' notice. Luce over there is a whiz with the delicates. If she was a wee bit older, I'd push her to try for a job with Agent Provocateur, but I think she's best with the frou-frou stuff for now. This is such fun! Back like olden days, customizing gowns, making underwear, almost like doing *haute couture*! You never know what life will bring to you.'

She bounced out to the back like a teenager, returning with a long purple silk dress with heavy bell sleeves. Nia surrendered her free will and spent the next few hours being measured and pinned, before leaving the store feeling much happier with a strappy purple cocktail dress wrapped up in brown paper and string. Her new boned, lacy underwear had been altered ever so slightly to give her a much sleeker shape even under her old clothes. She smiled as she thought about the little pink heart which Luce had sewed on the back of the basque - her trademark - Rachel had explained, when she showed her the same detail on each garment, before wrapping the dress in brown paper and string.

'Been shopping, have we?' said Glynn when she climbed back into the bus. 'Never you mind,' she pushed him away in mock outrage. 'Can you drop me back at my place, and I'll come round later for a show-and-tell.'

'Can't wait,' he said with feeling. The drive back to St Andrews was filled by lively conversation. Rose had found half a dozen rare books which she was planning to gift to the library, and Nick had bought some little men. Glynn and the other scientists had spent a productive day discussing professional gossip and speculating on the state of the job market. They were driving through Cupar, watching the last bright pink flashes of the sunset, when Nia's 'phone buzzed and she jumped at the text message. 'What's up?' said Glynn, noting her frown.

'I'm sorry, I need to get back,' she said. 'It's Ruth's midwife. The baby's coming early.'

Chapter Fourteen

By half-past-two in the morning Eilidh, Amira and Dr. Mosely were all half-asleep in Ruth's living room. Nia was huddled on the floor wrapped in a blanket, watching the tealights blink out around them, her brown paper parcel forgotten where she'd thrown it in the kitchen. She tried to believe Eilidh who reassured her that everything was fine, but she flinched every time she heard Ruth's moans from the next room, and her mind kept running through all the things that could go wrong. Her heart beat fast as she heard a sudden tangle of cries. Baby Eleanor came into the world with a long wail, and then settled down for a drink. A few minutes later the midwife came out to wake the circle from their vigil and give them the good news - a little underweight, but perfectly healthy.

While the others went home, Nia settled down on the sofa for the night. When she woke with the sunrise, she peeked into Ruth's room and saw a scene of Biblical calm, as the first milky sunlight formed a halo around the child sleeping peacefully in her mother's arms. Nia made sure that there was food available, and went back to her own flat, exhilarated and relieved by the last day's events.

After several long, cold showers, Glynn made it into work on Monday morning, berating himself for being jealous of a baby. He was immediately plunged into a day of briefings, as he was asked to 'cascade' his impressions of the meeting in Edinburgh. The problem of admissions, however, was pushed into second place, when Simon burst into the meeting mid-morning waving a sheaf of papers. 'You will not bloody believe this!' he yelled, passing them round. 'We've barely got these damn exams set and some sort of order imposed, and then this!' In disbelief, they all read the list of 'Students recommended for particular results.' What followed was an apparently random distribution of students into degree classifications, with a simpering note on the bottom, 'Strongly recommended for your approval.'

'But, we've only just marked the dissertations, and some of this lot won't be doing any exams, and haven't even submitted any work this year,' Tricia was very confused. 'How did they draw up the list? Oh …' she said, as Glynn pointed out footnote six, "Students who have paid their full tuition fees.' Got it.'

Confusion continued. They had planned an emergency meeting in a few weeks' time to assess the progress made by the final-year students, and see whether any of them could legitimately be awarded a degree. This pre-emptive strike from the Business Recovery Plan team took even Hobden by surprise. 'I don't understand,' Tricia tried again. 'I can sort of see how you're going to give them degrees, but how can you justify different classifications? I mean, surely we're the ones who decide that?'

The meeting adjourned while Eilidh went to investigate. They re-convened just before lunch, when she had some bad news. 'They're claiming it has an academic basis, looking at transcripts and then assessing this year's work. The second copies of dissertations went to the BRP office,' she said, simmering.

'But who's doing this assessing?' Even Hobden was indignant.

'Wait for it! Kath Christopher, the BRP deputy head

of Gestapo. I knew she was up to something!'

'What?' Glynn shrieked. 'That woman who told me my pencil was a health and safety risk?'

'Same one. She's been extremely efficient, it seems, so someone entrusted her with these decisions,' Eilidh said through gritted teeth.

'How can she possibly make these decisions?' Simon squeaked.

'Now, don't shout at me,' Eilidh warned. 'She's apparently been reading the dissertations, but she is a committed Christian who apparently feels that God has imbued her with excellent judgement.'

Tricia leaned over the table and said, 'So, she has a hotline to baby Jesus and he tells her who's worthy of a 2:1 does he?' Glynn smiled at her appreciatively, cursing that damn baby under his breath. 'This is outrageous!' Hobden stood, turning purple. 'She may be efficient, but the woman doesn't have a doctorate, does she? How can she possibly be taking decisions about academic quality? What next? Kath Christopher decides which students we admit, or what counts as good research, or what counts as plagiarism? This is intolerable.'

'Glad you feel that way, Malcolm,' said Eilidh. 'We're not the only ones up in arms. There's going to be an emergency meeting of the Senate after lunch. I was hoping you and Simon would go and make our voices heard.'

'Too bloody right!' Simon banged his hand on the table. 'This has to stop. We've been complacent, letting the damn BRP run things, but this is ridiculous. We'll not have a scrap of professional status left, if this continues. Now, I'm sure this Kath woman is a perfectly decent sort, and you know I'm a Methodist, but I'd respect her far more if she'd stay with what she knows, and give us some shred of credit for professional competence.' His blood was up, and he swept Hobden away to plan strategy over lunch. Glynn and Tricia double-checked the arrangements for assessment, noting with some satisfaction that a large number of the students who had stayed around had actually produced a good deal of work, despite the difficult circumstances. 'I think some of them *should* get a degree out of this,' Tricia said, looking through the notes, 'but I'll be damned if we should agree with that nonsense. Oh, I know it's nothing to do with me,' she said as Glynn looked concerned. 'They'll be chucking me out without a 'Thank You' in a few months' time, nothing but the dole come September for me, but you have to make a stand, right?'

'True,' said Glynn. 'If we think this isn't our fight, let them get on with it, who knows when it'll get us down the line. There's this poem, can't remember it all, it's about the Holocaust and it starts, 'First they came for the Jews', and this chap thinks, 'Oh, but I'm not a Jew, so I won't do anything.' Can't remember it all, but the last bit goes, 'Then they came for me, and there was no-one left to speak out for me.' Now I'm not saying this is the same, but it is, sort of.'

'Where do we draw a line?'

'If you tolerate this, then your children will be next.'

'Oh, now you *are* getting deep, getting your philosophy from the Manic Street Preachers!' she said in mock horror. He looked at her with interest, and she said defiantly, 'Don't look so surprised. My father loved them, had that on all the time when I was little.'

'Lots about you I don't know, isn't there? Ach, sorry,

sorry,' he groveled. 'I know, I'm an idiot. I owe you a huge apology. I'm an idiot, what can I say? Truce?' 'Apology accepted,' she smiled, as they collected up the papers for the next meeting, and tried to pretend there was real work to be done.

By the end of the day, the barbarians had been forced from the gates and it was agreed that only academic departments would decide on whether students graduated, and if so, with what degree. Some sections of the university did not feel able to award any degrees this year, and were hastily trying to work out whether any of their students could claim partial credit when things returned to some form of normal in September. Geography and Geology were far more positive, 'though Simon expressed deep concerns about the lack of fieldwork students had undertaken. 'It'll all come out when we write them references,' Eilidh had tried to reassure him.

The week passed slowly for Glynn as he held his final revision classes and tied up loose ends. He'd cooed at a picture of baby Eleanor and tried not to shout, 'But what about me?' when Nia excitedly told him how soft her skin was and how much hair she had. He was looking forward to the party, and his week was only partially disturbed by seeing Matt in town, hunting for booze, now that Finn's supply of home-brew had dried up in disgust. As he'd approached, Glynn saw that most people were treating Matt like an ordinary human being. 'Can they not see the horns?' he wondered, before he nodded an acknowledgement as he passed. He hurried by, not wanting to engage with the mixture of drunken scorn and pitiful loneliness he'd seen in Matt's eyes when he'd grunted a greeting. Glancing back at the long, matted hair sticking to Matt's collar, he cast his mind back painfully to the conversation he'd had with his father, when Matt was first in hospital. The old man had started by berating Glynn for having abandoned his brother, and when Glynn had started to explain what was wrong, his father had simply said, 'He needs to get a haircut,' and had hung up.

After another cold shower, Glynn was trying very hard to focus as he walked round to Ruth's for the naming ceremony, having found a clean shirt and shorts which he hoped weren't too casual. When he arrived, he kissed Nia a little too raucously for such a dignified event, but she had laughed and accepted his invitation for dinner the following Friday.

'I know you've needed to be here,' he said graciously, 'but what about me?'

'Anyway,' she said, as she'd agreed with his plan, 'I still have to show you what I bought in Edinburgh.' She was happy to sit by him throughout the ceremony, even though she had to quiet him when he expressed surprise at the choice of the non-religious guardian parents. 'I didn't even know Ruth knew Felix!' he'd whispered.

'Don't be daft,' Nia whispered back, 'Before she went away, Ruth and Abi were practically his big sisters when his parents died. Where've you been all this time?'

'Oh, well, I suppose I never saw them together much,' he ventured.

'And if you can't see it, it doesn't exist, does it? Wake up, Glynn, but no. Shut up for now.'

At the end of the ceremony Nia had looked anxious when Felix went to hand the baby to Glynn, 'Oh, it's alright,' he smiled at her alarm. 'She's much bigger than a hamster. Even bunnies I'm alright with. See? I'm a natural,' he said lowering his voice, as he he cradled the baby against his chest. He was very reluctant to hand her over when Hannah came to claim her non-religious god-child, but gave in with good grace and went to congratulate Ruth, 'This could be seen as Coals to Newcastle,' he shrugged as she opened the present, 'but I thought it's a mother-and-daughter crystal, so more appropriate than your common or garden bit of magic rock.'

'It's lovely,' she thanked him. 'It's good of you to come. We need as much positive energy to launch a life as we can in this climate. I appreciate it.'

'Oh, think nothing of it,' he waved it off. 'I love talking to babies. Captive audience, see?' He left early with a newly-strengthened resolve to finish his research on the Ludlow bone bed and publish it as soon as possible.

Several trades over several days allowed Glynn to assemble a reasonably balanced meal ready for Friday night. He was enjoying the town like never before, joyfully noticing small details, like the owl plaque on South Street and the peculiar angle of the mine-shaft in the castle grounds. Nia was in good spirits, too. Baby Eleanor was gaining weight and Ruth was coming back into the land of the living, greatly improved after spending a night asleep in Eilidh's guest room, while Hannah nobly stayed with the ever-wakeful child. When Nia unwrapped the dress from Edinburgh and tried it on for the first time, she was just as pleased as when she'd bought it. The dress called for a certain va-va-voom, so she'd dug out her newest make-up, taking advantage of the bright, warm summer evening to indulge in sparkles and a feather in her hair. She'd even decided to go the whole hog and wear her high red sandals, even though they squashed her toes. She was feeling some pain by the time she'd walked round to Glynn's, but the look on his face made it all worthwhile.

He was a perfect gentleman, as he led her into a tidy flat and offered her a glass of wine, 'Supermarket had a booze delivery a few days ago,' he smiled. 'Go on, one glass won't do you any harm.' She accepted happily and enjoyed the unfamiliar relaxation as he set out the meal. When he brought out two elaborate mousses from the fridge, she could almost hear him thinking, 'Mission accomplished,' as he leaned back watching her take the first bite.

'What you thinking about?' she said provocatively.

'Good news seems to be coming thick and fast,' he said, bursting to tell her. 'There's the baby, you've agreed to have dinner with me, and I heard something interesting a week ago. Maybe you're right about karma, after all. Thomas Masterson has finally had his comeuppance.'

'That's the bloke who got one of the jobs you wanted?' She remembered the name, but not the strength of Glynn's animosity.

'Southampton. That's the one,' he said gleefully.

'So what happened?'

'Well,' he began a practised narrative, 'he probably expected to sail through this, like Christian Marshall, masters of the universe stuff, but tragically he suffered badly from the depression, even tried to kill himself I hear, and then his devoted wife left him and went back to Oxford with the kid.'

'That's awful.'

'Isn't it?' Glynn grinned, 'but there's more. So his wife and baby are gone, not a marriage that could cope with anything less than perfection, it seems, but he's still got his job, so he gets better, and goes back to work, but tragically the world has changed. He picks up with his 'I'm alright, Jack' routine, not doing anything he doesn't have to, treating the students as a real inconvenience, going home at three, and the roof falls in on him. Not literally. That would have been too much, collapsing canopy, sorry, forget it, bad joke.'

Nia nodded, slightly bemused, as he continued, 'Thing is, Southampton had lots of students who'd turned up before they got ill, so there was more pressure to keep things running. So, the place was kept going through all this by some of the women in junior posts, who obviously had no love for lazy prima donnas like Thomas. So, when he's obviously not pulling his weight, they called in the higher authorities. He got a reprimand, and then, then, finally, there was a student complaint about sloppy marking. Turns out, he'd just put, 'Good, but watch the fonts' on her last piece of work, missed the fact the last three pages of her essay were a précis of a Simpsons episode. So, the university's desperate to keep its student fees, and decides to make an example of him, show how they value student input, dangerous I know, but poetic justice. He's about to face another disciplinary hearing and he resigns. Now I know he's got family money, so it's not such a big thing, but he's finished professionally.'

'So, this vindicates your position, does it?' Nia was a little uncomfortable, but glad to see him so happy.

'Well yes it does, but there's more to it,' he pulled his chair round to sit by her, then the 'phone rang. He picked it up in the living room, just out of Nia's line of sight, but she could hear that he frowned when he said to the image, 'Hang on a second!' before swinging back into view. 'Sorry,' he said to Nia with a look of tragic dejection. 'My dad. Won't be long. Tell you what, why don't you have a bath? There's lots of hot water, and I'll be with you very, very soon.' With a barely concealed passion, he pressed against her, kissed her and whispered in her ear, 'You look delicious!' She pulled away, smiling, and went into the bathroom, appreciating how he'd obviously cleaned before she'd arrived. Twenty minutes later, she slipped seductively out of the bathroom, wrapped only in a towel. Glynn was crunched up on the sofa, and she saw his father was reading something out from a newspaper. She slipped beneath the clean sheets and waited, warm and quiet.

The next thing she knew it was morning, the light was shining through the curtains and Glynn obviously hadn't joined her. She instantly thought something must have happened, and jumped up, wrapping the duvet round her. Glynn was snoring gently, sprawled across the sofa, an empty bottle of scotch on the floor by the 'phone.

Her heart sank, as she shook him awake and he groaned, 'My head. Turn that fucking light off.' He rolled over and suddenly woke properly. 'Oh shit, shit, shit, Ow!' he sat up. 'God, I'm so sorry. I was just so wound up and then I thought, I'd have a drink to loosen up, and Ow!'

'Is there any coffee?' said Nia slowly.

'Yeah, there's some instant stuff in the cupboard. Thanks,' he said, shutting his eyes.

She dressed quickly, cursing the tight zip on the dress, and made him a coffee. She was about to leave, when he said, 'No, no, I said I'd take you out to Amira's and I will.'

'Are you fit to drive?'

'Sure, yes, let me just drink this,' he slurped gulps of

coffee. 'God, it's the least I can do.' He pulled himself together, repeating almost to himself, 'I am so, so sorry. Damn,' he moaned, 'this isn't how I was going to tell you, but I haven't got long. I want you to come to Southampton with me. They've offered me a job and it could well be permanent.' She made to leave, and he sagged against the counter, running his hands through his hair. 'Please, just give me a minute? Try this again. I love you. I want this to work. I want us to have a fresh start, move way, start again. I know, I know, I don't deserve you, and you need to think, but promise me you'll think about it?' He looked at her pleadingly, through a hungover haze.

'I don't know what to say,' she said quietly.

'Perfectly alright,' he murmured. 'You need to think, I get that, and I know I've sprung this on you, but I really want you to come. Look, let me get you to Amira's.'

'Are you really fit to drive?'

'Yeah, yeah,' he moaned. 'Come on.' He pulled her outside, tripping over Tommy who was curled up near the front door. He suppressed a moan, and managed to make an exaggerated display of gallantly opening the car door for Nia. He pulled his hands through his hair again as he eased into the driver's seat, and muttered, 'Get with it!' to himself as he turned the ignition. 'Right. Let's be off!' he said, hitting the accelerator and shaking as the car jolted into reverse and scraped painfully along the wall before hitting a concrete bollard. 'Oh Shit! Shit! Shit! Oh god, my head!' he moaned, and pulled the car forward with a metallic crunch as the wing mirror fell to the ground. He turned the engine off and groaned again, as he saw the passenger door was too dented to open. Nia silently climbed out over the driver's seat, as he murmured, 'I am so sorry. I don't think I've ever done that before. Ah, just give me an iota of a minute. I'll get this sorted, I'll get you out there, I promise.'

'I'm going home,' she said, trembling.

'No, no,' he grabbed her arm. 'This is all my fault. I can't believe I just did that.'

'You shouldn't be driving with a hangover,' she growled, then walked away in her purple dress and high heels. For days she ignored his 'phone calls, and only anger stopped her from sinking into depression.

It seemed to be a time for irritation all round, and she wasn't surprised when a bunch of roses was delivered to Ethereal. 'Another one for you,' Nia said to Ruth. 'Persistent, isn't he, your architect?'

'Married, 'though isn't he?' Ruth replied, annoyed. 'Okay, let's see what we have this time. Probably sentimental pleas rather than threats of the law, but you never know. Ah,' she said, pulling out the card. 'Seems these aren't for me. Something you're not telling me?'

Nia read the card and said, 'It's an apology from Glynn.'

'Oh,' Ruth raised an eyebrow. 'What did he do now?'

'He asked me to move to Southampton with him.'

'Gosh,' Ruth rocked Eleanor gently on her chest, 'and that needs an apology?' When Nia didn't reply she said quietly, 'Sorry, none of my business.' Nia put the flowers in water and reluctantly answered Glynn's call later that afternoon, agreeing to meet him straight away outside his office.

'Terrible timing,' he said, pulling her into a run down the Scores, 'but you have to see this!'

They stopped at the railings looking out towards the West Sands. 'There. Best spot,' he said. 'You had to see this.'

'Wow,' she said, following his gaze upwards. 'That's weird, sort of like an oil spill in the sky.'

'Nice image. It's a nacreous, or mother-of-pearl cloud. Very rare. See, geology, weather, all mixed up.'

She stared as the pink, iridescent cloud changed shape slightly, lengthening and trailing individual strands of coloured light. As the brightest patch started to fade, he said, 'Whatever you have to say, I just wanted you to see this.'

'I'm glad you did,' she let out a long breath, turning to look out at the sea. 'Maybe it's an omen. Just as well it didn't turn up six months ago. People would have probably thought it was the end of the world.'

'Or just ignored it?' He took a deep breath. 'So, I know I kinda messed up the whole night, but the facts are the same. I'm an idiot. I love you. I'm an idiot. I want you to come with me to Southampton. And I'm sorry I'm such an idiot.'

She looped her arm into his, drawn by the hopeful sparkle in his eyes, but said, 'I don't think I can. This is sort of my home now.'

'But we could start again, set up a home in Southampton. I'm pretty sure they're going to offer me the job for real, and then we start again.'

'I have friends here, a community,' she tried again.

'A pretty ragged one.'

'No. It's all getting better. You know what they said, we've been a model community. Everyone's pulling together.'

'D'ya think? Seems to me people are just falling back into old habits,' he snapped, before pulling himself together. 'Nia,' he said more softly, 'You want to see

341

the best in people, hope all this will make people more thoughtful, kinder, but people want to forget. They want to go back to the way things were. Try to pretend it never happened. There's not going to be any great new kind world order. Yeah, we came off pretty lightly here, and maybe that's something good, but there'll be good things in Southampton.'

'This is a special place,' she said sadly. 'There's an energy here. The sea, the sky. I don't know. It brings out the best in people. I really want to stay here. I want you to stay with me.'

'I can't,' he said, more roughly than he'd intended. 'There's no job for me. Southampton is a real chance. It might be my only chance. I have to go, but I don't want to lose you. Please come with me.'

She said nothing, and he put his hands on her shoulders, 'I don't mean right away. I have to go next month, but you could take your time, get things sorted, come down at the end of the summer maybe, once I've got somewhere to live. Oh, don't cry. Come with me! I want you to come with me!' He hugged her tight.

'Is a job really so important to you?' Her voice was choked. 'I mean, you're always moaning about how badly paid you are, how there's this endless pressure to publish. And you hate the students.'

'Not really,' he was surprised by her view of his job. 'Oh, I know I moan, but most of them are hard-working youngsters trying to do their best. Being temporary's rubbish, but once I get a permanent job it's a great career. Not going to make a million, mind you, but that's not everything. We can have a life. Think about it? Alright? I've gotta get back, but listen to me. I love you, Ni. I want you to come with me. A fresh start. You could go to college in Southampton.

Hell, you'd be one up on the snooty bitches there if you were already engaged to a lecturer.' She sighed, 'I can't imagine I'll be thinking about anything else. But will you at least think about staying?' She looked at him, feeling all the muscles in her back tensing.

'It's not possible,' he risked a quick kiss on her cheek. 'I have to go. Call you tonight?' Glynn hurried back to his office, and she stood leaning on the railings until the flecks of rust cut into her palms, and the sky faded into a patchwork of ice-cream colours. She watched as normal life unfolded around her and wondered which compromise to make.

After a few more days of tortured indecision, Nia accepted Glynn's invitation for a walk one evening. She was slightly nervous about getting into his car, but soothed by his stream of self-deprecating jokes which lasted all the way to Kingsbarns. It was another beautiful evening, the sweep of the bay framing the shimmering sky. They watched a heron drift over the rocks, and the seagulls fled. Although the sea was calm, evidence of recent storms were still visible in a dark scar along the sand, broken branches tangled with bits of plastic and abandoned golf balls.

Everyone on the beach seemed lulled into a soft sense of unreality, as Glynn and Nia walked along, casually slipping their hands in and out of an embrace. The calm was destroyed when six fighter jets screamed across the sky towards Dundee. When the tremors subsided, Glynn said, 'There we go. Civilisation's back to normal. Glad to see our defences are in place. And I notice they've opened the toilets up there again. Civil servants, d'you think?' 'Could be,' Nia agreed. 'Amira says lots of the civil servants don't want to go back to their old jobs, so if they can keep the pay and perks, they want to stay as road-sweepers and home-helps. More job satisfaction, apparently.'

'Ah, but will they get to keep the pay and perks, once things change, I wonder?' Glynn doubted it. They hadn't discussed his proposal, and he waited until they were nearly back at the car before he said, 'I won't pressure you, but you can still change your mind. I'm just saying, once I go, that doesn't have to be it. You can still change your mind.'

'What, do the long-distance thing?' she said, briefly stabbed by hope.

'No,' he said bluntly. 'Trust me. Long-distance relationships don't work. All I'm saying is, I'm not going to go down there and shack up with the first girl I meet. So if you don't come now, but you change your mind, call me, okay?'

When Nia got back to her flat, she went round to see Ruth and rocked the baby in her cradle, saying nothing. 'All I'll say,' said Ruth, 'is that if you're still not sure, well, then keep thinking. But if you have decided, don't keep torturing yourself. There's no point in prolonging the agony. Pull the plaster off in one go.' When Amira came round for their meditation group a few days later, she stayed on to talk to Nia and tried to help her gain some perspective. '*You* must agree with me, that this is a special place,' Nia begged her, as they sat at the kitchen table.

'Of course I do, but things change. Even the sky, the rocks, erosion, it all changes.

'Do people change?' Nia was looking for a real answer.

'Depends.' Amira sighed. 'I mean, it's the solstice in a few weeks, so I always take the chance to look back on where I was six months ago. It was a dark, heavy time, this year; then look back six months before that, different world. We've all been trying to hang on to things, to put little hyphens between people and actions, but people change all the time. There are new things too. Little Eleanor, for a start. A whole new person. So the world is different.'

'I don't know what to say, what to think,' Nia's face scrunched until her muscles ached. 'I don't feel I sound like myself any more. Or maybe he doesn't sound like himself, I don't know,'

'Things have been worse for that lately, I reckon,' said Amira. 'It's like when you see a strange word in print somewhere, then you hear it on the radio the same day. Or when someone uses a term and you echo it later in the day, completely out of context. This depression changed the emotional climate, maybe for good. Maybe we'll all get back close to how it was, maybe better, maybe worse, but it'll be different somehow. I wish I could help, Nia,' she hugged her. 'Don't stay if you're wanting things to go back to the way they were, but don't go if you're hoping things with Glynn will be like they were six months ago, that's all I can say.'

'Everything seems to be speeding up. There've been times this year when every day seemed to take an eternity, and now … it's all rushing on so fast, and I have to decide and this is my whole life on the line.'

'Ah, but this is only one decision,' Amira consoled her. 'It's not THE ONE decision. No decision ever is. Whatever you do, that'll be the right thing, I promise.'

Nia wasn't the only one feeling the sea-change in town. After the CHLOE team had provided support to the forty-percent of local businesses which had stopped trading, a good range of the shops re-opened, with limited injections of stock helping the economy to grind slowly back to life. The *Chronicle* had a bumper month through June as news came faster than they could produce weekly editions of the paper. The first big story looked set to stay at the top of the charts for several weeks, beginning with the huge front-page announcement: 'Hollywood Is Coming To St Andrews!' The actual news was slightly less dramatic, as there were rumours of a documentary being made about communities which had survived the plague reasonably well, relying on strength of character and a dark sense of humour. St Andrews was on the list of sites to be visited, and there were hopes that a sci-fi blockbuster would be made, if the documentary was successful. When Glynn told Rory about this over a crackling transatlantic 'phone connection, he was sceptical, but promised to spread the rumour as far as he could to try to give it substance.

In a normal year, this story would have dominated the local paper for months, but it was pushed to the middle section the following week by the preliminary report on the local WHO survey. The headline was uninspired, 'Happiness: To do or not to do?', taking its cue from the opening summary paragraphs of the report. After discussing various philosophical considerations, the report had considered whether happiness was to be found in an essentially static or fluid state, a matter of being or doing. Should people be aiming to be or to do? Although the full report concluded the answer was, 'Both and Neither', the rhetoric of 'Action versus Contemplation' caught the imagination of the paper's editorial team, who quoted the relevant paragraphs at length. The editors even commissioned a series of illustrations to accompany the section on 'Mind as skyscape', discussing how clouds of depression could obscure the sun, but never truly changed the fact that the sky of happiness is blue. When Bob read the garbled version of this profound philosophical insight he became almost hysterical, and accused Hobden of providing the newspaper with its aerial photographs. He was only calmed when the paper allowed him to publish his own précis of the report in the following week's edition, *sans* pictures of clouds. Most people ignored this theoretical kerfuffle and were more interested in the detailed observations made by the survey's authors. The natural surroundings of St Andrews were seen as a significant factor in many people's good mental health, and the report suggested that even having pictures of the landscape in one's home could have a positive benefit. This was an unqualified positive from the survey, but most of the recommendations came with the cautions and warning that Felix had foreseen.

Most people, however, appreciated the range of ideas, as they looked ahead to the next winter when the light would fade and plunge them back into darkness. The *Chronicle* digest had a handy 'Pick and mix' pull-out sheet which found its way on to many fridge doors. Suggestions ran from 'Animals' and 'Contemplation', right through to 'Yelling out your frustrations' and 'Zoo-visiting.' Bob protested to the paper again, that many of the suggestions were repetitive and simplistic, so once again they allowed him to publish a newer, more intelligent version the following week. Fewer people kept this version on their fridge, because it took up considerably more space – even though there were fewer suggestions, it did come with lots of footnotes. 'Well,' Eilidh had agreed at the end of another meeting, 'if my husband hasn't made all of the town philosophically literate by Christmas, it won't be for lack of trying.' Glynn had smiled, but didn't join them for lunch as he was trying to detach himself psychologically. Keen to make a good impression on his new employers, Glynn had agreed to move down south as soon as graduation was over. He started packing as he marked the final exams, feeling each day pass with a sense of sadness mixed with exhilaration at the prospect of finally securing his goal. He hoped Nia would come to make his dream complete. Learning from his past mistakes, Glynn kept his distance, giving her time to make a decision.

Chapter Fifteen

'So,' she murmured, 'this is nearly it for you.'

He nodded as they clapped.

'Worried things aren't going to turn out how you'd hoped?' she whispered, clapping.

'Well, I'm pretty sure Nia won't come with me, if that's what you mean.'

'Bad luck,' she said, 'but you're still going?'

They clapped some more.

'Yeah, I'm pretty sure this job is the one, and then, get one piece of your life in order and everything else can fit round it, buy a flat, have the odd holiday, get a life.'

'Sure it works like that?' Applause.

'Hell, yes. Look at all the people who come to St Andrews, and within a year or so they get married and have babies,' Glynn's voice projected slightly too far and the Dean glared at him.

Glynn clapped loudly. Tricia smiled, 'That could be because this place is hell if you're single.'

'That as well.'

'Was it the night of graduation you broke up with your last girlfriend?' she asked casually.

He paused, planning to stay silent, but then he heard Sarah from Physics lean down from behind and say, 'Week after, I heard.'

'Shush!' Glynn clapped more loudly than before, and tried to ignore the conversation around him

By the end of the graduation ceremony Glynn's hands were aching. He'd hoped it would be shorter than the year before, as there were fewer graduands, but the university had decided to scrap the usual individual ceremonies, and run one mammoth session instead. By the time he'd cheered and applauded MAs in Modern Languages, Architecture and Horticulture, Glynn found it hard to summon much enthusiasm for his own students who flashed him toothy grins and waved their scrolls in his direction. He was keen to escape the crowds of overdressed parents and quickly fled to his office to continue packing.

Waves of brightly coloured graduates lapped the stone walls of the main streets and trickled down to the harbour. Escaping from the crush in town, Nia and Amira sat on the beach below the castle, watching the line of clouds forming a false grey horizon.

'No, I've made up my mind. I'm not going.'

'You sound pretty miserable about it.'

'I really thought we had something, but it's gone.'

'Well, you know what they say,' Amira mustered her optimism, 'better to have loved and lost, than to live with the psycho the rest of your life.'

'Are you going to tell me there are plenty more fish in the sea?' Nia tried to join in, 'because you know how the cod stock collapsed?'

'No. Seriously, if it wasn't right, then it wasn't right. Even if you ended up single for the rest of your life, you'd still be happier in the long run.'

'Are you?' said Nia, turning towards her, broaching a subject they'd only ever touched upon when they first met. 'I know you seem happy, but I can't believe you're still single. Are you really alright about it?'

Amira smoothed her hand over a large irregular stone, 'You know when people say 'Plenty more fish in the sea', you can laugh, but when a year passes and there's no fish, you can get a bit freaked. Then people say 'Give it time', so you wait, but after five or six years and still no fish, you can see how it can seem a wee bit desperate, and then you go mad. Marry the first bloke who has his own teeth.'

Nia laughed softly and let her continue, comforted by the strength of her narrative, so Amira told her more of the story. 'I think it was when I passed the ten-year mark I stopped worrying. I mean, if you'd told me when I was twenty-five that I'd be on my own for at least ten years, and maybe forever, well, I'd probably have died. Things were so great with him, in the beginning. But I know I'm happier than if I'd stayed once things went bad. I know I'm happier than if I'd settled for some comfortable substitute. Even if I spend the next fifty years alone, I truly believe I'll still be happier than if I compromised, and lived with a sense of something not right. Like shoes a size too tight. They can look great, make your legs look great, and I *do* have great legs, but if they're giving you blisters or crushing you, it's not worth it. Not that *you'll* be alone for long, unless you want to be, Ni,' she gave her a hug. 'You're a remarkable woman who will undoubtedly meet a real Prince Charming before you know it.'

'But you didn't!' Nia persisted.

'Ah, but I'm not a princess. Just an eccentric old hippy,' Amira threw a handful of shingle into the advancing waves.

'Oh, you are *so* a princess,' said Nia. 'Maybe you're the one who can't settle down to sleep because she's so sensitive she knows something's wrong.'

'The princess and the pea? So, I just need to find a man with very thick mattress, d'you think?

'Well, size does matter.'

'Atta girl. You'll be fine. This is so hard, but you'll get through it. You know, just how Ruth says, let it flow through you. Arise and pass away.'

'D'you think she's managing it, when Eleanor screams blue murder like that? Does she manage to let it go then?'

'I really don't know. Come on, let's walk, nothing seems so bad when you're travelling.'

'I just want it to be over,' Nia blurted out. 'While he's still here I keep thinking he might change his mind.'

'I've said it before,' Amira agreed, 'hope can be a terrible thing.' The wind rose and the waves' tiny white peaks blossomed across the sea.

'Sorry to see you go, old chap,' said Hobden, watching Glynn stagger down the stairs with another box of books for the post room to send on to Southampton. 'Good move for you, 'though. Strong department, and all that.'

'Thanks,' Glynn nodded and wiped his forehead before heading back up.

'Ah, ah,' Hobden paced in the hall, wanted to say, really appreciated all you've done here. Since you arrived, of course, but this past year … Not been easy. Well done.'

'Thanks,' Glynn said again, and Hobden nodded, before walking out into the sunshine. Six boxes later, Glynn staggered out of the building, and went to meet Felix who was sitting at one of the continental-style tables outside the Crown. 'Seen this?' Glynn said, handing over a magazine. 'Hot off the presses.'

'Ah, Rory's magazine. Not really my cup of tea, but good for him.'

'Hang on to it. I'm trying to declutter. First surprise is Page Six, a short discussion of the ethics of charity, by one Professor Robert Urquhart.'

'Really? Bob?' Felix flipped through. 'Well, I never.'

'Always does take things literally, so when Rory said 'Write something for us,' when he was leaving, Bob took him at his word, and obviously got on to it.'

'Funny,' Felix was amused. 'What's the other thing?'

'Well, I'd value your opinion on this one, but Rory's own piece looks suspiciously like a piss-take on the late, lamented Christian Marshall.'

'Oh, now that I *will* look forward to. So, just you then, is it?' Felix said kindly.

'Think so.'

'Aye, well, may be for the best.' They sat in silence, watching the light spectrum slowly shift.

'I'll keep an eye on Abi,' Felix said, as they got up to leave. 'And Matt. Call in when I can.'

'I saw him last week haunting the supermarket looking for booze. Wild man of the woods. D'you think he'll snap out of it?' Glynn masked his anger with feigned concern.

'Hard to say. People do pull themselves together, but they have to ask for help first. You never know. He has the bairns to think about.'

'Doesn't seem to have bothered him much yet.'

'No, well, I'll keep an eye on him.'

A few days later a long afternoon of laughter and emulsion drifted out from the backstreets on to the Scores, as Abi held her 'Housewarming-come-help-me-decorate-party' after she'd moved back into town. One of the first arrivals was Maisie, who had found a renewed enthusiasm for her wedding and was planning it for the end of August. She introduced Abi to a short girl with tight, dark curls and a serious expression. 'D'you know Lynsey? She's going to be one of my bridesmaids. Some of them dropped out, you know? She's been trapped in London, but now she's back we can get going again.' Abi greeted her and admired the strange bone belt Lynsey was wearing slung low on her hips. She found herself unprepared for the response. 'I had a dream a few weeks ago about how my pelvis is the gleaming white cauldron of my creativity. I could feel the bones moving in harmony, releasing spirits up through my cells,' Lynsey announced.

'Interesting,' Abi said, struggling to keep a straight face, 'and will your bridesmaid outfit be as, er, anatomical?'

'Peach taffeta,' Maisie stopped the conversation with panicked determination. Abi gratefully gave them paintbrushes and set them to work in the front bedroom.

By the time Ruth arrived, the party was in full swing and she heard the placid voice of Abi's mother coming from the garden, 'Bunnymeade was by the river, which was dangerously near. Mr. Bunney-Fluff was worried, Mrs. Fluff was sick with fear.'

'Learning through contextual activities,' Abi said with only a brief wobble, as they watched the small group of girls agog at the story. 'Understanding new homes through the medium of bunnies.'

'Although it should probably be 'Mr. Bunney-Fluff went to the pub while Mrs. Bunney-Fluff did all the work,' Ruth laughed.

'Aye. Wrong generation. It's an old Ladybird book about this family of rabbits who have to move house, and it involves a perilous journey across a river. If you get into the swing of it, we have similar horror stories of ducklings drowning in frozen ponds and baby squirrels getting lost in blizzards. The rabbit theme can continue also, with runaway pets and a very odd seaside story involving a green umbrella and some homoerotic duvet scenes.'

'Really?' Ruth was glad to see her friend had recovered her sparkle.

'Absolutely. These old books are full of innuendo. My mother had a whole box of them. Becky found them one afternoon. She's been entranced ever since.'

They sat down a short distance from the reading circle, and Ruth admired Abi's new necklace. 'Birthday present from Jamie,' Abi said with a shrug, 'He always remembers to get me something in Duty Free.'

'Do you mind if I take a look?' Ruth said with some interest.

'Sure,' she replied, unclasping the chain and handing over the pendant, a small pearl set in a circle of alternating green and purple stones. 'Isn't purple and green supposed to be a harmonious combination? No doubt Jamie picked it cheap on his travels.'

'I don't think so,' Ruth turned it over. 'We get some of the standard stuff in the shop, but this is pretty delicate workmanship, twenty-four carat gold, and you know these are the birthstones for June, right? These are alexandrites. I don't think he just picked this up in Duty Free.'

'Oh,' Abi was truly surprised. 'Right, better not let Becky have this for her dressing-up days, then?'

When Amira arrived she was already wearing old clothes for decorating and demanded to be led straight to the action. 'We're painting the bedroom walls, so I can get the bairns settled first,' said Abi, leading her through the boxes. 'I really appreciate this. Plenty of refreshments in the kitchen.' As they joined two of Abi's neighbours with tins of paint, she filled her in on the situation. The house was normally used as a holiday let, but there wasn't that much call for tourist accommodation that year. Relying on his celebrity as the man-who-fixed-things, or got-things,

Finn had persuaded the owners to let the place rent-free, in return for doing up the roof and decorating. 'We're having some furniture and stuff from Glynn,' Abi explained to Amira, 'and with any luck we might be making progress by the time the lease is up. My solicitor's hopeful.'

When Abi returned to the garden, the sun was strong and she was grateful for the delivery of sunblock the town had just received. She settled down beside Ruth and baby Eleanor as Eilidh was saying, 'Still calling, is he?"

'Oh aye,' Ruth said wearily. 'That noble instinct to tell him really worked out well. I don't mind if he wants to see her, or use those damn architectural skills to build a tree-house, but he's going to have to tell his wife. Can't have it both ways. Cannae keep anything this noisy a secret now.'

'Fine set of lungs on her,' Eilidh agreed.

'Funny thing is,' Ruth mused, 'one of my best friends, Dot, took an instant dislike to him when she met him. I was hurt, but she was looking out for me.'

'That's a true friend,' said Abi. 'My best friend from college made a best woman's speech at my wedding. She told everyone about the night she first met Matt, how he was tired after teaching practice, and had had so much to drink all he could do was keep telling her how much he loved me. And you know, she told that as a *nice* story.'

They shrieked with laughter, and she went on, 'Really, as if the salient point was that he loved me, regardless of how blotto he was. When of course the real point was that he turned up to meet my best friend completely paralytic and I didn't dump him on the spot.'

'Some wedding!' said Eilidh. 'What was the best man

going to say after that?' Abi groaned in reply, 'Oh, I'm such an idiot. He went on about how we were sat in the kitchen on the first floor at our engagement party, and something flashed past the window, and Matt said casually, 'Was that Lucca?' Then they calmly walked out and found he'd fallen from a second-floor window. Turns out he was so drunk he didn't break a single bone – he'd fallen like a big, sleepy blancmange.' She put her head in her hands, 'I cannae believe I've been such an idiot. How could I have not seen it?'

'Seriously, don't blame yourself,' Eilidh hugged her. 'After all, heavy drinking's pretty endemic, it's socially acceptable, and he was doing well, good job. Who'd think it was a problem?'

'Aye, and of course I was young and stupid.'

'So what am I?' said Ruth. 'Middle-aged and stupid? Is that any better?'

Once the bedrooms were finished, the workforce came outside for homemade lemonade. Baby Eleanor was fractious, and Ruth jogged her round the lawn to keep her from full-blown hysterics. She waved Amira over, and said in a soothing rhythm, 'Nia seems calmer since you spoke to her.'

'I'm glad. She'd already made her decision. I just wanted to help her feel better about it.'

'I don't feel I can really advise her, given the mess I've made of things lately.'

'Well, I'm hardly a role model, am I?'

'So, what did you tell her?'

'That she'd be better off dying an old maid than putting up with some loser who'd make her life a misery,' Amira explained. Ruth choked on her drink, and the baby gurgled happily as she was gently waved around by her mother's reaction to this tragi-comedy. 'Oh well, not quite that,' Amira relented. 'Just tried to convince her that single life, be it for six months or sixty years, is better than an endless string of compromises with the wrong man. Gospel according to Radiohead, Philip Larkin and Carol Ann Duffy.'

'Wise words,' Ruth caught her breath. 'Is that what you really believe?' Amira took a firm stance, 'It's what I want to believe. It's what the truest part of me believes. It's what I believe on my best days.'

'And on your worst days?'

'Worst days, when I wake up after treacherous dreams, wake up thinking I'll never be over the grief, well, we all have grief for something, don't we? So, I sit at home and watch *The West Wing*.'

'Don't think there's much harm in that.' Baby Eleanor calmed down and let Amira hold her, looking at her with wide-eyed fascination as they moved into the sunshine.

By the evening, the painting was done and Becky was impatient for the grand finale. 'Robbie'll be back soon, and he'll spoil it,' she whined to Abi. 'No, no, Uncle Finn said the best fishing's in the evening. He won't be back for hours. Come on, let's let them out, shall we?' The crowd took up their positions around the side of the lawn, as Abi released the rabbits. 'Okay, everyone, mind your feet!' After a few minutes investigating the onlookers, Lily and Barbie took full advantage of the long, winding lawn and started slaloming up and down, doing vertical take-offs and twisting in mid-air. Becky clapped her hands with delight and informed her little friends solemnly that this was called 'binkying'. 'When guinea pigs do it,' Emily offered shyly, 'they're doing 'popcorning', you know? Not quite as high, 'though,

Daddy said. Daddy's buying me a guinea pig for my birthday.' Becky was keen to learn more.

'Miraculous, no?' said Abi's mother, hugging her daughter. 'You've done the right thing here, hen, never doubt that.'

'Wow!' cried Eilidh. 'That must've been a good two-feet off the ground. Lively little things!'

'Aye, they got out of the run the first night we arrived,' Abi explained, 'and they just went mad. We've always let them have a good run in the house, mind you, they need to stretch their legs, but once you've seen how happy they are outside, it would be cruel to keep them in. And this garden is perfect, properly walled in. All we had to do was fence of the paeonies – poisonous, apparently.' She nodded towards the magenta blossoms, standing proud in a corner. 'Always reminds me of when you were little, paeonies,' said Abi's mother. 'They smell like that old medicine you used to have for your throat, remember?' They stood in silence, comparing the sharp taste of memory with the bright, joyful scene unfolding before them. The sun barely set that night and rose again bright and fresh a few hours later.

He'd missed the sunrise, but had been up early enough to welcome Tommy in for the last time and make his fond farewell. Glynn squashed a roll of maps into his rucksack and sighed over his last morning. He'd sold or given away most of his belongings, and Abi was going to buy his car. The books had been sent on ahead, and he was set up with the last few bits and pieces in his flat. He looked at the lump of chrysocolla on his windowsill, and decided to ask Abi to return it to Nia as a parting gift. He'd delivered a large box of cat accessories to his surprised neighbours, then cleaned up the flat as best he could. Abi and the children were coming to drive him out to Leuchars, ready for the long journey. He sat and twiddled his thumbs. They drove to Leuchars and Glynn got on a train.

Time passed, and the midday sun reflected off the screen as Abi drove down the narrow lane to Cambo Sands, having hidden the sentimental chrysocolla out of sight in the boot. The air was clear, but warm. A perfect day. She caught sight of them sitting a little distance from the long, rusty outflow.

'Hi!' Amira called out. 'I'd thought you'd still be unpacking.'

'Took a break,' Abi said sitting down. 'Becky and Robbie are having their Father's Day visit with Matt. Bob took them.'

'He's a good man,' said Amira, looking out over the sparkling waves. Nia said calmly, 'He's gone then?'

'Aye, we took him to the train. I tried to talk him out of it. Told him he was being a fool.' After a moment, she said, 'Jamie's coming over next month. I know he'll be glad to see you again.'

'Oh, he is *so* coming to see *you*!' Nia poked her.

'Don't be daft,' said Abi, throwing a piece of driftwood at her.

'She's right, you know?' said Amira. 'I mean, he brought you chocolates.'

'And that's a universal romantic flag, is it?'

'Pretty much, aye.'

'That would be a great story, wouldn't it? Tragic heroine in middle of nasty divorce, hooks up with her much younger brother-in-law?'

'Well, you never know,' said Amira, then frowned slightly, as she saw Nia concentrating too intently on the sand in front of her. Abi reached over and took

Nia's hand, 'Is this wise, being down here right now?' she said quietly. 'I know you and Glynn used to come down here a lot.'

'Actually, I'm fine here, better than in town,' Nia looked up and shook her head. 'It's odd, but it always seems different here, something special, you know?'

'Hmm,' Abi nodded, brushing sand off a limpet shell, 'I know what you mean. When I was in my teens I read a book which was set down here, and there was this scene with a young woman walking along with an older man. I can picture the scene just like a movie, and it's clearer to me than the memories of flying kites here for Becky's birthday.'

She seemed puzzled, as she continued, 'I don't know why it's stuck with me, but that's the only thing that stays constant about this place. They were walking along, not really talking, just lacing their fingers back and for. I think there was some tragic subtext, you know, they were in love, but he was married or she was dying. I don't really remember, but I can *see* them here. She had red hair and was wearing a green coat, and he was going grey. Sometimes I've even thought I've caught sight of them. Must be going mad, no?'

'Sounds like a good story,' said Amira watching the seagulls circle above. 'What happened in the end?'

'Oh, I don't recall,' Abi smiled sadly. 'She probably lived happily ever after.'